the
charm bracelet

the
charm bracelet

viola shipman

THOMAS DUNNE BOOKS
St. Martin's Press
New York

THOMAS DUNNE BOOKS.
An imprint of St. Martin's Press.

THE CHARM BRACELET. Copyright © 2016 by Viola Shipman. All rights reserved. Printed in the United States of America. For information, address
St. Martin's Press, 175 Fifth Avenue, New York, N.Y. 10010.

www.thomasdunnebooks.com
www.stmartins.com

Illustrations by Cameron MacLeod Jones

LIBRARY OF CONGRESS CATALOGING-IN-PUBLICATION DATA

Names: Shipman, Viola, author.
Title: The charm bracelet : a novel / Viola Shipman.
Description: First edition. | New York : Thomas Dunne Books, 2016.
Identifiers: LCCN 2015042048 | ISBN 9781250071323 (hardback) |
    ISBN 9781250101921 (international edition) | ISBN 9781466882485
    (e-book)
Subjects: LCSH: Mothers and daughters—Fiction. | Grandparent and
    child—Fiction. | Life change events—Fiction. | Domestic fiction.
    | Chicago (Ill.)—Fiction. | BISAC: FICTION / Contemporary
    Women. | FICTION / Family Life.
Classification: LCC PS3619.H5788 C53 2016 | DDC 813/.6—dc23
LC record available at http://lccn.loc.gov/2015042048

Our books may be purchased in bulk for promotional, educational,
or business use. Please contact your local bookseller or the Macmillan
Corporate and Premium Sales Department at 1-800-221-7945, extension
5442, or by e-mail at MacmillanSpecialMarkets@macmillan.com.

First Edition: March 2016

10 9 8 7 6 5 4 3 2 1

For my grandmothers

. . . and my mom

Thanks for teaching me that
the grandest gifts in life are the simplest
and for entrusting me with your charms,
which retaught me that lesson.

prologue

The Half-Heart Charm

To a Life Where We're Never Separated

July 4, 1953—Lolly

Fireflies blinked, illuminating the stepping-stones to Lost Land Lake.

"You see that, Lolly?" my mom laughed in the twilight. "Mother Nature is giving us a preview to the fireworks."

I smiled and inhaled.

My whole world smelled of summer: Suntan lotion and sparklers, barbecues and pine needles.

By our ears, dragonflies fluttered, as if an orchestra of violins had been sent, just for my mom and me, as we walked to our dock.

I had just blown out the candles on my tenth birthday cake, and my dad was busy building a bonfire for s'mores. He had given me his gift, my first fishing pole, so I could spend Sundays with him, but now it was time for my mom's gift. And she always gave it to me at the end of our dock.

In the quickening dusk, I felt for her hand as we walked, our wrists colliding, setting our charm bracelets jangling. I giggled. Out of habit, I began to feel for her charms, trying to guess each one by touch rather than sight. It was a game I had invented years ago.

"My baby shoe!" I said excitedly.

"To a life filled with happy, healthy children," my mom said.

"A key!" I yelled.

"Because you unlocked my heart," she said.

"Snowflake?"

"Yes," she said. "To a person of many dimensions."

My fingers kept flying, and my mom had a story and explanation for every charm. I knew almost every one by heart, and I spun my fingers until I found my favorites, the ones I always played with: The grand piano with the lid that opened and closed, the turtle with green gemstone eyes whose head moved back and forth, and a wishing well with a moving crank.

"To a life filled with beauty, a life filled with slow, meaningful decisions, and a life where all your wishes come true!"

As we neared the end of the dock, my fingers felt a charm I couldn't identify.

"What's this one, Mommy?" I asked. "I don't know it."

"That . . ." My mom hesitated, and her voice broke.

"Are you okay?"

"That's my rocking chair," she explained.

"What's it for?"

"It's for . . ."—again, she stopped, catching her breath, as if she had just finished a long swim across the lake—". . . a long and healthy life."

We took a seat at the end of the dock, and dangled our feet in the water, just as the fireworks started.

"Ooooh!" I said, as much for the chill of the water as for the fireworks. "Woooowww!"

My birthday fell on the Fourth of July, just like our nation's, and I was a child of summer.

"All those fireworks are really for you!" my mom would always whisper, the explosions booming overhead and echoing off the water. "The world is celebrating your uniqueness!"

Every year, for as long as I could remember, I received a charm from my mother on special occasions: Christmas, trips, school accomplishments. And every birthday, my mom would add another charm to my bracelet.

This year was no different.

"Happy birthday, Lolly!" my mom said, pulling me into her arms and kissing my head. "You ready to recite our poem first?"

I shook my head no.

"Why not?"

"Mom! I'm getting too old."

"You will never be too old. Let's do it together then!"

This charm
Is to let you know . . .

My mom's face lit up as she started the poem. Suddenly, it was like jumping into the lake on a hot day, I couldn't resist. So I joined in:

That every step along the way,
I have loved you so.
So each time you open up,
A little box from me
Remember that it really all
Began with You and Me.

My mom hugged me, radiating with joy. "Here you go," she said, pulling a small package from the pocket of her jacket.

I ripped open the tiny box, and, as usual, there was a silver charm sitting atop a little velvet throne.

"What is it, Mommy?" I asked, squinting in the darkness.

"It's half of a heart. To a life where we're never separated."

I pulled it out of the box and studied it, rubbing my hands over its delicate outline.

"Where's the other half?"

"Right here," she said, showing me her bracelet, which was as heavy with charms as our Christmas tree was with ornaments. Then she took my wrist, added the charm and placed my hand on her heart. "And right here. You will always be a part of me."

I smiled and leaned into my mom. She was warm, safe, and smelled like a mix of peonies and Coppertone.

"See, when you put our charms together," she said, connecting the two halves of our heart, "they read MOM AND DAUGHTER. They complete each other. So no matter what happens from now on, I will always be a part of you, and you will always be a part of me. Will you promise me something, Lolly?"

"Anything, Mommy."

"Promise me you will always tell our story and you will always be you."

"I promise, Mommy," I replied.

My mom smiled and looked out over the lake as fireworks illuminated the night sky, and put her arm around my shoulder, drawing me even closer.

"I will always be with you, Lolly. Especially when you wear your bracelet. It will always be filled with memories of our life together. No one can ever take that away."

She kissed my cheek as the fireworks exploded overhead.

"I will always love you, Lolly," she said.

"I will always love you, too, Mommy."

A breeze rushed across the water and over the lip of the dock to jangle our bracelets.

"You know, some people say they hear the voices of their family in this lake: In the call of the whippoorwill, the cry of the loon, the moan of the bullfrog," my mom whispered. "But I hear my family's voices in the jangling of my charms."

The way she said that gave me goose bumps. It was so beautiful, I had to look at my mom. Flashes of light from the fireworks illuminated her curly, blond hair and the freckles on her rosy cheeks. It was as if a million cameras with a million flashbulbs were taking her picture, so I'd never forget how she looked at this moment.

I looked even closer, and it was then that I noticed tears streaming down her face.

A year later, my beloved mother would be gone, dead of cancer.

July 4, 2013

Fireworks boom overhead, knocking me from this memory.

I am now seventy. My mother and father are long gone. My husband is dead, my daughter, Arden, grown and on her own in Chicago five hours away, my granddaughter, Lauren, is in college. For too many years now, I have celebrated my birthday alone. And yet when I look into the night sky, I am still mesmerized by the simple beauty of summer fireworks, overwhelmed by memories.

As my head tilts upward, I can feel tears trail down my face.

My mother may have taken half of my heart with her, but I got to keep all of her charms, and she *was* right: The charm bracelet is a constant reminder of her love for me.

I vowed to myself I would share our family stories with Arden and Lauren because none of us ever really dies as long as our stories are passed along to those we love. I started to tell them about our family when they were both little girls but then they got so busy, and life—as life does—quickly skips away like a flat piece of shale across Lost Land Lake.

I try to remind them of our history and traditions through the charms I still send, but my daughter has shrugged off our past and me, as if we were a jacket she no longer likes to wear. And her absence stings, like the first frosty day in October.

So while I pray they will return home, I continue alone: I still read my mother's poem out loud to the lake on my birthday every Fourth of July as fireworks explode. And, without fail, the wind will rattle my charm bracelet—now even heavier than my mom's ever was—and I will shut my eyes, and listen to the charms.

Happy birthday, Lolly, I can hear my mother say.

part one

The Hot Air Balloon Charm

To a Life Filled with Adventure

One

May 2014—Arden

A rden Lindsey realized too late that she was shouting.

She got up and slammed the door to her office at *Paparazzi* magazine, fuming over the terribly written article just submitted by her youngest online staff writer.

Beyoncé rocked her "recently unpregnant stomach" with sushi?!

Are you kidding me?

Simóne was always more interested in champagne and backup dancers than writing bubbly headlines and flowing sentences.

"And how many times can you use some form of the word 'sing'?" Arden continued to yell. "Sing? Sang? Song? Singer? Songstress?"

Arden took a deep breath.

"*And* could you even attempt to code the article for the website?" she mumbled to herself.

Arden plopped back into her chair, the momentum causing her black bob to swing in front of her face and her thick, black eyeglass frames to bounce on the bridge of her nose.

She removed her glasses, closed her eyes, and rubbed her temples. She could already feel the dull thump of a headache approaching even before it arrived, just like the vibrating tracks of the El train that ran outside the hip

River North warehouse offices of *Paparazzi* magazine announced the train's arrival.

You can't stop this train, either, Arden thought, pulling two ibuprofen from her bag as the El suddenly roared by her window.

Arden popped the pills into her mouth and drained the remnants of her latte. She inhaled deeply, attempting to channel her inner yogi, pushing her glasses high onto her nose and positioning her fingers over her Mac like a trained pianist.

Behind the Scenes with Beyonc[ACUTE "e"]!
(Only [ITALIC "Paparazzi"] Was There!)

By Simóne Jaffe
[P]
Are you ready to party, single ladies, because [CELEBRITY_LINK "Beyonc[ACUTE "e"]"] is!
[P]
The pop diva, who will perform her [LINK "Mrs. Carter Show"] Friday and Saturday at the [LINK "United Center"], held a private bash at [LINK "Sunda"] to celebrate her arrival in [LINK "Chicago"], where she dined on sushi and saki with [BUSINESS LINKS "hubby"] [CELEBRITY_LINK "Jay-Z"] and celeb BFF's [CELEBRITY_LINK "Gwyneth Paltrow"] and [CELEBRITY_LINK "Alicia Keys"].

When Arden Lindsey was in a zone like this, it was as if her soul had suddenly left her body and now hovered over her watching from above with the exposed ductwork and the wood beams of the drafty warehouse ceiling.

She could see her hands fly across the top row of her keyboard, using keys few ever touched.

Brackets and parentheses, number signs and ampersands.

Arden had a job few even realized existed.

Arden spent her day editing and rewriting, creating search engine optimization, click-throughs, coding, links, all the things that nobody considered when they read the magazine from their laptop, iPad, or cell, but which made advertisers happy and made *Paparazzi* the most searched celebrity website in the world.

Arden began to click through the pictures that *Paparazzi's* photographer had sent at dawn: Beyoncé hugging Gwyneth. Jay-Z in shades. Impossibly tall Kimora in high heels.

Of course, Simóne was stunning, too.

Simóne looked like she belonged in the pages of *Paparazzi*: Lush, dark hair, pale skin with emerald eyes, exotic yet accessible, a sort of step-Kardashian. In person, Simóne was maybe five feet tall, perhaps a hundred pounds. But in photos, she looked like a star.

And she acted like one, too. She could chat with celebs in a way that made her seem as if she belonged in their inner circle. She could get them to say things after a few drinks.

That is, if she remembered to take notes, Arden thought.

As Arden studied the pictures, she suddenly caught her own image in the reflection of her laptop screen, her pale face and dull dress juxtaposed against the beauty of Alicia Keys and Kelly Rowland.

She stared more closely at Kelly Rowland's hair, studying it, wondering if her sleek mane was actually a wig.

Now, that's a good wig, Mother, she chuckled, remembering the embarrassing wigs her own mother wore to entertain tourists in her resort hometown.

[PHOTO CODE: "TZQ]89&04L"]

Arden gave the article one final review, then uploaded it to Paparazzi.com, a stunning photo of Beyoncé and Gwyneth hugging the top of the page under a red banner that danced and screamed, "BREAKING NEWS!"

Arden picked up her coffee cup and arced it into her trash can. She stood and walked over to her eighth-floor window, which offered a peek—between the elevated tracks of the train and the high-rises around her—of Lake Michigan.

It was a beautiful, mid-May day, and the sunlight turned the surface of the water into a kaleidoscope.

Arden watched the deep green waves rock the boats dotting the lakeshore.

She had grown up on Lake Michigan, seemingly a million miles away—"on the other side," as Chicagoans sometimes referred to their Michigan counterparts.

It was only one lake, but it was, truly, a "great" lake to Arden, and it had seemed to separate her from the rest of the world when she was a kid.

"I can't smell salt," LA and New York celebrities would always say when they visited Chicago. Or, "You mean you can't see the other side?"—unable to comprehend the vastness and freshness of Lake Michigan.

"Nice job on the Beyoncé story."

Arden turned at the sound of her boss's voice.

"Thanks," she said to Van, noting his Zac Efron hair and bow tie.

"Online a couple of minutes, and it's already gotten a few thousand views," he said. "Jay-Z already texted me to thank us for adding all the links to his corporate ventures. We do a great job, don't we?"

We? You may be the editor of Paparazzi.com, and we may cover the royals every single day, but that still doesn't give you the right to use the "royal we" in regard to my *work,* Arden thought.

"Yes," Arden said, instead. It was all she could do to keep from rolling her eyes.

She hesitated.

"Is there a chance you'd let me cover her after-party tomorrow night?"

"Sounds like a great idea, but we need you here," Van said, smiling, in the same sweetly condescending way her ex-husband used to speak to her when she talked about writing her novel.

Even a decade later, Arden still couldn't believe that her ex fought with her about everything—writing, money, the news—everything except for his own daughter. In the end, he didn't even fight for custody. He didn't want Arden. He didn't want Lauren. His iciness had frozen Arden, paralyzed her ability to stand up to him and, as a result, she walked away with little financial support. Now, her ex had a new family, a new wife and a new life without them.

"How would we survive without you?" Van asked.

Arden smiled at the irony of his question, before turning to look out the window in an attempt to hide her disappointment and frustration.

"Let Simóne do that," he continued. "She lives for that sort of stuff. She's going to be our next feature writer anyway."

Arden winced, as if her boss had suddenly walked over and slapped her. Out of habit, she tugged at her earlobe, a quirk that had started years ago watching *The Carol Burnett Show* with her mom. It had morphed into a nervous habit when she first went to kindergarten and was too scared to leave her mom.

"Just tug your earlobe like Carol," Lolly had told her outside the classroom door. "It's your silent way to tell me—and yourself—that everything is going to be all right."

Arden kept her back to Van until she could hear him walk away. Van was—*what?*—a decade her junior and her seventh boss in the last decade? They all came and went, like pretty toy soldiers, putting in their time until the New York office called them up, or they landed at *People*, *EW*, or *Entertainment Tonight*.

No one wants to be a writer anymore, they want to be a celebrity, just like the ones they cover, Arden sighed.

"Mail!"

Arden heard a loud plop, and turned to find a mountain of mail already sliding across her desk. She walked over and began to rifle through it.

"Same ol', same ol'," she said, shuffling through press releases and early samples of celeb perfumes. A return address on a padded envelope caught Arden's eye, and her pulse quickened. Arden's desk began to rumble, and as she looked out her window to see the El screech by again, its tracks shaking violently, she could feel her headache begin anew.

Arden picked up the puffy package and nabbed a pair of scissors from a *Paparazzi* coffee mug on her desk to cut it open.

A little card came tumbling out.

Arden's heart leaped into her throat. Her mother's beautiful handwriting was no longer the looping, expressive cursive of her youth. Instead, it was jagged, slanted, hunched.

She read the card:

ALICE:
But I don't want to go among mad people.
THE CHESHIRE CAT:
Oh, you can't help that. We're all mad here.

How's the writing going, my dear?

Remember, we all must go a little CRAZY sometimes to find our happiness.

Hope you can visit this summer. I miss you and love you with all my heart!

 All my love to ~~Lorna~~ Lauren.

 Mom

Arden's heart began to beat in her temples, then in her eyes.

Lorna? Oh, Mom, Arden said to herself, seeing her mother's mistake. *How could you get your own granddaughter's name wrong?*

Arden picked up the envelope and turned it upside down. A little box rolled across her desk. She popped it open and sitting atop a velvet throne was a silver charm of the Mad Hatter.

"*Alice in Wonderland!*" Arden smiled. "My favorite book!"

Arden studied the charm, placing it in her palm and rubbing her fingers over it.

Still with the charms, Mom? Still believe they're somehow magical?

She thought of her mother's charm bracelet, thick with charms, the one she never removed, the one that drove Arden crazy growing up with its incessant jangling.

How long has it been since Lauren and I have been home to Michigan? Where does time go? Arden felt a tinge of guilt and then her laptop dinged.

Deadlines. That's where.

Arden picked up the card and reread it.

"*Hope you can visit this summer.*"

Her mother rarely asked for anything, much less a visit. Visiting home was tough for Arden, a lot like, well, Alice falling down the rabbit hole. It had not been easy for Arden growing up in small-town America. She had been an awkward kid, and it had not been easy having a mother like Lolly Lindsey.

"It's not that she's a bad person," Arden said to the charm, as if it were a therapist. "It's just that she's . . ."

"Debbie Reynolds!"

Yes! Exactly!

Bigger than life. Always on stage, Arden thought.

"Arden?"

Arden jumped and turned to find Van standing in her doorway, his blue bow tie adorned with yellow boats twitching around his neck.

Wait. I didn't say that? she realized.

"Debbie Reynolds is dating a twenty-five-year-old! Story's coming now! We have an exclusive. We'll need it online in less than fifteen minutes!"

"Of course," Arden nodded. Van was already walking away when she called, "But when I'm done, I think I'll take an early lunch, if that's okay. I need a little fresh air."

Van stopped, moonwalked back three steps, and checked his watch, before shooting a finger at Arden.

"Sure thing. We need you fresh. But it's still too early. Make it a late lunch, okay? We have a lot happening today. No plans tonight, right? Or this weekend? That promotion to web news director is still up in the air . . . ," Van added.

Arden opened her mouth to respond, but Van was gone.

Two

May 2014—Lauren

Pablo Picasso once said, "Every child is an artist. The problem is how to remain an artist once he grows up."

Lauren set down the quote she kept framed on her dorm desk and stared at her MacBook, her econ notes blurring in front of her eyes.

A warm breeze raced through the window of Lauren's dorm room and tousled her blond hair.

She inhaled deeply, the smell of Lake Michigan and the approaching summer air filling her lungs and her room, that sweet perfume of flowers and fresh water, newly cut grass and warmth, that smell of . . . hope.

She heard playful screams outside and stood, leaning over her desk to study the scene: Her dorm on Northwestern University's campus looked out at the lake and student beach. Even though the breeze off the water was still a bit chilly, boys played Frisbee without shirts and girls in bikini tops soaked up some rays.

There was something about the simple scene, of her fellow students enjoying a day free of care, which caused Lauren to stand, yank off her purple Wildcat hoodie, and walk over to the painting easel she had perched by her desk.

She lifted her brush.

"Ice cream!"

Lauren jumped, as her roommate twirled into the room like a tornado, dark curly hair flying, carrying two ice cream cones.

"I thought we could use these," Lexie said, speaking even faster than her typical New York style, "between being stuck inside studying for finals on this gorgeous day and . . . well, I just found out Josh is playing me again."

"What?" Lauren nabbed the ice cream from her roommate with one hand and wagged her paintbrush at Lexie with the other. "What did he do this time?"

"I found out that he's taking Grace to see Beyoncé at the United Center this weekend!"

Lexie licked her cone. "He was supposed to take me!" she said. Her shoulders drooped. "It was supposed to be our last big date before we go home for the summer."

"Dump the loser," Lauren said, setting down her brush. "Now!"

Lexie continued to lick her cone, when her brown eyes widened. Lauren knew instantly: Her roommate had a plan.

"Can't your mom get us tickets to the concert?" she begged. "So we can spy on him?"

Lauren rolled her eyes, took a big bite of her ice cream, and then took a seat on her bed. "She could, *technically*. But you know she'd never ask. That's so not her."

"I can't believe your mother works for *Paparazzi* and never uses any of those connections."

"She just would never take such a risk. I'm sure she's covering the concert . . . from her office," Lauren said, then added, "Lexie, you need to forget about him. He's not good for you."

Lexie stood, holding her half-eaten cone in her mouth, and began to text.

"Done!" she said a few seconds later.

"So romantic," Lauren said, and then began to laugh at her roommate. "By the way, you realize you look like a pregnant kangaroo, right?"

Lexie looked down at her distended belly and laughed, nearly choking on the cone still in her mouth.

"I foo-got," she mumbled through the ice cream, reaching into the over-stuffed pocket of her hoodie to unleash a flood of envelopes and packages onto her bed. "Here. Mail."

Lauren finished her cone, walked over, and began to rifle through the mail scattered across her roommate's bed.

With each envelope she opened, her heart closed a little bit more: Notices for internships at Fortune 500 businesses and banks, schedules for on-campus interviews, alerts for job fairs. It was late in the year, and she had ignored every notice. And had yet to tell her mother she was without an internship or job for the summer.

Lauren sighed. "I can't deal with this," she said, ducking her head, her blond locks cascading over her face.

"That's not going to block out the future," Lexie said. "Why don't you just tell your mom you're not happy about your major?"

"You've met her," Lauren said. "Happy hasn't been an important part of the equation in her life for a while now."

"If you're unhappy now," Lexie said, "just imagine how you're going to feel in twenty years."

Lauren sighed.

"Hey, what's that?" Lexie suddenly asked, pointing at a padded manila envelope on her purple NU comforter.

The envelope had Lauren's name on it, but she didn't recognize the labored handwriting at first, until she saw the Michigan return address.

"Grandma!" Lauren said, happily tearing open the envelope to find a card and a little box.

"I bet I know what it is." Lexie laughed, flopping onto her bed. "Open it."

Lauren popped open the little box to find a silver charm of a hot air balloon.

"Read it," Lexie urged.

Lauren smiled, thinking of Lolly. She adored her grandmother—her crazy wigs, her carefree attitude, her love of nature, her fiery spirit.

Lauren opened the card and began to read, her voice becoming emotional the more she read:

This charm is to a life filled with adventure!
Remember . . . YOLO!
Love,
Grandma

"She knows 'You Only Live Once'?" Lexie asked, opening her laptop before stopping as her voice cracked. "Your grandmother is so thoughtful. I miss my grandma. I loved her so much."

Lauren rubbed her roommate's shoulder, Lexie's words resonating deeply. "She is still with you," Lauren said.

"I know," Lexie said, biting her lip, before changing the subject. "Econ final. I guess it's time, isn't it?"

Lauren gave her charm a little kiss, before carefully adding the hot air balloon to her charm bracelet. She walked to her desk and placed Lolly's card next to her Picasso quote, running her fingers over her grandmother's writing. She looked over at Lexie and thought of what it would be like to lose her own grandmother.

Is she seventy now? Is that even possible? Lauren wondered.

Lauren looked up and studied her litany of academic, artistic, and athletic accomplishments lining the wall and sighed.

You are so right, Grandma. I do need an adventure.

Lauren stared out her dorm window again at the kids cavorting along the lake. She shut her eyes.

Growing up, she visited her grandmother every summer in Scoops, Michigan, at her cabin on Lost Land Lake. They were the best times in her life, although her mom's relationship with her own mother had always seemed as chilled as the ice cream cones she and her grandmother devoured nearly every day of the summer.

"Ice cream headaches are so worth it, aren't they, my dear?" her grandmother would say, massaging Lauren's temples with her fire engine red nails.

Every day was an adventure with her grandma: She taught her to swim, to paint, to believe anything was possible.

"Laughing and dreaming are the most important things in the world, my dear," she would always tell Lauren. "Those are the things we forget as adults."

Lauren thought about Picasso's words again, returned to her easel, and pulled out her paints.

She could see her grandmother's face, hear her laugh, feel her warmth. Lauren considered the econ final she needed to study for instead of painting.

I wish I could paint full time, Lauren thought, looking at her wall of accolades. *All of those times I made the honor roll, all of those times I won my track meets, and he didn't even care.*

There was no photo of Lauren's dad anywhere in her room. Save for the occasional note, the check on birthdays and Christmases, she hadn't seen her father in years. He'd abandoned her, and she had no intention of meeting his new family.

Being accepted into Northwestern was Lauren's own accomplishment: Her grades and awards had helped, of course, but it was her talent—her art—that had earned her admission.

But when Lauren was beginning to pack for her freshman year, her life had changed: She found the nasty letters from her father in the attic. She discovered the details of the divorce settlement in the garage. She came upon the overdue bills and financial statements in her mother's rolltop desk, and while her mother was at work, she read the diary her mother had stuffed in a shoebox under the bed. That's when Lauren learned the truth: Her father had refused to help Arden raise her.

Sometimes you must relinquish your passion in order to survive, her mother had written in her diary.

Guilt had overwhelmed Lauren. She took her mother's maiden name. She also never realized how much her mother had sacrificed until then, and she vowed that she, too, must do just that: A quarter million dollars for an art degree wasn't realistic. How could she expect her mother to pay all of that back? But a business degree, and then an MBA? With those, she could help her mother dig herself out of her financial straits. She could help undo the hell her father had created.

And then, if it wasn't too late, I could still paint, Lauren vowed.

Lauren now understood her mother's mantra: "Be sensible," she would say. "Be careful. Be planned."

It stood in direct opposition to her grandmother's: "Dream, my dear. Dream!"

Despite needing to study, Lauren began to paint, conscious only of her brushstrokes.

"Wow," Lexie finally said, knocking Lauren from her trance. "I mean, wow."

Lauren stopped and studied her emerging work.

When she was painting, the world fell away. She *lived* in the painting.

"You know how talented you are, right?" Lexie asked. "That's a gift."

Lauren smiled and tentatively touched the still-wet canvas, as if the painting were a bird she didn't want to frighten with any sudden movement. When it was completed, it would be an image of her grandmother licking an ice cream cone, the summer sun melting it quickly, her aging face a mix of childhood happiness and age lines.

"You have her eyes," Lexie added. "Same color as the sky right now. I'd have to wear colored contacts to make mine look like that, you know."

Lauren smiled. "Thanks for being such a great friend and roomie."

"Wasn't easy," Lexie laughed. "Remember?"

Lauren nodded.

When she started at Northwestern, Lauren's initial excitement had descended into near depression after discovering her mother's financial difficulties and changing her major.

They're going to make me room with some boring girl who refuses to go out, and loves statistics, Lauren was convinced.

Lauren had been icier than a Chicago winter to Lexie the first few weeks they lived together. They were taking Statistics One together, and Lauren's stress was palpable.

"How can they call this 'a friendly yet comprehensive introduction to statistics'?" Lauren asked in their dorm room, her voice rising. "It's not a puppy. Data mining? Quantitative strategies? Really?"

"Let me help you," Lexie said one night. Lauren could tell her roomie was trying to calm her down.

"I'm good," Lauren replied. "I'm not Suze Orman, like you."

"You know what?" Lexie had said. "I'm done. You don't want help. You don't want to talk. You don't want to get to know me. You just want a pity party. Fine. I'm outta here."

And, with that, she gathered her stuff and left, slamming the door behind her.

Frustrated, Lauren had begun to paint. Slowly, a little girl in a spinning inner tube emerged, a storm approaching on the horizon over the lake.

Lauren had fallen asleep at one in the morning and woke to find Lexie studying her painting.

"You never wanted to major in business, did you?"

Lauren had shaken her head and collapsed into tears.

"Tell me what's going on," Lexie said. "Please."

From that moment, the two had become inseparable. After Lauren shared with her grandmother how helpful Lexie had been to her, Lolly had sent the girls charms of two puzzle pieces, one that said "Best" and the other "Friends," which they wore religiously.

"Guess I can't avoid the inevitable any longer," Lauren said, shaking her head, bringing her back into the present. "Wanna go somewhere to cram with me?"

"Sure. Let me get ready first, okay?"

"For what?"

"I'm single again," Lexie said. "I can't go out looking like this."

"Hurry up, then," Lauren replied, pulling her hair into a loose ponytail and tying a light jacket around her waist.

"You don't have to do anything, do you?" Lexie sighed, heading into the bathroom that united their suite with the girls next door. "Give me five minutes, okay?"

Lauren shook her head and took a seat on her bed, knowing five minutes in Lexie's world meant twenty in real time.

She stared at the painting. *I miss my grandma. Why does life always get in the way?* Lauren felt her cell vibrate in her pocket and yanked it from her jeans.

Meet me for a late lunch? her mother texted.

Getting ready to study for econ final with Lexie. I can do really late lunch. 3?

OK. Meet me under Marilyn. Love you!

K. Me, too.

Lauren stopped and then began to text again.

Did you get a charm from Grandma, too?

Yes. A Mad Hatter.

I'm a little worried about her.

Lauren's heart raced as she thought of her grandmother so far away. Then her mother texted: *Me, too. We'll talk.*

Lauren chuckled. "Talks" with her mother were often more *Judge Judy* than conversation.

"Ready?" Lauren grabbed her purse and waited for Lexie.

"A few more minutes," Lexie said. "Hair's not cooperating."

Lauren fell backward onto her tiny bed, and glanced at her grandmother's note. The sun glinted through her dorm window and shined on the painting of her grandmother, her face seeming to radiate an internal light.

Three

May 2014—Arden & Lauren

The statue of Marilyn Monroe towered over Chicago's Magnificent Mile, her skirt blowing skyward in the Windy City's late spring breeze.

There were endless restaurants and landmarks downtown where Arden could have met her daughter—Water Tower, Millennium Park, Navy Pier—but the twenty-six-foot, lifelike sculpture of the actress and her scene on the subway grate from *The Seven Year Itch* captured for eternity somehow seemed right to Arden today.

Arden looked up at the shimmering stainless steel and aluminum mega Marilyn and thought of her shinier, bigger than life mother and her too small hometown.

Things haven't quite worked out as perfectly as I thought they would.

Arden sighed, thinking of Van and her job.

She walked directly between Marilyn's legs and patted her giant, strappy heel.

Sorry, Marilyn, Arden mumbled to the sculpture. *I feel like I get paid to look up celebrities' skirts.*

She took a seat on a concrete step facing the sculpture, as tourists leaned against the statue's legs and pointed up for the quintessential photo.

"Is she . . . ?" a heavyset, elderly husband and wife with rosy faces and fanny packs asked Arden.

"Yes." Arden smiled patiently. "She's wearing panties."

"Would you mind . . . ?" the cherubic-looking couple asked Arden at the same time.

"Sure," Arden said, standing to reach for the outstretched digital camera. "Smile!"

The couple pointed their fingers up Marilyn's skirt and laughed uneasily.

"That's a keeper," Arden said.

She watched the couple walk away, hand in hand, and for a second—in a city of millions—Arden felt so alone.

She shut her eyes and remembered taking a picture of her mom and dad in front of Lake Michigan at sunset. They had positioned their hands so it looked like they were holding the sun up to keep it from disappearing behind the water. Her parents' faces were as bright and happy as the exploding sky. Arden smiled at the memory before the thought of her own failed marriage popped into her head.

I was happily married like that once, she thought. *Before . . . everything . . .*

A small group of youthful protesters suddenly marched by, excitedly stabbing the blue sky with picket signs and yelling about college loans.

The word "loan" floated across the Chicago spring air and landed in Arden's ears, reverberating throughout her soul.

Arden's pulse quickened. *When is Lauren's next tuition payment due?* Arden wondered, feeling the familiar anxiety.

Arden briefly considered calling her ex to ask for additional help this month with the loan payment but quickly thought otherwise. She was about to stash her cell away in her purse when it rang.

Must be Lauren, she said to herself. *Running late.*

Arden glanced at the number. She was confused. It was coming from her mother's area code, but it wasn't her mother's number.

"Hello?" she answered. "This is Arden."

"I'm so sorry to bother you, Mrs. Warren . . ."

"It's Ms. Lindsey now," Arden replied icily at the reference to her former married name, thinking it must be a telemarketer. "I'm divorced. And I'm on the no-call list."

"Oh, I'm sorry. I forgot about that," the woman said in a Northwoods accent, adding uneasily, "Not about the no-call list, you know, but about the divorce."

"Who is this?" Arden asked.

"This is Doris Van Voozle. I own the fudge shop in Scoops where your mother works. I know it's been a long time since we've seen one another . . ."

"Oh, yes . . . yes," Arden said, as she tried to remember exactly how long it had been. "How are you?"

"Gearing up for another summer in Scoops," she said. "Our high season is almost here. And everyone's looking forward to your mother again . . ."

"I bet they are," Arden replied, trying to make it sound as if she meant it.

"The reason I'm calling is that your mother, well . . . she's missed a few of her shifts recently," Doris said, a hint of worry in her spirited voice. "She always comes in as soon as I call . . . and she always makes a joke out of it. Says she needs a lot more beauty sleep these days, or that her calendar is hard to update because she has to chisel it onto stone."

Arden laughed. That sounded *exactly* like her mom.

"That's so unlike her to miss work," Arden said. "She loves you. She loves working at Dolly's. It's her whole life."

"And we love her. That's why I was a bit worried about her," Doris said, before adding, "Oh, by golly, it's Lolly! Forget I called. Your mother just walked in."

"Look who the cat dragged in!" Doris yelled. Arden could tell her hand was over the receiver to muffle her shouts. But then Doris began to whisper, "Let's just keep this between us, okay? I wouldn't want to upset her. She's here now. No worries. I sure hope we get to see you someday soon. Your mom said it's been years."

Arden's worry about her mother immediately changed to guilt.

"I do, too," Arden said, trying to keep her voice steady. "We'll try and see you soon. Bye, Doris."

"Bye, sweetie."

Arden had just ended the call, but she was still thinking about her mother and what the call meant when she heard her daughter's voice.

"Oh, Mom!" Lauren called, stopping beside Marilyn's giant heels. "I didn't see you there. You . . ."

". . . blend with the concrete?"

"No," Lauren said, immediately embarrassed. "Well, sort of."

"You certainly don't, young lady."

Lauren laughed and pirouetted all the way around Marilyn's giant gam.

She was wearing a lime-green, off-the-shoulder top that billowed in the Chicago wind; tight, cropped lemon-colored jeans; large hoop earrings; a jangle of vintage necklaces; and a stack of neon jelly bracelets that would have made Madonna jealous in the eighties. Lauren's blond hair was tousled and past her shoulders.

"So? How are finals going so far?" Arden smiled at her daughter and asked.

"Intense, but fine. Business is . . . business," Lauren sighed.

"Fine?" Arden asked. "You don't sound fine at all. What's wrong?"

There had been an infinite number of times Lauren could have spilled the beans about knowing how bitter her mother's divorce had been and about finding all of the overdue bills and financial statements. So many times she could have told her mother she hated studying business, but she didn't want to add to her mother's pressure.

"Just stressed about finals, I think. I'm hungry. What do you want to do for lunch?" she added, changing the subject.

Arden raised her eyebrows, and Lauren knew that could only mean one thing.

"Garrett's popcorn?" Arden asked.

Lauren laughed and pulled her mother away from Marilyn. For most mothers and daughters, popcorn wouldn't constitute "lunch." But when Lauren and Arden were feeling stressed and when it was Garrett's famed corn, it did. "I'm guessing you want the Garrett Mix? Caramel and cheese?" Lauren said.

"You must be a mind reader," Arden joked. "I'll just double up on my spinning classes this weekend, or go for some really long runs."

"It's Garrett's!" Lauren said. "Totally worth it, and we'll walk as we eat it anyhow, right?"

The two zipped over to Michigan Avenue and got in the long line to nab a large, hot bag of the savory-sweet corn combo.

As the line snaked its way up to the counter, Arden thought about the many times they'd gone to Garrett's to ease breakups, setbacks, and disappointments. There had been Lauren's loss at the state debate tournament, her split from her boyfriend right before prom.

How many times did I come here after fighting with my ex, or after convincing myself I didn't need to finish my book? Arden thought.

"One large bag of the combo," the two said in unison when they reached the counter.

The duo rolled down the sides of the giant grease-stained paper bag, chomping, walking, and window shopping, leaving a trail of popcorn down the sidewalk.

"Look at these shoes, Mom!" Lauren yelled excitedly. "You should get them."

Arden stared at the strappy, sky-high heels. They were the kind celebrities wore in paparazzi pictures, but not Arden.

"Too dangerous," Arden said. "Too sexy."

The two were still studying the window when they heard, "Arden?"

"Zoe?" Arden said, surprised, her mouth filled with popcorn.

"Lookin' good, Arden," Zoe said, laughing and pointing at her mouth.

"You, too," Arden replied, swallowing hard. And she meant it: Zoe Sherman—all sassy, tousled blond hair, Pilates body, and glowing face— looked stunning.

"How long has it been?" Zoe asked.

Arden stammered for a reply.

Arden and Zoe had been members of a Chicago writing group called The Algonquin Wine Table, a humorous takeoff of the famed New York City writers' Algonquin Round Table that had included Dorothy Parker.

The writing group had been Arden's salvation at one time: They met once a week at one another's homes to write, talk, drink wine, and dream. When she was married, it had been literary therapy to Arden, although her then-husband had poked fun at the group and at her writing. And then came the divorce. It was the lowest point Arden had ever been, and it left her feeling like her writing was silly, and a book with the mounting expenses seemed frivolous when she didn't have any guarantee it would turn into anything concrete.

"Four years," Zoe finally said, answering for her. "Lauren was still in high school. How's Northwestern? Still focused on art?"

"Northwestern's great," Lauren said. "I'm a business major now."

"Business? I thought you were going to be an art major?" Zoe asked. "You and your mom were going to be artists. What happened?"

Lauren shrugged, looking back and forth between her mom and Zoe. "Life, I guess."

"And how's your book?" Zoe asked, turning to Arden. "Are you finished yet?"

"No," Arden replied too quickly, forcing a smile. "How about yours?"

"I did," Zoe said, breaking into a huge smile. "And I got an agent! She's going to shop it around once I do final revisions."

Arden felt as if she were going to faint.

"Congratulations," she said with as much enthusiasm as she could muster.

Arden suddenly caught her reflection in a storefront window, and the past few years flashed in front of her eyes: *I have a few more grey hairs and wrinkles but not a single new page in my book.*

Time had passed. So quickly, she thought again.

"You two look like you were on your way somewhere," Zoe said. "I don't want to keep you. I just wanted to say hello. And, Arden, we still meet every week. We'd love to have you back."

Arden tugged at her earlobe.

"I'll definitely try to do that," Arden replied. "It was great to see you, too."

"Stay in touch," Zoe said, hugging her friend. "I miss you."

Arden and Lauren continued their walk, making their way along the underpass below Lake Shore Drive.

"How *is* the book coming along, Mom?" Lauren asked encouragingly. "I think it would be great for you to go back to the writing group."

"Here," Arden said, handing the bag of popcorn to her daughter. "I'm not really hungry anymore."

Arden and Lauren walked in silence the rest of the way, before emerging on the running and bike path that stretched the entire length of the Gold Coast, the skyline and lakefront glimmering, Chicago coming back to life after a long winter.

Lauren stopped, kicked off her shoes at Oak Street Beach and tested the temperature of the sand with her toes.

"It's warm again!" she said happily, running toward the shoreline and finding a place to sit on the beach.

"C'mon, Mom!" she yelled back at Arden.

Arden slowly took off her shoes and sighed.

"I can't be sandy for work," she said, hesitating.

"Why not?"

Arden thought about it carefully before making her way over to her daughter.

"Impromptu beach day," Lauren said, yanking her mother to the sand.

Arden looked at her daughter, and followed her gaze out over the lake. Though the sun was shining brightly and the temperatures were warming, the waters of the Great Lake were still chilly, and the differential between the water and the air created a ghostly mist that seemed to haunt the waves. Arden wished she could relax, but between work and financial obligations, she had too much on her mind. Her body was always tense, her mind a hummingbird. And now she was worried about her own mother.

"I haven't shown you what Grandma sent me today, have I?" Lauren asked.

Lauren held up her wrist and jangled her charms. "A hot air balloon . . . for a life *filled with adventure!*"

Arden looked out over the lake and thought about her mother alone and so far from them. The Great Lake separated her from her mother, but it also connected them.

Lauren added, "I'm worried about Grandma. She's getting so old, Mom."

"Me, too," Arden admitted. "It's been awhile since we've gone to see her."

"Then let's have an adventure!" Lauren said suddenly, standing. "Let's head up there for Memorial Day. What do you say?"

With each sentence, Lauren's voice shot higher the more excited she became. "I miss her! I'll finish finals, and you request vacation. I mean, they owe you. You haven't taken a day off in years."

Arden hesitated. "But what about your internship?"

"I'm talking a week or two off, Mom," Lauren said. "Maybe head north the Sunday before Memorial weekend? Give ourselves a real break."

"But I have so many things to do," Arden said, thinking of Van and his veiled promise of a promotion. "How will they manage when I'm gone?"

"You deserve it, Mom. Let's surprise Grandma!" Lauren stopped and shook her bracelet in her mother's face. "Let's be *adventurous*."

Arden thought of the charm her mother had just sent her.

A mad hatter from the mad hatter.

The words from her mother's note echoed in her head:

Remember, we all must go a little crazy sometimes to find our happiness.

That's when some forgotten voice in the back of Arden's head—one that sounded an awfully lot like her mother's—overrode her logical one for the first time in a long time, and all she could say was, "Okay. Let's do it."

part two

The Dragonfly Charm

To a Life Filled with Good Fortune

Four

Main Street of Scoops, Michigan, looked like a live-action Currier & Ives portrait.

Arden watched as the little Victorian storefronts—filled with restaurants, coffee shops, clothing, jewelry, and handbag stores—drew in customers. Window boxes overflowing with petunias, marigolds, and begonias decorated every storefront.

"I forgot how quaint Main Street is," Lauren said. "It's just so . . . *sweet*, so quintessentially Norman Rockwell. Hey? Shouldn't we call Grandma?"

"Let's surprise her instead," Arden suggested, sniffing the air, smelling the sweet smell of fudge. "I have this feeling . . ."

Arden let her voice trail off. She grabbed her daughter's hand and led her down the narrow downtown streets canopied with white birch, sugar maples, and towering pines. An inland harbor—filled with bobbing boats, kayakers, and the last hand-cranked chain ferry in the United States—shimmered alongside Main Street, while in the distance they could see Lake Michigan and its towering dunes. It was a majestic backdrop.

They zipped through the bustling little downtown until they ran into resorters clotting the sidewalk outside Dolly's Sweet Shop.

"Wow! I forgot about all the 'fudgies,'" Arden said, using the nickname

Michiganders called tourists who took over coastal resort towns from Memorial Day through Labor Day. "They're like zombies. You just can't get rid of them. And they arrive earlier and earlier every year."

"Mother," Lauren said, whacking her mother on the shoulder, and nodding toward Dolly's nostalgic red storefront. "Ssshhh! You know why they're here."

"I do."

Arden walked up and tapped on the large window etched with Dolly's logo.

"Hi, Mom," she called through the glass.

Lolly looked up from the copper urns at the sound of her daughter's voice, her face changing from complete shock to total joy.

Lolly jumped up and down in the window, before handing her fudge-covered paddles to a young girl and running outside.

For as long as Arden could remember, her mother had been the center of attention in downtown Scoops. For decades, Lolly Lindsey had stood in the huge front window of Dolly's Sweet Shop, like Auntie Mame, a bigger-than-life personality in small-town America. While many flocked for the fudge, most came for the "show." Lolly was a regional treasure. She wore a variety of brightly colored vintage aprons: Red dotted with triple-scoop ice cream cones, white decorated with blueberries or cherries, pink with dancing cupcakes. But wigs were her signature look: Red, pink, white; bobs and beehives. Every hour on the hour, Lolly would dance and sing, "Hello, Dolly," entertaining vacationers and luring tourists into the shop.

Arden and her mother were total opposites: Lolly was as dramatic as Arden was buttoned down. And while Lolly's theatrics often embarrassed Arden, she was beyond happy to see her mother.

"My girls! What a surprise!" Lolly yelled, pulling Arden in for a bear hug. "What on earth are you doing here?"

Lolly turned to Lauren, pulled her close and began to jump anew. Lauren joined in, jumping up and down, screaming in unison with her grandmother, their bracelets rattling.

"We missed you and wanted to spend Memorial Day with you!" Lauren said, her words bouncing in the air along with her body. "I love you, Grandma!"

Lolly stopped jumping and pulled her granddaughter into her arms. "I love you, too, my dear," she whispered, before turning to Arden and raining her cheeks with kisses. "And I love you, too, my baby. It's been too long."

"I know," Arden said. "I love you, too, Mom."

As Lolly took her daughter's face in her hands to study it closely, Arden thought, *My God, she's aged.*

Even underneath the wig and all the makeup, her mother looked so much older than the last time she had seen her. Lolly's bright red lipstick trailed up the deep crevices that ran northward from her lips, like tiny rivers. Under all the foundation, Arden could still detect dark circles, and there was a hollowness in her cheeks despite her blush. Even her mother's eyes—long the color of the blue hydrangeas she loved so much—had faded. Her apron and sweat suit couldn't hide her shrinking body or rounding back.

"So? What brings my girls to Michigan unannounced?"

Lauren and Arden stared at each other.

"Okay, what gives, girls?" Lolly asked, hands on hips. "Going somewhere on a whim—even to the bathroom—is so unlike you, Arden."

Lauren couldn't help herself: She began to laugh, so hard in fact, she had to double over, until her face was near the sidewalk outside Dolly's.

"Thanks, you both," Arden said. "Really appreciate it."

"Spill the beans, or no one gets any fudge."

"Mom! Talk! Now!" Lauren said, suddenly very serious. "There's chocolate at stake!"

"Well . . . let's just say Lauren and I needed a road trip."

Lolly looked at her daughter with great skepticism. "That'll do for now," she said. "I'm just happy to see you both again."

Lolly paused, and opened her mouth to speak, but her cheeks quivered, and Arden could tell her mother was either ready to cry or to tell them something. Instead, she simply chirped, "Now . . . who wants candy?"

What is she holding back? Arden wondered.

Lauren took off for the fudge shop. Through the window, Lolly and Arden watched Lauren nab a little white sack and run through Dolly's like a kid in a candy store. The brick walls of Dolly's were lined with uneven wooden shelves and rickety tables covered with red gingham tablecloths and little red baskets overflowing with chocolate and sweets. Lauren grabbed all flavors of homemade saltwater taffy and licorice, before nabbing turtles and a mound of maple fudge. Without slowing, she headed toward the ice cream counter in the back of the shop, where high school kids in white smocks dispensed a rainbow of flavors.

"I bet she gets a triple scoop of Superman, Blue Moon, and Birthday Cake," Lolly said, her eyes twinkling as she watched her granddaughter. "I knew it! That's my Lorna."

Lorna? Arden wondered. *Again?*

Arden turned to look at her mother, waiting for her to catch her error. But Lolly only continued to smile and admire her granddaughter. Arden thought of the card she had received from her mother with the charm, containing the same mistake, and was about to say something when Lauren reappeared carrying a bag stuffed with sweets and a triple scoop ice cream cone.

"I'm glad to see you haven't changed," Lolly said, as her granddaughter licked the cone, the ice cream already beginning to trickle down her arm in the surprisingly strong May sunshine.

Lolly smiled at her granddaughter, and Lauren placed her head on her grandma's shoulder, sighing.

"My beautiful baby girl," Lolly whispered. "I've missed you so much."

Arden watched her mom hold her daughter, and she was nearly overcome with emotion.

It's been way too long since I've been home, Arden thought.

"Hey! It's the fudge lady!" a little boy with unruly curls suddenly screamed, knocking Arden from her thoughts. A group of children quickly gathered around Lolly. "When's your next show?" they asked, as Lolly pointed at the clock in the window.

"Five minutes," she chirped.

"Arden? Arden, is that you?"

A pretty blond woman in bright Lilly Pulitzer and a choker of pearls was holding the hand of a girl, while a gaggle of children trailed closely behind.

"It's Kathy," she said. "Kathy Van Wieren."

Arden felt like Alice again, falling down the rabbit hole. Suddenly, she was back in school, the lonely, shy, dark-haired girl who read too much, in a sea of tall, towheaded, beautiful and popular Dutch girls.

"Hi," Arden sputtered. "My gosh, it's been . . . so long."

"I haven't seen you since we graduated," Kathy said, her chirpy voice as happy as a robin's. "I heard you moved to New York to write for *People* magazine . . ."

"Actually, I live in Chicago and work for *Paparazzi*," Arden answered. "I . . . well, I . . ."

Arden stopped. She realized suddenly that, other than her job, she didn't really have a reason for staying away so long.

"Well, it sounds so glamorous," Kathy said. "Working next to all those stars."

Kathy gestured at her children. "My life is anything but. Not with five kids . . . my youngest is six."

Kathy looked at her youngest, ruffled her locks, and chuckled. "I'm such a good Catholic."

She continued, "My husband and I live in Chicago, too, but we spend our summers in Scoops at my grandparents' cottage, and he comes up when he can."

Lolly reached into her apron to grab some taffy. Kathy's son lurched for the candy while her daughter hid behind her mother's body.

"Sugar," Kathy sighed. "Just what they need. But they just love your mother. Everyone does." Kathy stopped and smiled at Lolly. "She has always been quite the character, hasn't she? You two are so different."

Arden couldn't help it, but she flinched at Kathy's words, which made her uncomfortable and reminded her why she had so much trouble coming back home.

"Can we stay and watch her show, Mom?" the little boy asked, his mouth stuffed with taffy. "Puh-leeeze!"

Kathy rolled her eyes at Arden. "Yes, yes, of course. But no more candy, okay?"

Kathy smiled, her eyes traveling southward to search Arden's left hand. "Are you married?"

"No . . . ," she started, before Kathy preempted her, whispering, "Oh, my goodness. I'm sorry. I forgot."

Arden nodded toward her daughter. "That's my daughter, Lauren. She's going to be a senior next year at Northwestern."

"She's . . . *beautiful*," Kathy said, looking back and forth from Arden to Lauren.

"Thank you," Arden replied, wondering if her comment was a compliment or veiled put-down. "Well, listen . . . We just got into town, and we're exhausted."

"Let's do dinner!" Kathy said.

"Sure," Arden lied.

"Does your Mom still live in that cute little log cabin?"

Arden nodded as Kathy walked on. Arden headed over to her mother and pulled her out of the circle. "Mom, Lauren and I would like to get a bite to eat and then head over to the cabin, okay? We're tired from the drive. And we need more than sugar for lunch."

Lolly looked over at Lauren, watching her granddaughter share some of her own taffy with the kids. "Listen, I have shows until seven. So grab a bite, and I'll meet you at home later on."

"Really, Mom? You still have *shows* so late?"

Lolly's face sagged like a sailboat's mast.

"Yes, I do," she said. "People are *counting* on me. It's almost Memorial Day. They wait all winter to see my Dolly act, and the weather looks perfect for big crowds. You two go shop, get a glass of wine . . . relax. I'll run home after I'm done.

"Now, scoot! Go have some fun. Get in some trouble. It's summer in Scoops, for goodness' sake."

Arden looked at her mother and laughed. "Trouble in Scoops? Now that's funny."

Lolly grabbed her daughter by the chin and gave her head a gentle little tug. "Always such a serious face! I'll see you later. I love you!"

Arden watched her mother immediately transform into Dolly as she walked away, blowing kisses to the crowd now gathering in front, anticipating the next show.

"Ready?" Arden finally asked Lauren.

"Really, Mom? We have to watch Grandma do her thing. She *is* summer."

Arden smiled at her daughter, and then nodded. "Okay."

In her wigs, makeup, and apron, Lolly was the spitting image of the real Dolly Van Voozle featured in the shop's logo.

Though her mother's alter ego had often embarrassed her when she was young, it was a perfect fit.

She's always had a lifelong flare for drama, Arden thought.

Lauren dragged her mother toward the front of the crowd, and Arden steeled herself, taking a breath, the smell of butter and chocolate filling her nose.

A white-haired man sat down at a player piano in front of the shop, pantomime-playing as he rotated sheets of paper music onto a large spool, polkas and tunes from a bygone era filling the street outside.

The old clock chimed in the rose garden across the street from Dolly's, and Kathy's little girl asked, "Is it time for the fudge lady?" The crowd giggled in anticipation, as Lolly adjusted her fire engine red wig and opened the double doors with a dramatic flair, the scent of wholesome sweetness trailing behind her.

"Greetings!" Lolly yelled.

"Hello, Dolly!" the crowd yelled back.

"What did you say?" She laughed, lifting her hands like a cheerleader to urge them on.

"HELLO, DOLLY!"

And, with that, she yanked off her pink apron dotted with singing lollipops to reveal a sparkly white sequined gown, cut on a bias, and a strand of pearls, all of which were haphazardly thrown on over a purple sweat suit and tennis shoes. Don, the elderly man from the player piano who had trailed along behind her like the sweet smells of the shop, handed her a feather boa. Lolly curtsied, taking it from his hands, before he returned to the player piano and rolled a new sheet of paper music onto the spool.

For a few seconds, there was silence, before the speakers on the street emitted a few squeaks as the spool rotated on the player piano playing the tune to "Hello, Dolly." And then:

Lolly turned to salute the fudge shop and its logo, before bowing to the crowd. She put her boa around the shy little girl who had asked about her moments ago and shimmied with her until the girl broke into a fit of giggles. Then she urged the crowd to sing: *"You're lookin' swell, Dolly . . ."*

"Thank you!" Lolly laughed.

Lolly moved into the center of the crowd and pulled some candy from a pocket on the side of her sequined dress. *"Take some fudge, fellas, and some brittle, fellas, 'cause Dolly'll never go away."*

She took a dramatic bow, flinging her boa behind her head, as the tourists applauded and went in for hugs and photos before flooding the shop to buy treats. As soon as the crowd had dissipated, Lolly walked inside to the paper clock adhered to the window and moved the hands up an hour.

NEXT SHOW: 2:OO.

She tied her pink apron back on, adjusted her wig, and began to stir the chocolate that had been added to the hot urns.

Lolly caught Arden's face through the window and smiled broadly.

"See?" Lauren said. "She's so happy we stayed and watched."

Arden smiled at her mom, then at Lauren.

I have to admit—despite my own feelings—the crowd loves her, Arden thought.

"Let's grab a little lunch and then do some shopping," Arden said. "There used to be a great local winery not far from here, and I'm sure there's a farm stand. Why don't we pick up some wine and fresh veggies after we're done, and I'll make dinner for you and your grandma?"

"You're cooking?" Lauren joked. "We might need two bottles."

Five

Arden didn't need GPS to find her way home again.

She simply followed the dragonflies.

Every year, as the cold spring rains ended and summer—ever so slowly—began to crawl onto the shores of northern Michigan like a forgotten castaway, the dragonflies arrived to signal summer had begun.

Arden navigated her car toward little Lost Land Lake away from downtown Scoops and the sprawling, historic cottages that lined Lake Michigan. Hidden in the woods, pirated away amongst the pines, Lost Land Lake is where she'd grown up.

The farther Arden drove and the nearer she got to Lost Land, the more the dragonflies darted alongside the car, serving as her guides.

"Tinker Bell?" she remembered having asked her mother when she was a girl.

"Yes!" her mother had said. "Magic is all around you! All you have to do is look!"

When Arden turned five, Lolly had given her a dragonfly charm as a birthday present.

"To a life filled with good fortune," her mother had whispered. "Just like Tinker Bell!"

Arden looked out her window at the dragonflies, shook her head, and pressed her foot down on the accelerator.

Arden drove until she saw the old red barn with WILSON FAMILY DAIRY painted on the side, took a little two-lane road until she passed the massive weeping willow that arched over it, then turned onto a narrow dirt road, canopied under soaring pines that choked out the afternoon sun. Finally, the little road opened onto Lost Land Lake.

"It's so beautiful, Mom!"

Arden looked over at her daughter, the wind from the open window blowing her long, blond hair.

"It is," Arden said, slowing her car.

She had forgotten how stunning Lost Land Lake was: The sandy-bottomed lake, loons floating, swallows swooping, birch trees bending in the soft wind, like a Midwestern version of *On Golden Pond*.

Arden eased the car over the many potholes that pocked the old dirt road, around an ancient pine trunk, past an old birch stump, and across a swinging bridge that sat over a creek winding its way to the lake. And, finally, they drove alongside seven old log cabins with lake stone fireplaces, stoops filled with fishing poles, wet swimming suits and inner tubes, and screened porches that faced Lost Land Lake.

Home.

Lucky #7.

The last log cabin on the lake.

Arden parked in a little area outlined by a fence of stacked logs. Before she could even stop the car, Lauren bounded out.

"I forgot how cute it is! It's so Walden Pond!" Lauren exclaimed, with more enthusiasm for the setting and little log cabin than Arden could muster. "I used to think Grandma's house was made of Lincoln Logs, remember?"

Arden smiled, yanking their suitcases from the trunk.

"Lauren, I need some help," Arden said. "Can you grab the groceries and wine?"

Too late. Her daughter had already kicked off her shoes and raced down the warped wood dock that jutted over the sandy shore, reeds, and blue-green water of Lost Land Lake.

"Thanks! Appreciate it!" Arden laughed.

Arden watched her daughter take a seat on the dock, whooping in delight as she stuck her feet into the water.

Arden relaxed for a second before she clamped her eyes shut, took a deep breath, and then willed herself to find her cell and make the call she didn't want to make.

"Arden?" her ex said. "What's going on? I'm about to go into a meeting."

Nice to talk to you, too, she thought.

"I'm sorry to bother you, but . . ." Arden hesitated, instantly feeling like a failure as a wife, mother, and daughter.

"Yes? What is it?"

"I took a couple of weeks off to visit my mom in Scoops. Lauren and I haven't seen her in years, and I was worried about her. She's missing work. She's just aged so much, Tom."

"Get to the point, Arden. I'm in a hurry."

You haven't changed a bit, she smirked to herself.

"Well, since I'm missing work, we're spending a little extra on vacation, and Lauren's tuition payment is coming up, I just thought . . ."

"Are you telling me you're not managing your finances? You received this month's deposit, didn't you?"

"Yes, it's just that . . ."

"I'm sure you'll be just fine. You've always been a hard worker. Why don't you ask your mom to help out?"

Arden could feel her anger rising.

"Tom, that's not nice! I can't believe you would suggest that."

"Tell Lauren hello for me. Hope she can visit this holiday season. I'm taking the family to Aspen. She'd love it."

"Always a pleasure, Tom. Have a nice Memorial Day."

Arden hung up and sighed, watching her daughter splash her feet in the lake.

Arden yanked the suitcases along the mossy steppingstones that hopscotched to the front screened porch and thought, *I'm glad Lauren doesn't know about any of this.*

After nearly every thunderstorm, polished lake rocks—in a myriad of muted hues—would wash ashore, and Arden had helped her mom gather the flat stones to finish a walkway. The stones were always mossy in May, before the summer sun had a chance to dry and warm the rocks.

Arden stopped and inhaled deeply. It was a habit every time she came home.

Green.

If Arden could describe the scent of Michigan in spring and summer, it wouldn't be a particular smell—blooming wildflowers or boat exhaust from the lake—it would be a color: Green.

Everything—after a long winter's hibernation—came alive, and it was that essence of life that permeated the state, like Mother Nature's perfume.

I'm alive, it screamed, *in every petal, leaf, reed! I'm green!*

As Arden came to the porch, she suddenly realized she had no key, but then remembered: Her mother never locked a door in her life. She gave the screen door a tug. It was unlocked.

She swung the creaking door open and dropped the luggage. The smell of wood and smoke—from decades of fires in the old stone fireplace—greeted her. Nothing had changed: Same old barn red glider, rocking softly in the breeze, same quilt over the white wicker couch, an odd array of jigsaw puzzles—shellacked, yellowed, and poorly framed—lined the walls, patchwork rugs and painted floor coverings—of pines, ferns, trillium—scattered across the slatted wood floor of the porch.

It's nice to be home again, Arden thought, *even with so much on my mind.*

Some of the screens were in need of repair. A couple had come loose from the frame, a couple had tiny holes.

The makeshift coffee tables on the screened porch—old milk crates, blueberry boxes, and shelves from neighbors' bee houses—were stacked with magazines.

Arden kicked off her sandals, instantly feeling sand on her feet just like she had as a girl, and walked toward the stacks.

Growing up, her mother had read *National Geographic, Life,* and *Newsweek* religiously. When Arden had told her mother she had gotten a job at *Paparazzi,* Lolly had stated, "I never knew celebrities interested you. I hope you're also writing about something that is deeply meaningful to you."

Arden picked up a copy and did a double take. She stooped with some effort and began rifling through the issues.

These aren't just any *magazines, these are* my *magazines.* Paparazzi. *Seemingly every issue. Even though I don't have a byline on any of the articles.*

Arden's lip quivered, and she clutched the magazines to her as if they were her mom.

A breeze through the screen door ruffled Arden's hair, and she heard a fluttering. She tilted her head, trying to determine the noise.

She walked into the cabin and that's when she noticed a myriad of Post-its fluttering in the wind. They were stuck to nearly every surface, almost like a Yellow Brick Road: The log walls, the refrigerator, the microwave, the pantry, the phone, even the floors. Arden followed the trail, plucking and reading the jagged handwriting aloud: "Eat breakfast!" "Get milk!" "Do laundry!" "Pay the phone company!" "Vacuum!" "Make dinner!" "Be at work by noon!" "Always put keys in basket by fridge!"

Arden drew her arms around herself.

She turned and walked into her mother's bedroom, a little log-filled nook that overlooked the lake, the long shadow of a pine falling across the middle of the worn mattress. More Post-its were stuck to the mirrors over the dresser and the bathroom sink.

"Take medicine!" "Take a bath!" "Brush wigs!"

Arden took a seat on her mother's bed and turned to face the window looking out at Lost Land Lake. The glass was cracked open, and the smell of water and pine filled the air. In the distance, kids screamed as they jumped into the still-cold lake. A dragonfly flitted onto the old wood windowsill.

Arden grabbed a pillow from her mother's bed and began to hug it.

Another scent overwhelmed her: Her mother's perfume.

Shalimar.

Arden noticed Lauren standing in the doorframe. In the shafts of light splaying off the lake and through the pines, her daughter looked so young.

"Mom?" Lauren asked, walking over to take a seat on the bed. "Are you okay? What's going on with all the Post-its?"

"No, I'm not okay," Arden said, her voice shaky. "And I don't know."

Suddenly, the screen door banged shut.

Lolly appeared in the door, smiling. It was then she noticed Lauren fidgeting with a Post-it and the look on Arden's face. Her smile began to fade.

"I didn't want you to see this. I didn't want you to see the cabin this way," Lolly began to mutter. "I'm so sorry. I'm so sorry."

"What's going on, Mom?" Arden asked.

Lolly walked over and took a seat on the end of the bed. She hesitated, as if she wanted to make up an excuse, but all she could do was blink back the tears pooling in her eyes.

"I don't know," she said, as a flood of tears trailed down her cheeks, clearing paths through her makeup. "I'm scared."

Six

I t's my belief she has MCI."

Arden was sitting with a geriatric doctor in an office at Lakeview Geriatric Center, grateful to have gotten an appointment on such short notice.

The beauty of living in a small town, Arden thought, before asking, "MCI?"

"Mild cognitive impairment," Dr. Van Meter said. "It's the stage between normal forgetfulness due to aging and the development of dementia."

Arden watched her mother through the window walking with Lauren in the immaculate back garden of the center, pointing out birds and flowers to her granddaughter, before the two took a seat on a teak bench. Arden knew this facade was, in essence, just like a pretty celebrity on a magazine cover. It made a great first impression, and helped distract people from the real issues in their lives.

"Are you sure?" Arden asked.

"Completely," the doctor said, patting Arden's leg. "We've performed a comprehensive series of physical and neurological tests on your mother, including a mental status examination."

The doctor stopped and smiled at Arden. "This isn't the end of the world, Ms. Lindsey. You need to know that. Not everyone with MCI develops dementia, but this does signal the need for significant changes in your mother's life and care. People with MCI have mild problems with thinking and memory, and they are often aware of their forgetfulness. Symptoms can include difficulty performing more than one task at a time, difficulty solving problems or making decisions, forgetting recent events or conversations, taking longer to perform more difficult mental activities."

"That explains the Post-its in her cabin?"

"Yes. And you should be aware that, over time, should your mother develop dementia, her life will become more complicated. She will have difficulty performing tasks that used to come easily, she will get lost, she will have language issues, she will misplace items. She could have personality changes that lead to inappropriate behaviors."

"She's had that for a long time," Arden said, trying to make a joke.

The doctor didn't laugh, and Arden realized that her mouth was moving as she stared at the doctor's face. She wasn't able to hear all that she was saying, because Arden kept thinking, *What do I do? I can't move to Scoops.*

Slowly, the doctor's voice began to play in her ears again, as if the volume on a TV were being turned up.

"As the MCI worsens, symptoms are more obvious and interfere with the ability to take care of oneself, like dressing, eating. One forgets current events, as well as one's own life history and awareness of who one is."

Arden took a sharp breath. Suddenly, the image of her mother's charm bracelet filled her head.

"Is there a . . . ," Arden began to ask.

"There is no cure," Dr. Van Meter said, cutting Arden off in midsentence with a polite but definitive smile.

No cure.

Arden couldn't feel anything, do anything more than stare at the doctor. She felt helpless.

"But there is hope," the doctor said. "I know this is difficult, Ms. Lindsey. Your mother has done a good job of not letting people know for a long time. She's made jokes, deflected attention. Like many people with MCI, it's hard for them to ask for help. She didn't want to burden you, or alter her life, but it's getting more serious now."

The doctor stopped and smiled reassuringly. "Ms. Lindsey, my hope is that—with the right diet, exercise, routine, mental stimulation, and ongoing care—she can have some normalcy in her life for a long while. But there will be good days and bad days. Right now, we need to focus on the good ones, okay?"

Arden smiled and nodded as the doctor continued to talk. Her heart broke.

"How much does my mother know?" Arden asked, still thinking about the doctor's words: *There is no cure.*

"Just that she's getting old and occasionally becomes confused," Dr. Van Meter said. "We like to leave how to tell a loved one up to the family, unless, of course, you'd prefer we do it."

In the distance, Lolly and Lauren had removed their shoes and stuck their feet into a fountain. They were threatening to splash each other.

What do I tell them? Arden thought.

Lolly's laugh echoed up and through the office window to her daughter.

If I tell her the truth, will she spin into a depression? Or would I be doing her a disservice by hiding her condition?

"Sorry to interrupt, doctor. You asked that I meet Ms. Lindsey?"

A bearish rumble of a voice surprised Arden, and she opened her eyes, a large shadow now cast over her body.

She saw that it was actually a bear of a man—well over six feet tall, bearded, muscled, soulful brown eyes—standing in front of her.

"Ms. Lindsey," Dr. Van Meter said, "this is Nurse Thomas. He's a geriatric nurse here who also does home care. I think it would be beneficial if he came by to assess your mom at home and help you establish a good routine for her."

Nurse Thomas smiled. "My first name is Jake, by the way. Not 'Nurse.'"

Arden chuckled, and tucked her dark hair behind her ears.

"Well, I have your number and will give you a call tomorrow to set up a schedule, if that works for you," Jake continued.

Arden nodded and tugged at her earlobe.

"Carol Burnett?" Jake asked, picking up on her nervous tic and mimicking the ear tug. "I love her, too."

"Yes," Arden said, flabbergasted.

"Everything's going to be all right, by the way," he said with a warm smile, giving his earlobe another tug in return. "Nice to meet you. See ya later."

As Arden watched Jake lumber away, she felt an immediate connection to him. There was something comforting and safe about him, like being tucked into a blanket next to a fire in the middle of a snowstorm.

"Arden," the doctor said, standing, signaling an end to their meeting, "all you can do right now is be patient with your mom. What you tell her is up to you. We usually think it's best to be completely honest. Nurse Thomas will help you get your mother into a routine that will help her, and he will be available to help coordinate home care as well, things like meds, meals, physical therapy."

Arden continued to nod, starting to feel overwhelmed.

"When you go home, make sure to talk about the past."

Arden's heart stopped for a beat.

"It's what we call 'reminiscence therapy,' and it may help her remember her past. You can pull out old pictures, play her favorite music, put together a memory album—a sort of life-story book—in order to encourage her to talk about the past. That can help jog memory—both long- and short-term. It will help keep her mind active and engaged, and helps allow Jake to incorporate routine without it seeming as a threat. This also lets you hear stories she might not be able to relay to you one day."

Arden winced. *The last thing I want is to return to the past.*

"Ms. Lindsey, I know it's hard, but please know this: Your mother needs you now more than ever."

Rosemary Clooney crooned from the car radio as Arden drove back to the cabin. Lolly had found an oldies station.

Arden kept looking over at her mom and in the mirror at her daughter. Arden felt as off course as the meandering roads that led to Lost Land Lake.

Arden could feel her hands shaking on the wheel trying to figure out what to tell Lolly and Lauren about Lolly's condition. She tightened her grip to keep herself from crying.

Overhead, the blue skies were quickly giving way to dark clouds and a rumble of thunder. Without warning, the skies opened, and Arden had no choice but to pull off the road by a farm.

The rain pounded the car and slid down the windows in thick sheets.

"Look how beautiful," Lauren said, putting her face to the back window. "All that green. The rain makes it look like a thick oil painting."

Arden's guilt magnified.

"How are you feeling, Mom?"

Arden tilted her head at her mom.

"So very serious," Lolly said.

"I am serious, Mom, because this is serious." Arden sighed. "I know the doctor didn't tell you much about your medical issues . . ."

"I'm getting old, Arden."

"Well, we need to address your memory issues," Arden started gingerly. "There are some big issues we need to discuss."

"You've said 'issues' about a hundred times in the last few seconds, my dear," Lolly said, turning down the radio. "As the kids say today: What's the 411, bro?"

Arden took a deep breath. "When I spoke to the doctor, she told me that she had diagnosed you with MCI, which is mild cognitive impairment. The doctor says it is a stage between normal forgetfulness due to aging and the development of dementia."

Lolly clucked her tongue. "MCI . . . CSI . . . HBO . . . LOL.

"YOLO," Lolly continued. "Right, Lauren?"

"That's right, Grandma," Lauren laughed, sharing a long look with her grandmother before Arden interrupted.

"Mom, I know you want to make light of this . . . I know that's the way you've always dealt with the difficulties in your life, but we're going to tackle this together, okay? I have someone scheduled to come out to help you get started with some new medication, a routine, meals, PT, and mental exercises . . . And we're going to start with some therapy, too. For the body and mind. We're going to share some memories."

Lolly chuckled. "Memories are very different from mental exercises, my dear."

Lolly stopped and looked her daughter squarely in the eyes. "I told you, I'm getting old, Arden. Period. Not really much of a surprise there."

"Mom, I don't think you want to talk about it because, well, maybe you're depressed. And that's totally understandable. We can get you help for that."

Lolly smiled and looked at the vista beyond the car. Her face—bright with makeup—shone with an inner light.

"I'm not depressed, Arden," Lolly said. "And I don't need help for depression. I've had an *amazing* life. One filled with blessings I could never have imagined. Depressed is the last thing I am. Realistic, yes. Sad, never."

Lolly reached out and patted her daughter's leg. "This is actually going to be more difficult on you and Lauren than it is on me. Yes, my life isn't a walk in the park, but whose is?"

Lolly cranked the radio back on, and Dean Martin came on without warning.

"I think that's enough talk about 'issues' today," Lolly said, ending the discussion. "I'm tired, and I have to work tomorrow. I'd like to get a little rest before then."

The rain began to slow, and sunshine filtered through the pines.

Arden rolled down her window—the smell of fresh pine invading her senses—and started the car. As she drove, she heard a soft flitter, and then she saw it—a flock of dragonflies rushing by her car.

Arden thought of the charm her mother had bought her so long ago, and shook her head at its erroneous premonition.

To a life filled with good fortune, indeed, Mom.

Seven

T he scent of cinnamon and sugar arrived before Arden had fully
woken up.

One of the quirks of growing up and living amongst a group of little log
cabins alongside a lake was that you could smell—and hear—nearly everything your neighbors were cooking and doing, especially in the summer
season: Scents and stories wafted through open windows and floated
from screened porches: Muffins and bacon, coffee and cookies, grilled
steaks, fried fish, and the latest local gossip.

This morning, Arden already knew she would be having her mother's
rhubarb–sour cream coffeecake.

"It smells delicious," Arden said, as she entered the cabin's tiny kitchen,
her foot coming to rest on an errant rhubarb leaf. "But it looks like a natural disaster."

Lolly's kitchen was always filled with life, and it had as much or more
character than its owner: Old, warped, and worn pine countertops, open
cupboards painted farmhouse red with vintage cherry-print fabric on tension blinds serving as the doors. A giant, white farmhouse sink sat below a
window overlooking the lake, while a center island of lake stones took up
the middle of the space. The antique appliances—the pink gas stove and

the aqua refrigerator—suddenly took on deeper meaning for Arden. She could picture herself as a little girl helping her mother bake, running back and forth from fridge to stove to island with ingredients and measuring cups.

Who would've guessed they'd outlast my mom? Arden couldn't help but think.

"She's messier than Julia Child, but I'm determined to make a baker out of her yet," Lolly laughed, nodding at Lauren.

Lolly had positioned a large, dark green rhubarb leaf on top of her red wig, like a sort of bizarre beanie, while Lauren's blond hair now featured two stalks of luscious red rhubarb holding a bun in place.

"It's my country nod to chopsticks," Lauren smiled, striking a super-model pose. "You like?"

"I'm hoping the coffeecake is better."

Lolly and Lauren looked at each other, surprised by Arden's sense of humor. "We have a third Musketeer?" Lauren asked with faux astonishment. She picked up three rhubarb stalks, handing one to her mother and the other to her grandmother. "Touché!"

"En garde!" Lolly laughed.

"We need to talk after breakfast," Arden said, putting her rhubarb stalk down, then turning to leave the kitchen. She added, "We need to finish our conversation from yesterday."

Lauren frowned, placing her veggie sword atop a cutting board and whacking it with a knife.

"Let's check the coffeecake!" Lolly said, winking at Lauren while opening the oven door. "Always insert a toothpick into the center. If it comes out clean, it's ready . . . *and it's ready!*"

"My first coffeecake!" Lauren said with amazement.

Lolly cut a little edge of the coffeecake—bright red spots against a fluffy white cake, all nestled under a golden crumb topping of brown sugar, cinnamon, and butter—and then blew on the fork to cool it. Lauren took a bite. Lolly followed suit and smiled.

"It won't be your last! It's delicious! Get the coffee. I'll bring out the cake!"

The desert rose dishes rattled a bit in Lolly's hands as she set them down, pushing aside a half-finished puzzle, which had seemed to occupy the mid-

dle of the trestle table on the screened porch for as long as Arden could remember. "It's lovely today. You know how Memorial Day weekends can be."

Arden scooted up the long wooden picnic bench and took a seat at the
small, pine green table. Her rear and arms sank into position: Years of use
had molded diners' arms and rear ends into the table and bench. You didn't
just sit at this table, it enveloped you.

"A little homemade whipped cream?" Lolly asked, placing a small container onto the table. "Just to gild the lily?"

Lolly took a big scoop of whipped cream and threw it on Arden's
coffeecake.

"So? What do you think?" Lauren asked. "It's my first coffeecake."

Arden took a bite, her face brightening with delight. "It's incredible."

Lauren's face lit up like the day. "Grandma's recipe."

Lolly and Lauren took a seat on the glider, and the three sipped coffee
while watching Lost Land Lake come alive as resorters returned to open
their homes for the long Memorial Day weekend: Boaters, floaters, and kayakers spilled onto the lake, grills were dragged into back yards, Adirondack chairs were lined up along the sandy beach, while inner tubes and
fishing poles were stacked on docks. Lolly's cabin sat at the end of Lost Land
Lake, and the water lapped just a few yards from the screened porch: It
was the perfect location. Loons and reeds were her closest companions,
while the commotion remained at a distance.

The loons moaned their soulful cry, and Lolly pursed her fire engine
lips and whistled, her mouth and throat eliciting a clucking moan exactly
like that of a loon. A few seconds later, the loons returned her call.

"You still remember how to do that, Mom?" Arden asked. "That's
amazing."

"I remember a lot of things from the past," she said. "Because I
choose to."

Lolly sipped her coffee and tossed a quilt over her and Lauren's legs.
"Speaking of which . . . you mentioned sharing some memories yesterday.
You said the doctor thinks it would be helpful for me to start 'mentally
exercising.' Well, ironically, I gave that a lot of thought last night. And I
think we should do that. All of us. The things I never told you, all the questions you never asked, all those little details that slid by, I guess it's time for

me to share them. And the best way to do that is by telling you about these charms around my wrist."

Lolly lifted her tiny wrist and shook her arm, which was as tanned and spotted as a bird's egg. Her fingers and wrists were knotted and gnarled, but still had a delicateness to them. The bracelet sagged with charms, singing with every little movement Lolly made.

"These charms capture every moment of my life . . . and yours, too. None of us would be sitting here today without them. They tell the story of where we've been, how far we've come, and where we still hope to go. I still believe that my life is like that dragonfly charm I gave you when you were a girl: Despite any sadness, it *has* been filled with good fortune."

Lolly held her charm bracelet up to her face and squinted.

"So, let's see . . . where's the best place to start?"

As her old hands rifled through each charm, her eyes grew misty, as if touching each one were unlocking some long-ago memory.

"I think the best place to start is with this one," Lolly finally said. "My sewing machine charm. And it's only fitting as we're covered with this quilt. Lauren? Are you ready?"

Lauren nodded.

"Arden, are you ready? I know how much you always hated that old sewing machine," she said. "But I think this will give you a different perspective."

Arden thought of the sewing machine and all the embarrassing home-made clothing she had to wear as a teen, recalling all the kids who teased her so much that all she wanted to do was run away from Lost Land Lake. Forever.

As if on cue, a breeze swept through the screened porch and rattled a wind chime, continuing its path to jangle the charms on the charm bracelet.

"I think they're ready, too," Lolly laughed. "This sewing machine charm was the first one I ever received. It was from my grandmother, Mary, and it's the reason we're all sitting here today."

part three

The Sewing Machine Charm

To a Life Bound by Family

Eight

1901

The ticket was nestled in the straw, right under an egg. Mary O'Connell looked up, her blond hair sticking through the top of the wire in the chicken coop, and blinked big tears out of her cornflower blue eyes.

"I don't want it! What if I never see you again?" Mary asked.

Her father, John, stood outside the hen house as snowflakes tumbled slowly through the air like forgotten confetti. He held out his gloved hand for the egg. When Mary handed him the ticket instead, he refused it.

"It's a miracle, Mary!" he said in his Irish brogue, grabbing the egg from her and placing it in a wire basket. "It's a ticket to America!"

America, she thought.

At seventeen, all Mary knew was this tiny plot of land, these chickens, and her parents' garden. She could hardly imagine a place so far away. And yet she knew there was no work in Ireland. Her job prospects were bleaker than the weather.

"We can barely survive as it is, Mary. We will follow you when we get more money."

John O'Connell called himself an "egg dealer," but even he knew that was generous: His few chickens gave him just enough eggs to sell from a ramshackle cart every weekend at the town market, and his garden gave him just enough vegetables to keep his family upright. The rest of the year, he worked as a laborer, but no one really had enough money to hire outside help.

Marian O'Connell had worked as a seamstress before the local factory closed, and now she made specialty dresses for wealthier families—communion and wedding dresses, a few times a year—but she mostly sold her quilts at market alongside her husband's eggs. Mary worked alongside her mother at the sewing machine, studying her, watching her, learning her mother's craft by the flicker of firelight in their tiny thatched cottage.

"Eggs and quilts, Mary, eggs and quilts," Marian would chant as she sewed. "Just enough of both to keep us from dying. That's no way to live."

Marian's sister-in-law and brother, a skilled wood carver, had traveled to America two years earlier, and he'd found work as a furniture craftsman in Grand Rapids, Michigan.

"Many immigrants are here," her brother would write, "logging or crafting furniture. You must come. There is work in America!"

And then one late winter's day—out of the blue—he and his wife had sent a prepaid ticket to the O'Connells with a note: "Only enough money for one. You must decide who sails."

It had never been much of a decision. "Mary," her parents cried when the ticket arrived. "Mary."

As the snow melted atop Mary's head—white on white—Mary crawled on her knees over to another chicken and roused it from its home. It cried and squawked, but reluctantly found another resting place. Mary felt its anguish and mouthed, *I'm sorry.*

She looked at the ticket as she felt for more eggs:

June 14, 1901.
Prepaid Passenger Ticket
Steerage to America

Four months later, she stood at the rail station, one suitcase and one ticket in hand, ready to board the train that would take her to the ship that would take her to America.

"We will try and send money, but you will need to work when you reach America," her father said. "Then you can go live with your aunt and uncle in Michigan."

"We love you, Mary," her parents said, holding her tightly, kissing her cheeks, her head, her eyes. "Write! And we will see you soon!"

Mary could feel her knees buckle and her heart crumble as her parents let her go, but she could see the hope in their eyes and that alone carried her forward.

Mary boarded and took her seat next to a window, watching her dark-haired, handsome father hold his tiny, blond wife. When the train began to move, Mary's parents ran alongside, waving goodbye, until the platform ended.

It would be the last time Mary saw her parents.

When Mary arrived at port, she couldn't believe the size of the giant hulled steamer ship and the number of people boarding. "It's as if all of Ireland are going to America!" she said to another young girl as she waited to board.

For a brief moment, as Mary boarded with hundreds of others, she walked the ship, wide-eyed at its opulence: Grand salons, flamboyant ballrooms, stunning dining rooms with white tablecloths, silver, and crystal. One of the ballrooms seemed as large to Mary as her whole county.

"Miss! Ticket?"

Mary jumped at the sound of the voice, and turned to find a man in a white uniform holding out his hand.

"Steerage," he said, before pointing toward a stairwell outside the ballroom. "Down. Down, down, down."

Mary disappeared down a steep winding steel staircase, her bag banging behind her, until she emerged at the bottom of the ship and was herded—just like she used to do with her father's chickens—into a tiny pen.

If the top deck were heaven, Mary learned, than steerage was more like hell: It was dark, noisy, smelly, and stuffy.

"Better find a bunk," an older woman cautioned Mary, as people jostled one another in a near panic.

Mary passed by a series of large bunk dormitories, with little or no privacy.

She peeked into bathrooms that were open to all. A sign read that access to the open deck was limited.

Mary tossed her suitcase on an upper bunk, crawled in, and stayed until the same elderly woman who had helped her before brought her soup that night.

"I'm scared," Mary told her. "I miss my family. Why is everyone leaving home?"

The woman smiled at Mary and swept her locks out of her eyes. Her touch was soft and gentle, like Mary's mother's. It grounded her.

"Hope," the woman whispered. "Hope."

And for seven days, Mary lay in the dark, eyes closed, fighting seasickness and homesickness whispering that word, "Hope!" to herself, as if it were a life preserver in the middle of the ocean, a parent in this vast world in which she now found herself alone.

"We're here!" she heard one day. "We're here!"

A flood of people rushed for the steps, swimming up the stairs, like salmon.

When Mary made it to the deck, exhausted, dirty, dragging her only belongings, she thought she was going blind: She had seen little light in days, and it took her eyes a while to adjust.

Slowly, slowly, the first thing that came into focus—as her hair blew in the early summer wind—was a giant woman, wearing a crown and raising a torch in her right hand, her sandaled feet trampling a broken chain.

"Is that . . . ?" she started.

"The Statue of Liberty!" people were yelling. "America!"

Mary didn't know why, but she started to cry, weep, and—for the first time—she didn't feel totally alone.

The steamship docked at Hudson's Pier to disembark first- and second-class passengers, while third class and steerage boarded a barge to Ellis Island. Mary stood on the barge, clutching her suitcase, the cool wind of America tossing her hair around her head, like the clouds above. The grandeur of the immigration station was unlike anything Mary had ever seen: Towering on Ellis Island was a stunning French Renaissance structure in red brick with limestone trim.

Is America so grand? Mary thought.

Mary was ushered with hundreds of other steerage passengers to the Great Hall Registry, where they waited to undergo medical and legal inspections.

Mary watched as doctors scanned patient after patient, listening to their hearts, looking into their mouths and eyes, studying their skin.

Each time a doctor would state, "Quarantine," and mark a patient with an *X*, Mary would struggle to hold back tears.

After hours of waiting, she heard: "Mary O'Connell?"

As a doctor began to look over Mary, her heart raced.

"You are nervous," he said. "Just take a deep breath . . ."

Mary inhaled, shut her eyes, and said a prayer.

"Next," the doctor said, pointing toward another man sitting at a desk, who then checked Mary's identity against the ship's manifest.

"Welcome to the United States," he said.

Mary didn't move. Tears came.

"Welcome to the United States," he repeated.

"What do I do now?" Mary asked.

"Anything you want," he said, smiling. "This is the land of opportunity."

"Mary," the girl heard a woman call. "Mary, this way!"

The older woman who had calmed Mary on the ship was motioning for her.

"My family is headed to a boardinghouse in New York City," she said. "You can come with us where you will be safe."

When they arrived, Mary was immediately overwhelmed by New York: It was loud and crowded. People moved at a pace Mary had never experienced.

The family set up a cot at the boardinghouse and Mary slept in a room with eight others. Between the snoring and the noise of the city, Mary was unable to sleep, so she arose and went to the living room of the boardinghouse where she sat in front of a fire.

Mary began to cry, as she thought of home, of her mother, of that sewing machine in front of the fireplace. And—just like the man at Ellis Island had promised—opportunity came to Mary.

"I heard you crying," the older woman from the ship said to Mary.

"I miss my family," she said.

"Do you have any skills?" the woman asked.

"I can sew," Mary replied.

"Then you will find work," she said. "Now, let's get some rest."

Mary rose at dawn and began blindly meandering from tailor shop to seamstress shop in New York, inquiring if they had any jobs available.

"We don't hire immigrants," they replied.

"How old are you?" others asked. "You're just a child."

By late afternoon, Mary was exhausted and hungry. She felt as if the pace and hubris of New York were eating her alive. As she stood outside a dressmakers shop, rejected again, a well-dressed woman emerged from a carriage carrying a sack. Mary watched as the woman entered the shop and began gesturing excitedly to the owner behind the counter, her giant, feathered hat and long, ruffled skirt moving in concert with her motions. She pulled beautiful white fabric that looked like clouds from the sack.

Mary walked to the shop door and cracked it slightly.

"We cannot do that," the man with the moustache said. "I'm sorry."

"Please," the woman asked.

The man continued to shake his head.

The woman exited and whisked by Mary, a look of disappointment etched on her pretty face.

"Madam?" Mary asked.

"I have no money for beggars," the woman said, brushing off Mary.

"I can make that dress for you!" Mary stated proudly.

"You can?"

The woman stopped before Mary, considering her, as her carriage driver opened the carriage door. "My baby will be baptized next Sunday, and I need a dress for myself that is as sacred as the occasion. The man said his shop didn't make communion dresses, and he knew no one that could."

"I can!" Mary said, lifting her head.

"You can?" the woman asked warily.

"Yes!" Mary said. "Except I have no tools or space. And the gentleman in this shop said he was not hiring."

"Wait here," the woman said. "I've been a client of his for a long time. We'll see about that."

The woman again entered the shop and began pointing back at Mary, whose heart had risen to her throat.

Finally, the owner gestured at Mary to enter.

"You will do fine in America," the carriage driver said to Mary, smiling.

Mary entered the man's shop.

"This is your only chance," he said, his moustache twitching. "I am Mr. Edwards."

The woman nodded at the man, and then handed Mary her material and a dress pattern.

"You have until dusk," he said, pointing toward a back room. "You will pay this lady back if you ruin her material, understand?"

Tears formed in Mary's eyes. "Thank you, madam. Thank you. And thank you, Mr. Edwards."

Mary nodded at the woman as she smiled and exited, and then pulled a curtain, revealing a back room where an army of women sat at treadle sewing machines—row after row—making men's suits, women's gowns, and little girls' dresses.

It resembled a ballet to Mary, as women moved in sewing syncopation and rapt rhythm with one another, feet flying, hands dancing, bobbins bobbing, and colorful thread spinning, which looked like fire exploding from their feverish work.

Mary scanned the room, and a woman with a tight grey bun nodded toward an ancient Singer sewing machine on a big treadle stand in the very back of the workspace. She pointed a thick hand with muscled fingers at the machine, a bracelet around her wrist jangling as if a hundred wind chimes had been rattled.

"Iz old, like me," she said in a thick Polish accent without a hint of irony, as the room of women tittered. "No one wants it, either."

She stuck out her old hand. "I am Rima Jablonski."

She helped Mary set up at the old machine, and Mary positioned the white fabric just so. Mary took a deep breath and studied the dress pattern. It was from a French magazine, *La Mode Illustrée*, and was one of the most detailed yet exquisite patterns she had ever seen: A floor-length dress with flowing arms fitted at the wrist, a high collar—with an intricately stitched, repeating pattern of a family crest—with an attached bow, a cinched waist with a fabric belt featuring a dogwood bloom on one side, suspended from which was a small cinched bag with tassels. The bottom of the dress was softly ruffled, with eyelets. The face was the only skin that showed in the pattern's picture.

Mary shut her eyes for just a moment and bowed her head in prayer.

I know it is nearly impossible to complete such an intricate dress in a matter of hours, but I am asking for your hands, and my mother's hands, to help me.

When Mary opened her eyes, the entire room of women had stopped and were praying with her.

Mary gulped, took a deep breath, and said softly, "To opportunity."

As if one chorus, the women sang, "To opportunity," and—though they worked at separate machines—they worked in unison for the rest of the day. Finally, hours later, Mary stood, walked to the front of the room, and held up her dress.

The room exploded into applause.

"You must show him now," a woman said to Mary, nodding past the curtain toward Mr. Edwards. "He must inspect it."

Mary's heart was in her throat as she took the dress to Mr. Edwards.

"Took you long enough!" he barked.

He unfolded the dress and began to examine the zipper and the stitching.

Mary felt as if she might faint. He was silent, save for the exhale of air that ruffled his moustache.

"I worked very hard on the ruching," Mary said, her voice filled with tremors.

"Ssshhhhh," Mr. Edwards said.

How will I ever pay the woman back? How could I have believed I could do this? How could I have ruined her material? Mary worried.

The owner studied the collar and waist, the bow and bag, his face slowly filling with admiration, his moustache twitching in excitement.

"Would you like to work here?" he asked.

Mary jumped at the sound of shouting, and turned to see a crowd at the curtain. "We have only the one machine you used today available."

Mary began to cry.

For the next few months, Mary worked in the dress shop and saved money, sending as much as she could spare to her parents while saving enough to earn fare west to Grand Rapids. Near the end of summer, Mary approached the owner and asked, "How much for the old sewing machine I have been using?"

"You want to leave?" Mr. Edwards asked. "You can't!"

"My aunt and uncle are in Michigan, and I must reach them before winter. I have finally saved enough money, and I would like to buy your sewing machine. It is a part of me now, and I will need it to earn money."

Mary used the last of her savings to purchase the treadle sewing machine, and on her last day at the shop, as Mary was saying her goodbyes to the women, she felt a tap on her shoulder. Rima Jablonski, who had introduced her to the machine, was pointing a bulbous finger toward the back door that led into the alley.

"I have something for you," she said. "A gift."

"No!" Mary protested. "I can't."

"You must," Rima said. "Is tradition of my country."

She began to tell Mary the tale of Jadwiga, who was a female monarch of Poland before queens were recognized. As a result, Jadwiga became king, renowned for her kindness.

"Jadwiga once took a piece of her own jewelry and gave it to a poor stonemason who had begged for her help," Rima told Mary. "When ze king left, he noticed her footprint in plaster floor of his workplace, even though ze plaster had already hardened before her visit. That footprint can still be seen in one of Krakow's churches."

The woman stopped and sighed, a rattle coming from deep within her chest. "My mother always told me, 'Give a piece of yourself. You will never realize how deep of a footprint you might make on a stranger.' So, to you, I give a piece of my life. I am old. I have little time left. But you . . . you have whole life ahead of you."

The old woman unlatched the bracelet from around her wrist. It sparkled in the alley's summer sunlight. The bracelet was filled with stones and pieces of amber, and charms of unusual design.

"Yes," the woman said, finally locating the right item on her bracelet. "Here it is!"

She handed Mary a small, worn silver charm with her aged fingers. Mary held it up in the air, until the sunlight illuminated it: It was a charm of a sewing machine.

"Just like the one you use here," she said, nodding. "Yes? Just like the one you will take with you."

"I can't," Mary said again. "It's too important to you."

"Which is why I must pass it on," she said. "You are like me: You come here from another place. You have left your family."

Tears began to form in Mary's blue eyes, and she lowered her head and cried.

"This simple charm has much meaning, my child," Rima said. She took Mary's young hands in her old ones, and held them tightly. "This is to a life bound by family . . . no matter how far away they may be. As long as you wear this, they will always be near."

The woman undid the naked slim bracelet around Mary's wrist, one her parents had given her when she was younger, and added the charm. Mary held up her wrist; the charm looked as if it had always been there.

As Mary traveled by covered wagon with others seeking family in the north and west, her bracelet danced, and Mary's fingers felt for the charm to calm herself. The charm made Mary feel safe, protected, surrounded by family. On her trek to Michigan, Mary stopped to do seamstress work in towns along the way, where she earned enough money from her sewing machine and her skills to get her to the next town.

When Mary made it to her aunt and uncle's tiny home in Grand Rapids, Michigan—exhausted from her many months of travel to join her family—it had just begun to snow.

"It's only November," Mary said.

"Welcome to Michigan," her aunt Sarah laughed, inviting her inside, where a tiny bedroom in the back of the house had been readied, keepsakes from Ireland placed around the room, and helped her unpack.

Mary thought of the day she found her ticket to America nestled under an egg, and of how the snow had stuck to her father's dark hair, making him look angelic. The memories, coupled with excitement and exhaustion, caused tears to flow.

"Are you feeling ill, Mary?" Sarah asked.

"No," she said, trying to explain her feelings. "I'm feeling . . . *blessed* by family."

Sarah held her close as they sat on her new bed, and Mary told her of her travels to America, her trip here, and her charm.

"It's ready," her uncle Sean said, interrupting the two.

"We have something to show you now, too," her aunt said, taking Mary's hand and leading her to the living room.

Mary inhaled sharply. Two chairs in front of a large picture window had been cleared, and Mary's Singer now sat there, framed by a hillside of snow-kissed pines. A fireplace burned nearby.

"This is where you will work," Sarah said. "You need a spot as inspiring as your work."

"Until you meet a husband and have a family of your own, that is," Mary's uncle laughed.

Mary sewed in that spot—through the dark days of winter that only the lake-effect snow could brighten, the spring bloom of daffodils so thick they made the hillside look as if it had been spun in gold, and the stunning summer when it remained light until nearly midnight—creating wedding dresses and business suits, quilts and coats. She sold them in shops around town, and before long many of the town's wealthy families hired her to do work just for them. Mary enjoyed the quiet of Michigan, and she saved money, sending it back to her parents, until one summer night she noticed that the dinner table was set for four.

Before Mary could ask why, a man resembling a wolf—an animal which Mary often observed through the window as she sewed—rumbled into the house. Mary screamed, and the man retreated.

"That's no way to greet our guest, Mary," her uncle laughed. "This is Web Falloran."

Wilbur "Web" Falloran owned a broad, burly body, and a face covered with an unkempt beard. When Mary screamed, the man curled his arms into his big chest as if he were going to have to engage in battle.

"I'm so sorry," Mary apologized. "You startled me."

"Web gets that a lot." Sean laughed. "He's a lumberman, Mary, from Scoops, Michigan, near the Upper Peninsula. He brings wood down to Grand Rapids for the furniture makers. And he's a fellow Irishman!"

Over a dinner of shepherd's pie and colcannon, Mary discovered the man she'd thought was a wolf was gentler than a pup. He spoke with a quiet rumble, almost like distant thunder, and he complimented Mary on her sewing and her bravery in coming to America. When dinner was over, he asked Mary's aunt and uncle if he could take Mary for a walk amongst the pines.

"Tell me about the charm on your bracelet," he asked as they walked.

Mary smiled, stopped suddenly under the boughs of an ancient pine, and ducked her head, her hair falling toward the green grass of the hillside.

It was a perfect Michigan summer night, warm and filled with the sound of peepers. Mary shut her eyes and inhaled deeply. The smell of nearby Lake Michigan filled the air. For a moment, Mary thought she was back in Ireland.

"You want to know about this charm?" she asked.

It seemed an odd question for a man to ask, much less a woodsman.

But Web only nodded his head and looked deeply into her eyes. "Yes," he said. "It must mean a lot to you."

So Mary told him, and he smiled a big smile underneath that bushy beard, his dark eyes twinkling in the last hints of day. "There is nothing more sacred than sewing," he said. "It is like the art of a lumberman. Both provide shelter for a family. Both require hard labor and long hours. Both, in the end, are works of art."

Two weeks later, Web returned for dinner, and they again went for a walk. Under the same pine boughs, Web stopped and pulled a small box out of his pocket.

"Open it!" he said.

Mary lifted the lid, and sitting atop a little velvet throne, was a charm of a four-leaf clover. "Luck of the Irish," he smiled. "It was my mom's. She sent it to me years ago, after I came to America. She said this charm is for luck in love and life."

He hesitated. "I think I have finally found luck in love and life."

Web softly pulled Mary's wrist into the summer air and added the charm next to the sewing machine.

And then with only the pines and the peepers as witnesses, Web leaned in and kissed Mary's lips. For a big man, the kiss was as tender and gentle as a soft rain. Mary collapsed into his arms. When Mary turned to walk home, she saw the curtain in the picture window move. Her aunt and uncle had been secretly watching.

Three months later, Mary was married. They moved into a little log cabin Web had built for his bride on a little lake—Lost Land Lake—in the woods outside of Scoops, Michigan.

Web set Mary's sewing machine up in the front window of the new log cabin, which was built with pine logs Web had felled and split, cured and carved. White mortar held the logs in place, and it was filled with windows.

"You can work here and always have a view of Lost Land," Web said.

The autumn vista inspired Mary, and—though the newlyweds had little money—she journeyed to the local feed store and picked out pretty patterned feed sacks, and to fabric shops where she fished out scraps, remains, and leftover material. Mary began to make quilts and curtains for the cabin. She began to make a name for herself in town, sewing for the locals. And when Mary found out she was pregnant a few months later, she ordered layette set patterns from McCall's and—inspired by the world outside her cabin window—sewed a yellow baby blanket, with intricate designs of floating swans, lake loons, tall pines, and tender tulips.

As winter turned to spring, and magical May breezes melted the winter's snow, Mary had to inch her stool back from her Singer, to give needed airspace between her belly and the bobbin. She became obsessed with handmaking items for her new baby, from socks and swaddling blankets, booties, beanies, and burp cloths, to onesies and a going-home-from-the-hospital outfit. Web made a tiny bassinette by hand, and Mary stacked it with their baby's clothes.

"The charms were right," Web told Mary one evening as they sipped iced tea on the screened porch. "We are blessed in America."

During the last month of her pregnancy in July, Mary felt something change in her body. One day, after months of internal kicks, she could no longer feel anything, and when she went to visit her doctor, his face went blank as he held a stethoscope to her stomach.

"What's wrong?" Mary asked. "Is something wrong with my baby?"

Mary was rushed to the operating room.

Her baby—a girl—was stillborn.

Mary could hear Web's sobs echo down the hospital's hallways.

"We can try again," Web said to Mary, as she recovered. "Doctor says you're fine. Just happens sometimes."

But Mary didn't respond, even after she had been released from the hospital a week later. Along with her baby, she had lost hope. She refused to talk, or eat.

The first thing Mary did as soon as she returned from the hospital was take a seat in front of her Singer and begin to sew. In the middle of the night, Web woke to find his young wife was not beside him. He could hear the soft whir of the Singer sing throughout the cabin.

"Mary, what are you doing?" he whispered in the night.

She simply looked up at her husband and continued to sew.

"Mary, what are you doing?" he asked again.

"Making our child's burial dress."

Web's heart shattered, and though he wanted to run away and cry, he said instead, "I'll keep you company while you sew."

The funeral dress was long and white, with full arms and pink stitching and little pink bows. The hem featured floating swans, lake loons, tall pines, and tender tulips.

A few days after the funeral, after Web had returned to work and the cabin was maddeningly quiet, Mary gathered every ounce of strength she had and carried her sewing machine to the lake. When she finally reached the shoreline, drenched in sweat, Mary edged into the water, up to her waist. Her clothes were heavy and wet. Step by step, Mary walked into the lake, still holding her Singer.

Suddenly, a swallow dove over her, flitting back and forth as if to draw her attention. Mary noticed the light on its wings. In the near distance, a loon moaned, as if commiserating with her. Mary stopped walking. She could feel the sun on her back. She swore she could hear Web's laugh echo off the water, as it did when he hooked a fish. Children were swimming, laughing, in the distance.

Slowly, Mary turned and walked out of the lake.

As she did, her bracelet jangled in the breeze even as her arms struggled to hold the sewing machine, which made her charms dance even louder.

She looked at the sewing machine and then the charms of the sewing machine and the four-leaf clover, their images reflected back to her from the lake.

This simple charm has much meaning, my child, Mary remembered Rima telling her when she first gave her the charm. *This is to a life bound by family . . . no matter how far away they may be. As long as you wear this, they will always be near.*

Suddenly, Mary screamed, a scream so loud the swans took flight and the loons quieted. And slowly, one step at a time, Mary trudged back to the cabin, carrying her sewing machine. She returned it to the window facing the lake, and never told her husband of her intentions.

A year later, Mary gave birth to a daughter. She would have four more children before she died at the age of eighty-seven.

"Bound by family" were the last words Mary uttered.

Nine

O ne of her children, of course, was my mother," said Lolly.

"None of us would be here without that charm," Lauren said, her own bracelet jangling with excitement.

"That's quite a story, Mom," Arden said slightly less enthusiastically than her daughter.

"I'm glad you wear yours," Lolly whispered to Lauren, touching her granddaughter's wrist. "You'll never know how much that means to me. I wish your mother would wear her bracelet."

Lauren reached out and grabbed her grandmother's hand, their bracelets resting against one another.

"Can you teach me to sew again, Grandma?" Lauren asked. "I remember trying to learn when I was younger, but I've forgotten everything."

"I'd love to, my dear," Lolly said, dragging her feet to slow the glider. "I still make all of my own aprons I wear to work . . . *and* I used to make all of your mother's school clothes."

Arden winced.

"I finally get it," Lauren said. "That's why you don't like color, Mom. That's why you dress the way you do. You were scarred by Grandma's wild designs."

"That's not true," Arden said, sitting up suddenly, a group of finches on a nearby bird feeder taking flight at the sudden commotion.

"Oh, it is, too," Lolly said. "I liked a lot of color."

"You dressed me like a hooker, Mother," Arden said. "Little girls aren't supposed to wear fire engine red dresses and purple bloomers."

"You were adorable," Lolly said. "I can't help that no one appreciated my fashion sense back then."

Arden shot her mother a look, so Lolly took her granddaughter's hands in hers and asked, "You want to help me get ready for work in a few minutes?"

"Really?" Lauren said. "Yeah. Let me clean up some of these dishes, and go take a shower first, okay?"

"Okay," Lolly said, patting her granddaughter's knees.

Arden watched her daughter pad away barefoot. When she was out of earshot, Arden said, "How do you know all of that, Mom? About Mary?"

"I asked," Lolly said simply. "Let me tell you something, my dear. My grandma sat at that sewing machine every single day, mending clothes, making wedding dresses for happy brides, tailoring suits for the town's businessmen, making all of my clothes. I loved the sound of that Singer. The whir of the machine sounded like a million hummingbirds, and it would lull me to sleep out here on the screened porch. She could take a feed sack and make me the most beautiful dress from a pattern. She could take the scraps of rich people's clothes and make us a quilt to keep us warm during long Michigan winters. My mom always tried to give her more charms, but my grandma always refused. 'I have the only two I ever need,' she'd say. My grandma had terrible arthritis in her later years, and it was hard for her to sew. Her knuckles looked like gumballs, her fingers like bent limbs on a sassafras tree. But she wouldn't stop sewing. One day, I brought her a cup of hot tea while she worked. She patted her lap, and I jumped in it. 'Let me show you how to do a running stitch,' she said, teaching me the magic of her Singer. When we finished, I looked up at her as she sipped the tea from her favorite desert rose teacup. 'Tell me about your charms, Grandma,' I said. And she did. Before she died, she gave me that sewing machine charm, and she was buried with her four-leaf clover, right next to her beloved husband. The quilt on our laps was made by your great-grandmother," Lolly finished, running her hand lovingly over the quilt.

Arden picked at her coffeecake. She stared out onto the lake, embarrassed by the fact she had never known this.

"Well, I need to go get ready for work," Lolly said, standing up.

"Work?" Arden asked, looking back at her mother. "Mom, you need to rest."

"No, I need to go to work. I need routine. Isn't that what you and the doctor said?"

"What about us? We're here and want to spend time with you."

Lolly gave Arden a look that a parent would give a child who just doesn't understand. She walked over and lifted her daughter's chin with her hand. "And I couldn't be happier that you're here. I *need* you so much right now."

Lolly hesitated, but continued, "I just wish it hadn't taken you so long to come."

When everyone had left, Arden took a seat on the glider. She felt chilled, from the inside out, and covered herself with the quilt. She fidgeted nervously with an errant thread on the edge, and pulled and tugged until a large seam split, and stuffing began to spill forth.

After a while, Arden fell asleep under the quilt, dreaming that she was drowning in Lost Land. But the lake wasn't filled with water, it was filled with charms. Arden tried to claw her way to the surface, but she slowly sunk to the bottom, until the only things visible at the surface were the charm of a sewing machine and letters on a wave that spelled out: *GUILT.*

part four

The Kite Charm

To a Life Filled with High-Flying Fun

Ten

Arden jolted awake after a fitful night of sleep, to the sounds of loud music and giggling, rather than the moan of loons and the gentle lapping of the lake.

She tilted her head, like the RCA dog, to listen.

She felt for her glasses on the bedside table made of old birch bark and twigs, kicked the quilt off her body, and groggily shuffled to the window of her childhood bedroom. It was cracked slightly, and Arden gave it a sleepy tug to open it fully.

The ancient window—still the original, wavy glass in a peeling wooden frame balanced on fraying rope pulleys—refused to budge.

Arden crouched, leveraging her palms under the bottom of the frame, and gave it a mighty push. The window went flying all the way up, like a strongman's bell at a carnival attraction.

A cool, morning breeze rushed into the upstairs room, and Arden was transported back to the days of her childhood. This room had been her refuge. Books had been her life raft. And they still lined her room—stacked haphazardly on shelves and on the floor—a sort of literary insulation from her bigger-than-life mother and the too small town where she felt trapped.

Arden scanned the room, and her neck suddenly popped from the stress of opening the stubborn window. She yelped, and reached for the ceiling, hoping a quick yoga stretch would relieve her suddenly screaming vertebrae.

Sun salutation.

The sun was rising over the lake, and Arden smiled at the beauty. She reached high yet again, her body mimicking the tall pines just out her window, whose sky-high tops were towering toward the light and gently swaying in the wind. The sun glinted through the pines and off Arden's glasses.

And that's when she heard—at an excruciatingly loud decibel—the screech of bubblegum pop music.

Katy Perry? "California Gurls"? she wondered.

Arden leaned out the window, studying the lake, and turned her head left and right to study the lawns and beaches of the surrounding cabins for the source of the music.

Okay, who's making all the noise? It's a tad early in the morning and the week for college kids to kick off Memorial Day with loud music, she thought.

That's when the floors beneath Arden began to shake violently, and for a second she believed she might actually *be* in California in the midst of an earthquake. The world outside her window, however, was serene. An off-key voice began to sing again.

Mother! she realized.

Arden tossed on a Northwestern University "Parents" sweatshirt, the static electricity causing her dark hair to stand on end, and carefully navigated the suffocatingly narrow stairwell that led from her tiny bedroom to the downstairs. She tiptoed down the stairs and stopped at the end of the landing.

Lolly and Lauren were dancing in the living room and singing into ladles. "California Gurls" blasted from Lauren's iPad.

Grandmother and granddaughter shimmied across the floor, before turning to kick in unison like Rockettes, their charm bracelets dancing along with them. Lolly was adorned in a platinum blond wig, while Lauren was sporting one of her grandmother's red beehives. Both—*both!*—were wearing bikinis. Lauren was teaching her grandmother "the sprinkler" and how to twerk, while Lolly was showing Lauren how to lindy and twist. They were having a blast.

A twinge of jealousy rose in Arden's throat. She loved that Lolly and Lauren were so close, but she wished she and her mother could connect so easily, like best friends. Her back stiffened, and the pain jolted her body, causing the wood step on which she had been perched to creak loudly.

"Morning, sunshine!" Lolly laughed, turning to her daughter while still shaking her rear as if it had been tossed into a blender. She pointed at Lauren's iPad. "Pandora. I learned something new today!"

Arden shook her head. "Not only is it too early to be playing loud music and dancing, but, Mom, you need to rest. You shouldn't be overdoing it."

Arden's criticism sliced through the music, and Lauren muted her iPad. Lolly reached for the robe she'd tossed over the side of an old rocker.

"Don't you dare," Lauren said, seeing her grandmother's joy turn sour.

Arden's eyes widened behind her glasses. "That'll be enough, young lady."

Bristling at Arden's words, Lauren yanked off her wig and tossed it across the room at her mother. "Mom, if you want to sleep in, fine, but you don't need to police us. Grandma and I got up to do a little yoga. I thought the stretching would be good for her. And then we decided to dance and have a little fun."

Arden suddenly felt bad for putting a damper on things, but the doctor had been clear about Lolly taking it easy, and she didn't want her mother to get hurt. She never wanted anyone—including herself—to get hurt anymore.

Arden knew Lolly wouldn't say no to Lauren; someone had to step in to keep everyone safe.

"It's six forty-five a.m. I'm exhausted."

Then, looking at her mother, Arden added, "Lauren, I don't want to talk about this right now."

Lauren exploded. "Well, I do. I'm sick of sweeping every emotion under the rug. I'm sick of having my life dictated to me. I've hated my life for the last few years. I'm a business major . . . a business major. What am I doing with my life?"

Silence engulfed the cabin. Just beyond the screened porch, loons cried their mournful song, matching the mood inside.

Arden was now wide-awake. Although her daughter's outburst seemed out of the blue, Arden realized—if she were honest with herself—that Lauren was deeply unhappy.

"I found the bills, Mom," Lauren finally continued, her cheeks quivering. "All the letters from Dad. The divorce settlement. That's why I switched to business. I . . . I just didn't want to add any more stress to your life."

Lolly looked at her daughter and granddaughter, pulling her robe tightly against her body.

Arden's face froze. She tugged at her earlobe nervously.

"Oh, honey. I never imagined," Arden gasped. "I'm so sorry. I have been totally oblivious to how you were feeling. *None* of that is your problem."

Arden again felt like Alice, falling into the rabbit hole. Only this time the hole seemed even deeper. It was all becoming too much—being back home, her mother's illness, Lauren's unhappiness. Arden felt as if she were doing her best to manage everything and take care of everyone, but it still wasn't good enough.

"It feels like it is my problem," Lauren said. "The bills are all because of me."

Lauren began to weep.

Lolly walked over and put her arm around her granddaughter, giving her a tender kiss on the cheek. Then she walked over and did the same to her daughter, before holding up her wrist and rotating through the charms on her bracelet, as if she were searching through an old Rolodex.

"Aaaah, here we go!" Lolly said, her face crinkling into a big smile. "My kite charm. My mother gave this to me . . ." Here, Lolly stopped and shut her eyes to hold back tears. ". . . before she passed away. This charm is to a life filled with high-flying fun. My mom gave it to me in order to always remind me that—no matter how difficult life can be—we must always remember to have fun."

"It's not that simple, Mom," Arden said, the words coming out before she could stop them.

"Actually, it is, my dear. We will resolve the money issues somehow, I promise. You can't eat an elephant in one bite. But, you must remember, unhappiness can consume you entirely, without you realizing. Happiness is a choice."

Lolly tilted her head at her daughter, and gave her a knowing smile.

"Let's have a little breakfast and then head to the beach. I don't have to be at work until late this afternoon, so let's enjoy the magic of this beautiful day," Lolly added.

"Mom, I probably need to work. We've already been here four days, and I need to reach out to my boss. I need . . ."

". . . to have some damn fun!" Lolly inserted. "I might have to stick to my routine, but you're on vacation!"

"Mother!" Arden started to argue.

"You're on vacation, my dear. Be! On! Vacation!"

Eleven

The winding road to Scoops Beach reminded Arden of the old Thanksgiving song, "Over the River and Through the Wood." It was an adventure to get there.

The tiny, two-lane road to the beach paralleled the river that meandered alongside the downtown, and eventually fed into Lake Michigan. The river dissected the beach road from downtown Scoops, which Arden could see was already jammed with returning resorters and fudgies already in town for Memorial Day.

The beach road wound past a series of cracker-barrel cottages—all shake shingles, shutters, and mossy roofs—which were among the original summer cottages built in the late 1800s. The road slowly climbed a tall dune to breathtaking, 360-degree views of the river, downtown, and Lake Michigan. Here, mammoth summer homes—multistoried behemoths with turrets, towers, and decks—perched on the dune.

Lolly had won the argument, and now they were all on their way to the beach, though Arden's mind was still preoccupied.

Dean Martin began to blare from the backseat, and Arden jumped.

"Found it, Grandma!" Lauren laughed.

"My Dean," Lolly sighed. "Ain't that a kick in the head?"

"What, Grandma? I don't understand."

"That's the name of the song, my dear. Time I teach you a thing or two about *my* music. Turn it up!" Lolly shouted.

Lolly began to sing, and Lauren rested her chin on the cushion of the front seat and beamed at her grandmother.

Why can't she just be quiet and relax? Arden thought.

Even over the music, Lolly's "Woodie" groaned as it continued to climb the massive dune.

"Attagirl." Lolly patted the dashboard tenderly. "You got it."

The 1950 Buick Roadmaster was as much Lolly's little girl as Arden and Lauren. Lolly's father had given it to her. The Woodie was the color of the lake, the ultimate beach car: pure nostalgia, unconventional, total fun.

"Your father spent years restoring this car for me," Lolly said to Arden, repeating the lines she said every time she drove the old car. "It's a part of the family."

Les Lindsey had indeed spent years restoring the car for his wife, re-turning the outside woodwork of white ash and mahogany trim to its pris-tine state, painting the car a vintage pearlized green, clear-coating the exterior to make it look as if it had been dipped in wax, and turning the interior into a white-and-pink leather wonderland befitting Lolly. The car was huge, with a backseat and trunk that could hold four kids and enough beach stuff to keep them entertained for a week. Lolly had even used the family sewing machine to add mismatched curtains in the back windows—vintage prints of cherries, stands of pine trees, and bobbing sailboats on a lake.

Yes, "Woodie" was Lolly's beach car, and—since her husband's death many years ago—the two had become nearly as famous as Scoops's fudge, two bigger-than-life personalities, both from bygone eras, roaming the resort town.

At the top of the dune, Lolly turned the Roadmaster like an old sea cap-tain changing the direction of his ship. Arden watched her mother—in her long, bright-white wig, a geometrically patterned scarf tied around her head like Doris Day—drive while singing "That's Amore." Arden gulped, fight-ing her instinct to grab the wheel and force the Woodie to the side of the road so she could take over.

Suddenly, a canopy of ancient sugar maples and pines choked out the sunlight, as the road suddenly cut through a dense forest that led to Lake Michigan, and Arden yanked off her sunglasses.

"Look!" Lauren said, pointing out both sides of the backseat window.

On the left, a family of deer stood at attention, like wax figures at Madame Tussauds, while on the right, a wild turkey high-stepped through the woods.

The Woodie slowly crawled down the other side of the dune, the brakes moaning loudly, until it was suddenly drenched in sunlight.

Lake Michigan stretched out in front of them like the ocean, the surface still as glass, sun illuminating the greens and blues of the water. Boats motored along the lake, Jet Skis zipped by, and some very brave souls had actually ventured into the still-frigid water. A golden-sand beach stretched out, dotted by bright umbrellas and towels, picnic baskets and sand buckets, people lounging in the sun. Dunes towered in the background, and dune grass danced in the wind. The Woodie stopped as cars ahead slowed pulling up to the one-room weathered guard shack to buy a beach pass.

"Hello, Dolly!" a young, blond girl in a red lifeguard T-shirt yelled from the guard shack. "Sorry . . . I mean, Lolly! Time for a new beach pass, I see!" she added, stepping out of the shack. "But the big question is: Where to add it this year?"

The girl giggled as she scanned the front and back windows of the Woodie. Decades of beach pass decals—designed in colors, fonts, and images that reflected the passing eras—were adhered to nearly every square inch of bumper as well as the front, back, and side windows, leaving Lolly only gaps through which to see the road.

"Ever thought about removing some of those, Mom?" Arden said, pointing to a window.

"Never!" Lolly said. "It would be like erasing a year from my life."

After a few seconds, Lauren called, "Found a place," and began thumping a few square inches of open glass on the back passenger window.

The lifeguard adhered the new beach pass and said, "That'll be sixty bucks for another year at Scoops Beach."

Lolly unzipped her jacket and reached into the top of her swimsuit, her hand disappearing, going deep into the unknown, as if she were a magician.

"Here we go," Lolly said happily, pulling out a wad of damp, crushed bills. "Let's just say my piggy bank has lost some of its oink over the years."

Arden's face turned red, but Lauren and the lifeguard laughed.

As Lolly began to pull away, the lifeguard yelled, "We all love you, Lolly! Have a great day at the beach with your family."

Lolly waved back and guided the Woodie down the narrow sand-covered road—people honking, yelling, and waving as if she were the queen of England—until she found a faraway parking place in a back row near a dune.

"We can probably get you a handicapped sticker, Mom," Arden said without thinking, popping open the trunk.

"Never!" Lolly said defiantly. "Now, make me a pack mule. Start piling it on, Lauren."

This was a game Lauren and Lolly used to play: After a day at the beach when she was little, Lauren would become so worn out and sleepy that Lolly would have to carry her and all the beach gear back to the Woodie. And she did, piling towels over her neck, chairs onto her back, all while carrying Lauren, beach bags, and a cooler.

Lauren spent a few weeks every summer with her grandmother, while her father worked endless hours and her mother worked to make him happy by creating the perfect home, the perfect daughter, the perfect wife, the perfect life. Lolly taught Lauren how to have fun, to relax, to be a kid, even for a short while. When Arden divorced, she began to work every minute and every summer. Lauren felt guilty leaving her mother alone and began to fade from her grandmother's life like a late August sunset.

Lauren began to pile four towels onto Lolly's neck until she looked as if she were wearing a brace.

They really bonded in the times I wasn't there, Arden thought. *I didn't spend enough time with either of them.*

Lolly began to walk—ever so slowly, like a camel from Lawrence of Arabia—across the sand-covered parking lot and boardwalk.

Arden's heart leaped in her chest. "Mother! Stop right there! You're going to hurt yourself!"

"My mind may not always be willing," Lolly said, turning around, windblown sand dancing around her ankles, "but my body is."

Arden shook her head, and she and Lauren hurriedly grabbed coolers, umbrellas, and lounge chairs while stuffing magazines and books into beach bags, shuffling in flip-flops to catch up with Lolly, just as she found a place near the water.

Lolly flicked a giant beach towel that read "LAKE MICHIGAN—UNSALTED!" into the breeze and settled it onto the sand, before sitting dramatically and posing, like Lana Turner. "I'm down!" she laughed. "And I may not get up again!"

Lauren laughed and pretended to kick sand at her grandmother, who screamed in protest, before the two began to slather lotion onto one another, leaving Arden to set up camp. Arden positioned two striped umbrellas against the sun, laid out sheets and towels, anchoring them with coolers and flip-flops, set out books and magazines and lotions, before arranging snacks in a row on a separate towel.

Lolly and Lauren stopped and looked at Arden. "Someone has to do it, Mom. Someone *always* has to do it," Arden said.

Arden's words hung in the wind and then drifted away, like one of the nearby seagulls. Lolly smiled tenderly at her daughter. "You never give anyone else a chance to do it, my dear."

Arden smiled at Lolly, but her mother's words made Arden think of her job. She had to orchestrate *everything* there, too.

Out of sight, out of mind, Arden thought, suddenly panicking and reaching into the beach bag to retrieve her cell. *I'll just check my email quickly in case there was an emergency.*

"Darn it!" she said after a few seconds. "There's no reception down here! I forgot!"

"This isn't your office, Mom," Lauren said. "It's the beach. We're supposed to have fun, remember?"

Lauren grabbed a little radio from the beach bag and found a crackly station playing country music.

Strains of Trisha Yearwood drifted into the lake wind, and softly intermingled with the voices of beachgoers and the lapping of the water. A young boy ran by on the beach, ahead of his mother, and plopped onto the sand. The mother handed him a sand bucket, and he began to dig.

Lauren was right, Arden thought, looking at the little boy and smiling. *Lauren used to do the same thing years ago.*

Arden thought about Lauren's words and felt guilty that her daughter had taken on so much responsibility so young.

Arden inhaled—the smell of summer filling her nostrils—and tried to relax. She stared at the Manitou Islands sitting just a few miles out into Lake Michigan.

Manitou was comprised of two islands—North and South—that rose out of the lake like humpback whales. Arden had never visited the islands. They were accessible only by boat and were popular for hiking and camping, but she always wondered how the islands came to be.

"You've always been such a serious girl," Lolly said, taking a sip of water and staring at her daughter, as if she were reading her mind. "Do you remember when we'd come here when you were a child, and you'd ask how many lifeguards were on duty, or if I brought enough books for you to read, or if there were sharks in the water?"

Arden nodded.

"While other kids were swimming, building sand castles, burying one another, or flying kites, you were always by yourself working and worrying. I always admired your drive and determination, Arden. *I still do.* You are so talented. But I always worried that you'd end up, well, like this . . . You still don't know how to cut loose, relax, have fun. And I worry that is your great undoing."

Arden stared down at her towel.

"The funny thing is, my dear, I was exactly like you as a child," Lolly added.

Arden perked up and Lauren tilted her head. A lake breeze ruffled Lolly's wig and she again found the kite charm and held it out, the sunlight illuminating the silver kite and its long tail.

"But this little charm freed me."

Twelve

1954

Vi Dobbs secured the geometrically patterned scarf over her bald head, twirled around in her bikini, and asked, "How do I look?"

"Beautiful, Mommy!" Lolly answered.

And she was being honest. Her mother—with her high cheekbones and freckled face, blue eyes, pink lips, and girlish figure—was still the most beautiful woman she had ever seen.

Even bald.

"You sure you're up to this, Vi?"

"Sssshhhh! Yes! Of course!"

Vi shot her husband a look that silenced him immediately. She had spent the morning in the cabin's tiny bathroom sicker than a dog, but it was a perfect beach day—low eighties, no humidity, slight breeze, pure sunshine—and Vi took little Lolly to Scoops Beach every perfect summer day.

Outside the cabin, Lost Land Lake glimmered with all the possibility of life.

An invisible calendar whirled through Vi's mind, and she shut her eyes to stop the tears that wanted to flow.

How many perfect summer days do I have left with my daughter? she wondered.

"Are you okay, Mommy?"

Vi bent down and took her daughter's face in her hands, the reflection from the charms on her bracelet casting her little girl in dancing light.

"I'm perfectly fine, my angel! Are you ready to have some fun today?"

Lolly gave her mother an uneasy smile. "I'm okay. Do we have enough water? Is it going to be too hot?"

Vi took a seat in a rocker next to the sewing machine by a window overlooking the lake, and patted her knees. She picked her daughter up and whispered into her ear, "We have enough water, and it's a beautiful day."

Lolly looked skeptically at her mother, and Vi's heart broke. Since she had been diagnosed with cancer, Lolly had gone from little girl to old soul almost overnight, consumed by worry.

"You don't need permission to have fun, Lolly," Vi continued to whisper in her daughter's ear. "Fun is the one thing we can do anytime we want. Fun is always free!"

"I don't feel fun," Lolly said. "I feel sad."

Vi bounced her knee, trying to shake a giggle out of her little girl, but Lolly clung to the arms of the rocker, refusing to be shaken out of her sadness.

"It's okay to be sad," Vi said, gently rocking her daughter. "But you can't be sad too long, or it will make everyone around you sad. Fun brings out the good in everyone. That's why we're going to the beach today. I always want you to remember this: When the world is too much to take and when you feel sad, go to the beach and dig in the sand. Run on the beach so the wind blows your hair around. Jump in the lake and scream like you did the first time you swam in Lake Michigan. And fly a kite into the summer sky, so high that"—Vi's voice trembled, but she rocked the tremor away—"I can touch it from heaven and make it dance.

"Listen to me, Lolly: Life can be hard. It can be downright awful and sad. But you must never forget to have fun. It's the most important thing. Okay?"

Lolly shook her head reluctantly. "Okay."

"Then let's go to the beach!"

As the Woodie backed out of the gravel driveway of the cabin, Vi honked at Vern, who waved as he headed—fishing pole, tackle box, and minnow bucket in hand—into the reeds of Lost Land Lake to work his job as a fishing guide.

"Fudgies have taken over the town," Vi said, as the Woodie wound down the beach road paralleling downtown. "Do you like my new scarf?"

The windows were down on the Woodie, turning the Roadster into a wind tunnel. Lolly's blond hair stuck out the window at a ninety-degree angle from her head, while the long tie around Vi's scarf rotated like a helicopter propeller. "It's very pretty. Did you make that one, too?"

"I did. Just like your Grandma Mary taught me. And just like I'm teaching you."

The Woodie moaned as it made its way up the giant dune.

"Attagirl," Vi cooed to her car, patting the dash tenderly. "You got it."

When they arrived at Scoops Beach, Vi opened the trunk, stuck her arms straight out, and said, "Load me down like a pack mule!" which was Lolly's cue to load her mother up with towels, beach bags, coolers, and umbrellas, a game they had played forever. As Vi made her way down the boardwalk, however, her pace slowed, and when Lolly caught up to her, she said, "I need a little help today, my dear," handing her daughter an umbrella and some towels.

"How about here?" Lolly asked. Vi nodded, and Lolly began to carefully set up their spot on the sand as if she were orchestrating a dinner party at the White House.

"We're at the beach, Lolly. We're supposed to have fun. It doesn't need to be perfect."

Lolly considered her mother's words, but continued with her routine, anchoring the towels, angling the umbrella just so, continuously knocking the sand from her feet and legs every time she took a step or two.

"Do you need anything, Mommy? Are you too hot?"

"What I need," Vi said, scooching over on her lounge chair, "is for you to come here."

Lolly squeezed in next to her mother. She started to say something, but her mother shushed her. Vi watched as the warmth of the sun seemed to relax her daughter, until her breathing became one with the rhythmic tide of the beach, the sounds of happy children screaming in joyous delight carried to her on the wind and then whisked away, as if on a magic carpet.

Lolly watched the shadows dance across the Manitou Islands, the clouds cloaking them in darkness before the sun illuminated their dense forestry and running streams.

"Do you know the legend of the Manitou Islands?" Vi asked her daughter. Lolly shook her head.

"Well, according to the Chippewa Indians, a mother bear fled across Lake Michigan to escape from a great forest fire in Wisconsin with her two cubs. When the mom finally reached the Michigan shore, she climbed a steep bluff to await her cubs. The cubs were so tired from their long swim that they never reached land. The mother bear waited day after day, but her babies never came. Eventually, she died. The Great Spirit Manitou marked her resting place with the Sleeping Bear Dunes and raised North and South Manitou Islands from the spot where her little cubs perished."

Vi halted, and she reached for her daughter's hand. "That is the love I have for you. That is the love I will always have for you. It will last forever. It will never die."

Lolly's jaw began to tremble, and a lone tear sprung forth from one of her blue eyes, but Vi said, "And I want your legacy from me to be this: Always wear your charm bracelet and always have fun. Here!" Vi said, grabbing a little box from the side of the aqua beach bag. "I got this as an early birthday gift for you."

Lolly began to open the gift, tearing at the paper, but her mother stopped her. "Don't forget the poem," she urged.

"Mom, I'm getting too old for this."

"You will *never* be too old. How about I say it along with you, okay?"

This charm
Is to let you know
That every step along the way,
I have loved you so.
So each time you open up,
A little box from me
Remember that it really all
Began with You and Me.

Lolly smiled and opened the little box, pulling out a silver charm of a kite with a long, dangling tail, the sun basking the charm in a glorious light.

"This is to a life filled with high-flying fun. Promise me—no matter how hard things get—you will always have fun."

Lolly began to protest, but her mother reached out to touch her, smiled, and said, "Promise me!"

Vi could feel her daughter's skin flare in goose bumps. She watched her daughter consider her question, look out over Scoops Beach as the wind tousled her hair, and finally nod her head.

"Attagirl!"

Vi winced as she rose out of the lounger, turning her face to hide the pain from her daughter. "Wait here," she instructed Lolly. "I forgot something. I have to get it from the Woodie."

Vi imagined that, from a distance, she must look like a ghost to Lolly, through the haze of the sun and the sand. She stopped, took a deep breath to quell the pain, and then ran, faster and faster, tossing something into the air, as if releasing a dove, still running toward Lolly.

A kite! Lolly gasped.

Lolly ran toward her mother, her feet kicking up sand. Together, they began to run in stride, the kite slowly going higher, higher, higher, the faster they ran.

Thwacka-whacka-whacka-whacka!

The kite made a ruckus as the wind lifted it higher.

"I made it from the funny pages!" Vi said. "It's a homemade newspaper kite!"

"And the tail is made from your sewing scraps!" Lolly said.

The tail danced by their heads, flipping and twirling. People began to stop and point as the duo ran by, clapping their encouragement. The two ran alongside the dunes, the grass dancing, before a gust of wind lifted the kite toward the clouds, and Lolly had to shield her eyes to see how high it had gone.

"Here!" Vi said, handing Lolly the guide, two popsicle sticks stuck through a ball of twine.

"I can't," Lolly panicked. "I don't know how."

"Yes, you can. You can do anything you want! Have fun!"

Lolly dropped her hands to her sides, refusing to take the kite.

Vi fell to her knees onto the sand, still gripping the kite. "Lolly, look at me."

Lolly turned her face toward her mother. Tears were streaming down her sweet little face.

"You're going to die! I'm going to be all alone! I will never have fun again!" Lolly wailed.

Vi looked her daughter directly in the eyes. "You're right, Lolly. I am going to die. But you will never be alone. You will have your father . . ."

"I won't have you!"

"Yes, you will. I will always be right here . . ." Vi nodded at her daughter's wrist, as her charms jangled in the summer breeze. "And I will always be up there looking over you like the mama bear forever looks over her cubs."

Vi looked into the sky, beyond the kite.

"I want you to take this kite and watch how it soars. That's how my soul will be. Now I want your spirit to sail free, like this kite, Lolly. Now, run, my dear. Run into the wind, and let your spirit fly!"

Lolly took hold of the kite, and the two took off running, faster, faster, until the world was a blur. When Vi could no longer keep up, she let go of Lolly's hand.

Watching her daughter run and giggle, Vi's spirit and soul soared, just like the kite.

Thirteen

Arden and Lauren sat in silence for a long time, unable to speak.

"I'm so sorry," Arden said softly. "I can't imagine. And I never knew the legend of the Manitou Islands. It's haunting."

"I've always thought of it more as a tribute. A mother's greatest fear is that her children will die before her," Lolly said, watching Lake Michigan roll in and out. "But my mom helped make me the person I am, even though I was so very young when I lost her."

Lolly stopped and looked at Arden and Lauren. "I can't say I taught you to have fun and that shakes me to my core."

"Mom, I know who I am," Arden said. "I have fun. I've just been so busy lately. Please don't ever think you let us down."

Lolly adjusted her wig, tucking a few tendrils into her late mother's scarf. "Then show me how to have some fun."

"What?" asked Arden

"Show me how to have fun," Lolly repeated.

"What do you mean?" Arden asked, her voice a bit nervous. "You know how to have fun."

Lolly scrunched up her face, thinking, before she smiled as big as the Grinch. "Run headfirst into Lake Michigan."

"What? Really? Are you serious? The sand is too hot. The water is too cold. I'm wearing an old swimsuit. My hair will get wet. I'm too old to be silly."

Lolly continued. "Arden, you can't schedule fun, and you can't put it off for the future. At some point, you just have to say to heck with everything and dive in headfirst."

Arden looked at her mother, stood, and slowly emerged from the shadow of the umbrella.

"Attagirl!" Lolly urged. "Go, Arden go!"

Ow!Ow!Ow!Ow!Ow! Arden thought, dancing to keep her feet off the sand.

"The sand is scorching, Mother!"

"That's what the water is for . . . Go!" Lolly waved toward the lake.

Arden ran to the edge of the water, her bobbed, dark hair as rigid as her body. She began to edge into the cold water like a zombie, body and arms stiff.

Oh!Oh!Oh!Oh!Oh! Arden repeated to herself, feeling the cold water hit her skin.

"The water is freezing, Mother!"

"We should rename you 'Ow!Ow!Ow!Oh!Oh!Oh!'—sort of like *Dances with Wolves*," Lolly shouted to her daughter, laughing. "It looks like you're being robbed! There is no etiquette to getting into the water! Miss Manners isn't here to judge you!"

Lolly grunted as she got to her feet. "Good gracious, Lauren. Let's show her how it's done!"

Lolly yanked off her wig, and she could see her granddaughter's surprised look.

"What? You expected perfection?" Lolly said, touching her curly, thinning, grey-white hair. "I know I look like a yard sale Barbie. Why do you think I wear a wig? But I'm not ashamed. It's just who I am. But I can't get my mom's scarf wet, and nobody cares what you look like at the beach anyway! Everyone looks bad wet . . . except for James Bond. Now, are you ready to show her how it's done?"

"I'm glad I'm here, Grandma. Until we arrived, I'd been so stressed. I feel bad about what I said earlier," Lauren said, a look of sadness on her face. "I'd never want to upset you or my mom."

Lolly sighed. "I'm so sorry the problems of others have affected your life so deeply. Humans are like dominoes. Once we start to fall, we tend to take everyone along with us. I promise we will work this out, okay? Now, we can't solve everything this minute, but we can have a beach day."

Lauren nodded, and the two sprinted hand in hand toward the water, both still in the bikinis they had worn earlier that morning. They rushed past Arden and into the lake like wild horses.

"Wheeeeeeeee!" Lolly screamed, jumping headfirst into the water, before coming up and shaking like a wet dog.

"Wheeeeeee!" Lauren echoed.

"There's only one way to tackle life, enjoy a day at the beach, and jump into a Great Lake: Headfirst!" Lolly yelled. "Okay, my dear! Your turn!"

"Mom, it's too cold!"

Arden was still standing at the edge of the clear, cold water, her arms overhead, her teeth chattering. Lolly began to splash her daughter. Lauren followed suit.

"Mom! Lauren! Stop it! Grow up!"

"No!" they replied. "You grow down!"

"Stop it!"

"No!"

"MOM!"

"ARDEN!"

"LAUREN!"

"MOM!"

Water was now running down Arden's face.

"I'm already wet!" she yelled at them, spewing water.

Arden gave her mother a menacing look, took off her glasses and tossed them back onto the sand where they landed with a soft whoosh, and sprinted directly into the lake toward her mother, screaming like a banshee.

Arden dove into the water, grabbing her mother as she submerged, the cold of Lake Michigan taking her breath away. The two opened their eyes as they plummeted toward the sandy bottom.

Arden—sans glasses—watched her mother through the prism of the rippling water, smiling, now laughing, the sun reflecting off her head and off the water, the ripples erasing her age, making her look smooth and young.

As the two rose to the surface, Lolly messed up Arden's hair, and laughed, huge air bubbles leaving her mouth and revolving around her head, like a character in a cartoon strip who has a lot to say.

And then Lolly reached in to hold her daughter, and, for the first time in ages, Arden felt safe, weightless, protected under water—even for just an instant—and when they came up and headed toward the shore, Arden watched their reflections—mother and daughter—dance in the water.

"I love you more than anything," Lolly said to her daughter, and Arden felt overcome with happiness.

Lauren was waiting with towels for her mother and grandmother as they came out of the water, the sun-dappled droplets shimmering on their skin like glitter.

"Are you ready, Grandma?" Lauren asked, smiling.

Lolly stared at her granddaughter. "For what, dear?"

"Our surprise."

Lolly cocked her head at Lauren as she dried her face.

"Grandma?" Lauren said, starting to frown. "Remember?"

Lolly studied her granddaughter's face, searching for a clue. She shut her eyes for a few seconds. "Oh, yes," she started. "The . . . the . . ."

Arden and Lauren stared at her.

"I can't come up with the word," she said.

For a moment, Lolly stared into her daughter's eyes, and they gave each other a look that seemed to say, "What are we going to do?"

Without warning, Lauren took off running across the beach. Arden walked over and put her arm around her mother.

"It's going to be okay," Arden said, as much for herself as for her mother.

"Here, Grandma," Lauren gasped a brief moment later, out of breath. "I think this is what you were looking for . . . the kite."

Lolly's face lit up. "Yes. Yes, my dear. That's it."

"Here," Lauren said, thrusting a handmade kite made from the Sunday funnies into her mother's hands. A long tail of fabric scraps that had been haphazardly tied together dangled onto the sand, leaving a shallow trail—all the way along the beach where Lauren had just run.

"What's this?"

"Haven't you ever seen a kite before?" Lolly laughed, shaking her head like a dog, her hair drying quickly in the sun and frizzing into an impossibly adorable version of cotton candy. "That's why I told you my story. I realized I never made you a kite."

"We made it for you this morning," Lauren continued, "but I didn't know the whole story until just now."

"What do I do with it?" Arden said, feeling a mix of emotions.

Lolly walked up to her daughter and put her arm around her goose-pimpled back. The two began to walk the edge of the shore, the waves churning at their feet, erasing their footsteps as quickly as they left them.

"We have so little in life that we can control," Lolly said to her daughter over the surf. "But our happiness is one of those things. That's what your grandmother was trying to teach me: That no matter what happens in life, we can still have fun and be happy."

Arden looked skeptically at her mother from behind her water-spotted lenses.

"Now, go fly a kite!" the two generations said at the same time.

Arden slowly began to walk the shore alone, the kite still in her hand. She felt silly.

Overhead, a few puffy, white clouds bounced along the horizon, occasionally blocking the sun, as if someone turned off the overhead lights without warning.

Arden began to trot, slowly at first, until her legs were turning as quickly as they did in her spinning class. Her trot turned into a jog that morphed into a run, which, finally, became a full-out sprint.

The strong lake breeze made Arden's dark hair dance, and spray from the lake coated her glasses.

But Arden, for once, didn't care.

She kept running and running, churning sand, waiting for the right gust of wind, until . . .

Arden tossed the kite into the sky, a gust off Lake Michigan caught it and sent it flying up, up, up.

Arden screamed in delight, and, for one moment, time stood perfectly still. As Arden continued to run with the kite, she turned and looked back at her family: Her mother was no longer getting older, her daughter was no longer unhappy, and Arden was no longer consumed by work.

For one brief moment, life slowed. Arden was simply a child, flying a kite, having fun.

part five

The Puzzle Piece Charm

To a Life Filled with Friends
Who Complete You

Fourteen

Any plans to cut your vaca short? We NEED you back . . . NOW! (Isn't
Michigan boring, btw?)—*Van*

Arden stared at her phone, her fingers poised over the keys, unsure
whether to reply to her boss or e-strangle him. Still, she was about to
give in to his request, tell him, yes, she would come back ASAP,
when she heard the outdoor shower roar to life.

Though her mother was hidden just out of view, she could hear her humming an old tune and watched as a cloud of steam danced its way toward
Lost Land Lake.

Arden felt as if she were caught in no-man's land. She wanted to stay
and help her mother, but Van's thinly veiled threats scared her.

Arden looked over at her daughter and watched her furiously texting.
Lauren felt her mother's stare and looked up.

"Grades haven't posted yet," she said. "I think I'll get all A's again. Don't
worry."

Arden's heart sank, realizing how much pressure Lauren must feel to
excel.

Before Arden could say anything, Lolly called to her from the stoop of the screened porch.

"Your turn!" Lolly stood, clutching her wig, drip-drying in a big towel tied around her body. "Water's warm."

Arden looked down at her phone, hesitating.

"You both need to wash that sand off your feet before you track it around the cabin," Lolly said, pointing at their feet.

Arden sighed. "Okay. I'll go."

Arden walked around to the shower, only slightly hidden from the world on the back side of the cabin, and tested the temperature of the water.

Lolly had already hung towels for her and Lauren on side-by-side hooks, one hook in the form of a fish, the other shaped like a pine tree.

Arden started to shower in her swimsuit, but then said, "Oh, what the heck," hanging her suit on one of the hooks and placing her glasses on the grass.

Arden washed the sand from her legs and then reached into an old minnow bucket holding a variety of mismatched shampoos, conditioners and shower gels to pluck a shampoo.

As she lathered up her hair, Arden squinted and took in the view from the shower, and the simple beauty caused her heart to skip a beat: Boats zipped across the hazel water, while smoke from grills cast the scene in an ethereal haze. Lolly's makeshift shower was, in its own way, as lovely as any luxury spa in Chicago.

Arden leaned her head back and let the warm water run over her hair.

There was something about showering outdoors—that mix of water and nature, body and soul, trees as your ceiling—that reawakened Arden's spirit.

Arden opened her eyes, her vision blurred by the steaming water and her lack of glasses, and saw something she couldn't quite make out which seemed to be coming toward her.

"Mom? Lauren?" she asked.

Arden squinted and fumbled for her glasses. Not finding them, she called, "Hello?"

No answer.

She shook her head and leaned toward the minnow bucket, plucking out an apricot scrub for her face. She shut her eyes and began to massage her skin, before turning her face to the water. As she opened her eyes, something big yet still very blurry seemed to be approaching.

Arden shut her eyes and quickly rinsed her face, rubbing her eyes. When she opened them again, what looked like a bear was standing directly in front of her.

Arden jumped.

"I'm sorry! I'm sorry! I didn't see a thing, I promise."

Arden screamed.

Lolly came running, Lauren by her side. "It's okay, Mom! We're here," Lauren said, handing her mother her glasses and shielding her as Arden hastily draped a towel around her body.

"It's not a bear!" Lolly explained. "It's a man!"

"You sound a bit too excited, Mother. Who are you?" Arden asked, pointing at the man.

"Jake. I'm here to check on Lolly, remember? We met the other day at Lakeview. I'm the geriatric nurse who will serve as her caregiver."

"Don't you call?" Arden asked. "You just show up?"

"I tried your phone several times today. There was no answer. I got worried."

"No cell reception at the beach," Lauren explained.

"I *swear* I didn't see anything," Jake said. "I'm so sorry. I can't apologize enough."

"No, you can't," Lolly said, her voice clipped, turning to walk back into the cabin. "The word 'caregiver' is downright awful. Don't ever use it in front of me again."

Fifteen

Y ou're right, Lolly. I shouldn't have said 'caregiver.' I apologize again. I'm
    so sorry."

Lolly scooched the jigsaw puzzle occupying the porch table to one side,
and began filling the table's center with sun tea, chips and dip, sandwiches,
bowls, spoons, and a gallon of Scoops County blackberry ice cream.

A now-dressed Arden knew her mother's small-town routine: *She may be
upset, but she's always cordial to a guest,* she thought.

Lolly looked at Jake warily, filling a glass of tea for him before doing the
same for herself.

"I'm a person," Lolly said, thrusting Jake's tea at him. "Not a plant.
I don't need 'care.'"

"You're right," Jake said, before nodding toward her gardens. "Although
I can tell you have a green thumb."

Lolly took a seat on the glider and regarded Jake, her face shifting from
overcast to slightly cloudy.

"I love gardening," she said. "It makes me happy. I love the feel of the
earth in my hands, I love . . ."

The trilling of Arden's and Lauren's phones stopped Lolly in midsentence.

"Where was I?" she said, looking out at the lake. "What was I just saying?"

Lauren looked at her grandmother, and Arden shot a look at Jake, the two nervously silencing their phones.

"We were talking about gardening and then technology interrupted," Jake said gently yet firmly, not missing a beat. "But technology isn't all bad. Do you mind if I show you something fun on my phone, Lolly?"

Again, Lolly regarded Jake, before reluctantly nodding her head.

"I've always wanted to try one of those," she said, "but I'm too old."

"Never," Jake said, walking over and taking a seat beside Lolly, causing the glider to swing wildly. "Here, let me show you what it can do."

Jake powered on his cell and began demonstrating the endless app's for Lolly.

"Here's how you get on the Internet," he explained, smiling.

Arden couldn't help but notice how big his dimples were.

"And," continued Jake, "you can check the weather, or pay all of your bills on here."

"No," Lolly said, amazed and shaking her head. "How?"

Jake pulled up his banking app and showed Lolly how, with a few clicks, she could manage her bills with Arden's help.

"And we can set up a shared calendar, with musical sounds like Lauren and Arden have, to remind you when you need to take certain medications, when you need to go shopping, even when you need to wake up. Now, hold on one second," Jake said excitedly, standing and walking outside, returning seconds later. "Look!"

Lolly grabbed his phone with one hand and covered her mouth with the other. "Pictures of my flowers! They're so beautiful," she exclaimed.

"And watch this," Jake said, tapping his phone.

A few seconds later, Lauren's phone began to trill. She looked at her cell, smiled, and answered. "Hi, Grandma."

"Here," Jake said. "Talk to your granddaughter."

There, on his phone, was Lauren. Not just her voice, but her face. "How is this possible?"

"FaceTime," Lauren said. "When you get a phone like this, you can call me anytime, and I can see your face. It's like we're together."

Lauren waved at her grandmother, and Lolly waved back, although the two were only feet apart. "Talk to you later, Grandma," she said.

"How do I get one of those?" Lolly asked.

"We'll get you one, Mom," Arden said. "That's such a wonderful idea, Jake."

Jake walked back, took a seat, and then took a sip of his sun tea. "Lolly, small cues and reminders to help your memory can really help you stay organized. Establishing a daily routine and maintaining regularity is important, and the phone can help. And I can help . . . if you will let me."

Lolly's face slowly lifted into a smile. "If you call first, don't ever say 'caregiver' again, and keep taking pictures of my flowers, you have a deal."

"Deal," Jake replied, laughing. "The important thing to remember is simply to take care of yourself, do what you love, and see Dr. Van Meter regularly. What I'm here for—what we're all here for—is to make sure you can continue living your life the way you already are."

"That's all I want," she said, smiling at Arden and Lauren.

"Well, you certainly have the right attitude," Jake continued. "In the early stages of MCI, you can do everything you already do: Drive, work, social activities. I'm here, like your daughter and granddaughter, to help you take care of yourself and plan as best you can for the future. On your own terms."

Lolly looked at Arden and Lauren. She'd never asked for help her whole life. Arden smiled at Lolly, who couldn't help but wonder and worry, *What happens when Arden and Lauren go home?*

As Lolly stared into Lauren's eyes, she felt loved, and that calmed her.

"The most important thing is to spend time with friends and family," Jake said. "To live in the moment. Enjoy every second."

"Good advice for all of us," Lolly added, smiling.

"Do you mind if I dig into this ice cream?" Jake suddenly asked, pointing to the container sitting on the table. "I love Dolly's ice cream."

"Help yourself," Arden said. "I don't need any more sweets. I haven't worked out in days."

Jake returned to his chair with a heaping bowl of blackberry ice cream. "You look like you're in great shape," Jake said, looking at Arden.

Arden's face flushed thinking about the shower now that she saw him clearly. *So do you,* she thought before catching herself.

"I couldn't help but notice the unfinished jigsaw puzzle on the table," Jake mumbled through a mouthful of ice cream. "And all the framed ones on the walls. Do you like puzzles? They are great for the mind, and great for the memory."

Lolly smiled.

"Oh, yes. I've loved puzzles my whole life. They're like"—Lolly stopped and held up her bracelet—"my charms. You don't really understand the whole picture until you understand the parts. Would you like to hear about how I got interested in puzzles, Jake?"

"Yes, ma'am," Jake said, using his spoon for emphasis.

Lolly lifted her charm bracelet, positioning it in a shaft of light shooting through the screen. She spun the charms as if she were playing roulette, before her fingers stopped—as if by memory—on a charm that resembled a single jigsaw puzzle piece that read BEST.

"Jo still has the interlocking piece that says FRIENDS," Lolly said with a smile, eyes shut, remembering something from long ago. "She always will."

When she opened her eyes again, they were damp and a tear trickled down her cheek. "This charm sums up the importance of friends in our lives: Friends are the pieces who complete us, the pieces that complete life's puzzle."

Sixteen

1954

Y ou have to get out of bed, Lolly. You have to go outside. It's summer."
Lolly Dobbs pulled the covers over her head and shut her eyes.
She only wanted to close out the world.

Lolly heard her bedroom door open and felt her mattress shift. She knew
her father was sitting on the edge of her bed.

"I know you miss her more than anything," Vern Dobbs said, his voice
barely a whisper. "I do, too."

When her father spoke softly, his voice sounded like a bullfrog. Or,
maybe, a pickup truck driving down a dirt road. He sounded exhausted.
Lolly knew—like her—he had been crying. Alone. In his bedroom.

Lolly couldn't leave her room. Every place in the cabin reminded
her of her mother. Memories of Vi were left dangling—aprons still on the
clothesline, cookies in the freezer, her scent in the air—like the last leaves
on a tree in fall. Her mother had even made the quilt on her bed. Lolly
felt like she was in quicksand, unable to move. Every breath was pain-
ful.

"We have to move on, sweetie. We won't ever forget her, but we have to
go on with our lives. She would want that. She would want you happy, not
sad. She would want you to have friends."

Lolly yanked the covers off her head and screamed, "I don't want any friends! I just want my mother!"

Vern's jaw quaked. He lay down on Lolly's bed and pulled his daughter into his arms. "I do, too, sweetie. More than anything."

His tears were hot as they dropped onto Lolly's face.

"I have something for you," he said. "Your mom wanted you to keep it."

Lolly heard the jangling and knew what it was before she saw it.

"I can't!"

"She wanted you to have it," he said, laying Vi's charm bracelet on Lolly's stomach. "Her memories are yours now. But you know what?"

Lolly shook her head.

"Now, you have to make some of your own. She wanted your bracelet to be as full as hers someday. But that means you have to get out in the world again and have some fun. Just like she wanted."

Lolly looked up at her father. He kissed her gently on top of her head.

Lolly gave her father a weak smile and held her mother's bracelet over her head. It shimmered and sparkled, and suddenly Lolly could see her mother's face, smiling down on her, as she had when Lolly was little, and the charm bracelet had seemed like an incredible mobile dancing above her.

"Would you help me put it on, Daddy?" Lolly asked, holding out the bracelet and her wrist.

Her father fastened his wife's bracelet around his daughter's wrist. "I'll always be here to help you, my baby," he said, giving her a hug.

As soon as her mother's bracelet was secure, Lolly felt safer and stronger, as if her mother were here in the room hugging her tightly.

"I have two charm bracelets," Lolly said, shaking both her wrists. "I have double Mommy."

"Maybe you can find a best friend to share your charms with," Vern said. "When you're ready, you get outside and be a kid again. Deal?"

Lolly hesitated. "Deal."

The next morning, Vern made blueberry pancakes, Lolly's favorite. "Feel like going outside today?" he asked, drizzling maple syrup on a large stack of cakes.

Lolly took a bite of her pancakes and looked seriously at her father. "I think so, Daddy," she said.

After breakfast, Lolly stepped onto the screened porch and took in Lost Land Lake. The finches—as yellow as the sun—still gathered at her mother's bird feeders, chirping happily; her mother's hydrangeas—in varying shades of blue, pink, and red—rocked in the morning breeze; the dock where Lolly and her mother exchanged charms, dangled their feet, shared s'mores, and dreamed about the future, still jutted far into the lake; and Lost Land still shimmered in the summer sun.

Lolly caught her breath and willed herself not to cry.

It's not fair! Lolly thought.

Lolly wanted to go back in time. She could feel the tears coming, so she closed her eyes, to shut out the world. And that's when she heard "Mr. Sandman."

Lolly and her mother had loved that song. They had sung it together when she was sick, when they had prayed for a miracle, a dream.

Lolly flew off the porch, the screen door banging behind her.

A little boy with short black hair was facing the lake, about four cabins down, hunched over, as if in deep prayer, singing and humming.

"That's my favorite song, too," Lolly said. "What's your name?"

"Jo! Why?" the boy said in a startled voice, before spinning around hurriedly, like he was about to get in trouble.

Lolly didn't mean to, but she giggled. There, in front of her, sat a little girl with a ragged pixie cut.

"Jo, without an *e*," she explained, already seeing the look on Lolly's face. "Jo Roseberry. And it's okay. Everybody thinks I'm a boy. My dad wanted a boy. I'm named after Joe DiMaggio."

"My dad likes Joltin' Joe, too," Lolly said, extending her hand, as her mother had taught her to do when she met someone. "Hi! I'm Lolly. Lolly Dobbs."

Jo's dark eyes filled with storminess, and she nervously turned away, her gaze scanning the lake. "Everyone's talkin' about your family," she said. "I'm real sorry about your mom."

Lolly had heard those words—over and over, at the visitation, the church, the funeral, when townsfolk brought over pies and casseroles—but they sounded so different coming from a little girl her own age. To Lolly, the words sounded genuine, and not rehearsed, for the first time.

"Me, too," Lolly said. She shut her blue eyes to keep the tears at bay, but when she opened them, Jo was standing and facing her. "You can cry if you want. Sometimes, it helps when I cry. I don't mind."

Lolly began to heave with all the force of a sudden summer thunderstorm, before Jo reached out and hugged Lolly, holding her, letting her tears soak the shoulder of her jumper.

"My mom says tears are just too much emotion, like when the bathtub overfills," Jo said, whispering into Lolly's ear and patting her back. "And she says hugs are like Band-Aids."

For once, Lolly didn't feel the need to act brave for anyone, or to apologize for her sadness.

As Lolly held on to her new friend, she finally saw—just over Jo's shoulder—something on the ground.

"What is that?" Lolly asked. "Is that what you were working on while you were singing?"

Jo walked over and took a seat on the grass. Scattered in front of her—on a piece of plywood—were hundreds of puzzle pieces, only a few of them connected.

"Uh-huh," Jo said, grabbing the top of the puzzle box and handing it to Lolly. "That's what it's supposed to look like."

"That's Lake Michigan!" Lolly yelled, shaking the photo of the puzzle excitedly. "That's a photo of Scoops Beach! See all the umbrellas and kites? My mom and I used to go there all the time!"

Jo looked up at Lolly, and it was now her eyes that were filled with tears.

"My parents got me this puzzle and said this was my new home, and we would never be moving back to Chicago," Jo said, big tears plopping like raindrops off the plywood. "I miss all my friends. I miss my house. I miss Chicago."

This time, it was Lolly who held Jo in her arms, until she could cry no more.

"I've got an idea," Lolly said, looking Jo right in the eyes. "I miss my mom, and you miss your friends, so why don't we start trying to be happy together? What if you help me stop missing my mom so much, and I'll help you stop missing your home?"

"How?" Jo asked, her eyes wide.

"Well, let's start by finishing this puzzle. That way, we can do something new together. I can tell you about my mom, and you can tell me about Chicago."

Lolly sat down next to Jo.

"Okay, let's start looking for all the umbrella pieces first," Lolly said. "They're colorful and will be easier to put together than the beach and water ones. See this red-and-yellow one?"

"I found a yellow piece!" Jo yelled.

"Oooh, and here's a red piece!" Lolly said. "Let's see if they fit!"

Lolly placed one piece down on the board. Then Jo did and—*click!*—they snapped together easily.

"It's like they were meant to be together!" Lolly said.

"Just like us!" Jo said.

That evening, Lolly came rushing home at dusk and immediately flew into her father's arms. Vern put down the charcoal just in time to catch his daughter.

"Daddy, you won't believe the day I had!" Lolly exclaimed, as her father began prepping the grill for hot dogs. "I met a girl named Jo, and she is my new best friend."

Lolly told him about the puzzle.

"I have an idea," Vern said. "Why don't I help you shellac and frame it when you are finished? That way, you can treasure it forever."

Lolly screamed her delight, and the two went in search of more jigsaw puzzles stored in the tiny attic over the cabin, finding a few old ones, including one of the Bobbsey Twins and one of the state of Michigan.

Every day for the next two months, Lolly and Jo sat by the lake and worked on a puzzle, taking breaks to swim in the lake, float on inner tubes, or beg their parents to take them to the beach or for ice cream in town.

On the Fourth of July, Vern made Lolly a birthday cake and had Jo and her parents over for a picnic.

"Open your presents!" Vern said.

Lolly clapped: Her father had wrapped and framed a few of the girls' completed puzzles.

"They're just like art!" Lolly said. "Can we hang them on the screened porch?"

"Sure," Vern said. "But why outside?"

"Because that's where I first heard Jo singing!" Lolly explained.

At dusk, after everyone had gorged on barbecued hamburgers, potato salad, chips, s'mores, and cake, Jo asked Lolly if she would like to walk to the end of the dock to watch the fireworks.

As they walked, dragonflies followed and fireflies blinked.

The two sat on the edge of the dock and swung their feet into the lake. Frogs called around them.

"I have a present for you, too," Jo said suddenly, pulling a little box from her pocket. "Happy birthday!"

"Jo!" Lolly squealed. "What is it?"

"Recite the poem first."

"What?"

"The poem you told me you always said to your mom on your birthday." Lolly's face froze.

"I can't," she said.

"Yes, you can," Jo said. "You need to."

Lolly was overcome with emotion, but Jo was right. She shut her eyes and began to recite. She had to stop and start, because her voice kept cracking, but saying the words reminded her of her mother and a feeling of happiness and comfort came over her.

Jo handed Lolly her gift, and Lolly ripped open the wrapping paper on the tiny box. Sitting atop a little velvet throne was a silver charm.

"What is it, Jo?" Lolly asked, squinting in the twilight, holding the odd-shaped charm into the darkening sky.

"It's a puzzle piece that says BEST FRIENDS because we are and always will be," Jo said. "See . . . your piece says BEST, and . . ."

Jo stopped and lifted her arm up to show Lolly her wrist.

". . . My piece says, FRIENDS. They fit together. Just like us!"

Boom!

Fireworks began to explode overhead, their colors reflecting in the water.

Lolly added the charm to her bracelet, and then reached for her best friend's hand.

Seventeen

J o and I were inseparable throughout our school years," Lolly said, taking a seat again on the glider next to Jake. "Everyone called us the 'Jigsaw Twins' because we were never apart: We double-dated, played basketball, and took dance classes together. She helped me get through those hard years without my mom.

"After high school, she begged me to go to college with her, but I just couldn't leave my father alone. So I stayed and helped him with his fishing guide business. Jo ended up becoming a teacher, and she married an engineer and lived in Chicago. She had three children. I married and had Arden. We saw each other every summer, and . . ."

Lolly nodded vigorously toward the framed jigsaw puzzles on the walls of the screened porch.

". . . we never stopped doing puzzles. Even apart, we kept our tradition alive: One of us would start a puzzle, finish and shellac half of it, and then wrap it and mail it to the other one to finish. Whoever finished a puzzle kept it and framed it. Jo sent me puzzles from her travels all around the world—jigsaws from Paris and London, old puzzles she'd find in antique malls. I sent her mostly puzzles of home—of Michigan and Scoops, of ice cream cones and the lake."

"How is Jo?" Arden asked. "I remember visiting her, but I haven't heard you talk about her for a while. Is she still in Chicago? Are you sending this puzzle to her when you're done?"

Lolly scanned the expanse of green in front of Lost Land Lake, before closing her eyes. She blinked hard.

"Wait!" Arden said suddenly, bolting upright and heading to the table. "Oh, Mom! I know what this puzzle is going to be: A pink ribbon. I'm so sorry!"

"This was our last puzzle." Lolly tried to swallow. "Jo did the first half in the hospital and then sent it to me to finish. I just can't bring myself to finish it yet. I miss her so much."

"Jo's husband told me she wore her puzzle piece charm every day," Lolly said. "She was buried with it."

Quiet enveloped the cabin for a few minutes. In the distance, a dog barked, followed by children shouting to one another and then splashing in the lake.

Arden's heart shattered. She felt terrible and guilty that she didn't know her mother's best friend had passed away.

"Mom, why didn't you ever tell me this?" Arden asked.

Lolly looked at her daughter. "You were so busy . . . you were already worried about so much . . . I didn't want to burden you any further."

How did we grow so far apart? Arden thought, looking at her mother.

"Life goes on." Lolly sighed.

Lauren ran to her grandmother and hugged her tightly.

"Grandma, the puzzle piece charms you and Jo had . . . that's why you sent them to me and Lexie, isn't it?" Lauren asked.

Lolly nodded, and she looked at Lauren.

"You are my light," she said. "You complete me, too."

Lauren smiled and thought of the painting she had started of her grandmother, the light seeming to radiate from her face. "You're my light, too, Grandma."

Lauren began to text furiously, her fingers flying over the keypad on her cell.

"What are you doing?" Lolly asked, gesturing at her granddaughter's phone.

"Lexie," Lauren said, looking up at her grandma, her long lashes damp. "I had to tell her the story of you and Jo right away."

Lolly nodded, as Lauren continued to text and talk.

"We just finished finals, and she's back in New York. I miss her, and just wanted to tell her . . . I just wanted to tell her I love her."

Lauren's voice choked.

"Stop for a second," Lolly said. Lauren's fingers quieted. "What do you hear?"

"Nothing."

"You're not listening closely enough," Lolly admonished. "Now, what do you hear?"

"I hear kids screaming, boats zipping across the lake," Lauren said. She stopped and tilted her blond head toward the screen. "I hear a hawk. I hear loons moaning."

A smile lit up Lolly's face, illuminating her from the inside out, as if she'd just swallowed a million fireflies.

"When you stop, you can also hear your heart, your thoughts . . . you can hear *you*," Lolly said. "A best friend is just like that: They listen closely. They hear your heart, your thoughts, *you*."

Lauren was overcome by Lolly's words.

"You want me to call Lexie, don't you, Grandma?"

"It's important to hear a friend's voice," Lolly said. "I know it's easier to text, but it's so much nicer to hear your best friend's laugh and to capture every nuance of every word she is saying to you, especially when you're still around to hear it. Why don't you do that face thingy we just did?"

"FaceTime," Lauren said, moved by her grandmother's suggestion. "Good idea, Grandma. Excuse me for a few moments. It was nice to meet you, Jake."

Lauren sprinted off the porch, the screen door slamming behind her, and—without knowing it—ran to the exact spot where Lolly and Jo had met, taking a seat on the grass to call her best friend.

Lolly smiled and turned to Arden. "What about you? Any friends you want to talk with today?"

Arden continued to stare out over the lake, unable to meet her mother's gaze. Lolly's simple question hit her hard. "There's been so much work, I've really lost track of my friends," Arden admitted sadly.

"A job can't hug you," Lolly said, touching her daughter's arm, letting her words sink in. "Lauren told me about your writing friend you saw in Chicago. And Kathy was so sweet when she saw you at the fudge shop."

Lolly hesitated. "You have to invite friends into your home. No one is ever going to kick the door down and just walk on in."

She tilted her head at her daughter before changing the subject. "Well, I need to go get myself ready for work. And we all know how much time that takes. When will I see you again, Jake?"

"Friday, if that works. Just before the holiday weekend?"

"Works just fine," she said. "Maybe you and Arden can help me get one of those fancy phones like you all have. You can put a calendar on that, right? One with little sound effects to remind me of things?"

"You and technology? This is a miracle, Mother!" Arden joked.

Lolly disappeared into the cabin, leaving Jake and Arden to sit in silence for a few seconds.

"Well, I best be going," Jake said. "I'm sorry . . . well, you know . . . for . . ."

"Seeing me naked?"

"Yes."

"That will take more than an apology," Arden said, her face flushing. "It might take a partial lobotomy, or a lot of drinks." She couldn't believe she'd just suggested drinks, but the words were out before she knew it.

Jake laughed, stopping at the screen door. "Speaking of drinks, and since we've been talking about friends, I'm meeting some tomorrow night at the Rendezvous Bar & Grill, if you care to join us."

Arden's face flushed again. She wanted to say yes—she wanted to scream yes, actually—but it had been a very long time since she had gone out with a man other than her ex, and she wasn't sure she was up to the possibility of a new romantic relationship just yet, especially with all that was going on in her life.

Arden thought about her mother's story, and it hit her again how limited her time was with her mother.

"Oh, thank you for the invitation, but I don't think so. I need to spend some time with my mom. I appreciate it, though."

Jake ducked his head. "Just thought I'd ask," he said, opening the door. Arden could see the disappointment shadow his soulful dark eyes. "Have a great rest of your day."

The screen door slammed, and the sound resonated in her head, just like her mother's advice: *No one is ever going to kick the door down and just walk on in.*

Arden watched Jake walk down the steppingstone path toward his car, and wondered if she'd made a mistake not accepting his offer.

Jake stopped, turned, and opened his mouth.

For a second, Arden thought he was going to shout back at her—*Please ask me again!* she thought—but Jake seemed to change his mind and turned back toward his car.

Arden shook her head, tugged nervously on her earlobe, picked up the melting gallon of Scoops County ice cream, and headed inside the cabin, where she ran directly into her mother, grinning from ear to ear.

"What's so funny, Mom?" Arden asked.

"Life," Lolly replied. "Life can be very amusing."

As her mother turned to finish getting ready for work, she began to hum—*Frank Sinatra? "Summer Wind"?*—and Arden couldn't help but wonder what her mother was up to now.

part six

The Loon Charm

*To a Life Filled with a Love That
Always Calls You Home*

Eighteen

L olly Lindsey allowed herself only one moment of melancholy every
day.

After she had retired to her bedroom for the evening, Lolly removed
her wig, makeup, lashes, and Dolly costume, every bit of plumage—save
for her charm bracelet and her wedding band.

She put on soft, flannel pajamas and positioned her body in the middle
of the big, birch bed that took up most of the nook overlooking the lake.

Lolly's nightly routine never changed: She grabbed a long-ago photo of
her and her husband that sat on the nightstand—one taken at sunset on
the beach of Lake Michigan, their young bodies framed by an explosion of
color and light—and kissed it gently. She then tucked her body into a question mark under the sheets, grabbed her husband's pillow and held it. If
she inhaled long enough, Lolly swore she could still smell the Old Spice
he loved to wear.

When the skies were clear and the moon was bright, the long shadows
of the pines outside her window fell across the middle of the water-blue comforter, and the pine needles took the shape of moving fingers. Lolly would
sigh and pretend the needles were her husband's fingers, and that he was
holding her, massaging her tired old body.

Lolly would then stare at another picture that hung haphazardly from an old log—another of Lolly and Les, this one when they were older, taken just outside the screened porch, two loons floating in the inlet behind them.

Lolly would sear that image into her brain, shut her eyes, and feel for the loon charm on her bracelet until its smooth, shiny beak and feathers revealed themselves to her fingers.

And then Lolly would wait.

Whooo-dooo-ooooh-ooooh!

The loons' mournful wail outside her window transported Lolly back in time. She hugged her pillow and could now hear her husband's voice.

"Listen," Les would say to her, as she rested her head on his chest. "Fred and Ethel are going to bed, just like us."

Whooo-dooo-ooooh-ooooh!

The two loons had seemingly been married and living on Lost Land Lake as long as Lolly and Les Lindsey had. Their home was the reeds and inlet that pooled just feet from the bedroom window and screened porch of the cabin.

"Tell me about the loons," Lolly would always reply.

And he would.

"They mate forever, just like humans," he would tell her. "They always come home, to the same place, same lake, every year, as soon as the ice thaws. They are territorial, and mates will defend their home from other loons. Small lakes can only accommodate one pair of loons, so they are always together, and they always talk to each other. Sound familiar?"

"What do they say to each other?" Lolly would ask.

"Well, it depends, my love, just like us . . . on their mood, what they have on their minds," he would say in his husky rumble. "That sound we hear right now—that wail that sounds like a wolf's howl—is the way they talk during their night chorusing. It's just like what we're doing now: It's their own way of saying, 'Good night. I love you.'"

Lolly would sigh and spoon even tighter to her husband's side as he continued.

Lolly knew all of this, by heart now, but she was comforted hearing her husband's voice hum in her body, his heart beat in her ear, just like hearing the loons call.

Whooo-dooo-ooooh-ooooh!

"I guess it's now time for me to do my night chorus to you, my dear," Les would whisper, before softly singing "Let Me Call You Sweetheart."

Lolly would hum along, until her husband would stop and say, "If you live to be a hundred, I want to live to be a hundred minus one day so I never have to live without you."

The screen door banged, jolting Lolly from her memories.

"Why is the reception so spotty out here?" she heard her daughter say.

Lolly's heart sank as she thought about Arden's confession that she had no friends, only work. Lolly never felt Arden had married for love, and since her divorce, Arden had been married to work.

Will she ever find what we had, Les? Lolly worried.

Lolly's memory of her husband's nightly lullaby recalled when she used to sing "The Bare Necessities" from *The Jungle Book* to Arden. She had sung it to her very intense little girl to calm her and get her to sleep, but she had also chosen the song to try to teach Arden to be happier with the simple things, as when a cheerful Baloo explains in the song how "a bear can rest at ease with just the bare necessities of life." But—even at a young age— Arden had not seemed to care much for her mother's stories or songs, and seemingly only wanted to get moving, to leave her mom, this cabin, this lake, her home.

Lolly heard the loons sing "good night" to one another: *Whooo-dooo-ooooh-ooooh!*

Will she ever find what they have?

Suddenly, Lolly's heart began to beat rapidly. She panicked and sat straight up in bed.

Whooo-dooo-ooooh-ooooh!

What are their names? What are their names? Oh, Lolly, you old fool!

She began to bead in sweat, so much so that she got out of bed and opened the window all the way. A cool breeze calmed her, and she inhaled.

Whooo-dooo-ooooh-ooooh!

Lolly felt again for the charm of the loon on her bracelet. "Fred and Ethel!" she said. "Fred and Ethel!"

Lolly repeated the loons' names as she nestled back into bed. She grabbed her husband's pillow and held it tightly.

"Les," she whispered to herself. "Les."

Lolly never regretted a day she had with her husband. *No regrets*. She knew few could say that.

No, Lolly didn't fear dying alone, because she wouldn't. Les would always be with her, until they were reunited.

"For better, for worse, for richer, for poorer, in sickness and in health, until death do us part."

No, Lolly's fear was much deeper: She worried there would come a day when she would not be able to remember her husband, or the loons, no matter how much their voices tried to remind her.

Lolly shut her eyes and whispered, "Good night, I love you," into her husband's pillow.

And then she dreamed of standing beside Les—just like in the picture on her nightstand—the loons alongside, all four mates forever in love, forever home, forever together.

Nineteen

B e ready by seven!" Lolly announced, walking onto the screened porch the next morning.

Arden was furiously texting and jumped when she heard her mother's voice.

"For what?"

"I'm taking you and Lauren to dinner after work. My treat! Rendez-vous has music on Thursday nights!" Lolly said, holding up two aprons. "Now, which one?"

Arden had returned to texting and gave her mother a distracted look. "Aren't they the same?"

"No!" Lolly said. "One has dancing cherries on it, and the other has dancing strawberries on it!"

"Too early for cherry season," Arden said, without looking up.

"You actually have a point. What are you doing, by the by?"

"Working."

"On . . . ?"

"Work."

"A conversation involves conversing, my dear," Lolly replied.

Arden stopped and looked up at her mother.

"I'm texting my boss to see how things are going." She looked up at her mom and then back down at her phone. "Without me."

"I thought you were going to take some time off?" Lolly asked, concerned.

"I need the hours, Mom," Arden said. "I need the money."

"You need to stand up for yourself, then good things will follow," Lolly said. "Don't send that message. Just be in the moment for a bit. Then clarity will come."

"I can't," Arden said. "I wouldn't know how."

"Just be," Lolly said. "*Just be*, my dear."

Arden continued to text.

"Arden, it worries me that you have no friends and put your needs to the side for work," her mother suddenly said. "You need to love and respect yourself."

All the sound seemed to be sucked from the cabin, like when Lolly finished placing the airtight seal on when she canned preserves. Lolly could actually sense it, hear it, feel it. But she couldn't take the words back now.

Arden winced and narrowed her eyes behind her glasses. Her mother was right, but her words still stung.

"I'm sorry. I'm just worried about you. I want you to be happy," Lolly said. "I want you to find true love and lead a full life *beyond* work."

Lolly stopped and looked out at Lauren, sunning on a striped towel on the dock.

"Have you ever told her about your first love?" Lolly asked suddenly.

Arden looked at her mom, shocked, and then shook her head. "She doesn't need to know all that."

Lolly smiled sweetly and folded the cherry apron into a neat square before tying the crisp apron dotted with bright strawberries, trimmed with a white border, around her neck and waist. She watched her granddaughter spray her body with suntan lotion before flipping over.

"She doesn't?" Lolly finally said, turning to look at her daughter.

"Why would you bring that up, Mom?" Arden asked.

"I just want the same things for you both. I'm getting older, and I want you both to be happy."

Lolly stopped and looked back out at Lauren. "I've been thinking about what Lauren said, about how she switched majors. She needs to know you're human, you've made mistakes, and that it's okay for her to make some, too. She's trying so hard to be perfect, and she's not happy, my dear."

Arden's head whirled.

Is she right? Has my carefully crafted life been built on a cracked foundation? Arden thought. *And now Lauren is crumbling, too?*

Arden stared at her mother, seeing her differently for the first time in a long time: Solid. Strong. Sage.

Lolly nodded at her daughter and then pinned a large plastic nametag onto her apron featuring the logo of the sweet shop and the name "DOLLY!" in a capitalized script, the exclamation point in the shape of an ice cream cone.

"See you at seven," she said, ambling off the screened porch with a large bag stuffed with Dolly's costume, and blowing Lauren a kiss. She stopped on the stoop and turned back around. "And try to look . . . well . . . a bit less serious for dinner."

"You don't like my wardrobe, Mother?" Arden asked.

"Why not let your daughter help you get dressed tonight," Lolly sang, walking away from the cabin. "Just for fun."

Fun, Arden thought, suddenly picturing herself in her office at *Paparazzi*, images of the magazine's most beautiful women—Kerry Washington, Angelina Jolie, and Princess Kate—whirling through her head.

Out of the blue, Arden chuckled, watching her mother walk away: In a surreal, alternative universe sort of way, all of this made sense. One of the most bookish women in the world—bespectacled, bobbed, little makeup, drab clothes, no jewelry—working at one of the glitziest consumer magazines in the world, and the daughter of a true character.

As Arden's mind continued to whir, her life quickly became Photoshop clear: *I am the Spanx underneath the glitz, the unseen glue that holds it all together.*

As soon as Arden heard the soft crush of gravel of her mother's Woodie pulling away, she bolted upstairs, changed into running shorts and sneakers, and zipped past Lauren without saying a word.

"Hi to you, too, Mom!" Lauren said, but Arden didn't hear her.

Arden jogged around the edge of the lake, hoping she might be able to outrun the ghosts from her childhood.

Have I always been this lost?

Then she saw it: That tiny opening within the large stand of white birch. She tried to resist, but it called to her, and Arden found herself running directly into it.

Here was the secret jogging trail that skirted Lost Land. It meandered through the woods and hopscotched around summer cottages. The path had been formed when Arden was young, when wealthy Chicagoans had seen *On Golden Pond* and flocked to Scoops for a taste of the simple life, snatching up cottages as quickly as fudge. Thin white women with severe bobs introduced running to the resort area along with Pottery Barn and Martha Stewart, and their lithe bodies and Nike-clad feet eventually cleared a trail along the memorable little lake.

As Arden ran, she recalled how fascinated she had been with this influx of status into the long-overlooked lake that sat miles from the money of downtown and the Lake Michigan coast.

Arden remembered watching from her bedroom window during high school as construction workers descended onto Lost Land—earthmovers replacing herons—and transformed tiny log cabins on the opposite side of the lake into Ralph Lauren–chic estates. The wives followed, decorating and running, running and decorating. They would meet in their yards, which fronted the lake, stretching, doing this thing called "yoga," before dashing off—*Zoom!*—an angry army of hornets in pink.

Arden had followed. She not only began to run, she began to want clothes and shoes that Lolly and Les just couldn't afford. Arden began to yearn for a life in the city she had never known.

"They aren't real. You can't live your life wanting to be a projection of someone else," Lolly would repeatedly say to her shy daughter. "You have to be you, Arden. And they wear *tennis* bracelets, not charm bracelets. They don't know who they are or where they came from anymore."

Lolly had fought to preserve the original seven cabins along Lost Lake and had come out victorious. She knew these women didn't like her, but she hadn't expected her daughter to envy them.

"They aren't happy, Arden," Lolly told her daughter. "They are never content enough to enjoy their lives."

Arden picked up her pace, trying to outrun her thoughts, and sprinted along the trail, shadowed and cool under a canopy of birch and sugar maples. She breathed deeply as she ran, her lungs filling with an ease she rarely experienced in the city.

Arden approached a tiny stream—a "crick" as her mother called it— that ran into Lost Land, and decided to jump it like a show horse. She picked up steam and . . .

Whap! Splash!

Arden's left foot caught on a tree root, and she yelped, her glasses flying from her face, her body falling hard and coming to land directly in the water. Arden's heart raced, and she scrambled up to assess the damage.

Face?

Palms?

Back?

Knees?

Arden exhaled and looked up toward the sky.

No damage, she thought, relieved.

Arden reached for her glasses and found them sitting on the edge of the bank she'd never reached. She rubbed the dirt off her lenses with her shirt and, as she placed the glasses on her face, the world came back into focus. Arden gasped.

In front of her stood a tiny forest of gnarled sassafras, their trunks dark, knotted and bent, like witches' fingers. The weight of the scene forced Arden to take a seat on the damp embankment, her feet resting on a stone in the stream.

This is it! Our "secret spot," she realized, amazed.

Arden tried to catch her breath, but memories came rushing back.

"Meet me by the sassafras grove," read the notes that Clem used to shove into her locker, Arden recalled.

Clem Watkins, a quiet farm boy who raised cattle and showed goats, had appeared as suddenly into Arden's life as her father had left it.

Clem and Arden had never talked much in school, outside of the occasional hello in the hall, but he came to the cabin after her father's sudden death from a heart attack, with a casserole from his mother and a rose for Arden. No other classmates had come to visit, so when Clem asked Arden to go for a walk, she agreed. She had no one else, it seemed. They ended up sitting for hours in this sassafras grove, Arden crying until she could cry no longer, Clem patiently holding her until her tears subsided.

"How will I move on?" Arden had gasped. "What will my mother do? I can't imagine living alone with her. She's already crazy enough."

"Your mother is not crazy. She's unique. That's a wonderful trait. Can you imagine what she is going through, too? Arden, you need to take all the time you need to mourn the death of your father," Clem had said in the quiet of the woods.

His words had stunned Arden. They were not only more mature than anything she expected a boy his age to utter and more heartfelt than any she had ever read in any of her beloved books, but they also echoed her mother's.

She began to tell Clem about her father's and grandfather's work as fishing guides, their love of the lake, the land, Lolly and Arden, Fred and Ethel.

"They mate forever," Arden said to him of the loons. "And they always return home. Forever. Do you think my dad will ever come back to visit?"

"He never left you," Clem had whispered. "He's right here . . . in every leaf and in every wave of the lake."

For the first time since her father had died, Arden felt a sense of peace.

From that moment on, they met whenever they could.

The farm boy who Arden would have never previously talked to had suddenly touched her broken heart and made her consider a life that wasn't part of the elite set or the city.

To a girl who had lived with her head in books, Clem was real. Too real. Six foot four inches of tall Dutch ancestry, a body chiseled by farm labor, tousled hair made blonder by the summer sun, pine green eyes with chips of gold, and a deep voice that sounded like the engine of the family Woodie. When they talked about their futures, Clem's always included Arden. When they kissed, Arden could actually picture their futures.

One October afternoon, as they lay in the grove of sassafras, angling their faces just so between the red-leafed branches to catch the last of the Michigan sunlight before winter returned, Clem said, "Marry me?"

Arden's first thought—as she lay on her back, still too stunned to move— was that Clem's words sounded more like a plea than a question.

When she sat up, Clem was on his knees in front of her, holding a little box.

"No," Arden said. "No, Clem."

"It's not a ring," he said. "Just a promise that I'll be with you forever."

Arden opened the box: A charm of a loon sat nestled on top.

"Have you been talking with my mother?" Arden said.

"Maybe," Clem said. "Can I add it to your bracelet?"

Arden held out her wrist, and Clem added the charm to her bracelet and then kissed her hand, as if she were a princess.

Arden stared at the charm. It was just like the one her mother had on her bracelet.

Arden looked into Clem's green eyes, the breathtaking fall background of the woods, filled with sugar maples exploding in gold, red, yellow, and orange behind him.

And that's when Clem leaned in and kissed Arden. She hadn't expected the proposal. She hadn't expected her heart to leap from her chest. She hadn't expected her head to began to twirl, like the Tilt-A-Whirl that came to town with the traveling carnival every year. She hadn't expected, at the young age of eighteen, to want to say yes.

But when her lips left Clem's and she began to speak, a pack of Chicago women visiting for the fall color tour suddenly ran by, talking about "that crazy charm bracelet widow" in the old log cabin who had lost her husband. "Probably faked his own death to get away from her," one cackled.

"That daughter has just as many charms," another one laughed. "She's going to be just like her."

"Ignore them," Clem replied.

But Arden couldn't. These women were everywhere: They descended on auctions of foreclosed homes and farms like vultures, picking and plucking possessions, while tired families watched from behind curtains.

"Could you ever see yourself in a city?" Arden asked Clem one day. "What does our future look like?"

"God, no," Clem scoffed. "A city? I can't live like that. I'm a farm boy. I love this town. I want a simple life with a big family. Don't you?"

Farm boy. Simple life. Big family.

For weeks, Arden was panicked, haunted by Clem's dreams. She avoided him at school, hid out on weekends, made up excuses.

But when Arden was without him, she was haunted even more.

At a school assembly, Clem was honored by his chapter of the Future Farmers of America for service, and in his acceptance speech, Arden could hear his joy when he talked about farming. When he showed her his medal after the assembly, his face beamed.

Arden shut her eyes, but no longer saw Clem: She saw the tired faces of broken families. She saw her mother.

"Meet me after school," she told him. "In our spot."

"I can't marry you," Arden said when they met, bursting into tears. "I love you, but I just can't live here. I will die here, just like you'd die in the city."

And so, like the city women, Arden ran—from Clem, from Scoops, from her mother, from her past—toward the city.

The next summer, Arden left for college. She thought of Clem every day for years as she finished school, started as a journalist, worked on her book, and became a part of Chicago.

Arden was working at the *Chicago Reader* when her mother sent a letter that included a clip from the local paper, *The Scoop*, that read, "Local Boy Killed in Farming Accident."

Even after so many years, Arden's heart shattered.

She sat in her cube and wept, thinking of the boy she had left, of the most vulnerable time in her life, when Clem had made her feel so safe.

Clem had married a local girl and had three children, two boys and a girl. The paper ran a picture of the family: The kids looked like Clem. The family looked happy.

In the bottom of the envelope was the charm of the loon, dangling on the bracelet Arden had left at home, her past hidden in an old shoebox in the closet.

"My heart breaks for you, my angel," Lolly had written in her looping script. "He loved you so much, didn't he?"

Arden took the next day off work. She held her bracelet for hours, before removing the loon charm. Then she wrapped her bracelet in a *Pen-*

nysaver ad that was shoved into her mailbox and hid it away in a shoebox in the back of her closet.

Arden went to the Lincoln Park Zoo to visit the animals in Clem's memory. She walked the park and buried the posting of Clem's death under a stand of sassafras, using her hands to dig a shallow grave. When she had finished, she walked to the bridge overlooking the zoo's pond—the Chicago skyline framed in the distance—and sat, her legs swinging over the side.

Arden thought of Tom, the man she had just begun to date. He was the exact opposite of Clem: A businessman, urban and polished, driven by a desire for money and success.

The two are as different as, well, Chicago and Scoops, Arden thought, staring at the skyline.

That's when Arden heard the familiar sound. At first, she thought she was hearing a siren. But, no, running across the pond, calling, crying, singing their soulful song, were two loons, right in the middle of Chicago.

It's a sign! Arden thought. *I made the wrong decision! I should have married him and had his children. No man could love me like he did.*

Arden watched the loons take flight, wondering if they were already beginning to migrate south for the winter.

Clem will always be with me, but I have to let him go. I have to move on somehow, too, even if it will never be the same.

Suddenly, she stood and, without thinking, began to catapult the loon charm her mother had sent from her bracelet into the lake. But just as she was about to let go, the loons circled overhead and wailed. Arden stopped, retracted her arm, fell to the earth sobbing, and clutched the tiny charm to her chest.

Whooo-dooo-ooooh-ooooh!

Loons sounded their mournful wail as Arden realized she was still sitting on the embankment of the creek. She rubbed her knees, now shivering as she remembered falling, remembered all of this. Her tears made the sassafras trees appear to move, wiggle in front of her, like ghosts.

Yes, Mom, you were right: I loved him. And I never allowed myself to feel that again after that pain.

"Mom! Are you okay?"

Arden jumped and turned to find Lauren behind her.

"I fell," she mumbled. "I don't know if I'm okay . . . I don't know."

Lauren took a seat on the damp ground beside her mom, checked her mother's knees and head, before laying an arm around her mother's shoulder. The two listened to the burble of the creek.

"Wow," Lauren finally said, "those sassafras are magical, aren't they, Mom?"

Arden smiled, clenched her jaw, and turned away, trying to hide her tears, but it was too late.

"Mom? What's going on?"

Arden thought of her mother's words earlier, and suddenly the story of Clem tumbled out of her mouth, along with more tears.

When she was done, Lauren hugged her mother.

"Mom, I never knew. I'm so sorry."

The two sat in the quiet of the woods, before Lauren spoke again. She started and then stopped before finally getting the words out. She started tentatively, "I want to change my major, Mom."

Lauren took a deep breath and continued. "I want to be a painter. I mean, life is too short for us to turn our backs on our unhappiness. You and Grandma are finally teaching me that."

Arden listened closely, before lifting her head and looking into her daughter's eyes. "Business *will* allow you to be in control of your own life, though, Lauren. You will make more money than I did. And you won't be reliant on anyone, like I was. You can always just paint on the side, can't you?"

Arden watched her daughter's eyes fade into a distant place. She nodded and turned her head, but she wasn't able to hide her tears from her mother.

"Life is filled with difficult decisions," Arden said.

Arden wanted Lauren to be happy, but most of all she wanted to protect her. She didn't want Lauren to worry about money or supporting herself.

"I know," Lauren said, standing up. "I know."

Twenty

Beep! *Beep!*
Lolly honked the horn of the Woodie to sound her arrival at the supper club, something she did every time she pulled into the small gravel lot.

"The Rendezvous?" Arden asked, suddenly remembering where they would be having dinner. Arden had eaten at the Rendezvous nearly every week growing up, considering her mother loved it and—in the winter— it was often the only place around that was still open. "Really? Everything here is fried."

"Except the beer!" Lolly chirped. "Best brew and perch in Michigan!"

The three exited the Woodie, and Arden took in the exterior of the ancient supper club, a dark, dingy building in the middle of the woods that looked like it had seen better days.

LVE MUSC TONGHT! a shoddy sign in the parking lot read.

"Did they run out of money to buy *i*'s?" Arden asked.

"It's like *Wheel of Fortune*," Lolly laughed. "You have to buy a vowel, or solve it, to enter."

Lauren swung open the door of the Rendezvous, a waft of grease and liquor overtaking them.

"Are you okay?" Lolly whispered to her granddaughter. "You seem awfully quiet tonight."

Lauren nodded.

The three entered, and Arden quickly was blinded: The Rendezvous was pitch black, save for a few weak overhead lights and some candles flickering on the tables.

The Rendezvous had originally been built as a bar for local hunters and fishermen. The only windows in the place were narrow and sat high, like eyebrows, at the top of the restaurant. It became known as "The Hunter's Mistress" because the "widowed wives" of the outdoorsmen couldn't tell whether or not their husbands were inside unless they entered. And few had the nerve to do so.

Over time, the Rendezvous morphed from hunting bar to supper club, with jazz musicians from Chicago and Detroit heading north for summer getaways to jam together and test out new songs. A lot of the greats had played here—though they may not have remembered they did—including members of The Rat Pack.

Arden braced herself.

"I had drinks with Sinatra," Lolly said loud enough to get the attention of a few diners. "We were quite a pair!"

Lolly told the same story every time they came to the Rendezvous.

"There's our picture!"

Lolly pointed to an old framed photo on a wall over by the narrow bar that fronted the small stage where musicians still jammed.

"What a place! What a dame! Can't wait for my next rendezvous at the Rendezvous!" Sinatra had written.

The supper club's walls were crammed with mounted deer heads and big fish, glassy-eyed wildlife meant to be showcased in all their outdoor glory, but dressed over time by drunken customers in Santa hats, leis, and sunglasses. Autographed photos of musicians sat alongside the wildlife, the singers and piano players looking even more glassy-eyed than their counterparts.

The bar was stuffed with stools, the restaurant with small tables and mismatched chairs.

"We have your usual table reserved, Lolly," an elderly waitress with sky-high hair said while chomping on a piece of gum.

"Thanks, Trudy," Lolly said.

The trio followed Trudy's ample rear, which bumped the tight tables—drinks wobbling unsteadily—as she moved quickly to the back of the restaurant.

RESERVED FOR LOLLY LINDSEY

Trudy picked up the yellowed sign from the table.

"You still got that old sign?" Lolly asked.

"This old thing will never go away," Trudy hacked, grabbing her big behind, "like this old thing. Now, what'll I get for you ladies?"

"Three mugs of your summer pale ale," Lolly said. "Make 'em icy."

"Back in a flash," she sang.

Lolly had barely been seated when she looked up and said, "Well, well, well! If it isn't Nurse Ratched."

Arden turned and gasped. "Mother!"

"What?" Lolly said, mocking confusion.

"Your memory is a little bit better than any of us thought, isn't it? Tonight's dinner isn't a coincidence at all, is it?"

Lolly shrugged like an innocent child.

Sitting a few tables over—downing an icy mug of beer and laughing with a big group—was Jake. He smiled, waved, and then began ambling toward their table, like a good-natured version of the stuffed black bear that sat near the bar with a perpetual grin on its face, a mug of beer in its paw, sunglasses on its snout, and a Scoops hat on its big head.

Arden dropped her head into her hands as Jake approached.

"Back of your head isn't an appealing look, my dear," Lolly said.

"What are you ladies doing here?"

"Well, we thought we'd have a quick drink and bite . . ."

Arden cut her mother off. "Don't dig yourself a deeper hole, Mom. I know this is all a setup."

"Doesn't matter," Jake said sweetly, as Trudy reappeared with beers. "I'm just glad you're here. It's such a fun place. Would you two mind if I stole Arden for a few minutes? I'd love to introduce her to some of my friends."

Arden shot a glance at her mother and daughter, hoping they might intercede to save her. Neither was biting.

"I'm here with my family," Arden said. "I promised my mom I'd have dinner with her."

Lolly tapped her daughter dramatically and then gave her granddaughter a wink. "I think we'll be okay, won't we, Lauren?"

Lauren laughed, winked back, and then lifted her mug of beer to salute her mother. "We will, Grandma. Have fun, Mom!"

"We can get beer and perch together any old time, can't we?" Lolly said, winking again, her fake eyelash softly landing like a butterfly on her cheek.

"I'm buying," Jake said as incentive.

Arden stood hesitantly. Jake pulled out her chair, put a hand around the middle of her back, and escorted her to his table, where he began introducing her to his friends.

Lolly polished off half her beer in one big gulp, then held up two fingers to Trudy before she dashed away. "We're gonna need them to watch this train wreck."

Lauren smiled, in spite of herself.

"So what's going on?" Lolly asked Lauren. "You're definitely not yourself."

"Mom told me about Clem today," she said, taking a sip of her beer. "And I told her I wanted to change my major. I want to paint, Grandma."

"I know you do, my dear," Lolly said. "I take it your mother didn't like that idea."

Lauren nodded. "I told her life is too short to be unhappy. We have to follow our passion, right?"

Lolly nodded. "You're setting me up for a story, you know. Can I tell you about the loon charm? I think it will help you."

Lauren nodded again, before taking a big gulp of beer.

Lolly smiled, her old face beaming. She felt again for the charm and to Lauren, her grandmother looked like a young girl again, decades washing away, a light surrounding her body and emanating from her soul as if a spotlight had been focused on her in this dark bar.

"Your grandfather gave me this charm, my beautiful girl," Lolly said, shutting her eyes as the band took the stage and began to play. "Oh, my goodness! They're playing 'Summer Wind' by Frank Sinatra. Do you know this song?"

Lauren shook her head no.

"Listen to the song's story, and then I'll tell you mine. It's a story about summer love, a story about a love that forever calls you home," Lolly said, shutting her eyes and swaying her body as the honey-voiced crooner began to sing. "Your grandfather is with us tonight!"

Twenty-one

1962

Whooo-dooo-ooooh-ooooh!

The loons woke Lolly just seconds before the predawn rustling of her father. The nineteen-year-old rubbed her eyes, navigated the cool, narrow wood steps in the log cabin and padded into the kitchen, where her father stood illuminated in the darkness by the weak light from the refrigerator.

"Lemme help you, Dad," Lolly said.

"I can get it," he groused.

"You can? It's okay to turn on a light," she said, hitting the switch over the sink. "It's not gonna wake me up."

"I like to watch the sun rise over the lake," her father said. "That's my morning light. Along with you, of course."

Lolly smiled and hugged her father, her blond head coming to rest on his flannel overshirt.

As the two pulled apart, they looked at each other closely in the burgeoning light from outside and smiled, hiding their deeper emotions: Vi's too early death had aged both of them. There was a constant weight, like an invisible brick, pressing down on them. Vern's hair was now more grey than black, and Lolly often woke with circles under her eyes.

Lolly started the coffee, grabbed a skillet, and pulled out three eggs and two slabs of bacon.

"Toast?" she asked.

"Yep," Vern said.

She yanked the jam and butter from the refrigerator and bread from the bin on the counter, and plugged in the toaster. She plopped the bacon into the now-hot skillet, and when it began to bubble and grease began to fill the bottom of the pan, Lolly cracked three eggs into it.

The sun was just beginning to reflect off Lost Land when Lolly handed her father his breakfast. For a moment, the eggs' yolks matched the early summer sunshine. Her father lifted his fork and cut into them, the yellow spilling forth and flowing haphazardly around the plate.

"You can't take care of me forever," he said, sopping up the yolks with his toast.

Lolly looked out at the lake, a long sigh her answer.

It was summer, and the resorters were returning. Although it had been nearly a decade since her mother had died, the first weeks of summer always stung like an angry ground hornet. Lolly knew her mother would never be coming back.

Even Jo was gone. She was staying in the city, living in her sorority house and working.

"Who are you taking out today?" Lolly asked, breaking the silence.

"A group of guys from Chicago," Vern said, snapping off a bite of crispy bacon. "They want to fish Lost Land for musky, and then the big lake for salmon. Full day. Good money."

Vern stood. "Mind filling me a thermos of coffee?"

"Sandwiches?"

Vern nodded. "I'll go gather up my stuff."

An unspoken routine between the two had developed over the years. Lolly met her father on the screened porch, thermos and cooler filled, picked up a tackle box in her free hand, and accompanied her father to his johnboat at the end of their dock.

The morning was crisp but would warm quickly, as they did in Michigan, the chill giving way to humidity-free warmth and skies as blue as the indigo buntings that dove over the lake in search of mosquitoes.

Whooo-dooo-ooooh-ooooh!

"New couple, I do think," Vern said, nodding back at the cabin, where two loons nestled in the inlet by the screened porch. "I think Lucy and Ricky might have passed on this winter. I think we may have some new lovers."

"Loud ones," Lolly said, handing her dad the thermos and cooler. "Woke me up again this morning."

"You got names for them?"

Lolly jumped at the sound of a strange voice.

She turned to find a mop-headed kid, with eyes as green as the lake reeds swaying in the breeze behind him.

"Oh, Les! Right on time!"

"Thanks for letting me help you out this summer, sir."

Lolly's head pivoted between her father and the young man, her eyes wide, waiting for an explanation.

"Oh, I'm sorry, Lol. Didn't I tell you about Les?"

"Umm, no."

Les laughed, his face breaking into a huge smile, before quickly covering his mouth with his hand. "Sorry."

"Les, Lolly. Lolly, Les."

The two shook hands tentatively. "Les is on summer break from Michigan State. He's majoring in . . . what was that again?"

"Forestry."

"You study forests?" Lolly asked.

"Fish and wildlife, actually. I'm in the College of Natural Resources and Agriculture."

"So then my dad is sort of your 'outdoor' professor this summer?" Lolly asked.

"That's right. I'll be helping him with his fishing excursions this summer, which will give me a chance to study our state's northern lakes, especially the musky and salmon population."

"His parents have a summer cottage here," Vern explained. "His dad contacted me about this."

"Can you change a hook? Cast? Clean a fish?" Lolly asked in quick succession, a bit jealous that a college boy was about to take over some of her usual summer duties with her father.

Vern doubled over at the sudden barrage of questions from his daughter, booming laughter echoing off the lake and causing a group of herons nearby to take flight.

"My daughter has a point," he said, looking Les—and his crisp khaki pants, ironed polo shirt, and deck shoes—over closely. "Lolly, you should do all the interviewing from now on. So, can you do any of that, Les? It's kind of important, since most of the city folk can't."

"Ummm . . ." Les hesitated, looking between Lolly and Vern.

Vern leaned into the boat and nabbed a pole and his tackle box. "Here ya go. Tie on a lure and cast into the lake for me."

Les pursed his lips as if he were going to whistle, or maybe cry, and then exhaled a puff of wind heavenward, blowing his flaxen bangs out of his eyes. He did this over and over, as he fussed with the lure. He tried tying the lure for five minutes, his eyes crossed in concentration, until Lolly couldn't take it anymore.

"Here!" she said. "Let me show you!"

Les's face reddened, as Lolly continued. "It's okay that a girl's showing you. Don't be embarrassed. It's easy: This is a figure eight tie. See, you twist and twist, until an *eight* forms, then loop the end through the bottom of the eight and then the top of the eight and pull tight, like this. There!"

Les looked at Lolly as if she were a magician. He yanked and yanked on the lure, but it stayed in place, as if it had been cemented onto the line.

"Do it again," he said, incredulous. "Please."

Lolly showed him again, and when she was done, cast a perfect toss alongside the edge of the reeds, hooking a smallmouth bass in under a minute.

"You'll get the hang of it," Lolly said, pulling the fish off and tossing it back into the water, where it immediately dove to the bottom of the clear lake. "It's like having a dad who's a butcher. You learn how to grill a steak, right?"

Les nodded, and again blew his bangs toward the sky.

Lolly finally studied the boy. Yes, he was gangly. Yes, he was a bit green. Yes, he was a college boy.

But there was no denying, he was very cute.

Suddenly, Lolly's face flushed, as if everything she just thought had been said aloud, for the entire world to hear.

"Now, you try casting," Vern said.

Les picked up the pole, moved to the edge of the dock, hitched up the rod, and flicked his arm like a robot. The lure sailed the wrong way, screaming backward, where it hooked Lolly directly in the charm bracelet.

"Lolly! Are you okay?" her father yelled, rushing toward his daughter.

"Oh, my gosh! No! I'm so sorry!" Les yelled, following suit.

"Mom was watching over me," Lolly laughed, holding up her bracelet and beginning the process of untangling the lure from amongst the knot of charms it had hooked. "As for you," she continued, staring at Les, "I think the only thing you might catch is a cold . . . or a lawsuit from one of the guests."

Les gave a wobbly smile, his humiliation giving way to the comforting fact that at least his boss's daughter had not been injured.

"What are all those?" Les asked, moving forward to help Lolly untangle the mess he'd created.

"Charms," she said. "Most from my mom, who died. All of them have a story."

"I think I just added a new one to your bracelet," Les said, blushing.

"A charm or a story?" Lolly asked, cocking her head. "I'm guessing story, since that lure is too dangerous to add to my bracelet."

"My mom and grandma have charm bracelets," Les said, finally fishing the lure free from her bracelet. "They are just so . . . beautiful, aren't they? They have so much history. Your mother *was* protecting you."

Lolly stared in shock at Les. She had never heard someone so young, much less a boy, say something so profound about her bracelet.

"Does your girlfriend have a charm bracelet, too?" Lolly managed to ask, her mouth suddenly feeling as if it were filled with cotton.

Les smiled. "I haven't hooked one yet."

"We gotta get going, Les," Vern said from the dock. "You just observe today, got it?"

Les ducked his head and nodded, his hair flopping.

"I love you, Lolly," Vern called. "See you tonight."

"Okay, Dad. Catch a lot of fish to fry for dinner!"

Vern got into the back of the boat and lowered the engine into the water.

"So? You never answered me," Les said to Lolly, before he turned to leave.

"About what?" Lolly asked.

"What are the names of your loons?"

"Oh! Well, they're new here," Lolly said. "And they're loud. They sort of squabble, but in a nice way. The old loons were named Lucy and Ricky. Got any ideas?"

"What about Fred and Ethel?" Les said. "They squawk at each other, but you know they couldn't live without the other one."

Lolly's face beamed. *I Love Lucy* was the one TV show that could always make her laugh.

"That's perfect," she said.

"You know what I learned about loons in college?" Les asked.

Lolly shook her head.

"They mate for life," he said. "And they always return home, to the same lake, every summer."

Vern revved the engine on the boat, and Les left Lolly standing dumbfounded on the dock. Les climbed into the boat unsteadily and took a seat with a big thud. As the boat left the dock and zipped across Lost Land Lake, Lolly waved goodbye, her bracelet jangling, as Fred and Ethel, alarmed by the commotion, ran across the top of the lake after each other, their legs churning, until they took flight into the morning sky, craning their necks to look at one another. Lolly strained her eyes to watch them fly; she could swear they were smiling.

And just like Fred and Ethel, Les returned to Lost Land every summer for Lolly and, eventually, he never left home, either.

Twenty-two

Y ou can't leave me hanging like that, Grandma," Lauren said, her eyes wide. "When did he finally ask you out? How long did you date? When did he propose?"

Lolly laughed and took a big gulp of her second beer as another Sinatra song ended.

"Your grandfather, Les, asked me out the next summer, and we went steady long distance until he finished college. The summer after he graduated, he secured a job with the state parks department and helped my father on weekends, before taking over his guide business," Lolly said. "He proposed to me that summer at the end of the dock on my birthday in the midst of the Fourth of July fireworks. It was so romantic and so thoughtful. He told me he had asked my dad—and my mom—for their permission. Les gave me the most beautiful engagement ring, and then he pulled out another box."

"What was in it?" Lauren asked, on the edge of her seat.

"The charm of the loon," she said, holding up her bracelet and finding the silver bird instantly. "I was so happy and honored that any man would value my past so beautifully. I asked him what the charm meant, and he said, 'This is to a forever love that always calls you home.'"

Lauren was now weeping uncontrollably, sloshing beer out of the mug she was holding. "That's the most beautiful love story I've ever heard, Grandma."

"Here, my dear," Lolly said, handing her another napkin. "You could use this."

"I'm so sorry, Grandma," Lauren said, putting her beer down and blowing her nose. "People are staring."

"That's my granddaughter!" Lolly laughed. "Causing a scene, just like me."

"I'm sorry I never got to meet him. I'm sorry he died so young."

Lolly reached out for her granddaughter's hand and took it in her lap.

"He would have loved you! He was such a good man. He was such a great husband and father. He would have made a wonderful grandfather, too."

Lolly squeezed her granddaughter's hand. "But I want you to know something: Although I miss him desperately, I don't regret a day of my life. One year, thirty years, fifty years: I found *the* love of my life, and that is the greatest blessing. You do know, my dear, that all my tragedy has affected your mom in so many bad ways: My mother dying so young, my husband's premature death, and never having enough money. That's why she's so strict with you. That's why she feels she has to control life, so it won't come unhinged on her. The only things we can control are our happiness, our destiny, our impact on others. Rest is up to God."

Lauren sniffled and nodded.

"Are you crying because you don't have someone to love like that?" Lolly asked. "Have you ever been in love?"

Lauren looked toward her mother. "No, I haven't been in love. I think I may be a bit like my mom . . . wanting to control life too much."

"Well, don't," Lolly admonished. "You'll find someone special, and when you do fall in love, let me help you plan your wedding! I had a charm pull at mine . . ."

"What's that, Grandma?"

"Cake pulls are an old tradition. My mom and grandma both had them. My wedding cake had a satin ribbon for each of my bridesmaids," Lolly said excitedly. "Before Les and I cut the first slice, my bridesmaids each pulled a charm that was popping out from the bottom two layers of the cake. It was her keepsake for the day. I picked each one especially for every girl— ones for good luck, fortune, or romance—and prayed they would pick the right ones. And they all did! Jo picked the charm of little silver bells, mean- ing she would be the next to marry, and she did—the very next year!"

"I'd love for you to help me when I'm ready," Lauren said. "I've been too focused on school to be open to love, but maybe that will change."

"It would be my honor," Lolly said, before looking over at her daughter and Jake. "And I'd be over the moon to see your mom fall in love again, too."

Twenty-three

My mother must be in heaven right now," Arden said to Jake, nervously sipping her beer, as the lyrics to "The Way You Look Tonight" played in the background.

"She loves Ol' Blue Eyes?" Jake asked.

"You haven't heard the story?" Arden asked incredulously. "You must be the only one. See that picture by the bar? That's my mom with Frank in the Rendezvous."

"Wow!" Jake said. "She's something else."

That's an understatement, Arden thought, surveying the table of Jake's friends, all of whom were very polite, well-spoken, and nice. Almost too nice. It had been ages since Arden had sat at a table where it didn't involve work or where someone didn't have an agenda.

"Would you care to dance?"

Jake's words interrupted Arden's thoughts, and when she turned to look at him, the restaurant behind him whirled.

"Oh, me? No! No! I can't dance!" Arden stuttered.

"Can't or won't?" Jake asked directly. "Those are two very different things. Everyone can dance. Most people won't."

Before she could say a thing, Jake was already on his feet, hand extended, leading Arden to a tiny square of warped parquet flooring just to the side of the jazz band.

Arden's body was stiff as Jake took her into his big arms.

"It's okay," he whispered in a husky voice. "Loosen up. Just follow my lead."

Arden felt dizzy and unsteady on her feet, but Jake was strong, more muscular than Arden had imagined. She held on tighter, one arm around his neck, the other around his back. He was solid, like a tree, and smelled of outdoors, a mix of fresh air and—*what was that?*—Fahrenheit cologne. A tuft of lustrous black hair spilled forth from the top of his plaid button-down.

"I gotcha, I gotcha," Jake whispered above the music.

Still, Arden couldn't help but hear the Sinatra line about "breathless charm."

Must everything in my life have to involve the word "charm"? Arden thought, stealing a look toward her mother, who blew her a big kiss.

"I did a little research on you," Jake said, swaying to Sinatra. "I'm impressed by all that you've accomplished. *Paparazzi* magazine . . . that's huge."

"Thank you," Arden said softly.

"Do you write those articles?"

Arden hesitated. "Sort of."

"Do you write books?"

"I . . . well . . . I did."

"Did?"

"I stopped."

"Why?"

The room again spun, this time as Arden was suddenly reminded of her failed marriage and stalled writing career.

"Life," she finally said, looking into Jake's stormy eyes.

Jake seemed to sense the sadness in Arden's voice, and he tightened his grip around her waist.

Again, the room spun as Jake began to twirl Arden. She laughed suddenly, a small yelp falling from her mouth as she twirled.

Jake slowed as the song ended and another began.

"How about you?" Arden asked. "Why are you here? In Scoops?"

Jake flashed Arden a smile that was seemingly filled with as many secrets and as much depth as the waters of Lost Land Lake.

"Well, the *Reader's Digest* version of my life is that I grew up in Green Bay, and my parents were both factory workers. I saw the toll that took on their health, so I always wanted to be a doctor. I was the first to graduate college, but I could never afford med school, so I became a geriatric nurse. It's a calling to me. I moved here from Chicago because I came here on my honeymoon with my ex-wife . . ."

"Ex-wife?" Arden asked, stopping in the middle of the floor, her jaw dropping like an anchor.

"Yes," Jake said with a rolling laugh, like thunder across the lake. "Ex! I knew it was over before it began, really. I grew up with her. She was my high school sweetheart. But she never liked what I did. She always wanted to live in Chicago, or New York. She wanted bigger, I wanted smaller. She never left the cabin when I brought her here on our honeymoon."

"That's a bad thing?" Arden laughed.

"Not usually on a honeymoon, but, for us, it was. We had nothing in common but our past. I've learned as a geriatric nurse that if you only focus on your past, you're doomed. You have to honor your past but be focused on the future. You have to believe that there are always happier days to come."

The words struck Arden in the heart, and she shut her eyes as Jake moved her across the small floor.

"I'm an 'ex,' too," Arden whispered into his ear.

"Can't spell 'next' without it," he whispered back, holding her closely, until the music stopped. "Band's taking a break."

"Oh, my gosh, I'm so sorry," Arden said, breaking free from his embrace. "I didn't realize."

"Seems like you enjoyed dancing," Jake chuckled.

"Actually," Arden said. "I did."

Jake led Arden back to Lolly and Lauren's table. "Thanks for letting me steal her. It was a lovely evening. I hope we can do it again soon."

Silence gripped the table. "Tomorrow!" Lolly finally said. "You're coming by Friday to make sure I'm alive, right? Even though it's the start of the holiday weekend?"

Jake laughed heartily. "Wouldn't miss it. Ladies, drive safely. And, Arden? I had a wonderful night."

Arden's face flushed, and she fidgeted with her eyeglasses.

"Me, too," she replied softly.

The ride home was quiet, save for the chorus of early summer peepers that lived in the surrounding farms, fields, and ponds.

Another chorus greeted the Lindsey ladies as soon as they returned to the cabin and Lolly had turned off the Woodie's engine.

Whooo-dooo-ooooh-ooooh!

Lolly smiled in the darkness and thought of her husband. "I'm wiped out, girls. Off to bed. I love you dearly."

"Good night, Mom."

"Good night, Grandma. Thanks for sharing your love story," Lauren said, hugging her grandmother.

"My pleasure. Night night."

A few seconds later, Arden and Lauren saw the lights in Lolly's bedroom come on. The two remained quiet, watching the lake dance in the moonlight, until they could see Lolly crawl into bed and turn off the lights.

"She told you about your grandfather? And the loons?"

"She did. It is so beautiful, Mom. I hope we can both find that one day."

Whooo-dooo-ooooh-ooooh!

"I'm sorry about my reaction today," Arden said. "I just want to protect you."

Her voice surprised the loons, and they took off running across the lake, before awkwardly lifting into the air.

"I know," Lauren said, nodding at the loons. "But at some point, I just have to take off, like them, no matter how hard it might be to watch. I'll either fall or fly."

Arden took her daughter's hand, Lauren's bracelet jangling, and the two walked to the end of the dock and dangled their feet into the water, where they talked about first love, risk, and an ache that still called, like the haunting sounds of Fred and Ethel.

part seven

The Ice Cream Cone Charm

To a Sweet Life Filled with a Passion
for What You Do

Twenty-four

G ood morning! Happy Memorial Day weekend!"
Lolly pulled an old ceramic mug dotted with blueberries from an open cupboard overflowing with mismatched cups and saucers, and filled Arden's mug to the brim with coffee.

"How'd you sleep?" Lolly asked, looking at Arden and her white sweatshirt emblazoned with the slogan WE GIVE YOU THE STARS AND THE SWOON underneath the famed *Paparazzi* logo.

"Like a rock," Arden replied, blowing on the steaming mug before taking a generous sip. "A rock that had three beers and danced with a complete stranger."

Arden's sweet, unguarded admission surprised Lolly and immediately sent her into a fit of giggles, which caused her arm to twitch and scatter the chocolate chips she was sprinkling into the pancake batter across the kitchen floor.

"Oh, my dear! I'm so proud of you. It feels good to have friends and a little fun again, doesn't it?"

Arden took another sip of coffee and tilted her head, contemplating her mother's words. "It does."

Arden hesitated. "And I told Lauren about Clem yesterday, too."

The new admission surprised Lolly again, causing her to smile brightly. "How did Lauren react?"

"She said she'd never felt closer to me," Arden said, smiling. "I'm beginning to think she never thought I was human." Arden's words were tinged with the regret she felt for waiting so long to open up to her daughter.

Lolly turned to look at her daughter. "Every generation can benefit by learning from the one before," she said, nodding toward Arden's sweatshirt. "And I'm sorry to say you *can* seem closed-off at times, my dear. That job of yours takes up so much of your time and attention."

Lolly lifted the chocolate chip–coated spatula from the batter and offered it to Arden to lick, just as she had always done when Arden was a little girl. Licking the spoon always made Arden feel better instantly.

Arden smiled at her mother's offer, quickly grabbed the spatula, and walked to the kitchen sink. As she licked the spatula, she looked out at Lost Land coming awake. The waters were calm, the sun's early morning light turning the lake alternating colors of brilliant blue and sea glass green. White swans floated on the surface, craning their necks as they swam, while sparrows dove like The Blue Angels around the lake.

Arden thought of her father and grandfather, and closed her eyes. When she opened them, her eyes were greeted by the warped wooden dock jutting into the lake.

So many memories—good, bad, happy, sad—on that little dock. It had, literally, been the jumping off place for my love of books, my love of writing.

Her mother's charm bracelet jangled as she flipped the pancakes.

This is where my mother's love of charms began, Arden thought.

"I've forgotten how beautiful it is here," Arden sighed. "I've . . . well . . . I've just forgotten."

Lolly smiled at her daughter, retrieving her own mug of coffee and refilling it.

"I'm glad you're remembering as I'm starting to forget," Lolly said. She hesitated but continued quietly, "You know, names slip me sometimes."

Arden wrapped her arm around her mother's waist. "I know, Mom." She pulled her close. "I'll always remember. I promise you. And I'll always help you remember, too. Didn't you say that we have to live in the moment? That's all any of us can do, right?"

Lolly nodded.

"Well, then, I'll finish the pancakes, if you make more coffee," Arden said. "It won't be pretty if Lauren wakes up without caffeine."

Lolly smiled and hugged her daughter.

"Let me get a broom and dust pan first," she said, looking down at the errant chocolate chips still scattered across the wood floor. "It won't be pretty if she walks in without caffeine and thinks ants have invaded the cabin."

The two laughed, and then mother and daughter finished making breakfast together.

Twenty-five

"I'm so glad you two decided to join me," Lolly said, as the wind tossed tendrils of her blond beehive about her head wildly.

The Woodie's windows were down, the wind whipping through the car as Lauren drove. "It's going to be a madhouse in town, what with this perfect weather. I thought I'd go for Brigitte Bardot today," Lolly laughed from the passenger seat, fussing with her wig.

"Who?" Lauren asked.

"Oh, that's right," Lolly said, looking at her granddaughter. "Wrong generation . . . by about four decades. I thought I'd look—what do you kids say today—very 'retro.'"

Lauren laughed, nodding her appreciation. "YOLO, right, Grandma?"

"YOLO!" Lolly repeated, sticking her face out the window.

Memorial Day weather in Michigan was as unpredictable as a kitten. It could be sunny and seventies, or raw and rainy. Scoops had even experienced a handful of Memorial weekends where the angry skies spit snow, the coast refusing to let go of winter.

But today was perfection. And having her family here for the first time in ages made it even better for Lolly.

She pulled down the ancient visor in the Woodie and looked into the wavy mirror, more to steal a glance at Arden, reading emails in the back-seat.

Lolly's body suddenly ricocheted into the door, and Arden's cell flew all the way from the backseat to the front seat.

"LAUREN!"

Lauren screamed and regained control of the Woodie, which had briefly gone off the side of the narrow two-lane road and skidded on gravel.

"Sorry," she said, guiltily flipping up her own visor. "I thought I'd check my hair, too, since Grandma was. This steering wheel has *a lot* of play in it."

"You have to keep a tight grip on the big wheel," Lolly said, reposition-ing her granddaughter's hands at "10" and "2," their charm bracelets col-liding. "It's sorta like steering the space shuttle with a kite string."

Arden shut her eyes and inhaled, willing her heart to slow. "Can you hand me my phone, please, Mom? It seems to have a mind of its own."

Lolly retrieved the phone from the floorboard by her feet, and then slipped it into her purse.

"Hey! What are you doing?" Arden asked in a panic.

"*Why* are you working today?" Lolly asked. "It's an official holiday."

Lolly turned to look at her daughter. "You're missing this gorgeous day by keeping your head down to read your emails. Those can wait. This," Lolly said, gesturing with her hand out the window, "can't. Remember what you said just this morning about how you've forgotten how beautiful it is here?"

Arden sighed and nodded. "You're right, Mom."

The Woodie passed a local tourism billboard featuring a woman read-ing a book on the beach.

"Remember how you used to love to write?" Lolly asked Arden. "You *dreamed* of being a writer. Your little face would light up when you told me about the stories you were writing. You were so talented. Whatever hap-pened to your novel?"

Arden thought of her recent conversation with Zoe and her long-lost writing group days.

"It sort of took a backseat," Arden said, "to life."

"Did you get the charm I sent you?"

Arden smiled at her mother's persistence. "Yes. It was such a sweet ges-ture, Mom, but you realize those charms are purely sentimental."

"Mom!" Lauren yelled.

"Well, it's true. They're sweet, but they don't change anything."

Lolly turned around again in her seat, her face now as white as her wig. "They do! You just don't believe in dreams anymore. Where did all that girlish enthusiasm and talent go? If you love what you do . . ."

"I know, Mother," Arden said, interrupting her. "You've told me this a million times."

"Then say it again. Out loud. To remind yourself."

Arden let the warm wind whip across her face. "*If you love what you do, you will never work a day in your life.*"

Twenty-six

Downtown Scoops was jammed to its gills.

Even larger hordes of fudgies had descended on the town, like a swarm of hungry locusts.

By the time Lauren found a parking space and the courage to parallel park the giant Woodie, Lolly had to dash to the fudge shop and enter through the back door to avoid the snaking line in front.

"Hi, everyone!" Lolly said to the crew at Dolly's while firing up her dueling copper urns and scrambling to pull together ingredients to start the fudge. "It's crazy out there!"

"Hi, Lolly!" the group yelled, many of whom applauded her dramatic arrival.

"Yeah! The holiday weekend can really start now!" a young girl with dark hair layered with dyed purple streaks said.

"Do you wanna help?" Lolly asked Arden and Lauren. "I need to touch up my makeup before my first show."

Lauren and Arden were nearly paralyzed as the crew sprinted around preparing the shop to open. To Lauren, the scene reminded her of a Christmas cartoon special, in which elves ran around Santa's workshop making sweets, building toys, filling stockings, and essentially spreading happiness.

"Sure," Lauren said. "What can we do?"

"Stir the pots!" Lolly instructed, pulling on a set of long, pink gloves. "Don't let the cream scorch!"

Lolly ran to the front windows and moved the hands of the **NEXT SHOW** clock to **NOON**. The sight sent the waiting crowd into a frenzy.

"Dolly! Dolly! Dolly!" they chanted.

"This is crazier than a Justin Bieber concert," Lauren said, her eyes wide. "This is such a rush."

"You're still high from the chocolate chip pancakes, maple syrup, and coffee," Arden said, stirring the urn of fudge with her paddle.

"Mom, this is a blast," Lauren said. "You can't deny that."

Arden started to say something, but Lauren cut her off. "Do you think it's against the health code to stick my face into this pot?"

Arden laughed, as her mother dashed out of the bathroom in full Dolly Van Voozle costume. In addition to her blond beehive and clownish cheeks, Lolly had chosen a flapper dress covered in shiny red paillettes and ending in fringe, with strands of multicolored Mardi Gras beads and dangling earrings in the shape of ice cream cones. Over that, she had tied her favorite vintage apron, red dotted with dancing ice cream cones.

Dong! Dong! Dong!

The old clock chimed in the rose garden across the street. The crowd outside counted, "One! Two! Three! . . ." as the chimes climbed to a dozen. When they finished, the spectators once again began to chant, "Dolly! Dolly! Dolly!"

"How do I look?" Lolly asked her girls.

"Like a dream," Lauren said. "Like my grandma!"

Lolly winked a big fake lash at her, slapped Arden on the rear, and turned to the old man at the player piano. "Ready, Don?"

"Is fudge sweet?" he laughed. "Another Memorial Day weekend together, eh?"

The old man's jaw quivered a little, his voice filled with emotion. His little face resembled that of an apple doll's. Lolly walked over and gave him a side hug.

"We've got a lot of years left, Don," she whispered, adjusting his giant red bow tie. "Don't go all soft on me now."

Don smiled, his thick grey eyebrows twitching in delight.

The workers at Dolly's applauded the duo, and began to chant with the crowd.

"Let's go!" Lolly said, taking Don's hand.

The blinds lifted.

The door opened.

The crowd screamed.

Lolly emerged, still in tennis shoes, the sweet smells of the shop and Don trailing along behind her.

"Greetings!" Lolly yelled.

"Hello, Dolly!" the crowd yelled back.

Lolly yanked off her apron to reveal the sequined dress, shimmying just so to make the fringe dance.

The crowd roared.

Don handed Lolly her feather boa, and she curtsied as he ambled away. Through the windows, the shop and its treasures were now on full display, the sun like a spotlight illuminating the copper urns, fudge, ice cream, taffy, and candies as well as Don, now seated at the player piano, started the piano and the music began.

Lolly walked up to an elderly man leaning on a cane, and placed her boa around his neck. She began to sing and his face broke into a smile as bright as the midday sun. Then she urged the crowd to sing along with her.

Arden shook her head from inside the shop and walked away as yet another group played along, putty again in her mother's hands.

But, suddenly, there was silence.

Arden tilted her head.

Nothing.

Arden raced back to the window.

Music from the player piano continued to squeak from the speakers. Lolly turned and looked back at Arden, panicked. Without thinking, Arden began to pantomime the lyrics, swaying back and forth. Lolly's face instantly brightened.

"We feel the shop swaying 'cause the piano's a-playing," Lolly sang, the crowd none the wiser, nodding back at Don, *"one of your favorite songs from way back when!"*

When Lolly finished, she took a dramatic bow, flinging her boa behind her head, as people in the crowd applauded and went in for hugs before flooding the shop to buy sweets.

Lolly posed for pictures, and as she did, her mind flashed, like the cameras: *Actually, Dolly is going away, fading, one day at a time,* she thought with sadness.

"Thank you," a young mother said, stroking Lolly's back. "My whole family has adored you for ages. You will live forever in our photo albums and memories."

Lolly's jaw quaked, but she steeled herself and hugged the woman. "Thank you, my dear. You have no idea how much that means to me today."

As soon as the crowd outside had dissipated, Lolly walked inside to the clock adhered to the window and moved the hands up an hour.

NEXT SHOW: 1:00, it now read.

She put her apron back on, adjusted her wig, and took over the paddles from Lauren and Arden.

"Thank you," she whispered to Arden.

"You're welcome," Arden said. "You will get through this, okay? Even if you have to use a sheet to remember the lyrics. People will still love you."

Lolly smiled and began to stir the chocolate.

"Look at her smile," Lauren whispered to her mom. "She's not just punching a time clock, is she?"

As Lauren walked over to help her grandma stir the fudge, her words struck a chord in Arden and, as if led by an external force, she found herself walking directly over to Doris Van Voozle, Dolly's granddaughter, who now owned the shop.

"It's good to see you!" Doris said, hugging Arden. "Glad you could make it up this year."

"Me, too," Arden said, before nodding toward her mother. "Act never changes, does it?"

Doris's doughy face considered Arden's question. "Some things never should," she said, straightening her own white apron with Dolly's logo emblazoned on the front. "There's not enough innocence in the world. There's not enough nostalgia. The world is all bad news and ticker tape terror. Your mother makes people feel safe and happy. She reminds them of the way the world used to be. Escapism, like in those celebrity profiles you do, right? If that's not a necessary gift today, I don't know what is."

Arden's mind shifted, and she smiled at the woman's words.

"Still can't believe your mother came up with this whole Dolly idea," Doris said matter-of-factly, before turning to head to the cash register, jammed with customers. "Sure been great for our business all these years."

"Wait! What?" Arden asked, confused. "What do you mean she came up with this whole idea?"

"Didn't you know?" Doris asked, ringing up a family laden with sweets. "The whole she-bang, from the Dolly song and act to making the fudge in the front window. She just walked in one day off the street, introduced herself, and told us she was lonely and needed hope. I was a bit skeptical at first, and sort of let her try it out, because I felt sorry for her. But she was a huge hit, so I gave her a job. I don't want anything to change. Especially your mom. She is a gift."

Arden's jaw dropped. She turned to watch her mother work the urns.

"Doris, do you mind if my mom takes a break after her next show?"

"Not at all."

"I think I want to buy her an ice cream cone."

Twenty-seven

S coot your rear over a little more." Lolly laughed, hitting Arden's bottom with a cheek of her own. "There."

Lolly, Arden, and Lauren squeezed onto a teak bench in the rose garden across from Dolly's, three generations crammed together and eating triple scoop ice cream cones. Sun squeezed through the thick, verdant branches of the dogwood, birch, and redbud trees that canopied the small park.

"After these, we may not be able to fit on this bench anymore," Arden said, licking a scoop of cappuccino chocolate chunk.

"Hey, this was your idea, Miss Fitness," Lolly laughed, licking her Blue Moon cone, her tongue and lips turning blue. "What gives?"

Though it was early in the growing season in northern Michigan, sunny daffodils and color-drenched tulips lined the small park's border, and nuclear-size azaleas and rhododendrons flowered. But the park was known for its roses, and the early varieties in virginal white, deep violet, and pretty pink danced in the breeze for passersby.

Arden took a big lick of her ice cream, wiped her mouth, and put her hand on her mother's leg. "So, a little birdie just told me about how you masterminded the whole Dolly showcase."

Lolly stopped licking her cone for a second, craning her neck dramatically to scan the branches above. "Bad birdie!" she said.

"Mom," Arden said, suddenly very serious. "I want to know: How did that come about? I had no clue. I guess I just thought Dolly's had always had a Dolly and that you were the latest to be cast in the role."

Lolly chuckled. "So you actually want to hear one of my stories?"

"Yes . . . no . . . well, I mean . . . I guess I do, Mom."

A little girl, no more than five or six, wearing the most adorable pink and white dress skipped into the park with a bubblegum ice cream cone as big as her head. Her parents trailed behind, the mother pushing a stroller, the father carrying a camera and cone.

"Rose!" he shouted. "Slow down! We want a picture."

The little girl, her curly red hair starting to come loose from the colorful barrettes and big bow that held it back, stopped in front of the roses.

Lauren glanced over, and her artistic senses whirred. It was as if the scene had been perfectly coordinated in cotton candy colors, everything washed in pinks and whites. On instinct, Lauren shut her eyes and her hands began to move, to sketch and to paint, invisibly.

Lolly and Arden watched Lauren, until the little girl screamed, "We're done!" and Lauren opened her eyes.

"Nothing sweeter than a child with an ice cream cone in the summer," Lolly said. "It was that very simple thing that changed my life, in fact." She paused.

"Here, hold this," Lolly said, handing Arden her cone, "so I can show you this."

Lolly looked through her charm bracelet until she found a charm unlike the many silver ones that ringed her wrist, one that mimicked the design on her apron: A glittery ice cream cone, with one blue scoop atop a pink scoop sitting in a golden sugar cone.

"This sweet little charm gave me purpose, passion, and meaning," Lolly said, smiling and waving at the family now leaving the park. "This charm made Lolly Dolly."

Twenty-eight

Memorial Day Weekend, 1985

Fog hung over Lost Land Lake, heavy and thick, like a moving curtain, choking out the daylight and making even the dock and water impossible to see from the screened porch of Lolly's cabin.

She shivered and pulled a blanket over her body, gripping her warm mug of coffee closely.

Save for the loons, there was not a sound coming from the lake.

Typically, on the first summer holiday of the year, the lake was teeming with people and activity. Summer—like life—was ready to begin again, filled with hope and optimism. Now, however, the world was cloaked in darkness.

The weather matched Lolly's mood: She was in a grey place, on the verge of depression. It had only been a short time since she found her husband, dead. This was her first Memorial Day without him.

Arden would be leaving Scoops for college in a few short months, and Lolly had a feeling deep down that her daughter would not return.

My whole life has been an endless ellipsis: I have gone, in the blink of an eye, from little girl to motherless daughter, from daddy's caretaker to wife and mother.

My whole life—nearly every single day—has been spent caring for someone else.

Now, in the blink of an eye, I am alone.

How could You, God? How could You?

Despite wanting Arden to be happy and to pursue her dreams no matter where they led her, Lolly couldn't help but feel stung by Arden's rejection of everything dear to her.

Tears came, and a great weight rested atop Lolly's body. She was exhausted, unable to even sit up and move. Lolly set her mug on the slatted wood floor, propped a pillow under her head, and stretched her body out on the glider, adding another quilt over her weary bones.

The chilly fog seeped through the screens of the porch, almost like sleeping gas, and, quickly, Lolly was unconscious, nightmares of death and loneliness causing her body to thrash on the glider.

In the midst of her nightmares, Lolly was startled awake by the sounds of boat engines and children screaming. She sat up, and the world was gleaming in sunshine.

She squinted at the old, glittery kitty-cat clock she had on the porch—eyes moving left, tail moving right, eyes moving right, tail moving left.

Two o'clock? I've slept for four hours?

Lolly shook the cobwebs from her head and walked to the screen facing the lake. The fog had cleared, the skies were now blue, and a warm wind blew. Everything glistened with dew, as if Michigan had been dipped in wet silver. She held her face to the sun.

"Who wants ice cream?" Lolly heard a mother a few cabins down call to her children.

"I do!" they replied, sprinting to the cabin in their wet swimsuits.

I do, too, Lolly thought.

She searched the fridge first, and then the big cooler in the garage, but she was out of ice cream. She was out of everything.

Lolly willed herself to get dressed, put on some makeup, and walk out of her cabin.

She revved the Woodie and pointed it toward Scoops, parking it along a side street on the edge of town in the only spot she could find.

As she strolled, she started to see her hometown through fresh eyes.

Scoops was founded in the mid-1800s, and while the lakeshore teemed with new construction, the hilly town remained quaint: Little, shingled bungalows and white clapboard cottages sat tucked behind huge gardens and walls of rhododendrons.

Lolly inhaled deeply as she walked. Scoops smelled of lake water and wood, pine needles and fudge.

As she neared downtown, her pace slowed as soon as she passed the little hardware store, packed to its wooden rafters with tools, bolts, mowers, and birdseed.

Scoops was filled with fudgies, who had foregone the beach due to the bad weather earlier and flocked to town, instead.

Women trailed into dress and purse shops, while their husbands took seats in the Adirondack chairs that sat outside the stores, patiently waiting until it was late enough in the afternoon to hit the Sandbar Saloon or Old Crow Bar for a happy hour beer.

Lolly headed into the old Scoops drugstore, which had been around forever and was once the epicenter of the tiny town. Resorters loved the drugstore for its cheap sweatshirts and Scoops souvenirs, and locals loved it for Dr. Philbrook, who had been the pharmacist before—the town joke went—aspirin was invented. Few folks knew, however, that way in the back of the congested store—behind the rows of Scoops T-shirts, hats, and mugs, beyond the trinkets and key chains, and tucked behind the pharmacy and towering rolls of toilet paper—sat a narrow old ice cream counter on a patch of red-and-white tile. The short counter held only eight worn leather stools that rotated slowly even when no one was seated on them, behind which stood two soda jerks, who barely had enough room to turn from griddle to counter. The old-fashioned drugstore served up only a select few items in the tiny space: shakes, malts, phosphates, *real* cherry cola and homemade ginger ale, along with sundaes, floats, banana splits, hamburgers, onion rings, and French fries.

Lolly used to come to the drugstore with her mom and pick out charms, before they would head to the back for a treat. Lolly had done the same thing with Arden. She thought of her daughter's suitcases, sitting in her room, already half filled to leave for college.

Lolly looked up and down the counter at the happy people eating ice cream and making the best of what had started as a rather dreary Memorial Day weekend.

An elderly man using a walker slowly made his way to the counter and took a seat next to Lolly, grunting with every effort he made.

"Ma'am?" asked a young man wearing a brightly striped paper hat tilted on his head.

"Could I get a chocolate malt?" Lolly said. "And a cherry phosphate, please."

The man nodded and went to work, scooping ice cream into a silver blender, before starting work on her drink, pouring cherry syrup into a mineral water glass and squirting dashes of acid phosphate into it, and then topping it with a steady stream of carbonated water, the mixture bright and bubbling. Lolly fidgeted in anticipation, causing her charms to dance.

"That'll be four-fifty, ma'am," the soda jerk said, pushing Lolly's sweet concoctions in front of her.

Lolly reached for her purse, but it wasn't on her shoulder.

No! You old fool! she thought, embarrassed.

"I . . . I . . . I . . . ," she stuttered to the boy, as a few patrons—chomping burgers and rings, and slurping shakes—turned to stare.

Lolly was suddenly foggier than she had been earlier in the day, more alone than she had ever felt her whole life.

How could I forget my purse?

"I'm so sorry!" she cried, rushing out and onto the teeming street, the little bell on the door tinkling like her charms.

Near tears, Lolly searched for somewhere, anywhere, to hide, but every chair in town was held hostage by a man holding packages for his wife.

Everyone, Lolly realized, had someone.

I have no one anymore, Lolly said to herself. *How did my dad do it after the love of his life died?*

"I bought your malt and your phosphate."

Lolly jumped at the sound of a man's voice. When she turned, the man with the walker was standing beside her.

"We all have bad days," he said, as the soda jerk rushed up to hand Lolly her drinks. "Some worse than others."

Lolly tried to respond, but her lips felt sealed shut.

"You have a good holiday, ma'am," the man said, following the soda jerk and slowly making his way back into the shop. "Make it a sweet one."

One step at a time, it suddenly dawned on Lolly, as she watched the man. *That's how my father did it: One slow, steady step at a time.*

Lolly walked down the street, lost in thought, before coming to a deserted metal bench that was dotted with sticky napkins, empty candy wrappers, hardened chocolate, and dripping ice cream.

"For heaven's sake," she said, taking the unused napkins and cleaning a spot big enough for her to sit.

Lolly sipped her malt and phosphate, but they didn't taste the same as they had in the past. She shut her eyes and let the emotions of her day roll out. She began to cry, then weep, her shoulders slumped.

"Are you okay?"

Lolly looked up, and an angelic little girl—blond ringlets, rosy cheeks, bright blue eyes—was staring at her, licking a pink ice cream cone.

Lolly suddenly laughed, finally noticing that the little girl was wearing a princess costume: A sparkly pink sleeveless top over a glittery silver skirt fluffed with mounds and mounds of pink tulle. On her head sat a tiara that glistened in the Scoops sunshine. In one hand, she held her giant ice cream; in the other, she held a glittered wand.

Lolly's eyes grew wide in surprise.

"Your eyes are the same color as mine," the girl said, rotating her cone, and licking every side to keep it from dripping. "Except a little redder. Why are you sad?"

"I'm lonely," Lolly said, setting her drinks down on the bench.

The little girl plopped down next to Lolly, oblivious to the chocolate and ice cream on the bench, her tulle making her body tilt sideways as if she were sitting on a mountain of fabric. "My mom tells me that when I'm lonesome to 'member that I'm never alone. She's always with me."

Lolly's heart raced. Her mother used to tell her the same thing.

"I do have memories. Great ones! See!" Lolly said, showing the little girl her charm bracelet. "They're all right here."

The little girl screamed in delight.

"Lookie!" she yelled, jumping up. "Me, too!"

She held out her delicate wrist, and around it sat a charm bracelet, already filled with many trinkets.

"This is my birthday cake charm!" the girl said, showing Lolly the candles that popped up from the charm when she touched it. "I'm five!"

"Congratulations!" Lolly said.

"And this is my ballerina slipper charm, and this is my diving board charm, 'cause I wanna be in the Olympics!" the little girl said excitedly. "And this is my lucky star charm, so I can wish on it and be anything I dream of being! What do you dream of being?"

The child's words caught Lolly off guard.

"I don't know," Lolly answered honestly.

"Can I see your charms now?"

Lolly held out her wrist, and the girl giggled as she flipped through Lolly's charms, one by one, asking about them as she continued licking her ice cream cone.

"You know what you need?" the little girl suddenly asked.

"What?"

"An ice cream cone!"

"Oh, I already had some ice cream in my malt," Lolly whispered to her, nodding toward the drinks on the bench beside her. "And I don't have any money with me right now."

"No, not one of those," the little girl said, nodding back at the ice cream counter through a nearby shop window. Lolly looked, finally realizing she was sitting in front of Dolly's Sweet Shop. "One of these!" she said.

"Hold this!" the girl finally said definitively, giving Lolly no other option than to take charge of her cone. She took a seat again, her tulle spilling over Lolly's lap, and removed her bracelet. With sticky fingers, she removed a charm of an ice cream cone as glittery as her outfit, two scoops of blue and pink ice cream atop a sugar cone. "Now, hold out your wrist!"

"Oh, I can't take that from you!" Lolly said. "It's one of your special charms."

The little girl looked at Lolly and said, "You need it way more than me!" Then she lowered her voice into a whisper. "And, besides, I have lots of ice cream charms. We come to Scoops every summer."

Lolly held out her wrist, and the little girl carefully added her charm to it.

Lolly held it up to her face, her eyes wide. She no longer felt so alone.

"Your eyes look a lot prettier with no sad red in them," the girl said, before pointing back at Dolly's. "Hey! You look just like the ice cream lady!"

Lolly didn't understand what the little girl was trying to tell her, but she smiled and said, "Thank you for this." While holding her bracelet and new charm to her heart, she handed the little girl's ice cream cone back to her. "It's so sweet of you," Lolly said.

"Good one." The little girl giggled, finishing off her cone. "Sweet! Now, shut your eyes."

"What?"

"Shut your eyes! I'm a fairy princess, so I'm going to grant you a wish. But you have to shut your eyes."

Lolly closed them tightly. The little girl lifted her glitter wand and brought it down lightly, touching Lolly on the top of the head with it. Lolly kept her eyes shut, until she heard the little girl giggling. When she opened her eyes, the girl was nestled in the crook of her mother's arm, who was carrying a big bag of Dolly's fudge.

"I hope she wasn't too much of a bother," the little girl's mother whispered.

"Not at all. She's an angel," Lolly said, still in a trance. "Do you mind if I ask her a question?"

"No," the mother said, cocking her head.

"What wish did you grant me?" Lolly asked.

"I can't tell you," the little girl said very seriously. "But if you believe, it will come true."

"Well, we best be going," the mother said. "Have a great day!"

"You, too," Lolly said, as the two made their way down the street, the little girl's pink tulle floating in the wind. "Oh! Excuse me! I'm sorry to bother you, but can I ask one more question?" Lolly called, suddenly chasing them down the street.

The mother turned and smiled, a quizzical look etched on her youthful face. "I guess. Sure."

"What's your daughter's name?"

"Honey?" she said, looking at her daughter. "You can tell the nice lady."

The little girl turned, her tiara shimmering, her face bright. "Hope!" she said.

The mother waved, and the two disappeared into the crowd of fudgies. Lolly felt dizzy and returned to take a seat on the bench in front of the shop. She shut her eyes and felt the top of her head, which she could swear was tingling.

Lolly heard a door chime, and when she opened her eyes, she was staring directly at the big sign on the fudge shop's front window, where an image of the original Dolly Van Voozle appeared.

You look just like the ice cream lady!

Lolly's heart raced again. She now understood what the little girl was saying. She did look like Dolly.

Beyond the fudge store, the backdrop of the coastline—a triple scoop of shoreline—caught Lolly's eyes, and she stood, finally understanding the wish Hope had granted her.

Believe! Believe!

Without thinking, Lolly rushed into Dolly's, asked for the owner, and began to explain—in a rush—her vision for a show and front window display to lure customers into the shop.

A half hour later, Lolly emerged into the sunshine not only with a job but also a cone—on the house.

And the ice cream tasted just like it had when she was a little girl.

Twenty-nine

N ever underestimate the power of ice cream!" Lolly said, polishing off her cone, and jostling the knees of her daughter and granddaughter. "The purity of that little girl made me realize I could still dream, that I could still be anything I wanted, that my world wasn't ending. And I believe my gift to the world is to make others happy, to forget about the real world for a little while, to be a kid, just like Hope. My simple, silly little job fills me with purpose. It keeps me young."

A pair of fat robins chirped happily on a nearby branch. Lolly sighed.

"Do what makes you happy. It sounds so simple and yet it's so hard, because few of us do. We live out of fear. We live for others, their hopes and expectations. We do what makes everyone else happy."

She stopped and looked hard at her daughter and granddaughter, before continuing. "Why do we make it so hard? Our purpose *should be* our passion. We should sing every day as happily as those robins. My job may not change the world, but at the end of the day, I am complete. And that's all we can hope for, isn't it?"

Arden and Lauren shifted uncomfortably on the narrow bench.

Lolly stood and softly mussed up her girls' hair. "Well, enough preaching! I've got to get back to work. I'll leave you two to talk. See you later for dinner. Let's barbecue tonight! Hamburgers, chicken, foiled potatoes, corn on the cob. I'll bring the ice cream!"

"And Arden," Lolly said, stopping, "thank you for today."

The two watched Lolly amble slowly down the brick path and out of the garden. They followed her wig as it bounced above the rhododendrons, and a few seconds later they heard the fudgies across the street yell, "Dolly!"

Arden scooched over on the bench and reached out her hand to her daughter. Lauren took it, tentatively at first, her hand open, her fingers unbound.

"The arts are full of such risk," Arden said. "I just wanted you to be safe and protected. My mom tells a great story, but we struggled after my dad died. I worked a lot of jobs to make it through college."

"I know, Mom," Lauren said. "I have such guilt about adding any more financial burden to your life. I know that Northwestern is expensive. I know that you have a lot of debt. I know that you need your job to make ends meet. And I promise I will help you with my student loans."

Lauren stopped and took a deep breath. "But what happens if I hate my career so much I can't even hold a job? Isn't that worse than trying to be a painter? Then what? I can always get a 'real' job, can't I? I think there are still going to be people interested in hiring a Northwestern grad with a business and art background."

Arden smiled. She studied her daughter in the garden: She was as beautiful and fresh as these flowers. She was still so tender, so young. Arden thought of how much she loved to write.

Arden removed her glasses with her free hand and shook her head.

"I only want for you to be happy, and I'm having the opposite effect in your life."

Lauren squeezed her mother's hand tightly.

"I know you have worried about Grandma's 'unruly' influence on my decisions in life and I know that you have lived much of your life in Grandma's shadow, but I've lived in your shadow, too," Lauren said, the wind catching her blond hair and blowing it around her head. "What if we started over, right here, right now? Let's believe what that little girl told Grandma a long time ago: We can be anything we dream of being."

Arden leaned in and hugged her daughter.

"Deal."

"That means you have to uphold your end," Lauren said, pulling free and wagging a finger at her mom. "That means you need to dream again, too."

"Double deal."

Mother and daughter stood and strolled around the park, hand in hand.

"I think I'm going to help Grandma for the rest of her day, if you don't mind," Lauren said. "I had so much fun earlier. Wanna come?"

"You go on ahead. She'd love that," Arden said, as they exited the park and stopped in the street across from Dolly's, where a crowd had already gathered for Lolly's next show. "I think I'm going to stroll over to Third Coast Books. I haven't been there in ages."

Lauren zipped across the street, giving a backward wave, just beating a pair of neon-colored scooters that the fudgies loved to zip around town on. The riders gave a loud toot to Lauren as she passed.

Arden stood motionless in the street, forcing fudgies and Segway riders to part around her like salmon swimming upstream, and watched Lauren surprise Lolly with a hug and then take one of her paddles to stir a copper urn.

Arden took off jogging down Main, taking to the street to avoid all the vacationers. She was out of breath when she reached Third Coast Books and had to remove her glasses to wipe the perspiration off the lenses. Arden stopped and studied the giant windows, filled with exquisitely artful book displays and event posters, fronting the old bookstore.

Third Coast's old wooden floors creaked under Arden's feet as she entered. She went to the back, ordered a latte, and wandered the store's cramped aisles sipping and scanning. Her mother had bought countless books for Arden here. Between Third Coast and the local library, Arden had traveled the world without leaving Scoops, progressing from Nancy Drew to Judy Blume, from Michener to Hemingway.

Arden meandered into "classics," took a seat on the floor, and placed her latte between her legs. She began to pull some of her favorite authors from the shelves, reminding herself of how much reading and writing meant to her.

Arden was so engrossed that she didn't hear the footsteps behind her.

She was so enraptured that she jumped when Jake's rumbling voice began to read:

ALICE:
But I don't want to go among mad people.
THE CHESHIRE CAT:
Oh, you can't help that. We're all mad here.

Arden looked up, and Jake laughed, slowly folding his big body, like an accordion, and taking a seat next to her on the floor. "Great book. Even better advice."

Jake cocked his head at Arden, lifting his big, black brows, and let his dark eyes search her soul.

"That's why you're here, isn't it?" Jake asked, nodding around the store. "And not just here, but *here* . . . in Scoops . . . right?"

Arden's heart raced.

"You've gone mad," he said, "but not in a good way."

"Yes," she said softly, returning the book in her hands to the shelf and taking a sip of her coffee. "My daughter and I came to help my mother, but I think she's helping us even more. We are starting to find our passion for life again here."

"Have you?"

"I don't have an ending to my story yet."

A bell on the door of the bookstore jingled, and Arden smiled.

"The sound of my mother's charm bracelet is everywhere," she said. "Now that—*that*—used to drive me mad."

"Maybe you're just ready to listen now." Jake's face broke into a smile as big and white as a Scoops blizzard. "You're not quite the cynic you want people to believe you are, huh?"

Jake laughed, suddenly placing a hand on Arden's leg. "Would you like to go out with me?" he asked.

His hand felt warm and natural on Arden's leg.

"Okay," she said, surprising herself.

"I'm off Memorial Day. Maybe we can go to the beach or something. Weather looks beautiful. I'll call you."

Jake leaned forward, took Arden's face in his sturdy hands—her chin resting in his palms—and kissed her on the lips. For a big man, his kiss was as gentle as the spring rain.

For a second, Arden thought she was dreaming. She was pleasantly stunned.

Jake stood, towering over Arden, and said, "I had to. You're just so darn cute. I'll call you later."

"Okay." Arden smiled.

After Jake left, Arden tried to piece together what had just occurred. Her heart was still pounding.

She leaned over and picked up the copy of *Alice in Wonderland* that Jake had left sitting beside her.

Arden ran her hands over the cover.

She smiled, again reading the words her mother had read to her so many times, the words her mother had tried to emphasize to her growing up.

She shut her eyes, and could feel her mother sitting beside her on her bed in the cabin. Arden could hear Lolly's voice reading:

ALICE:
But I don't want to go among mad people.
THE CHESHIRE CAT:
Oh, you can't help that. We're all mad here.

Arden smiled.

My mother was trying to teach me the secret to life long ago, but I never listened!
She lovingly carried the book to the counter and bought it.

part eight

The Snowflake Charm

*To a Life in Which You Become a Person
of Many Dimensions*

Thirty

A rden sat on the edge of her childhood bed and clicked on the lamp. The lamp—like her mother—was made up of an amalgam of mismatched, colorful parts: The base was an old red lantern while the shade was fringed like a skirt from the musical *Chicago*. The light and the fringe both moved and flickered as if dancing together.

Arden propped up a few pillows against the birch bark headboard and picked up her copy of *Alice in Wonderland*, smiling at the memory of Jake and of purchasing the book earlier in the day. Without thinking, she opened the book to a random page, something she used to do when she was a child. She once regarded it as a sort of an omen, the page and its words a sign meant to tell her something meaningful about her life. Arden had learned in journalism school, however, that there were three kinds of readers: Ones who always opened a book or magazine to page one, and started from the beginning; readers who always read the last page first (Arden could never understand those readers); and readers who randomly opened to a page somewhere in the middle to gauge their interest.

I still see it as an omen, Arden thought, *shutting her eyes and turning to a page.*

"Begin at the beginning," the King said gravely, "and go on till you come to the end: then stop."

Arden gasped, and then reread the line she had just stumbled upon.

Life really is quite simple, Arden thought. *Begin at the beginning.*

She suddenly thought of Jake's kiss earlier in the day.

He is giving me a new start, she thought.

Arden drew her arms around herself and shivered at the invisible breezes that always seemed to find their way through the cracks in the logs of the old cabin.

Is it the chill? she thought. *Or his kiss?*

She hopped out of bed and went in search of a blanket to ward off the chill. Arden unlatched the trunk at the end of the bed. It was stacked with childhood memorabilia: Yearbooks, plaques, ribbons, as well as other mementoes from her past. A signed picture of Shaun Cassidy, a Wonder Woman belt, a "drinking happy bird" sipping from a glass of water she'd always had sitting on her desk, a corkboard covered with old pins.

Arden started to pull out her old yearbooks, but stopped herself, dropping the trunk lid and moving her search to the dresser. Every drawer was filled with long-ago Dolly costumes: Dresses missing half their sequins, threadbare boas, snagged gloves.

Arden's heart skipped a beat.

Memories shoved away for far too long, she thought.

Arden moved toward her old closet, the warped door opening with a loud squeak. She zipped through hangers filled with her old clothes and her mother's winter jackets, thinking a blanket might be somewhere in the midst.

Nothing.

That's when she noticed, illuminated by the bare bulb that hung from the ceiling, the bottom of a quilt, its ends dangling over the edge like her feet on the dock.

She reached up, standing on her tippy toes, but the quilt was just out of reach. Arden turned, searching the bedroom for a stepping stool or a sturdy chair. She walked over and pressed down on the top of the trunk, but it felt flimsy to the touch.

I can do this myself, Arden thought, turning back to the closet. *This is why I run and spin.*

Arden crouched and jumped, but in midleap, her arms got entangled in the hanging clothes. She made it only a few inches off the ground before the hangers came flying off in a shocking jangle that sounded like a wind chime in a hurricane.

"Mom?" Lauren yelled from the bedroom next door. "Are you okay?"

"I'm fine," Arden yelled back. "Just dropped the book I'm reading."

"Sounds like you dropped a library." Lauren laughed.

That was as graceful as my dance with Jake, Arden murmured to herself.

She picked up the fallen clothes, and then pushed all the hangers to one end of the closet to give herself room.

Here we go again, she thought, leaping into the air.

Arden's fingers snagged the end of the quilt, and, at the very last minute, she yanked it off, grunting at its unexpected heft.

As Arden descended, she saw white, and wondered if she had hit her head.

But as she looked up, she smiled: It was snowing.

Falling all around her were hundreds of homemade snowflakes—their lacy silhouettes softly drifting about, as if she were trapped in a snow globe.

Mom and I made those decades ago, Arden thought, remembering when they used to hang the snowflakes on the cabin's windows at the holidays.

Arden sat down on the floor as if pulled by force, and pulled the quilt around herself, watching it snow, finding herself in the middle of an unexpected blizzard of memories.

When it stopped, Arden gathered the snowflakes into a pile and stretched out, resting her head on them.

She held up a snowflake—the paper yellowed, the edges bent—and ran her fingers over it, before doing the same to the quilt. Arden shut her eyes, and listened to the sounds of the cabin. It always seemed to have a life of its own, like the seasons in Michigan.

Arden sighed and slowly drifted to sleep in a pile of newly fallen pretend-snow.

Thirty-one

November 1977

I t's a winter wonderland," Lolly yelled from the front window of the cabin. "Arden, hurry! Come look!"

Arden padded downstairs in her stocking feet and peered toward Lost Land Lake. She couldn't even see the dock.

"But it's not winter yet," Arden said. "It's only November."

Always so logical, Lolly thought, smiling at her daughter.

"C'mon! We have to check this out," Lolly said, pulling Arden by the hand and opening the door to the screened porch. "Wow!"

Snow was blowing through the screens and already drifting onto the wood floor. Lolly pulled her daughter out onto the porch and said, "Ssssh! Listen."

The snow hissed in the air as it fell, but, beyond that, the world was silent, hushed, buried.

Snow was as common in Scoops as pine trees and deer. The first snow typically fell around Halloween, grew heavier in November, and often continued into early April. The town received over two hundred inches of snow a year, thanks to its close proximity to Lake Michigan. Much of the heavy snow—like today's—came from a weather phenomenon called lake effect, in which arctic air routinely moved across the relatively warmer waters of the big lake, causing a dumping effect, almost as if the town were located at the wrong end of a snow blower.

"Scoops should have been named Shovels." Les laughed from the cabin. He put on his gloves and pulled a ski mask over his face, until only his eyes and lips were visible. He grabbed his red plaid thermos of coffee and said, "Time to make some cash. I'll see my beautiful girls later."

In the winters, Les Lindsey led ice-fishing excursions for the hearty, or, as his wife put it, "the crazy." Locals loved to ice fish in the many inland lakes, like Lost Land, that dotted the area. It was as popular as skiing, snow-shoeing, and building snowmen. The weather didn't matter much to sports-men because Les did most of the work anyway. He put up the shanties that kept out the snow and wind, and which kept the fishermen warm; he cut the hole in the ice; he kept them fed and jovial with his "special" coffee; and he told them all the stories of the big fish he had pulled from holes in the ice, just like the ones that were about to jump on their dangling lines any second now.

Arden watched her father trudge through the snow, which was already up to his knees. After only a few feet, he became a ghost. And then, he was gone.

It was snowing so hard that the world had become one-dimensional, white on white.

Arden felt as if she were trapped in a snow globe that had been shaken. There was no color differential between the sky, the ground, the world. It was a blur of white.

The happy screams of children shattered the silence.

"They refuse to get up on a school day"—Lolly laughed, mussing Arden's hair—"but they will jump out of bed on a snow day."

Although the joke in town was that the school district only called a snow day "when the bus drivers could no longer see the stop signs or the school," there were days when the kids might have gotten to school but could never have gotten home.

This was one of those days.

"Isn't it beautiful?" Lolly asked, a big smile etched on her face. "Every-thing looks so fresh and new. And it makes me feel like a kid again."

Lolly hopped up and down. "Let's get ready to have some fun!" she said, pulling Arden by the hand back into the cabin. "How about some pancakes first, and then we'll build a snowman . . . and then a snow fort . . . and then make snow ice cream . . . and . . ."

"Mother!" Arden interrupted. "It's only snow. And I don't really like snow. I only like the days off school."

Lolly stopped and stooped in front of her daughter. "What a silly thing to say. Who doesn't like snow? It's magical."

"It's cold and wet," Arden said. "How's it magical?"

"Let's have some breakfast, and then I'll show you!"

"The secret to a great snowman," Lolly said to Arden, her words coming out as big puffs of smoke into the frigid air, "is its pack-ability. See?"

"The what?" Arden asked, folding her arms around herself, her glasses fogged over from the cold.

Lolly smiled at her daughter. At first glance, the ten-year-old looked as if she was seemingly trying to ward off the cold, but Lolly knew it was more than that: She was trying to ward off the frigidity of the world.

Arden had always been that way.

Lolly bent down and picked up two huge handfuls of snow, recalling all of the comments Arden's teachers made on her report cards: *Arden is smart and a great writer but is very sensitive, shy, and unaware of her beauty, talents, and dimensions that make her unique. She seeks to please others too easily. She doesn't stand up for herself.*

"See?" Lolly said, pushing her hands together to make a ball. "Lake-effect snow is too dry, so you have to put some extra heat into it to make it melt a little. Then it's perfect. Your turn," Lolly said.

Arden gathered a tiny ball of snow, which disintegrated in her hands.

Lolly again smiled at her daughter, and trudged through the snow. She kissed her daughter's stocking-capped head. An inch of newly fallen snow toppled off the top of Arden's head as if her mother had just knocked it off with a broom.

"Follow my lead," Lolly said, turning in a wide circle to gather the base for the snowman, pushing snow into a large mound.

Mother and daughter worked silently in tandem as the snow hissed around them, their grunts and pats echoing in the quiet, white world. When they were finished, a nearly four-foot round, plump sentinel stood quietly on the hill as if to protect their little log cabin and the frozen lake below.

"Is it time for hot chocolate?" Arden asked. "I'm getting cold and wet."

"Oh, we're not done yet, my dear," Lolly said. "We still have to give her a little personality to bring her to life, just like Frosty. Wait here!"

Her? Arden thought.

Lolly trudged through the snow, now hip deep on her, leaving a meandering trail behind her. She returned a minute later carrying a plastic bag.

"First things first," Lolly laughed, setting the bag atop the snow and plucking out a feather boa. "To keep our snow woman warm and stylish."

"Frosty is a *boy*, Mom!" Arden protested. "*He* can't wear that!"

"Ours is a snow *woman*! And snow women can be even more magical, my dear," Lolly said. "She just needs a piece of us—our history—a little extra dimension to make her shine in this world."

Lolly pulled out a pair of large blue buttons and stuck them on the snow woman's face followed by a pair of fake eyelashes as big as butterflies. Next came a carrot for a nose and smaller red buttons for lips. Pink buttons trailed down the snow woman's front.

"Over there," Lolly said to Arden, motioning to a pine tree. "Get us a couple of those fallen branches."

When Arden returned, Lolly attached them as arms, placing an old purse in her piney hands.

"And now? The finishing touch!" Lolly said, yanking out a straw hat—drenched in spring flowers—and placing it on the snow woman's head with a flourish. "Voilà!"

Lolly and Arden took a step back to admire their work.

"What do you see when you look at our snow woman?" Lolly asked.

Arden's face still registered confusion.

"I thought snowmen were *men*," Arden asked. "That they couldn't be women."

Lolly let out a deep sigh that lingered, frozen, in front of her face. She grabbed her daughter's hand. "You can create and be anything in this world that you want to be," she said, shaking her mitten, her bracelet jangling in the silence. "Your imagination should be limitless."

Lolly continued. "Didn't you know that people are just like snowflakes? No two are alike."

"Really?" Arden asked.

Lolly lifted her face to the sky and let the snowflakes gather on her eyelashes. When she blinked, they caught in the wind and went flying.

"You bet," Lolly said. "As snowflakes fall from the sky, they each take a different path to reach the earth. They float and flicker through clouds and cold, taking shape in a unique way, just like us. Every snowflake takes a different journey to the ground that makes it unique. Sometimes it's hard for them to make it all the way here to us, but they do, still holding on to all those wonderful dimensions that make them different from every other snowflake in the world."

Arden held out her hand and waited for a snowflake to land in her palm. "You mean this one is different from every other one out here?"

Lolly stopped and stooped, her knees slowly sinking in the snow until she was at eye level with her young daughter. "Yes! Isn't that amazing? But what we try to do is to fit in and conform, so we're like everyone else. We lose all of our unique angles . . ."

Lolly grabbed her daughter's hand and held it in the air, snowflakes gathering in Arden's mitten. ". . . that make us special, just like these snowflakes. It's up to us to remember how multifaceted we are and to celebrate all those odd little angles we have which make us who we are."

Arden smiled and nodded.

"What a dumb snowman!"

The words cracked through the air, breaking the frozen silence and making nearby cardinals take flight. Lolly stood and turned, her arms protectively in front of Arden.

Two boys were standing a few feet away, one dragging a sled and the other a toboggan.

"You boys know better than that," Lolly said, turning. "Watch your tone."

Arden remained behind her mother. That's when the wind-burned faces of these two boys registered in Lolly's mind: Arden had pointed them out to her once after she got off the bus, saying how they always teased her at school.

"Sorry," one said without any remorse. "Let's go, Ted."

The two boys trudged off into the snow, until they disappeared into the fog.

Arden was still standing behind her mother, when Lolly suddenly dropped like a dead weight onto the ground.

"Snow angels!" she yelled, trying to distract her daughter's mind from the boys. "Let's see yours!"

Arden fell into the snow with a soft whoosh, and began sliding her arms and legs through the snow, giggling as the powder flew into the air.

Lolly stood and carefully helped Arden step from the silhouette she had created.

"Two angels," Arden said. "A big one and a little one."

"Both unique," Lolly said, hugging her daughter. "Both perfect, right?"

"Right!"

"Want some hot chocolate? With extra marshmallows?"

"Yeah!" Arden yelled.

The two trekked inside and shed their wet winter gear, pulling on robes and warming themselves in front of the lake stone fireplace with their hot chocolate. They sipped, while the snow still fell heavily, making the windows appear as if they had white curtains hanging outside.

Bam! Bam! Bam!

As the two sipped, they suddenly heard a barrage of rapid shots hit the cabin, as if a hunter had missed his target and sent errant buckshot flying.

Lolly and Arden ran to the window and looked out. Two figures in hooded coats were trying to run, but the depth of the snow and the drag from their sled and toboggan held them back.

"Stop! Stop! Right now!" Lolly yelled as she threw open the door to the screened porch, her shouts making snow slide from the roof.

Lolly quickly yanked on her mukluks, coat, and gloves and sprinted off the porch. "I mean it," she yelled. "I see you. Come back here!"

As she heard the boys' laughter echo across the lake, Lolly turned to see that the snow woman she and Arden had just built was on its side, as if it had gotten tired and wanted to lie down for a long winter's nap. Its head had rolled off to one side, its hat had already blown against the house in the wind, and its face was now expressionless and blank, the carrot and buttons now deep in the drift.

Arden stood as frozen as the snow woman on the screened porch. She watched her mother turn her face toward the heavens—snowflakes gathering on her youthful face—and then suddenly take off in a flash, her anger seeming to make her fly across the top of the snow.

As if on cue, the sun peaked out through the thick layers of lake-effect clouds that rolled by in the sky, illuminating Lolly as she bent down, hurriedly made a snowball as hard as a baseball, and whipped it at the two boys, where it smashed against the back of one's coat, shattering on impact.

"What the . . . ?!" the boy yelled.

The two bullies turned, their faces growing even redder, their surprise turning into anger. "You shouldn't have done that, lady!"

"You shouldn't have ruined our snow woman!"

"Snow woman?" they mocked. "Ha! She didn't really stand up for herself!"

The boys quickly began to make snowballs, and Lolly now stood as helpless as their snow woman had been. They picked up snowballs in each hand, and Lolly turned to brace herself for the attack.

Whap! Whap! Whap!

I don't feel anything, Lolly thought. *Am I too cold to feel the sting?*

Whap! Whap! Whap!

That's when Lolly turned, and her mouth fell open. Arden was standing—back straight, chest puffed—a series of snowballs stacked in front of her, like cannonballs on a battleship. She was firing them rapidly and accurately, each snowball making direct contact to the boys' chests and, now, backs.

"Never touch my snow woman again!" Arden yelled. "And don't you dare ever hurt my mother!"

The boys dropped their snowballs and took off running.

Tears of love and pride ran down Lolly's face, before stopping, frozen, in midtrack.

Lolly hugged her daughter, and then the two made their snow woman come alive yet again before heading inside to finish their hot chocolate.

"I'm so proud of you for what you just did," Lolly said, as they sat again in front of the fire. "That took a lot of courage, and it showed another dimension of who you are as a person. I want to show you something," Lolly continued, returning a minute later with two pieces of white paper and pairs of scissors. "I thought we'd make some paper snowflakes to hang in the window, since the holidays are coming up soon and we're getting our tree this weekend with your dad."

Lolly handed Arden a pair of scissors and a sheet of paper. "Doesn't look like much right now, does it? Just a plain ol' piece of paper. But we're going to make magic, just like we did with our snow woman."

Lolly took a sheet of paper and folded it three times until it formed a tiny triangle. "Now, take your scissors and lop off the tip, and then begin cutting little designs into the edges. The lines can be curvy or straight, whatever you feel like. Your turn."

Arden slowly followed her mother's directions, using the tip of her scissors to make intricate patterns.

"It still doesn't really look like anything," Arden said, scrunching her face and looking at the tiny piece of folded paper, chock full of cuts.

"Not yet," Lolly smiled. "Now we have to unfold it, very carefully."

Arden gasped when she was finished. "It's . . . beautiful!"

"Just like you," Lolly smiled. "Let's hang them in the window. They will welcome your dad when he comes home, just like our snow woman."

Lolly taped the snowflakes in the window, and they danced, the peekaboo sun illuminating their intricateness.

"See how different the two are?" Lolly asked, putting her arm around Arden. "Wholly unique, just like us. And see all the different angles and curves, patterns and designs? We all have that inside of us. But it's up to us to make sure the world sees all of our beauty. We have to learn it's okay not to conform, to be our true selves."

Arden ducked her head. "It's hard to be different sometimes."

"I know it is, Arden, I know," Lolly said, pulling her daughter tightly into her body. "But without showing the world all of our dimensions, we're just a flat piece of paper."

Arden smiled and hugged her mother.

"Want to make some more?" Lolly asked.

"Yeah!"

Lolly returned a moment later and set a stack of paper on the coffee table in front of the fire. On top, one piece was already folded and cut.

"What's this?" Arden asked.

"It's a special snowflake for you," Lolly said. "Open it carefully."

Arden unfolded the paper, and, as she did, a charm came tumbling out.

"It's a charm of a snowflake," Lolly said. "For your bracelet. My mom gave it to me a long time ago on my birthday. She used to tell me on my birthday that the world was celebrating my uniqueness. I still believe that. And I want you to celebrate yours, too. This charm is a reminder to live a life in which you become a person of many dimensions. Only that way will you become a whole, happy person."

Arden leaned in and hugged her mom. "Will you help me add it?"

"Of course," Lolly said.

And then the two made a drift of snowflakes, no two alike.

Arden awoke with a start. She sat up quickly, snowflakes tumbling off her head and back.

A person of many dimensions, Arden thought. *What happened to my angles, my muchness?*

She went to bed, dragging the quilt, snowflakes trailing behind her, and dreamed of winter and the time in which she had the courage to fight for what she loved in life.

Thirty-two

Arden stopped in the lobby of Lakeview Geriatric Center and checked her hair in the mirror. She had "borrowed" a pink top from her daughter, which didn't go unnoticed when she tried to sneak out of the cabin.

"Where are you off to in such a hurry?" Lolly had asked, as she and Lauren sipped coffee on the screened porch and worked a puzzle.

"And in *my* clothes," Lauren added.

"A quick errand," Arden had said, trying to rush by them.

"You look very pretty for a quick errand," Lolly said. "Looks like more of a mission."

"And I'm taking the Woodie, too," Arden added, jangling the keys.

"But I have to work later," Lolly called.

"Take our car," she yelled, jumping into the Woodie. "I need this . . . for luck!"

Arden had watched as Lauren and Lolly gave each other a suspicious look and bewildered shrug—both mouthing *for luck?*—as Arden pulled the Woodie past the screened porch.

"Can I help you?" the receptionist asked, jolting Arden from the memory as she was applying some of Lauren's "borrowed" gloss to her lips.

"Oh, I'm sorry," Arden said, suddenly embarrassed. "I'm here to see Jake Thomas."

"Is he expecting you?" the receptionist asked.

"No . . . well . . . no, he isn't," Arden fumbled, grabbing a big bag brimming with food off a table in the lobby and giving it a shake for emphasis. "It's sort of a, well, surprise. I brought him lunch."

"Oh, you must be Arden," the receptionist said, smiling.

"What? How . . . ? He's talked about me?" Arden finally noticed the little gold sign in front of her that stated the receptionist's name. "Really, Patty? He has?"

"He has. Many times," Patty said. "All good things. He really cares for your mom, too."

Too, Arden thought, biting her lip to keep her from saying it out loud.

"Jake's in the music therapy room right now," Patty said. "Big room next to the cafeteria. You can go on back. Surprise him."

Patty gave a dramatic wink that Arden immediately believed could imply a million things. "Thanks," she said.

As Arden walked down the brightly lit hallway, music bounced off the walls and echoed in the corridor.

Arden stopped and tilted her head.

"Frosty the Snowman"? she thought. *To kick off summer? Am I still dreaming?*

She stopped at the edge of the music room, poked her head around the corner, and did a double take.

Jake was playing a trumpet and sporting a Santa hat while standing in front of a group of roughly twenty seniors, all of whom were clapping and bobbing their grey heads vigorously.

His eyes were closed, and his body was one with the trumpet, swaying, swooping, dipping with each crescendo as his fingers flew over the keys and the brass instrument danced.

Arden immediately thought of famed trumpeters like Louis Armstrong, whose music her mother loved, and Doc Severinsen, who Lolly had watched for decades on *The Tonight Show Starring Johnny Carson.*

He looks so handsome, Arden thought. *So lost in the music.*

Arden began to nod her head along with the seniors, and she shut her eyes, again remembering the day her mother taught her to build a proper snow woman.

She didn't notice the music had even stopped until she heard Jake's voice boom, "Any requests?"

Arden popped open her eyes, her face immediately turning red, as twenty grey heads turned her way.

Arden vigorously shook her head no. Jake chuckled and walked over, wrapping one muscular arm around Arden's waist and pulling her into the room. Upon her entrance, he lifted the trumpet to his lips and played a dramatic flourish, as if she were royalty.

Arden giggled.

"We have a surprise visitor!" Jake announced in a faux English accent. "A queen of words!"

The seniors smiled, some giggling along with Arden.

Jake gave Arden a surprise peck on the cheek and whispered into her ear, "It's good to see you. I'm in the middle of music therapy. It can really help patients with MCI and dementia recall memories from their past."

Arden again thought of the snow woman, and then of the snowflake charm.

"Actually," Arden said aloud, surprising Jake as well as herself, "I do have a request: 'Let It Snow.'"

A few of the seniors clapped their approval.

Jake bent at the waist. "Anything for m'lady."

And, with that, Jake lifted his trumpet, and Arden could have sworn she was once again in the middle of winter, happy for the holidays.

"So? What prompted this surprise?" Jake asked, taking a healthy bite of the roasted turkey sandwich that Arden had picked up at a farm stand and deli on her way to see him. "This sandwich is awesome. It's like we had planned this."

Arden smiled at the deeper meaning of his sentence. As she watched Jake eat, she thought of the little farm that had seemed to call to her—like the dream she had last night—as she was driving. The farm stand was beyond adorable. It was lined with baskets overflowing with homegrown produce: blueberries, early white asparagus, eggs, fresh herbed chèvre, beets, lettuce, and spinach. The deli was operated out of a restored barn, its old doors pushed open so you could see right through to the fields beyond, which were filled with bleating goats jumping around like excited children.

A man and woman draped in aprons ran the stand and deli, and they seemed to communicate to one another without saying a word.

Just a few weeks ago, I wouldn't have stopped there, Arden thought. *I wouldn't be here. I want what that old couple have. I want what my parents had.*

"I was supposed to call *you* for a date."

"What?" Arden asked, returning from her thoughts.

"I was supposed to call *you* for a date." Jake stopped, his eyes twinkling. "Remember? So? Is this a date?" he continued, raising his eyebrows and nudging Arden with his knees.

"I'm the writer," she said. "Let's call it a meet-and-greet."

"Wow," he said, taking another bite of his sandwich. "So romantic."

The two were sitting on facing benches outside Lakeview. It was one of those stunning May days, as Lolly used to say, that made her "soul ache."

Arden took a bite of her kale salad dotted with tart Michigan cherries and shook her head. She couldn't contain her smile.

I feel as giddy as a schoolgirl, she thought.

Arden lifted her face to the sky and let the sun warm her. The sun was playing hide-and-go-seek through the branches of the apple trees that circled the patio where they sat. The two had it all to themselves. No one else was eating outside. A clematis vine was just crawling to life on a trellis next to them, its green arms slowly stretching heavenward. Soon it would be filled with luscious, white blooms.

Arden inhaled.

It's not the only thing coming to life, she thought.

The scene felt so romantic, so sweet, that the two could have easily been dining on a tree-lined street in Paris.

It just feels so right, Arden thought.

As the two ate, their knees touched. Each time they did, a sudden sensor of heat and excitement pulsed through Arden's legs and body. She tried to act nonchalant, although she felt as if her heart were thumping out of her chest.

"I didn't know you played the trumpet," Arden said. "Why didn't you ever tell me?"

Jake smiled. "I'm a man of mystery, I guess."

"Did you take music in college?" Arden asked.

"Minored in music," he said. "Played trumpet all through college . . . orchestra, jazz band, marching band . . . you name it."

Explains the muscular lips, Arden thought, again turning red.

"A real Renaissance man, huh?" she asked.

"I never thought of it like that," he said, gesturing with his sandwich. "I always just pursued what I liked."

Jake shot Arden a look as he finished the sentence, and then winked at her to reinforce the double entendre.

Arden's heart raced again.

"I like you, Arden," Jake said suddenly. "I know all of this—me, your mother's health—is a lot to take in, but I just want to be honest."

Arden's eyes met Jake's, but she couldn't match his words for some reason.

Being honest with my feelings has never come easily, she thought.

"Do you even realize how much you've changed over the last week?" Jake asked.

Arden nodded. "I think I'm starting to see."

"You're becoming a whole person again," Jake said. "Daughter, mother, friend, caregiver, reader, writer, . . . *date* . . ."

Arden laughed. "Again with the date?"

"That's why I play the trumpet," Jake said. "It's an important part of me that I need to express. That's why you need to write again. It's an important piece of you. It doesn't matter if I ever play Carnegie Hall, but it matters that I let the world see *me.*"

He stopped and set down his sandwich, before standing and taking a seat next to Arden, their legs now pressed against each other.

"So many of my patients are haunted by the things they never did in life and the people they never became," Jake said, looking into Lakeview. "They didn't have the power to stand up for themselves, to battle their fears, to show the world who they really were, all those beautiful . . ."

"Dimensions?" Arden asked.

"Exactly." Jake smiled. "The worst thing in the world is to have regrets. You will always have a few, but they shouldn't be ones that keep you up at night."

Jake stopped, and Arden knew instantly that he was going to kiss her. She could sense it, almost as clearly as she could smell the sweet, perfumed scent of the apple blossoms that filled the air.

Arden shut her eyes and let the moment sweep her away, images of a future life—season by season—pirouetting in her mind.

As their kiss ended, Arden put her hands on Jake's face and looked tenderly in his eyes.

I can see myself with this man, she thought.

And then she laughed.

"That bad of a kiss, huh?" Jake asked. "I tend to have that effect on women."

"No, no, no," Arden said. "I'm sorry. I just noticed you still have a little circle around your lips from the mouthpiece of your trumpet when you played earlier."

Jake touched his lip self-consciously.

"No, it's cute. Really cute," Arden said, before grabbing his face and kissing him again. "You have great lips."

"So do you," Jake whispered, grabbing her hand.

Arden put her head on his shoulder. "The apple blossoms smell so heavenly, don't they?"

"They do," Jake said. "That's why they're our state flower. And Michigan is one of the top apple producing states in the country."

"You *are* a person of many dimensions," Arden said.

"You are, too," he replied. "Hey? Can I ask you a question?"

Arden lifted her head. "Sure. Anything."

"Why did you request 'Let It Snow'?"

Arden smiled and tugged nervously at her earlobe.

"There's no need for that, Ms. Burnett," Jake joked. "Just tell me."

Arden tightened her grip on Jake's hand and then told him the story of her mother, her own fears, and the snowflake charm.

"She's right," he said, when she finished. "We just want you to be the best, most well-rounded person you can be in this world. A whole person is a happy person."

"That sounds like a bumper sticker." Arden laughed.

"I just want you to be 'muchier,'" Jake said softly, pulling Arden in for another kiss, the wind knocking a few delicately colored cherry pink and white petals off the trees, as if the two were kissing in a snowfall of blossoms.

Thirty-three

Arden's fingers hovered over her cell phone. She was having trouble hitting SEND.

"Do you want me to do it for you?" Lolly asked, walking in from her afternoon at work, dressed in a bright purple sequined Dolly gown. "Jake is teaching me a lot about technology. All you have to do is . . ."

"I know how to send an email, Mom." Arden laughed, thinking of her "date" earlier with Jake.

He's teaching me a lot, too, Arden thought.

"It's a work email," Arden explained. "I'm trying to tell my boss to stop bothering me while I'm gone . . . and that I want to write for the magazine."

"Good for you!" Lolly said. "I'm so proud of you!"

Lolly's face beamed with pride, and she took a seat next to her daughter on the glider, her sequins announcing her every move.

Arden looked at her mom, smiled, and then hit SEND, giving a squeal of nervous excitement after her cell had sounded its exit.

"No matter what," Lolly said, nodding her head toward the lawn, "you're fighting for what you want, just like you did during that snowball fight so long ago. Remember?"

Arden's eyes widened at her mother's clarity and intuition.

It's like she can read my mind, Arden thought.

"I do," she said, smiling, hugging her mom before giving the glider a gentle push with her feet.

"Wheeee!" Lolly said.

Before the glider had stopped swinging, Arden's cell trilled.

"Simóne's doing a GREAT job filling in for you," Van replied.

What a jackass. No "Have a good time, you deserve it," or "How's your mom?" Not even a "Let's talk when you get back after your vacation." Just a thinly veiled threat, Arden thought, annoyed.

Lolly patted her daughter's leg. "You don't need anyone's permission to be who you dream of being. You are here—right here—because of the journey you took."

Lolly stopped, her voice quaking along with her sequins. "There is no one else in the world like you, my beautiful girl. *No one.* Please know that. You are made up of so many dimensions. Now it's just up to you to let the world see that beauty."

Arden began to cry, without warning, her tears a downpour, a sudden thunderstorm of emotion.

"There, there," Lolly said, comforting her daughter, holding her tightly. "There's no need for tears. Why don't you go write?" she added, brightening. "Just go sit and write. Lauren knows clearly who she wants to be. No one tells her to paint. She just paints. Remember when you used to write because you loved it?"

Arden sat straight up.

"Are you okay?" Lolly asked.

"Yes!" Arden replied. "I am!"

"Are you off to write?"

"I am," Arden said, standing. "But I have to do something first. Where's your paper and scissors?"

"What? Why?" Lolly asked, before seeing the determination in her daughter's face. "In the kitchen. Junk drawer."

Arden gathered her materials, sat in front of the living room fireplace, and made a blizzard of snowflakes for her mother, which the pair then hung in the cabin's windows.

And then Arden sat on the dock and wrote until dusk, until the dragon-flies called her home for dinner, summer snowflakes twinkling in the cabin's lights.

part nine

The Shooting Star Charm

To a Life in Which You Are Lucky in Love

Thirty-four

Arden yawned in sync with Lauren, their eyes fluttered, and then their heads dipped, until their chins were resting on their chests.

Lolly clapped, waking her dozing daughter and granddaughter with the subtlety of an earthquake, their eyes shooting open in alarm.

"Here, girls, have some more coffee," Lolly said, rushing into the kitchen and returning with a pot of coffee. "You can't go to sleep yet!"

Arden looked at her watch and slumped deeper into the couch. "It's nearly eleven o'clock, Mom. I need to be in bed, not chugging caffeine. Do you really think this is such a good idea?"

Lolly filled the three mugs sitting on the coffee table in front of the fireplace and turned to look at her daughter. "There has never been a better idea, my dear," she said with complete conviction. "We may never have the chance to see the Northern Lights again together."

Lauren shook her head and said, "You're right, Grandma. I've heard about them my whole life. Now it's the right time to see them. Together!"

Lolly smiled. "It's a perfect night. Clear as a bell. The weatherman says it might not happen again for a while. Wanna help me with some snacks?"

Lauren nodded. "Grab us some sweatshirts, my dear," Lolly said to Arden. "It'll be chilly on the beach, especially if we have to wait awhile."

Arden considered protesting what she felt was likely a wild-goose chase, but her mother's face said there would be no discussion. Instead, Arden nodded, too, and grabbed some sweatshirts.

Thirty-five

L olly, Arden, and Lauren were stretched out on a giant quilt, lying side by side, staring up at the starry sky, the sound of the waves from Lake Michigan lulling them into a trance.

There was an out-of-body experience to being on the beach at night. A few other hearty stargazers were camped out on the sand, but no one had lit a fire or had flashlights shining. Everyone was waiting for the show, almost reverential in anticipation of what might occur.

"It's so dark and quiet out here," Lauren said. "In Chicago, there's always light—streetlights, headlights, apartment lights—and noise from people, airplanes, sirens, the highway, the city."

"That's why it's so perfect to see the Northern Lights here," Lolly said. "There is no pollution in the sky to hide the show. And you can see from heaven to earth, and east to west, forever."

Seeing the Northern Lights in Michigan was akin to seeing Bigfoot, Arden thought. *Everyone in Michigan said they had seen them at some point in their lives, but few could ever offer up specifics, or even a great photo.*

Arden had studied the Northern Lights in science class. If she remembered her studies well enough, the Northern Lights—or aurora borealis—were a natural light phenomenon in the sky, mostly seen in high latitudes.

They were named after the Roman goddess of dawn (Aurora) and the Greek god of the north wind (Boreas) by Galileo. The Northern Lights are the result of collisions of gaseous particles in the earth's atmosphere with charged particles released from the sun. The effect was akin to a 3-D kaleidoscopic light display in the sky. The light displayed in many colors and forms, including shades of green, pink, red, yellow, blue, and violet—in arcs, streamers, rippling curtains, and shooting rays that lit up the sky in an eerie, otherworldly glow.

The three stared into the sky. "Isn't this exciting?" Lolly asked, her voice high.

"Are you sure this is going to happen, Mom?" Arden asked after a few minutes of silence.

"Oh, it'll happen," Lolly said, grabbing Arden's and Lauren's hands in the dark. "When you least expect it. It's like love. You just have to be patient and then—BOOM!—you see lights."

Lauren laughed. "Did you see lights when you first met Grampa, when he hooked you with his fishing lure?"

"I think I saw my life flash before my eyes first," Lolly laughed. "But, yes . . . I know this sounds a little silly, but I immediately saw light radiating from him when we met. I just knew."

Lolly smiled to herself and continued. "You know that photo I have in my bedroom? The one taken at sunset on the beach? It was taken right here. Your grandfather brought me here on a date. He roasted hot dogs and we made s'mores, and then he told me the date wasn't over. He said he'd asked my dad if he could show me the Northern Lights. But my dad didn't like me staying out so late with a boy, so Les invited my dad to join us. And the lights were spectacular."

Lolly stopped and closed her eyes. She was silent for a moment. "And in the middle of the Northern Lights—right in the middle of all that color and those shooting stars—he gave me a charm."

Lolly sat up. "Your phone has one of those flashlights on it, doesn't it? Jake's taught me all about those—what are they called?—apples?"

"Apps, Grandma." Lauren laughed, turning on her phone. "Here you go."

Lolly held her charm bracelet in front of the light and shook it. She held out a charm and sighed. "It's appropriate the light is shining off it so brightly," Lolly said. "This is my shooting star charm. When Les gave it to me in the middle of the Northern Lights, he whispered, so my dad wouldn't hear, 'To a life in which you are lucky in love.'"

"And I whispered back, 'You will always be my lucky star.'"

Lauren sat up. "Don't make me cry again, Grandma."

The three listened to the waves crash onto the beach, and owls hoot from the aspen and pine trees in the dunes behind them. "Did you see light when you met Dad?" Lauren asked her mother.

Arden considered lying to her daughter, but she sat up and said to the lake, "No, I didn't, sweetie. I saw . . . stability. I saw . . . a life of ease. I saw . . . well . . . no fireworks, nothing that had anything to do with love, sadly."

Arden stopped and put her arm around her daughter's shoulder. "But the greatest love of my life resulted from our marriage. So I can never be sorry about that decision. And you certainly light up my life."

"Thanks, Mom," Lauren said, hesitating before forging on with a question. "Did you see lights with Clem?"

"I did," she said. "I didn't just *see* fireworks, I felt them. I felt like I'd eaten a million lightning bugs when I was with him. He made my soul brighter, and that's all you can ask for when you're in love."

Arden inhaled the lake breeze. "Your grandmother is right. There is a bit of luck involved in love. You have to be open to it."

"Open to what?"

The three women jumped and screamed at the deep voice booming over them.

"I didn't mean to scare you," Jake said. "I'm so sorry."

Lauren beamed her flashlight at his face. "Light," she said, suddenly laughing. "I see light coming from him, Mom."

Arden wrestled the phone from her daughter's hands and clicked off the app. "What are you doing here?" she asked, pleasantly surprised. Then it hit her. "This isn't coincidence, is it, Mom?"

"I invited him," Lolly admitted. "I texted him, as you kids do these days. Surprise!"

Arden couldn't help but smile in the dark.

"Mind if I steal Arden away for a minute?" Jake asked. "Wanna go for a walk? I promise I'll keep a tight hold on your hand, and the moon will light our way."

"So romantic," Lolly and Lauren said in unison, sighing dramatically.

Thirty-six

Have you ever seen the Northern Lights?"
Arden and Jake were holding hands and walking barefoot along the edge of the water, where the lake naturally "scooped" into the land. Locals said this giant half-circle in the lake had been created when God—in the midst of all His hard work—attempted to dip a giant ice cream scoop into the dunes, believing the golden sand was ice cream that could cool Him off. Scoops was named after this natural wonder.

"I have," Jake said. "Many times. It just takes timing and a little patience."

"Like love?" Arden offered softly, her hair rustling in the breeze.

"Just like it," Jake said. "And I've seen lots of shooting stars, too."

He stopped walking and turned to Arden, gently taking her face in his hands. "But I've never seen one as bright as you."

Jake stopped. "I know we've only just met, but there's something between us, Arden, that is as special and wondrous as the Northern Lights. I can feel it. Can't you?"

"I can," Arden said, her voice quivering.

Jake pulled her into his arms to warm her, to hold her. "Lolly and Lauren are such bright lights, too. For your mom to invite me tonight . . ."

Jake stopped. "Do you know how much that means to me? And do you know what a good mother and daughter you are?"

"No," Arden said, her voice suddenly breaking and tears forming in her eyes. "Sometimes I don't."

"You are," Jake said. "You're such a whole person now. You need to see that."

"Thank you for saying it to me," Arden said. "Thank you for seeing it."

"Sometimes people think they're lucky in love or life when really they've just made themselves open and aware to the incredible possibilities and gifts that life has to offer."

"Deepak Chopra?" Arden joked.

"No," Jake said. "Just my little old philosophy on life and love."

"I like this little old philosopher."

"Old?" Jake laughed. "Little?"

Arden looked into Jake's face. The moon and stars were illuminated in his eyes, as if he had swallowed the whole night sky so it would shine in his face for only Arden to see.

"I know we have a lot of things working against us," Arden said. "Distance, careers, my mom's health issues, obligations, exes, family . . . I mean, I don't even know that much about your family yet . . . but I want to give this a chance. I really do."

"I'm so happy to hear you say that. I've never wanted anything more in my life, either," Jake said. "And on Memorial Day? We'll have a proper date, okay? No more surprises. I'm officially asking you. What do you say?"

"Let me think about it." Arden laughed, quickly adding, "Okay, I thought about it. Yes!"

"I think it's only right that we come back here, to this beach, just the two of us, like your mom and dad did on one of their first dates. How's that sound?"

"Perfect," Arden said.

"I hope this is, too," Jake said, leaning in and kissing Arden.

As if on cue, Arden saw a shooting star arc across the night sky. "You make me see stars," Arden said.

Jake lifted Arden off the ground and twirled her around in the air, until they were one star in their own universe.

Thirty-seven

L olly pulled an old thermos with a red tartan plaid design from the basket sitting on the quilt and poured some steaming liquid into the lid.

"Want a sip?" she asked Lauren.

"Oh, Grandma, this smells so good," Lauren said, lifting the lid to her nose, steam rising. "What flavor of coffee is this?"

"Infused." Lolly laughed. "It has a little—how shall I put this?—'kick' to it, if you get my drift. Don't tell your mother. It was your grandfather's secret recipe."

Lauren acted as if she were locking her lips in secrecy and then took a sip. "Mmm, this is good. You think of everything, Grandma."

As soon as the words were out, Lauren wished she could take them back.

"Not quite everything anymore," Lolly said, trying to make a joke out of it.

Lolly patted her granddaughter's leg and looked out onto the horizon. The wind ruffled the scarf that secured her red wig, long tendrils flipping to and fro in the breeze like streamers on a kid's bicycle handle.

"I do remember something you told me the other night at the Rendezvous, however, when I was telling you about the loon charm and you said you'd never been in love," Lolly started. "You said you wanted to control life a bit too much, like your mom."

Lolly took the thermos lid from Lauren and sipped. "Are you telling me the whole truth? Is there another reason you're not dating anyone?"

"Men are dogs, Grandma," Lauren said without thinking.

"That's not a good thing?" Lolly asked. "Aren't dogs sweet?"

Lauren laughed and shook her grandmother's leg. "You'd think so, right? But I mean dogs as in . . . well, you know . . . they tend to wander."

"Oh!" Lolly said, finally understanding. "Dogs!"

Lauren stopped laughing and turned serious.

"If I'm being totally honest, it's just that I'm really scared to put myself out there, Grandma," Lauren said. "I'm a little gun shy after Mom and Dad's divorce. I mean, they have hurt each other so much. And, Lexie's boyfriends have all cheated on her. I want so much to find true love, but I don't want my heart to get trampled."

Lolly scooched over on the quilt and put her arm around her granddaughter. "Oh, my dear sweet, sensitive girl. Your heart is going to get trampled a little bit, whether you put it out there or choose to lock it away."

Lolly ruffled Lauren's hair and continued. "If you put yourself out there, you're going to get hurt at some point. Yes, your boyfriend or husband could leave you. He might stray. He could die way too young like your grandfather. And, at some point, you will both probably say things to one another you immediately want to take back. But, if you remain alone, your heart will ache for all that you never experienced. Love is filled with great beauty *and* great pain. But there is no beauty to life if you don't put your heart at risk. The ability to love is one of the greatest gifts we're given. It's the reason we're here."

Lolly stopped and pointed up at the sky. "Think of when you paint . . . say, like a scene of shooting stars in the sky. You lose yourself in that work, don't you? You experience the sheer beauty of what you're seeing and feeling. It's the same way in love. You must never lose who you are, but you also must be willing to lose yourself entirely in the depth of the relationship. Does that make sense?"

Lauren leaned into her grandmother. Even though Lolly's body was fragile, Lauren could feel her strength. "It does, Grandma. The relation-ship you and Grampa had is my role model. I want that."

"And you will," Lolly said. "So will Arden. I think she may have already found it, in fact."

"I do, too," Lauren agreed. "And I *will* find love. I *know* I will, especially having two strong women role models like you and Mom. What I've learned is that the best way to find love is to have your own inner light shine through first."

"So true," Lolly said. "The world is a mirror. You attract what you re-flect."

Lauren stopped and pulled her grandmother closer. "I've learned that sometimes family can also be a great love in a person's life, especially when she needs a guiding light to help her find her way in the world."

"I love you, my dear," Lolly said.

"Me too, Grandma," Lauren said, before shouting, "Look!"

In the distance, a shooting star flew across the horizon.

"A guiding light, indeed," Lolly said.

Thirty-eight

D id you see the shooting star?" Lauren asked excitedly when Arden and Jake returned.

"It was beautiful," Arden agreed, taking a seat next to her daughter, Jake plopping next to Arden.

"Symbolic," Lolly added.

"I think that might be all we see tonight, though," Arden said. "It's getting late."

"Hold on to your horses," Lolly said, grabbing Lauren's phone and tapping it to check the time. "It's only twelve-thirty. And we've got each other for company and lots of coffee to stay warm."

Arden laughed. "Is that your *special* coffee, Mom? I know your secret ingredient. We won't care what time it is after we drink it."

"In that case, I'll take a cup!" Jake said, his deep voice rippling with laughter.

"Attaboy," Lolly said, handing him the thermos.

Lauren shivered, and Lolly pulled a blanket over the group's laps, and the four sat in silence, the muffled waves singing to them.

I can feel the whole world out there waiting for me to change it, even though I can't see it right now, Lauren thought, staring out over the dark lake. *Love makes it possible to believe you can change the world.*

"Did you just see that?" Arden asked, turning her head left, then right.

In the distance, a curtain of glowing light began to dance in the sky, as if a lava lamp had been poured onto the horizon.

"You're right, Mom," Arden said, her voice rising in excitement. "It's happening!"

The glow slowly got bigger, richer, brighter, until all the heavens were filled with ghostly, colorful lights. Purples, pinks, greens radiated from every corner of the sky, alive, dancing, unveiling their mystery for all the world to see.

Lauren grabbed her phone and began to take pictures with her camera, oohing and aahing like it was the Fourth of July.

Lolly secretly turned her head to watch the reactions of her family. The lights played off their faces, whirled in their eyes, twinkled off Arden's glasses, wonder etched on their faces like it was Christmas morning.

The amazing beauty of life and family, Lolly thought, smiling, *if only we take the time to see it and cherish it.*

Arden caught her mother looking at her, and she grabbed Lolly's hand and squeezed it before following her gaze back out to the lights.

"Native Americans believed that the lights were the spirits of their people," Lolly said softly. "I believe that. Right now, we can clearly see all of our family who came before us and shared the same earth, water, light, and air."

Lolly stopped, the lights dancing off her face.

Lake Michigan reflected the Northern Lights, too, the waters dancing in delight. In the distance, the Manitou Islands seemed alive in the glow, and Arden's heart overflowed thinking of the story her mother had shared earlier in the week.

Arden squeezed her mother's hand again, and Lolly's bracelet jangled as her daughter cradled her hand.

"These lights are like my charms," Lolly said. "They remind us of our past and how blessed we are by the precious moments in our lives."

How long will all of this last? Arden thought, looking at her mom and then again at the lights.

And, then, as quickly as it had started, the sky grew dim and the show was over.

"Is that what love feels like?" Lauren asked, her eyes still wide with wonder.

"If you're lucky," Arden and Jake said in unison.

"And we are," Lolly said, as the four gathered their stuff and headed home.

part ten

The Mustard Seed Charm

To a Life Filled with Faith

Thirty-nine

Lauren jumped awake, her mind whirling like the Northern Lights, unable to sleep.

I feel as if my life is at a crossroads. I feel like all of our lives are at a crossroads, ran through her mind.

It was still dark, and she leaned over to read the alarm clock by her bed. *5:47.*

She laid back down and shut her eyes, but her mind would not cooperate. She was still energized by what she had seen and experienced just a few hours earlier.

Lauren yawned, stretched, and went in search of coffee. As she was waiting for the pot to brew, she leaned against the counter in the kitchen, watching the lake come to life.

That's when she saw it in the dusky dawn light: An easel, canvas, and paints were set up on the dock.

Grandma!

Lauren nearly shouted in excitement, and had to cover her own mouth to quiet herself. When the coffee was ready, she walked outside, looked out over the lake, and sipped from her cup, the sky and her senses coming alive.

She bowed her head to say a small prayer before dipping the tip of her brush into the paints, the sky quickly brightening over Lost Land.

She looked at the clear Michigan sky over Lost Land Lake and blew her bangs out of her eyes with a great sigh.

This isn't just beautiful. It's ethereal, she realized. *The Northern Lights and now a heavenly sunrise.*

The morning light shimmered through the trees and gave the lake an otherworldly hue. Everything in this Michigan world seemed to have a soft shimmer to it, as though God had hung gauze over the sky and softly scattered glitter on all his creations.

A little more gold? White? Blue? she considered.

This simple, little lake was filled with so much beauty.

It's the light, my grandmother always told me. It's the magical light, Lauren thought.

Scoops sat along the forty-fifth parallel north, a circle of latitude often called the halfway point between the equator and the North Pole.

Some of the world's most stunning vistas rested along this line, and they were considered by many to be not only spiritual spots but also places of incomparable beauty. At this latitude, the sun stayed in the summer sky in these parts of northern Michigan for nearly eighteen hours. Artists believed the angle of the sun and the magical light it produced made the world glow. Artists traveled from around the world to paint here for decades, and local galleries housed in former barns now dotted the lakeshore. Art collectors in smart spectacles, linen pants, and silk scarves came to Scoops from across the country every summer, snatching up works both by famed and yet-to-be-discovered talent.

Farmers and vintners had followed the artists in recent years. Vineyards and wineries sat along rolling hillsides overlooking the bay, producing exquisite chardonnays and Rieslings, while produce farms and farmers' markets sold the freshest cherries, blueberries, asparagus, heirloom tomatoes, beans, and peaches. Farm-to-table restaurants had replaced dingy diners and smoky bars, and from Memorial Day through Labor Day, diners needed to—*gasp!*—make reservations.

Lauren studied the simple scene in front of her: The lake at dawn. The dock jutting forth over the quiet waters, reeds rustling on the banks, swans waking, smoke from stone fireplaces in log cabins mixing with the morning light.

And that sky! That sky! She exhaled.

"It's the light," Lolly said.

Lauren jumped.

"I know, Grandma. You taught me that."

"Need a refill? We were up so late, but it was worth it, wasn't it?"

Lolly was standing in a fluffy pink robe, already in wig and full makeup, holding the pot of coffee. Lauren nodded yes to both questions.

"Didn't mean to startle you," she said.

"I was just so deep in thought," Lauren said. "I lost track."

"Passion!" Lolly winked, filling her granddaughter's Scoops mug.

A pang of guilt filled Lauren, and she nervously stole a glance toward the window of the bedroom where her mother still slept.

"No need for guilt," Lolly said, filling her own mug and setting the coffeepot on top of a sun-faded dock. She tilted her face toward the emerging sun, and it, too, was cast in an otherworldly light. "You've known what you were born to do since you were a little girl. You just fought it. We all do. You just needed faith. And a little push."

Lauren grinned at her grandmother and winked. "And a little 'Hope,' right, Grandma? That's how the ice cream charm led you to find your job at Dolly's, isn't it?"

Lolly smiled and nodded, shutting her eyes to remember her granddaughter as a little girl filled with hope, faith, and unbridled talent. Lolly had bought Lauren her first set of crayons, first set of sidewalk chalks, first paint-by-numbers project, first set of watercolors.

Lauren looked over at her grandmother, whose eyes were still shut, and she closed hers, too. She could still feel her grandmother's hands on hers, as they had been when she was a child, guiding her, helping her.

"Don't worry! It's even better when you go outside the lines. That makes your vision unique!" Lolly used to tell her. *"Make the sky purple instead of blue! That's the way it looks to dreamers!"*

"I can't thank you enough for this, Grandma," Lauren said, gesturing at the easel and paints. "I don't know what to say."

Lolly clucked her tongue. "Oh, my dear, I didn't do this. Your mother did."

"What?"

"She wanted to surprise you," Lolly said. "Encourage you. I think my stories, and your and Jake's influence are doing wonders on her," she said. "But now it's up to you. You have to believe in yourself."

Lauren turned and watched a heron break the surface of the water, stretching for a fish, before taking its catch to the shore. "I love to paint, but what if I can't cut it? I can't imagine doing anything else, but what if I don't make a living at it?"

"There's no doubt, it's scary to try to make it as an artist," Lolly said. "But as I always say: If ifs and buts were candy and nuts, oh, what a merry Christmas it would be!"

Lauren cocked her head, confused.

"It's an old, old phrase, my dear." Lolly laughed. "Older than me, even. What it means is: You can't worry about all of that. You can only control the now, your own happiness. Let me ask you, what if you didn't try? How would you feel in ten years? Twenty years?"

"You sorta sound like Lexie," Lauren said.

"Life is filled with risk and uncertainty," Lolly continued. "I face it every day battling my memory. Your mom is learning to let her walls down with Jake and to listen to you. And you have all the talent in the world."

Lolly walked to the easel and studied the canvas.

"What are you painting?" Lolly asked. "If you don't mind me asking?"

"No, not at all!" Lauren said, taking a sip of her coffee. "I'm painting our dock. I'm painting the generations who have been joined by this place, this water, this light."

There was silence. Too long of a silence, Lauren thought, for her grandmother. A whippoorwill sang, and Lolly pursed her lips and returned its call, a beautiful whistle that matched the bird's: *Whip . . . or . . . wiiiillllll!*

"Are you okay, Grandma? Is anything wrong?"

"Nothing is wrong," she said. "You just . . . understand this place. You *get* me. I'm a little sentimental. I guess I'm just happy to have my girls home with me for a little while."

Lauren gave her grandmother a kiss on the cheek and noticed that she smelled wonderful, like flowers.

"What is that perfume you're wearing?" Lauren asked. "It's amazing!"

"Wish I could take credit for that, but it's not me. It's those!"

Lauren looked to where her grandmother pointed and saw a little garden perched at the front of the dock, between the warped wood and the lake.

"Peonies!" Lolly said. "The most beautiful flower in the world!"

The two walked over, and Lauren leaned down to inhale the sweetest scent she'd ever smelled.

"Those are early blooming," Lolly said. "Stunning, aren't they?"

The just-opening buds were the size of small eggs, and the flowers smelled like heaven. The flowers were as white as a bridal gown, save for tinges of pink along their edges, and they were dense and thick, row after row of petals, woven together to create a round ball of beauty.

Lauren crouched down and held a heavy bloom in her hands, admiring its beauty, watching a chorus line of ants journey to its scented center. She smiled and lifted the peony to her nose, inhaling deeply.

"Now, that's a picture *I* need to paint!" Lolly said. "Those started from a simple seed."

Lauren stood and stretched. "I feel a story coming on!" She laughed.

"You know me too well. In a while. But, right now, you should paint, and I need to water before I head off to work. These flowers can't grow without a big drink and lots of verbal encouragement."

Lolly grabbed the coffeepot off the pier and turned to head inside, but not before Lauren grabbed her arm.

"Thank you, Grandma."

"For what, my dear?"

"The encouragement."

Lolly smiled and disappeared into the cabin. Lauren turned and began to paint. Inspiration came quickly, the light her guide, and Lauren swore she could feel her grandmother's hands, right now, right here, on top of her own, helping her paint just like when she was a child.

Time seemed to stop, and Lauren became lost in her work. Slowly, three generations of women appeared in front of the lake, seated together at the end of this warped dock, the images of the women in the foreground as they appeared now—older, wiser, damaged but strong—while their reflections in the water were from their youth—younger, sadder, lost but hopeful. The connection?

This place.

Home, Lauren thought happily.

As the morning passed, the scene around her seemed to change and grow deeper.

Just like my family, Lauren thought.

In the stronger sunlight, the lake began to turn a million shades of the Pantone chart: the deeper water a midnight blue, the shoals aqua, the sandy shallows caramel, the wind turning them all forest green and midnight black when it churned the waves. Ducks drifted across the lake, as if they were sliding on ice, their feathers ruffled by the breeze. White swans—as white as newly fallen snow—bobbed. Fishermen veered their colorful johnboats in and out of the reeds, searching for the right spot, nets at the ready. Kids in bright swimsuits splashed in the water, teens sunned on Crayola-like float rafts, while their parents readied barbecues or sipped beers in retro-colored lawn chairs and Adirondacks.

I am home, Lauren thought again.

Lauren heard the screen door slam, and she was back in the present. Her mother emerged with a cup of coffee, dressed in shorts and a T-shirt.

Lauren glanced at her watch.

"You slept until ten a.m.?! I'm proud of you, Mother!"

"For what? Being a slacker?"

"No. For taking care of yourself. It was a late night." Lauren stopped. "And thank you, Mom."

"For what?" she asked again.

"This," Lauren said, nodding toward the easel. "For listening."

Arden ducked her head. "You're welcome."

"Mom?" Lauren started. "I just want you to know that I'll help pay off my loans, I'll do a work study next year, I'll . . ."

"You let me worry about that, okay?" Arden said. "I gave up my dreams, and I regret it. I've been trying to ensure you'd never worry about money, but I realize now that it's more important that you never have the regrets I do."

She stepped forward to study the painting. "It's stunning, Lauren. It really is. Not just your talent but your understanding of subject. There's depth on so many levels."

Lauren's face flushed, and she hugged her mom, leaving a trail of paint down the back of her T-shirt. "Sorry."

"Your grandma bought me this shirt years ago," she said. "Speaking of which, where is she?"

"Watering, I think."

The two stopped and tilted their heads. They could hear the faucet running on the backside of the cabin, where Lolly had a large yet still emerging cottage garden of phlox, hydrangea, lilies, dinner plate hibiscus, bellflower, daisies of all colors, foxglove, coral bells, and hollyhocks. Lolly cut from the garden all summer long.

"What's that?" Lauren asked, looking down at a tiny, but growing, river of water, rolling downhill toward the lake.

"Mom?" Arden yelled.

The tone of Arden's voice intensified from question to panic, when there was no response.

"Mom!"

The two took off running, Lauren dropping her brush and Arden her mug, until they saw Lolly, sitting on the ground holding the hose, a peony in her hands, the water running. She looked like an old garden statue, a fountain come to life, sitting there, expressionless.

Arden sat next to her mother, put her arm around her shoulder, and removed the hose from her hand while Lauren turned the water off.

"Mom, are you okay?" she said quietly. "Are you hurt? Can you talk? Tell me what's going on, okay?"

Lolly looked at her daughter very seriously and said calmly, "I'm sorry. I forgot what I was doing. And then I got tired."

Without warning, Lolly began to shake.

"I'm so scared," she said, as Arden held her tightly. "I just forget sometimes."

"We all do," Arden said, placing her arms around her mother. "We all do."

A whippoorwill called from the lake.

Lolly didn't return its whistle.

Lauren and Arden helped Lolly to the screened porch, where they lay her on the couch, covered her with a blanket, and made her some tea. She quickly fell asleep, the soft light off Lost Land basking Lolly in an ethereal glow.

She looks like she's wearing a halo, Lauren thought, holding her hand.

Arden retreated to the kitchen and called Jake. Then she went upstairs to the bathroom, turned on the faucet and the shower, and began to weep.

Forty

H ow are you feeling, Lolly?"
Lolly's false eyelashes fluttered, and she slowly opened her eyes—
one at a time.

"I was dreaming of loons," she said with a dry voice, still holding the
peony from the garden. "Looks like I still am!"

Dr. Van Meter, Jake, Arden, and Lauren were all hovering around her,
anxiously waiting for her to wake up. They all laughed at Lolly's words,
greatly relieved.

Lolly noticed that Arden's cheeks were quivering, as she tried to hold
back tears. She gave her earlobe a weak tug to show her daughter everything was going to be okay. Arden smiled and repeated the gesture.

"We're going to try you on some new meds, Lolly," Dr. Van Meter said.
"I think they will help with your clarity and not make you as confused.
Might make your mouth dry, but that's about it. And I want to see you again
in a couple of weeks."

Lolly nodded. "Thanks, Doc," Lolly said. She looked to Arden and Lauren. "I am thirsty. Could I get some water?"

"I'll get it," Lauren said.

"I'll walk you out," Arden said to the doctor.

"I'll keep you company," Jake said to the others.

"I've always had that effect on men," Lolly laughed.

"So, what's really going on, Doctor?" Arden asked out of earshot, as they approached Dr. Van Meter's SUV.

"MCI patients will have good days and bad. This is a bad one. Unfortunately, there can be more like this as the months progress, especially if your mother's condition should ever deteriorate into dementia. You need to be ready for that, just in case."

The doctor looked at the inlet, where Fred and Ethel were floating. She turned and considered Arden with a serious expression. "Living so far away, you need to begin to think about where your mother might live long-term."

"Long-term?"

"When, and if, she's ever unable to live on her own way out here," the doctor said. "Right now, you just might consider having someone check on her regularly."

Arden turned toward the lake to hide her emotions.

"I know it's hard," Dr. Van Meter said. "But dementia is like thunderstorms in the brain. Lolly's short-term memory will be affected, so she will have trouble with daily activities as some time progresses: bathing, cooking, eating, paying bills. No need for immediate alarm, but—like we all do—your mother has to prepare for the future."

Arden extended her hand to the doctor, who was looking toward the lake.

"Can I ask a personal question?" Dr. Van Meter asked. "Who painted that picture of your family that is on the dock? It's stunning. It would be perfect at Lakeview. I think it would inspire a lot of people."

Arden felt instantly proud. "Lauren painted that."

"Do you think she would ever consider selling it?" Dr. Van Meter asked.

"It's not for sale," Arden responded without thinking.

"Well," the doctor started, "your daughter is very talented."

Arden returned to the screened porch to find her mother sitting up, the peony now behind her ear, a natural embellishment to the rather unnatural wig she was still sporting. Lauren and Jake were seated at the little table, sipping tea and fidgeting with the unfinished jigsaw puzzle on the table.

"I see that look on your face, Arden," Lolly said, smiling. "But I'm not scared, my dear. My only fear is that I might forget you. But I'm not scared of the future. I don't regret a single day of my life."

Arden looked at her mother and shook her head. "You are remarkable," she said. "Why didn't I ever realize that before now?"

"You were never the brightest bulb in the box," Lolly quipped with a wink, her joke breaking the tension. "I'm just teasing you, my dear. It's just that you've always been so intelligent, but sometimes you have to believe in the things you don't understand."

"Like you?" Arden said, returning the wink.

"Exactly!" Lolly laughed. "I have faith. You need to have faith, too. So does Lauren. I didn't, for the longest time, however."

Lolly set her water down on the floor and began to flip through her charms, until she found one of a tiny yellow seed encased in a little bubble of glass and surrounded by a frame of woven silver.

"If you have faith as small as a mustard seed, then you can move mountains. Nothing will be impossible."

Arden shot her mother a suspicious look.

"There's a difference between faith and religion," Lolly said, wagging the charm and a finger at her daughter. "We are all given a tiny seed of faith. What we do with it is up to us. How did I survive such heartache? How did you end up with such a special daughter? Faith. You believed. Even if you didn't know it at the time."

Lolly removed the peony from behind her ear, held it to her nose, and inhaled deeply. "Heaven," she sighed. "This is what heaven will smell like!"

She tossed the flower to her daughter, who caught it just before it hit the floor of the porch.

"My peonies started from seeds," she said. "They were planted by my grandmother Mary. They can bloom for hundreds of years. Those flowers will outlive all of us."

Lolly sat up on the couch and stretched her arms high toward heaven.

"There was a time when I had very little faith," she continued. "I felt lost, like I didn't have a compass. And then one day, I met a poor man whose soul made him richer than Donald Trump."

Forty-one

1988

L olly cast her line into the lake, close to the reeds, and gave the lure a quick tug.

Nothing.

She reeled in the bright, wooden lure and gave it another cast—*whiiiirrr!*—into the water, where it hit with a soft splash.

There was something about the act of fishing—the repetitiveness of motion—that relaxed her. It had the same soothing effect as sewing.

It, too, connected her to her father, her husband, her past.

Lolly set the rod down on the dock, her legs dangling over the edge, and zipped up her hooded jacket. Though it was only early October, a fall chill had settled over Scoops. Lolly inhaled and—*whoosh!*—blew out a gasp of air to test the temperature.

I can already see my breath! Winter is around the corner, she thought.

The giant sugar maples that rimmed Lost Land Lake were already losing their leaves. The lake, in fact, glowed, looked as if it were on fire, between the reflection of the maples' delicate orange, gold, and crimson leaves off the water and the ones already floating on its surface.

Lolly was happy she had found a job that occupied her on fall color weekends and kept her busy over the summers and holidays. She was happy that Arden was doing well at school. Lolly missed Arden and Les, but there was something deeper that seemed to be missing, too. Something that made Lolly ache, even more than the damp chill that surrounded her.

"You gotta have a lot of faith to fish."

Lolly let out a yelp, nearly dropping her pole, before turning to see an elderly man with a white wisp of hair jutting forth from the middle of his forehead.

"Didn't mean to startle you," he said. "My name is Joseph."

"I usually don't scare so easily," Lolly said, leaning back on the dock—pole in hand, line in water—to extend her hand. "My name is Lolly. It's just so quiet these days. Everyone has left for the season."

"Quiet don't mean lonely to me," the man said, shaking her hand.

If Michigan were dressed in its Sunday finest—drenched in brilliant Technicolor—the old man was dressed in his work clothes: worn Dickies work pants, tattered coat and torn overshirt, muddy boots, hands and fingers that were red and curled, knotted as the sassafras that dotted the woods.

"What brings you to Lost Land?" Lolly asked. "Come to fish?"

Lolly was a trusting soul, but there was something about this man—almost an aura, if you believed in such a thing—that made her feel a bit off-kilter.

"Came to build," he said.

"Build?"

Lolly reeled in her line and pushed off on the dock to stand. After the buying boom of the 1980s, Lolly hated the word "build." Scoops—and Lost Land—didn't take kindly to renovation, gentrification, and escalation. Things were just fine as they were. She took a step toward the man, and nervously zipped and unzipped her jacket.

"Just a little house," he said. "A peaceful place, somewhere near the lake."

"Do you have property?" Lolly asked.

The man laughed, revealing perfect white teeth that didn't fit his aged, whisker-stubbled face, Lolly thought.

"Yes," he replied.

"Where are you staying?" Lolly asked next.

The man's eyes twinkled, like the lake, and seemed to turn a hundred shades of grey, before settling on slate. "In an old stable just up the road."

"Whose barn?" Lolly asked. "I grew up around here. Know pretty much everyone."

"Just some nice folks," he said. "I help look after their animals in exchange for room and board. Gives me a chance to build in the afternoons. I'm looking for some help, if you're interested."

Lolly narrowed her eyes and gave the man a wary look.

"I'm sorry," he said, sensing her distrust and stepping slowly backward until he was off Lolly's dock. "I didn't mean to overstep any boundaries. Just looking for someone who might have some skills to offer. You have a good day, ma'am."

"I don't have any skills!" Lolly called, surprising herself. She hadn't even considered responding. The words just came out as if she couldn't control them.

"We all have skills, but most of us don't have faith in ourselves," the man said. He pointed a swollen finger that hooked at the knuckle. "Meet me on the opposite side of the lake tomorrow—over there by the weeping willow, see?—around three."

Lolly knew the willow well, but turned just to make sure. When she spun back around, the man was gone, not even a puff of breath hanging in the fall air to indicate he had even been there.

The next day, Lolly walked the edge of the lake, arriving at the willow promptly at three. A stack of two-by-fours and knotty pine wood sat under a tarp, alongside bags of concrete, saws, hammers, wheelbarrows, buckets, a spade, and a rusty toolbox. The man was already up to his waist in the wet ground, digging up shovelfuls of Michigan sand mixed with dark mud.

"You own this land?" Lolly asked, looking around the spot. "Millers own that cabin up the hill from here."

"This is the right spot," the man replied.

Lolly considered his response odd but conclusive. She glanced back up at the Millers' cabin.

I could call them. Do I have their number? she considered.

"Why don't you start hauling up some water from the lake?" the man asked, distracting Lolly from her thoughts. "I'll need it for the concrete. Need to finish fast, before the ground freezes."

"What are you building, exactly?" Lolly asked once more. "Seems small."

"Tiny of space, huge of inspiration," the man said.

Lolly began hauling water, and asking the man questions: Was he married? Where did he live? Why did he come here? Did he have a family? What did he do for a living?

The old man worked feverishly, with the inexhaustible drive of youth, dispensing little personal information but much wisdom.

"I have no family," he would say, "save for the world."

And, "I come from everywhere. My home is wherever one will accept me."

The man never tired, only stopping on occasion to drink water from the lake, like one of the deer. Once, when he lifted his shirt to wipe his brow, Lolly gasped: The old man had the body of a young one. His stomach was taut, muscles rippled.

Over the next few weekdays, at three, Lolly did what she could to help the man: Hauling water, raking dirt, stacking lumber. She didn't know why she returned, but she felt compelled to do so. She found the hard labor as comforting as fishing or sewing.

"Told you I don't have any skills," she would tell the man over and over.

"You have many gifts," he would repeat. "You just need to believe in them."

The following Monday remained drizzly and cool, and Lolly walked around Lost Land Lake, her galoshes leaving sloppy, wet footprints in the muddy grass. When she neared the willow, she looked up, stopping dead in her tracks: The structure was complete.

In front of her stood a tiny white chapel, no bigger than a back-yard playhouse for two children, a cross made of birch jutting from the roof. There were small windows on each side, empty pine window boxes underneath both. The back—facing the lake—was all glass. The front double doors were painted red, and a steppingstone path led to the lake.

"What?" Lolly stammered, as the man emerged from inside. "How did you? When did you?"

"Labor of love," he said. "Come inside."

Lolly ducked to enter the front doors and again gasped once inside: The cathedral ceiling soared toward heaven, and was outlined with wood beams. It was tall enough for Lolly to stand fully and stretch her body. The walls were knotty pine, the floors painted white. Four tiny pews, two on each side, big enough to hold two people each, were burnished and lacquered to a high shine. One step up led to a tiny altar that was lit with candles. A single Bible sat in a wood stand in front of the glass window, the lake shimmering beyond.

"I don't understand," Lolly said. "It's beautiful, but I thought you said this was going to be your home."

"It is my home." The man smiled, showing those perfect teeth. "It is yours, too. It is everyone's."

"I still don't understand," Lolly stammered.

"Now it's your turn," he said. "What skills can you offer to make this place your own?"

Lolly looked at the man. She knew she should have felt scared, but instead she felt incredibly calm. This felt like a place she wanted to be.

"I can sew curtains for the windows," Lolly said. "I have an old Singer at home. Oh! And I can make a garden, too."

"See," the man said. "You have many talents. It's a deal. I have some things to finish here. Come back when you are done with your work."

Lolly scurried home, working round the clock to make sweet curtains from sheets her mother had loved, a pattern dotted with deer, pine trees, steeples, and little lakes. When she was done, Lolly went into her garden, which had died back but whose flowers still held their pods for spring, and gathered seeds from her peonies, daisies, foxglove, coral bells, and hollyhocks. She returned the next Monday at three. The man opened the doors when she arrived. He looked younger to Lolly, although he was cloaked in the same dirty work clothes.

"These are gifts from your mother," he said. "Gifts from your family."

"How did you know?" Lolly asked.

"Because they tell a story, just like your bracelet."

He helped Lolly hang the curtains, and then the two went outside, turned over the earth, and planted the seeds.

"If you have faith as small as a mustard seed, then you can move mountains," the man said when they were done. "Nothing will be impossible."

"Excuse me?" Lolly said.

"We have all been given a seed of faith, but it is up to us to spread that

around. We must believe in ourselves, have faith in what we don't understand. When we do, the world will open. You will no longer fear."

Lolly stared at that man.

Was he getting younger? I must be tired, Lolly wondered.

"It's time I went home," the man suddenly said.

"I thought this was your home."

"My home is everywhere. See you tomorrow at three?"

Lolly nodded. She bent down to retrieve an extra curtain rod she had
brought, and when she stood, the man was again gone, not even a footprint
to track his departure.

At three the next overcast day, Lolly returned. The man was not outside waiting. When she opened the doors of the chapel, it was aglow in
candlelight.

"Hello?" she called.

Nothing.

Lolly looked around, again admiring the incredible craftsmanship of
the building: the angles, the beams, the woodwork. She walked to the front
and took a seat in a pew. The candles flickered, like the lake, and that's
when Lolly shut her eyes and prayed.

She stayed that way forever, it seemed, and when she opened her eyes
she felt at peace. Her internal ache was gone. Lolly stood to blow out the
candles, and that's when she noticed a little box on the altar next to the
Bible.

She sat on the step and untied the bow. Inside was a little charm of a
tiny yellow seed encased in a little bubble of glass surrounded by a frame
of woven silver.

Lolly ran the charm between her fingers, confused as to what it was and
what it signified. As she rolled the little seed to and fro, the man's voice
popped into her head:

*"If you have faith as small as a mustard seed, then you can move mountains. Noth-
ing will be impossible."*

Lolly added the little charm to her bracelet, and when she walked out
of the chapel, she felt—for the first time in her life—a great sense of peace.

Over the course of the winter, Lolly returned to the chapel at three—
trudging through several feet of snow—to see if the man had returned. She

asked around Scoops if people had seen the man, and stopped at farms around Lost Land Lake asking if anyone had let an elderly man stay with them.

No one had seen such a man.

When spring came, and Michigan thawed, the resorters returned. All that is, save for the Miller family, who Lolly would learn had been killed in a tragic car accident that fall.

Over time, the chapel became a playhouse and hideaway for the children who lived around Lost Land Lake.

On fall and winter days, when everyone had left Lost Land for the year, Lolly would return, around three, and bow her head in prayer.

Forty-two

No matter what happens—in your lives, in my life, with my health— you need not fear anything," Lolly said, giving her charm a little kiss. "Faith will see you through it all. My only fear is forgetting. That's why I'm telling you these stories."

"That's so beautiful, Grandma," Lauren said, walking over to give her grandmother a little kiss. "Let me get you some more water."

"Mom, are you sure you weren't depressed?" Arden asked once Lauren had left for the kitchen. "Or taking something?"

"Oh, ye of little faith!" Lolly said, wagging a hand at her daughter. "You have all the talent and brains in the world, my dear, but you've always lacked faith."

Lolly glanced at Jake, who was still staring at her, riveted by the story. She cupped her hands around her mouth, and said in a Shakespearean whisper, "Especially in love."

Arden's face flushed.

"You're as red as a cardinal." Jake winked, nodding toward the bird feeder.

"I think I need some air," Arden said, rushing off the screened porch, embarrassed.

Jake hesitated, but Lolly said, "Go after her!"

"Are you sure?" he asked.

"Are you?"

With that, Jake raced out the door. Lolly watched Jake scan the dock and grassy hillsides that rolled to the lake. They were teeming with holiday revelers.

Then, in the distance, Arden rounded the bend of the lake, like a fleeing bat. Jake zipped after her.

"What's going on?" he huffed, gently grabbing Arden by the arm.

"My mother has always had this way of embarrassing me," she said, turning, her cheeks flushed, her eyes wide. That's when Jake could tell she had been crying.

"I'm sorry," he said in his low voice. "I don't think she means to embarrass you. I think she just wants to shake you up a bit because she cares."

"Do I need shaking?" Arden asked, taking off in a hurry once again.

"Maybe," Jake said. "Do you?"

Arden stopped. "Maybe I do," she conceded.

"Well, your mother certainly has a flair for the dramatic," Jake said, gesturing ahead of Arden. When she turned, Arden could see the chapel-turned-playhouse—now warped, the doors aged to a faded red, a birch cross still emerging from the roof—standing in front of the lake.

Jake took Arden's hand and led her into the chapel, the two stooping to enter. Once inside, he led her to a front pew, where they took a seat and stared out the front windows.

"Do you think she's telling the truth about this place?" Arden asked.

"Do you?"

"Please don't answer a question with a question," Arden replied. "I'm sorry. I didn't mean that. I just feel a little overwhelmed."

"I do think she's telling the truth," he said, putting his arm around her back to calm her. "But now I get to ask you a question: Do you pray?"

"No," Arden said.

"Why?"

"What's the point in praying to something that isn't there?"

Jake looked closely at Arden, and then out the side window, to the lake shimmering beyond. "Religion is like a blind man looking in a black room for a black cat that isn't there, and finding it."

Arden cocked her head.

"Oscar Wilde," Jake said. "Even a literate cynic believed."

A breeze tossed around the delicate flowers planted in the window boxes. "Do you think my mother still plants these boxes?" Arden asked.

"Of course," Jake said. "She found the black cat."

Arden stood and raced out the chapel.

"Always on the run!" Jake called.

Before he could exit, he saw Arden's hand pluck a peony from the window box. By the time he was out of the chapel, Arden had raced halfway around the lake and had already entered the screened porch of the cabin before Jake finally caught up with her. As he entered, Arden was handing the peony to her mother.

"Would you like to decorate graves for Memorial Day, like we did when I was a kid?"

Lolly was touched by Arden's suggestion, and her tears told her daughter she did.

Later, after Lolly had rested and Jake had left, the three women all put on respectful clothes and sensible heels, packed some Kleenex, American flags, and a slew of fresh flowers they had dug up earlier from Lolly's garden and they loaded into the Woodie, and began to make their "rounds."

At Scoops Memorial Cemetery, the three parked under a series of narrow pines that lined the gravel drive. Arden opened the trunk and handed her mother some flowers and her daughter some flags. Arden took a box of Kleenex, and the three began to walk, arms interlocked, until Lolly said, "I think it's this way."

"Are you sure?" Arden asked.

The two argued for a few seconds, before they set out over the soft grass, wending their way through headstones—some of which were new, marbled, impressive, while others were worn, cracked concrete.

Cemeteries along the lakeshore of Michigan were not lush, lavish, or large. Graveyards, as they were simply called, were compact and rested on a rolling foothill, a quiet piece of country land next to a pasture, or on the edge of a sandy dune overlooking Lake Michigan. They were not filled with marble headstones. The graveyards and headstones were simple, like the people.

"Here she is!" Lolly said.

MARY FALLORAN
Wife, Mother, Grandmother
Sewer & Adventurer
1884–1971

Lolly bowed her head, reaching her hands out to Arden and Lauren. The three clasped hands and prayed. Lolly nodded to Lauren, who kneeled and planted a tiny American flag by Mary's grave. Then Lolly bent to the ground on her knees, dug her hands through the wet earth, and planted some peonies. When they were done, Arden handed Kleenexes to Lauren and Lolly.

"Next!" Lolly said, pointing north.

Lauren and Arden helped Lolly stand, and she smiled. As the three walked, arms interlocked like sentinels in a graveyard, Lauren asked, "How long have you been doing this, Grandma?"

"Forever."

"Why?"

"Smell!" Lolly said, holding out a peony for her granddaughter.

"I know! It smells like heaven!" she said.

"Exactly!"

Lolly stopped on a slight embankment, under the shade of a pine. Gravestones were artfully arranged in perfect symmetry on the hillside below. The flags and flowers adorning the grass were beautiful. Lolly held the peony up to her own nose, and the memories came flooding back.

"These peonies started in Ireland, where Mary was born," Lolly said. "Since Mary couldn't return home, her parents sent her starts of their peonies, so that a piece of home would forever link the family. Those long rows of peonies on the backside of the cabin? Mary started those, rotating bushes of white and pink, babying them until they grew big and strong, until the flowers grew so heavy that they simply exhausted the stems that valiantly tried to support them. And, oh! The smell!"

Lolly held a peony in front of her face.

"Before my mom died, we would decorate graves on Memorial Day, and she told me Mary's stories. This place," Lolly said, nodding at the cemetery, "is where I learned so much about my family and friends, those who passed before me, or those I barely knew.

"My mom told me that Mary planted two types of peonies, early and late blooming. Mary planted the early bloomers for just one reason: So that she could decorate the graves of her family and friends on Memorial Day with not just real flowers, but with flowers that came from her family's garden, flowers she considered to be the most beautiful in the world."

Lolly halted, but couldn't stop a tear from trailing down her cheek. "You know, the earth is what grounds us in life for a very short time. The starts from Mary's family remain forever in my garden. They represent a way to keep the memory of those we love alive, no matter where we live, or how much time has passed."

"Like your charms," Lauren said.

"Exactly, my dear."

Lolly turned with a purpose, pulling Arden and Lauren alongside, and meandered until she found her husband's gravestone, images of the lake and two loons etched into the stone.

"My Les," she whispered, planting a peony.

The trio of visitors continued their rounds, stopping at Lolly's mother's grave next, and then continuing on as if they were greeting guests at a party, Lolly telling stories about people her granddaughter and daughter never knew.

Finally, Lolly said, "I think we're done with our visits."

Arden hesitated. "I think there's one more, Mom."

The three meandered around the small cemetery until, perched under a sassafras, they found the stone: *Clem Watkins.*

Arden took a flag from her daughter and a peony from her mother, knelt on her first love's grave, planted a flag, and then said a prayer.

You were the first man to love me. I'm so glad you found your happiness. I pray you help me find mine. And I pray that someone takes the time, like my mother has done today, to share my story, to visit me on occasion, to plant a seed of hope, to pass along my legacy.

And then Arden dug through the new grass, mud, sand, and clay, and she planted some peonies.

part eleven

The Tiara Charm

To a Life in Which You Get to Feel
Like a Queen, Even for a Day

Forty-three

T*he Scoop* hit the stoop with a bang.

The noise startled Arden, who was in the midst of checking in with her office. She jumped, coffee sloshing over the edge of her mug and onto her stomach.

"Owww!"

She looked up in time to see the local paper take a big hop and fly end over end across the lawn, as if it were a piece of shale that the paperboy had skimmed across the lake.

Arden set down her coffee and hit SEND on a message to her editor that read, "Van, c'mon . . . it's a holiday! I'll be back WHEN MY VACATION IS OVER."

Before she had even set down her phone, Van replied: "Simóne's still doing a GREAT job filling in for you."

Arden's heart raced as she retrieved the paper. She thought about responding but instead took a deep breath and rolled the rubber band off the paper. Arden opened the paper and laughed sarcastically at the front page:

Happy Memorial Day, Scoops!
75th Annual Tulip Queen Celebration Today!

"The universe must be telling me something today." Arden chuckled, reading the lead story. "Wow. This hasn't changed at all. *The Scoop* ain't the *Trib*. Or even *Paparazzi*."

"This isn't Chicago, my dear," Lolly replied, walking onto the porch with her own cup of coffee. "And we're not celebrities, thank goodness."

"That Tulip Queen thing sounds fun!" Lauren said, following her grandmother. She took a seat on the glider, crossing her legs and balancing a bowl of cereal in her lap. "How come we've never gone?"

Silence engulfed the porch.

"I mean, every little town has a dairy queen, or cheese queen, or something, right?" Lauren said between mouthfuls of the Lucky Charms her grandmother always bought for her. "I always wanted to be queen of something."

"All girls should be a queen or princess, even for a day," Lolly said, sipping from her mug, and giving Arden a wink. "But, my dear, there's a reason why you've never gone and why your mother is being so quiet. Isn't that right, Arden?"

"Mother!"

"What am I missing?" Lauren squealed, bouncing on the glider, her cereal sloshing to and fro in the bowl. "Yet something else my mother forgot to share with me?"

"I can't wait to hear this!" a disembodied voice that sounded like a bear's rumble boomed from outside the porch.

For the second time, Arden jumped, again jostling her coffee. Jake's handsome face appeared at the screen.

"I was just trying to have a quiet cup of coffee and read the paper," Arden said, exasperated, taking a seat at the table with a sigh, as Jake entered the cabin. She took an errant piece of the jigsaw puzzle and gestured with it as emphasis. "*Alone!*"

"I'm shocked there aren't *Paparazzi* paparazzi swarming this cabin!" Jake said, jostling Arden's shoulders playfully. "You're famous in Scoops! You should be featured in your own magazine!"

"Enough mystery!" Lauren yelped. "Somebody talk."

Arden bounced a hard look off her mother, who returned her visual volley with a withering glance. "Go on," Lolly said with a smirk, taking a seat and folding her arms satisfactorily.

"Well . . . ," Arden started. "My mom felt it was important that I meet some friends my own age. She felt before I went to college that I needed to come out of my shell, so I wouldn't be so shy."

"*And* that we do something together as mother–daughter," Lolly added. "To bond, after Les died."

"So," Arden continued, "in typical Lolly fashion, she came up with this harebrained idea . . ."

"Hey!" Lolly interrupted. "You're a journalist. Stick to the facts!"

"I am!" Arden said with a groan. "So . . . she decided to enter me in the Tulip Queen contest. Unbeknownst to me, of course."

Lolly shrugged her shoulders innocently, eliciting giggles from everyone but Arden.

"So, I agreed, just to make her happy. She ended up sewing this hideous Day-Glo yellow dress . . ."

"It was the color of a spring tulip!" Lolly interjected.

"I looked jaundiced, Mother," Arden said. "And the bottom of the dress was made of all these different-colored panels . . ."

"They were all the colors of spring tulips!" Lolly interjected once more.

". . . and the dress featured this long train she filled with fresh tulips cut from her garden. I looked like a melting bowl of sherbet. Of course, she put me in one of her blond wigs—adorned with more tulips . . ."

"You needed to look all-American Dutch!" Lolly interjected yet again.

"That's an oxymoron, Mother," Arden said to more giggles. "And enough makeup to make me look like a hooker."

"A good hooker wouldn't have fallen in her heels," Lolly said, wagging a finger at her daughter.

"Okay, we're getting somewhere now," Lauren said.

"Hold on," Arden said. "I'm nearing the big finish. So, for talent, my mom suggested I sing 'Tip-Toe Through the Tulips' by Tiny Tim . . . while PLAYING A UKULELE!"

"It was perfect," Lolly said, her eyes shut, as if in a dream.

"The only problem was the crowd started laughing, I got embarrassed, and when I tried to run off the platform, which they build to jut out over the river, my train got caught on a warped board, my heel caught, and I fell backward into the river. They had to rescue me."

"And my wig," Lolly laughed.

Jake stood and put his hands on Arden's shoulders, giving them a gentle squeeze.

"Everyone called me Ar-don't," she said. "Essentially I became a warning to every other girl in town: If you enter the Tulip Queen pageant, don't do anything that Arden did."

Lauren clapped her hand over her mouth in shock, but a smile still spilled forth. "Oh, Mom. I'm so sorry. Why didn't you ever tell me that?"

"Why would I tell anyone that?"

"It explains a lot about how guarded you are, and the way you dress," Lauren said. "I'm glad I know now. Thanks."

Arden gave *The Scoop* a hearty shake. "You're welcome, but I'm still having a quiet Memorial Day," she said, hiding behind the paper.

"You know why I entered you in that pageant, don't you, Arden?" Lolly asked seriously, cocking her head like the wren that sat on the feeder outside the screen.

"Yes. To humiliate me."

Lolly stared out at the lake, her blue eyes reflecting the idyllic scene. "No, it's because I could never enter it. When I was young, you had to have your mother sign the consent form. I always dreamed of entering because they had the most beautiful charm of a tulip tiara. I thought . . . well, I thought it would be fun to do it as a mother, if I couldn't as a daughter. I thought it would be fun for someone in our family to feel like a queen just once in our lives, even for a day."

Arden softened and smiled at her mother, and Lauren followed her grandmother's gaze out the screen in order to hide her own tears.

"So what brings you here?" Lolly asked Jake, suddenly changing the subject. "Besides to meet the famous Ar-don't in person?"

"I just wanted to check on you, see how you're feeling."

"I feel much better, thank you, sir," Lolly said. "I plan to head to work at noon. It's a big holiday. Lots of fudgies in town."

"And . . . ," Jake said, hesitating dramatically. "I'm here to pick up Arden for our date."

"Date?" Lolly repeated, her face lighting up.

"Date?" Arden echoed, smiling.

"We're going to the beach," Jake said to Lolly, "just like you and your husband did on one of your first dates."

"I love it," Lolly said. "Don't you, Arden?"

Arden nodded, but immediately thought of Van's text.

"I probably need to check back in with work first," Arden said. "There's a lot going on. I might need to work remotely from here for a few hours."

"But it's a holiday," Lolly said, her words flying out with a sigh.

"There's always less coverage on a holiday and more happening, it seems," Arden said.

"Remember what we talked about?" Lolly asked.

Arden hesitated and looked down at the table, to avoid the stares of her mother, daughter, and Jake.

"I'm going to put the finishing touches on my painting, Mom," Lauren said. "And then lay out and catch some rays. It's a perfect beach day . . . for a date!"

Arden thought of Dr. Van Meter's offer to buy Lauren's painting, and just as suddenly her mind shifted to Van. Arden looked at her mother, as silence engulfed the screened porch.

What will I remember when I'm her age? That I worked? Or that I went to the beach? Arden reminded herself. *My new life begins now.*

"You're right," Arden finally said. "I'll go get ready."

"Don't trip," Lolly teased.

Arden tugged her mother's wig off to the side as she passed. When Lolly heard the stairs creak, she looked at Jake. "Thank you," she said.

"For what?"

"Everything."

Forty-four

Scoops Beach was jammed worse than Lake Shore Drive in the middle of a January blizzard.

Cars snaked up the narrow beach road perched between the tall dunes, music of every genre—pop, rock, country, jazz, oldies—booming from open windows.

Arden looked down at the dial of Jake's old pickup. In the strangest juxtaposition, this big man in the rusting truck was listening to classical, and he was whistling—on pitch—to Beethoven.

Arden watched Jake's dimpled cheeks puff, his perfect lips purse as he whistled.

The truck inched forward, and sun glinted through a set of birch, blinding Jake. He reached for his sunglasses on the console, catching Arden's stare as he turned.

Jake smiled, strumming his fingers on the wheel to the staccato of violins.

The strings reached a crescendo on the radio, and Arden's heart raced higher along with them.

I like this man, Arden thought, before whispering it to herself, as if she needed to say it to believe it. "I like this man."

"What?" Jake asked, sliding his sunglasses down onto the bridge of his nose to look at Arden. "Did you say something?"

Arden was about to say it—say "I really like you," to Jake—when a horn blared behind the truck.

"The smartest people always act so dumb on holiday weekends, don't they?" Jake asked, sticking his head out the window, and shaking it with bewilderment, before saying to Arden, "You have three options: Buy a season beach pass, buy a day pass, or turn around and go home. Pretty simple."

Life should be that simple, Arden thought, opting to remain quiet.

Slowly, the traffic began to inch forward. The lifeguard saw the season pass on the front of Jake's window and waved the truck through, Jake settling his old Ford into a narrow space tucked in front of a small dune that separated the back lot from the one nearest the water. Arden could only watch as Jake began to load himself up, draping towels around his neck, bags around his shoulders, chairs on his back, coolers and umbrellas in his strong hands, and slowly make his way up the dune, churning sand in his wake. "I got it!" he yelled back at Arden.

Once over the dune, the boardwalk greeted them. Jake lumbered down the warped boards, before turning right at the end to huff along the shoreline. After a few yards, he stopped suddenly and shrugged everything off his body and onto the sand.

"We're here!" He laughed, his face lathered in sweat. "Sorry, but it's as far as I could go."

The two began to set up their beach camp in earnest, silently choosing chores that fit them best—Jake pounded beach umbrellas deep into the sand with a rubber mallet while Arden lay out towels, anchoring them with flip-flops and coolers, arranging books, magazines, and drinks on each.

"We make a good team." Jake laughed.

Arden could feel her face flush as Jake smiled at her, and was thankful the sun was out in full force to disguise her redness. She took a seat on her big beach blanket—which featured a huge image of Dolly's Sweet Shop.

Arden looked out over Lake Michigan and sighed. It was one of those high seventies, low-humidity, northern Michigan afternoons that made locals' endurance of endless dark, lake-effect-snow-driven months of winter worth all the pain.

Such days in Michigan were magical but numbered, running typically from the Fourth of July until Labor Day.

One hundred days of summer, Arden remembered the locals calling their summer season, which started with Memorial weekend.

The odds of getting a perfect Memorial Day weekend were about as good as winning the lottery.

Arden lifted her face to the sun and suddenly smiled, feeling thankful.

Puffy, white clouds lazily floated about, mirroring the people in the water, the sky an almost unnatural, surreal blue, the sun seeming to smile, the light saturating every detail—the lake, the boats, the sand, the swimsuits, the grass on the dunes—so that it took on an almost magical quality, like when *The Wizard of Oz* switched from black and white to color. It was nearly too much for her eyes.

"You look . . . different," Jake said, jolting Arden from her reverie. "Happy."

Arden turned to him, as he finished pounding the last post into the sand.

"Sorry," he said. "Didn't mean to scare you. Worried about your mother?"

"Yes," she said. "But I'm actually thinking how beautiful this is."

Jake smiled, his bearded face opening brightly, his white teeth appearing like pearls in the daylight. He suddenly took off his tank top and dropped his long, khaki shorts to reveal a tight, box-cut swimsuit.

Arden's jaw dropped.

She couldn't help but stare at his body. In his scrubs and street clothes, Jake had appeared stocky, but now—bare chested—Arden could see he was pure muscle. His biceps bulged and his shoulder muscles lurched toward the sky like mini-mountains. His chest rippled, and etched into his stomach wasn't just a six-pack of abdominal muscles, but a full eight-pack. A trail of hair tousled in the lake breeze and led down to a set of thighs like marble pillars. In the sun, with the sand dunes behind him, Jake's skin was the color of gold.

Jake dropped the mallet into a beach bag and then sank onto a blanket on his knees like a falling pine. He popped open a LaCroix water that Arden had set out for him. With each motion, Arden's eyes followed him, transfixed.

"Aren't you going to change?" Jake asked casually.

Arden's heart jumped, and she looked down to assess her chosen outfit: A long-sleeve black T-shirt, yoga pants, and a Cubs ball cap, her dark glasses sitting atop a nose sporting enough gloopy, white suntan lotion to protect a small town.

She thought back to her days at school in Scoops. Whereas her mother wore wigs and garish makeup, Arden had tried to make herself invisible. Over the years, that look had become her trademark—the blunt bang, the dark glasses, the dull clothes—but she now realized she had been hiding under all of these layers as a way to insulate herself from any pain. She had made herself impenetrable to the tough world of Lolly, the tougher worlds of Chicago and *Paparazzi*, and the toughest world of them all: single men.

Arden desperately wanted to throw her arms around her body, protect herself, and take off running across the beach. But there was a magnetic quality to Jake, one that could make Arden do anything he asked.

Arden pulled off her black T-shirt and kicked off her yoga pants to reveal a red bikini she had borrowed from Lauren, just like she had the pink top and lip gloss when she'd surprised Jake.

I've never felt so naked, physically or emotionally, Arden thought.

"I don't know what I was thinking," Arden babbled. "I pulled it out of my daughter's suitcase . . . I just thought . . . I guess I . . ."

"Sssshhh," Jake said, putting a big finger over his lips to quiet her. "You look amazing."

"I spin. I do yoga. I run."

"It shows," Jake said, his eyes slowly taking in Arden's shape. "Do you mind putting some lotion on me?"

Jake stood, pulling Arden to her feet, and handed her a bottle. She was a little nervous, but she squeezed some lotion into her hands and began rubbing it onto Jake's broad back, across his muscled neck and shoulders, her heart racing.

He feels like steel, Arden thought, feeling butterflies in her stomach.

"Thanks," he said, giving her a smile that was equal parts innocent and sexy. "Your turn."

Arden stared at him, suddenly feeling herself flush.

Jake massaged lotion onto her shoulders and neck.

His hands! Can he feel my heart pounding through my skin? I hope not! she worried.

Jake tossed the lotion onto a towel and said, "Let's go for a swim."

"No. Too cold. Tried it already with my mom."

"It's Lake Michigan," he said. "It's always, shall we say, *refreshing.* You know that."

Without warning, Jake picked Arden up into his arms and sprinted into Lake Michigan, taking huge, romping steps like a pony. When he was waist deep, he dove headfirst—still holding Arden—into the water.

As Arden sunk, so did her glasses. Under the clear water of Lake Michigan, she watched her signature black frames sink to the bottom, where they came to rest on the sand and a few colorful lake stones. Without them, her vision became wavy, as if she were viewing everything—the sun above, the ripples, her own body—through a prism.

As Arden ascended, she could see her childhood reflected in the ripples. She remembered seeing her mother's face above the water when she taught her to swim. She pictured her mother waiting on the dock every time she floated on an inner tube.

She was always there for me, Arden remembered.

Arden came to the top, gasping for air, her body covered in goose bumps.

Perhaps my mother never left me. Perhaps, just perhaps, I had abandoned her when she needed me the most.

Jake swam over to Arden and reached out to her. "Are you okay? I'm sorry. Just wanted to have some fun."

"I'm fine. But I lost my glasses," she said, running a hand through her dripping hair. "I must look a mess."

"Actually, you look . . . beautiful," Jake said. "Wait here."

Without warning, Jake dove down.

Arden leaned forward to get a better look, but only her reflection stared back.

Arden gasped when she saw herself in the glassy surface of the big lake. Without her glasses and with her hair wet and tousled, she looked years younger. She looked softer, more feminine.

She looked like her mother and her daughter.

"Got 'em!" Jake yelled as he surfaced, holding Arden's glasses over his head like a prized pearl he had just plucked from the ocean's depths.

Suddenly, Arden leaned in and kissed Jake. Jake took Arden's body into his arms and chest. Her body exploded in more goose bumps.

Arden had never kissed or been kissed like this—with such abandon—and the blood rushed through her body, warming her even in the chilly lake water.

She looked up into the sky, the water rushing down her face.

"I'm right here," Jake said, holding her tightly. "You're safe."

For the first time in a very long time, Arden knew he was right. She thought of her mom and dad, of their first date here so long ago, and how life seems so big and yet is really made up of the smallest of moments, the most intricate of memories.

The two began to splash each other in the water, and that's when Arden realized something else, too: She was actually having fun.

Suddenly, she yanked her glasses out of Jake's big hands and tossed them into the sky.

"How can you see?" Jake gasped.

"I have contacts back at the cabin," Arden said. "I'll rely on you for now."

She hesitated, then continued, "But, with or without my glasses, I finally realized something."

"What?" Jake asked.

Arden smiled at Jake, but didn't respond. Instead, she dove back into Lake Michigan and let loose a happy scream that seemed to release decades of insecurity, unhappiness, obsessiveness, and worry. It was a scream that answered Jake's question of what she finally realized, even without her glasses:

I can see everything clearly for the first time in my life.

Forty-five

Lolly's voice drifted from her bedroom window and floated out to the dock where Lauren was painting.

Her grandmother was humming an old tune with which Lauren wasn't familiar, but it didn't matter: Her happy, lilting voice delighted Lauren, as well as the birds zipping about the lake, and they began to sing in unison with the oldest bird on Lost Land.

Lauren smiled and studied her painting of the three Lindsey ladies.

Something is missing, she pondered.

And that's when she heard it: The echo of her grandmother's charm bracelet jangling like the backbeat of a drum's cymbal to all the chirping.

That's it! Lauren exclaimed.

Lauren dipped her brush in the paint and began to add bracelets to the wrists of her and her grandmother, before slowly adding in the charms her grandmother had given her over the years as well as the charms whose stories her grandmother had shared the past week.

Oh, why not?

Lauren laughed and began to add a charm bracelet to her mother's wrist, too.

She stopped and studied her work, and then looked out over the lake.

Hundreds of tulips were in bloom—a crayon box of colors—giving the lake a paint-by-numbers feel.

Lauren stared at the flowers, tipping to and fro in the gentle breeze. Suddenly, her heart began to race. She picked up her paints, palette, and easel and began to run toward the cabin, screaming, "Grandma, Grandma, Grandma!"

"What is it, my dear? Are you okay?" Lolly yelled, alarmed, from her window. Her face, painted as brightly as the tulips, appeared at the screen. "Are the ground hornets already out? Did you get stung?"

"No!" Lauren yelled, stopping, out of breath. "Can I go with you into town?"

"I have to work until six," she said. "Are you sure?"

"Never been surer of anything in my life," Lauren said.

Forty-six

E xcuse me! Excuse me!"
        Lauren wove through the crowded sidewalks of downtown Scoops, weaving through fudgies moving at the pace of zombies.

"Sorry," she said, bumping arms laden with ice cream cones and lattes. "Pardon me!"

She had escorted her grandmother to Dolly's, acting casual but checking the time on her cell every minute, her pulse racing each time a group stopped Lolly to get their picture taken with her character, Dolly. As soon as her grandmother had entered the sweet shop, Lauren told her she wanted to go shopping and took off like a bullet, darting through the resorters like a crazed salmon swimming upstream. She zipped down the main drag before cutting toward the river, taking off in a sprint down the warped boardwalk, zipping past pontoon boats and yachts, sailboats and paddle boarders, outdoor bars jammed with revelers.

And that's when Lauren saw the brightly colored banner whipping in the wind, the reason she had decided on a whim to come to town with her grandmother:

75th ANNUAL TULIP QUEEN PAGEANT!
5 p.m., Memorial Day

Lauren stopped and caught her breath, taking in the scene. Scoops Park, the little town square overlooking the river, was rimmed in blooming tulips. The old Victorian pavilion, elevated on a white wicker platform and decorated in flowers and lights, served as the judges booth, while the parking lot that sat between the pavilion and The Mermaid, a popular waterside restaurant, had been filled with bleachers. In a corner of the park, an ancient weeping willow bent its arms into Scoops River, which swept them forward, giving the branches the appearance of a slow-moving street cleaner. Beyond the willow, a makeshift wooden platform jutted into the river.

Lauren nervously pulled her hair into a loose ponytail and made her way up the steps of the pavilion.

"Am I too late to sign up?" she asked.

A heavy woman with long white hair that had been pulled onto the top of her head, making it look as if she had a honey bun resting on her noggin, looked up and smiled. She was wearing a Tulip Queen sweatshirt and bright red sweatpants.

"You're a bit late, sweetie," she said, checking her watch. "It's one o'clock."

Lauren began to speak, but no words would come. Only tears.

"There, there. It's okay. What's the matter, sweetie?" the woman asked, reaching out to touch Lauren's arm. "You just need to fill out an application, give us the twenty-five dollar entrance fee, and have family that lives in Scoops."

Lauren wiped her eyes. "My grandma lives here. And my mom grew up here."

"Perfect," she said, pushing a form forward on the table and handing Lauren a pen. "It's just that a lot of these girls have been working on their gowns and talents for months."

"Gowns? Talent?"

"It's a pageant," the woman said, tapping her nail where Lauren needed to sign. "Miss Tulip is like Miss America. Except . . ."

The woman lowered her voice into a whisper and looked around suspiciously. ". . . except, well, some of our girls don't always look like Miss America."

Lauren laughed and handed the woman her form. She scanned it before surprising Lauren by shouting, "You're Lolly Lindsey's granddaughter? You're Ar-don't's daughter?"

Lauren nodded.

"Well, welcome, sweetie. This is sure gonna give this year's contest a little added drama now, isn't it?"

The woman leaned over the table and, for the first time, took a long, hard look at Lauren. "You sure don't look like your mama." She stopped and scanned the application again closely, lowering her half-glasses to the tip of her broad nose. "Just wanted to make sure you signed the waiver, sweetie. Just in case, given your family history."

"I'm very proud of my family history!" Lauren said defensively.

The woman gave Lauren a wink. "I'm just teasing you! Now, you best scoot, so you can go get a gown and work on your talent. See you at five!"

Lauren smiled, and then took off running, down the steps of the pavilion and then down the boardwalk, but not before turning around to take one last look at the platform.

"Excuse me! Excuse me!" she shouted at the fudgies, as she retraced her steps all the way back to Dolly's Sweet Shop. She reached the store just as her grandmother was finishing her one o'clock performance.

"Done shopping already?" Lolly asked, her eyes wide, surprised to see her granddaughter again so soon.

"Oh, Grandma," Lauren said, running directly into her arms. "I need your help."

Lolly's chin was quaking before her granddaughter had barely gotten the words out of her mouth.

"You're doing all of this for me?" she asked.

Then she stopped, grabbed Lauren's chin—her charm bracelet rattling—and looked deeply into Lauren's eyes, seeing her fierce determination.

"Time's a' wasting! We have a lot of work to do!"

Forty-seven

I wonder what this is all about?" Arden said, more to herself than to Jake. "You don't think? No."

She looked at her phone again, as Jake drove toward downtown Scoops in his pickup.

Arden reread aloud the text that had finally come through from Lauren as soon as she and Jake had just gotten back to the cabin.

"Meet me at Scoops Park at 5! DON"T BE LATE!"

"What do you think that means? What do you think is going on?"

Jake laughed, a rocky rumble that matched the engine of his truck. "I don't know, Agatha," he joked. "Maybe she wants to do a surprise dinner downtown. It is Memorial Day. Why are you making it into such a mystery?"

Arden's voice rose in surprise. "Because it's my daughter. You know girls her age. They're *always* up to something."

The truck bumped along the top of the dune road. To one side was the majestic view of Lake Michigan, stretching out to infinity like an ocean, its blue water meeting the blue sky, making it appear as if one huge, heavenly canvas had been stretched across the entire horizon. On the other side sat the river and the town—jammed with vacationers—and beyond Scoops were squares of green and ovals of blue, Mother Nature's patchwork quilt of farms, lakes, pastures, and vineyards.

Jake reached out and touched Arden's forearm. She dropped her phone in her lap and grabbed his hand. They drove that way until traffic into town became snarled, the tiny, two-lane road—no wider than a country bridge—unable to handle the giant SUVs sporting license plates from Chicago, St. Louis, Detroit, and Indianapolis.

"Over there!" Arden suddenly shouted, pointing at an empty space.

"I think your contacts work better than your glasses," he said, parking his truck. "And you certainly look even prettier without them."

The two took to the Scoops streets, falling into flow with the slowly meandering summer resorters, on their way for drinks and dinner. Arden grabbed Jake's hand and cut down a small alley between two restaurants, which spit the pair out just down the street from Dolly's.

"I became quite the expert at avoiding crowds my whole life in Scoops," Arden explained in a matter-of-fact way when Jake stared at her for taking the impromptu shortcut.

Arden peered through the window of Dolly's, but didn't see her mother. She looked at the clock on the window, but there was no time designated for the next show.

Alarmed, she zipped into the sweets shop and asked a young girl with two shades of hair—white on top, black underneath—"Where's my mother? Lolly? I thought she worked until six?"

"She said she had an emergency," the girl said, looking up as she rang a customer up.

"Was she okay?" Arden asked, alarmed.

"Totally," she responded. "Very happy. She took off with some young girl."

"Let's just go to the park," Jake said, pulling Arden out of the shop and toward the boardwalk. "That's where she said to meet."

"Something's just not right," Arden said, checking her cell as they walked.

4:59.

And that's when she saw it: The giant banner above the park announcing the Tulip Queen pageant.

Strains of terrible music suddenly began to blare over a pair of squeaky speakers. Pimply, ragtag members of the Scoops choir—dressed in hideously bright colored T-shirts—stood in front of a row of mics and began to sway like flowers in the wind, singing off-key The Andrews Sisters' song that had kicked off the Tulip Queen pageant for decades:

Tu-li-tu-li-tu-li-tulip time!

"Oh, no," Arden said, stopping in her tracks so quickly that a family of four nearly tripped over her body. "This is like reliving a nightmare."

Jake put his arm around Arden and led her to the bleachers. Arden squinted in the late afternoon sun, the reflection bouncing off the river, and yanked sunglasses from her purse.

From behind the bleachers, a row of girls dressed in colorful, sequined gowns began to walk in a line toward the platform in front of the pavilion. From a distance, they looked like one, long, undulating glittering snake seeking sun.

"Why am I here?" Arden asked out loud.

And then she saw why: At the very end of the snaking line stood her daughter.

"Lauren?"

Without thinking, Arden was on her feet.

"Lauren?!" she yelled at the top of her lungs. "Lauren! What are you doing?"

The crowd around her stared, alarmed by her shouts, cautiously sliding their rears away on the aluminum benches from the crazy woman.

In the distance, Lauren heard her mother yell, and she waved back enthusiastically, just like she had done when she was little and had to perform in a band concert.

"Don't alarm her," said Lolly, who was hiding under the last rows of the bleachers. "Just keep her calm."

Arden saw her daughter laugh. She put her hands around her eyes, scanning the narrow slats between the bleachers to get a better look.

Was that . . . ?

"Mother!" Arden yelled, standing on her bleacher. "I knew you were behind this!"

As Arden's screams traveled toward Lolly, she tried to hide behind a stranger's body, shadowing the surprised observer like Wile E. Coyote might in a cartoon.

"I can see your wig, Mother!"

Though Lolly's body was small and fragile, there was no mistaking—even from a distance—her mother's teased, flame red wig and rainbow makeup. From a distance, Lolly looked like a falling meteor.

Arden watched her daughter motion with both arms for her to take a seat. When Arden refused, Lauren crossed her hands in mock prayer. "Please!" she mouthed.

Arden stepped down off her bleacher and sat with a thud, crossing her arms in displeasure.

Tu-li-tu-li-tu-li-tulip time!

The choir finished its song with a weak warble, and was immediately replaced by an Up North bellow:

"We begin da pageant with da evening gown competition!" the emcee yelled, reverb causing the crowd to cover their ears. "Contestant number one is Molly Von Mancipher!"

Slowly, the contestants walked the runway, stopping in the center to pose, turn, and smile. One by one, Dutch blonde after Dutch blonde winked, blew kisses, tossed tulips, and pirouetted.

This is like the movie Groundhog Day . . . *I have to watch my life over and over again,* Arden thought, grimacing.

"Our final contestant is Lauren Lindsey from Chicago *and* Scoops! We have quite da world traveler!"

As Lauren took the stage, Arden watched her daughter gracefully float across the platform, as effortlessly as one of the white clouds bouncing overhead. Lauren stopped in midstage, posed, and turned.

Don't fall! Don't fall! Arden thought, tugging her earlobe and clamping her eyes shut in a panic, reciting the line in her head like a prayer, fingering the handle on her purse as if it were a rosary.

Don't fall! Don't fall! she prayed.

She opened them as Lauren continued to walk—beaming a smile with complete confidence.

NO! Is that . . . could that be . . . ? Arden's eyes widened.

Arden stood again, her hands over her mouth. She realized her daughter was wearing the same dress she had worn, the *exact* gown her mother had made for her decades earlier. And yet the yellow dress with the train of tulips that had looked so garish on her looked totally different on her daughter. Lauren was happy, beautiful, confident.

Arden's negative thoughts were swept from her head and replaced with a positive one:

The difference is my daughter is happy to be here, proud to wear that dress, proud to be a Lindsey.

From a distance, Lauren resembled a beautiful tulip come to life, sunshine radiating on her. Lauren's long hair had been pulled into a soft updo, blond tendrils falling around her face, chandelier earrings dangling to complement the simplicity.

All around her, the crowd buzzed. "Who is that?" "She's beautiful!" "Lindsey? No! Is *she* related to Lolly Lindsey? Was her mother Ar-don't . . . ?"

As the applause and whispering subsided, one other sound caught Arden's ears. In fact, she could hear it even in the bleachers, yards away from the platform. As Lauren crossed the runway, Arden noticed the only other jewelry Lauren sported was her own *and* her grandmother's charm bracelets.

Arden could feel her heart in her throat. Without thinking, she gripped Jake's hand. He put his arm around her.

"She looks just like you and your mother," he said, reaching out to kiss her on the cheek.

Arden smiled as Lauren exited the platform as if walking on air.

"Now for da talent competition!" the speakers boomed.

Arden's stomach lurched. The memory of her debacle—Tiny Tim, the ukulele, the wig, falling into the water—overwhelmed her, as the contestants began to dance, sing, and twirl batons on the platform. She tugged furiously at her lobe.

"Everything is going to be all right," Jake said, pulling her in close to reassure her. "*Everything!*"

"Our final contestant . . . Lauren Lindsey."

Arden gritted her teeth, her molars emitting an audible grinding sound.

As Lauren walked out, two pageant workers zipped onto the deck. One hastily set up an easel and placed a canvas on it, while another placed paints, a brush, and some water on a little table.

"I know this isn't as exciting as singing, or dancing . . . or my mom," Lauren said, eliciting a few titters from the crowd, "but I've never really put my talent on display for the world to see, or followed my calling. But I learned that now is the time."

Arden watched her daughter look offstage, and then Lauren began to paint.

"Picasso once said, 'Every child is an artist. The problem is how to remain an artist once he grows up,'" Lauren said to the crowd, as her brush danced over the canvas. "I never understood what he meant until recently . . . until I've gotten to know my grandmother—my family—a lot better."

Lauren quieted and continued to paint, the jangling of her charm bracelet carried on the breeze.

"Painting is like life," she said. "It requires a lot of patience, a lot of faith, a lot of passion. The beauty in great painting is capturing the emotion underneath the subject."

Lauren set her brush down, picked up the canvas, and began walking toward the crowd.

"This is the story of my family."

Lauren stopped and turned the portrait toward the audience, three generations of women seated together at the end of a warped dock, their images in the foreground older, wiser, damaged but strong, while their reflections in the water were from their youth—younger, sadder, lost but hopeful.

"This is a story of home . . . of *here*."

The crowd erupted in cheers, many standing to yell, "How much?" or "I want that."

"I'm overwhelmed," Arden said into Jake's strong shoulder, as he drew her in. "I thought . . . I expected . . ."

"Then stop," Jake said, as the crowd continued to cheer. "Expectations are just preconceived resentments."

Arden pulled away, her face etched in surprise. "Let me guess? Not Deepak Chopra?"

"No," Jake said. "Just a guy who has seen a lot of life and death. In the end, I think we all just want the same things: Family, happiness, love, faith."

"I've always felt like the world was stacked against me," Arden said.

"The world is stacked against everyone, Arden," Jake said. "But now I'm here for you."

He patted his shoulder, and Arden rested her head on it, as the emcee's voice squeaked over the speakers.

"Last up," the announcer said, "da Q and A."

"I never made it this far," Arden said.

"Really? I'm shocked. Your question could have been, 'Is that the backstroke or the dog paddle?'" Jake teased, giving Arden a hug.

Arden melted into a puddle of laugher.

"My question to today's contestants is this," the emcee stated. "Name da most influential person in your life."

Girl after girl responded: "Daddy," "Jesus," or "Tom Izzo, the Michigan State basketball coach."

"Finally, Lauren Lindsey," the emcee said, as the group of contestants stood on the platform over the river. "Please name da most influential person in your life."

Lauren stepped to the mic in the middle of the stage, stared out over the river and then scanned the crowd.

She stopped and caught her breath. When she began again, her voice was as wavy as the current of the Scoops River.

"My grandmother," she said. "Life has not always been easy on her: She's lost everything and everyone, at one time, and yet she has somehow managed not only to survive but also to believe in the beauty of the world. She has remained an optimist. She has fun in this life, no matter what. I've learned that you can plan your life all you want, but you can't control it. You have to dive headfirst into it, experience its joys and pains . . . you have to live . . . and then you have to share those stories with the ones you love before it's too late."

Lauren stopped and cleared her throat. Quiet enveloped the bleachers. Lauren could hear the wind float across the water, and, as it did, catch her charm bracelets and make them sing. She looked over at the ancient weeping willow, whose arms were sweeping in the river, singing in the breeze, joyously telling the secrets of its own past. Lauren smiled and said, "Grandma, would you join me on stage?"

Lolly—as bright as the sun—slowly made her way out to the platform. Lauren took her hand, and brought her into her body.

"This pageant has long been my grandmother's dream. Her whole life, she's supported everyone else's dreams, sacrificed herself to make others happy. I wouldn't be standing here today without her."

Lauren hesitated but continued. "We need to take time to get to know our elders, because they have led lives we can barely imagine. I've come to appreciate that our elders—our grandmothers—are not only the pillars of our families, the charms in our lives, but also the bridges to our past and the steppingstones to our future. Today is not only for my grandmother, but for all the grandparents in the world who fought for all of us to have better lives."

There was silence for a few seconds, before the crowd began to clap. That applause turned into a roar, and, quickly, the crowd was on its feet, screaming. Arden looked around: Many were wiping tears from their faces.

"That's my daughter!" Arden began to yell, pointing toward the stage. "And that's my mother! Lolly!"

As the applause died down and the judges began to deliberate, Arden looked up at the pines and the birch that circled the park, and she smiled. Arden could see her mother in those trees: They bent but never broke; they believed good days were to come in spite of the often bad weather; they loved the simplicity of nature and life; and they were always reaching toward heaven.

"What is it?" Jake asked.

"Is this what it's like to be happy?" Arden asked.

Jake studied her face, uncertain of what she was asking.

"To just be in the moment?" she continued. "Not running or planning or working. Just enjoying this very second of life, without trying to perfect it, change it, or run from it?"

"Yes," Jake said.

"I like happy," Arden replied. "It's a very nice place. Like Michigan."

She stopped.

"And I also . . . well, I also . . . really like you," Arden said, finally saying the words she had longed to get out.

Jake grabbed Arden's face and kissed her, inhaled her, held her, and
didn't stop even after the crowd began to catcall. Jake removed a hand from
behind Arden's neck and began to encourage the crowd with it.

"And I really like you, too, Arden," Jake said, pulling Arden into his big
body.

"Da judges have da decision!" the emcee announced over the loud-
speaker.

Arden jerked upright. "Here we go!"

"I didn't think you wanted to be here," Jake razzed her.

"Ssshhhh!"

"Ladies and gentlemen, it's now time to announce da first runner-up and
new Tulip Queen. Are you ladies ready?"

The twenty girls clutched hands and clamped their eyes shut. "The first
runner-up is . . . Tara Milligan!"

A pretty blonde in an eggplant-colored gown claimed her tulips and a
new sash, and stepped to the side.

"And, now, da moment we've all been waiting for . . . the Seventy-Fifth
Annual Tulip Queen is . . . Lauren Lindsey!"

The crowd screamed its approval, and Arden didn't realize she was
crying until she could taste her mascara.

The emcee placed a Tulip Queen sash across Lauren's shoulder while
the outgoing queen placed a crown atop Lauren's blond head and handed
her a huge bouquet of colorful tulips and a little box wrapped in a bright
ribbon.

"Introducing your 2014 queen, Lauren Lindsey! Lauren, you may take
your coronation walk!"

Lauren raised her arms and waved to the crowd as she made her way
across the platform. At the end of the platform, she held out her arms, and
her grandmother came running into them. The two then walked—hand
in hand—back across the stage. Lolly raised her left arm, and cupped her
hand, waving it like a true queen.

She's waited her whole life for this moment, Arden thought, and smiled.

She stopped, watching her mother and daughter, and then amended that thought: *Lauren has waited her whole life for this moment, too.*

Lauren stopped in the middle of the platform, removed the crown, and bent over and placed it on her grandmother's head, securing it to her wig. Lolly touched it, ran her hands over the points and rhinestones, as if it were magical, and then hugged her granddaughter tightly.

Both returned to the coronation area, where the contestants mobbed them. Arden grabbed Jake's hand and began dragging him down the bleachers.

"Congratulations!" Arden screamed when she reached her daughter and mother. "What a surprise! How did you two manage to pull this off?"

"Teamwork," they both said in unison, laughing.

"And Spanx," Lauren added.

Arden smiled and took the hands of her mother and daughter in hers.

"Seriously," she asked, giving their arms a gentle shake. "How did this happen?"

"I was painting this morning—I was painting *us*, all of us—and I could see everything so clearly for once," Lauren said. "Everything seemed—oh, I don't know—*possible* and *exciting*. I thought of all the stories Grandma has been telling us. I thought of all she had done for us, and I thought, there has to be something I can do for her. And there was."

Lauren dropped her mother's hand, repositioning the tulips to her other arm, and handed her grandmother the gift box she had been given after her win.

"I think this is for you, Grandma," Lauren said.

Lolly opened the little box with shaking hands. Inside sat a silver charm of a tiara. "Oh, I can't, Lauren," Lolly protested.

"I insist, Grandma," Lauren said, handing her mother the tulips and carefully adding the charm to her grandmother's bracelet, which she took off her own wrist and placed back on Lolly's slender wrist.

Lolly held up the bracelet to her face. "Every woman deserves to feel like a queen, even for a day," she said quietly. "You know, this is the one charm I always wanted. It's the one I never thought I'd get, and one day it will be yours, my dear."

She hesitated.

"It's the one I'll never forget."

Lolly gave her bracelet a robust shake and then pulled her granddaughter close.

"I love you, more than anything," she whispered.

"Me, too, Grandma."

"I've had the best time this past week," Lolly smiled, surveying her girls' faces. "It's nice to have my family back for a little while."

"I've had the best time, too, Mom," Arden said. "It's nice to have my mother back. I'm just so sorry . . . for . . . well . . . everything."

"Can't change the past," Lolly said. "But you can change the future."

"Speaking of which," Lauren said, "can I talk to you for a minute, Mom?"

Jake picked up on Lauren's need for some privacy. "You look like a real beauty queen with that crown, Lolly. Mind showing me how you do that pageant wave so well?"

Lolly smiled broadly. "Of course," she said, walking toward the river with Jake, the two looking like a modern version of Abbott and Costello. "First, you have to cup your hand . . . like this."

Lauren laughed, as she led her mother over to the corner of the park, where they took a seat on a bench underneath the massive weeping willow.

For a few moments, the two watched boats—big and small—float by on the river, some heading out to the big lake for sunset, some heading back to the dock. Finally, Lauren broke the silence.

"I'm staying with Grandma, Mom."

Arden shook her head, not comprehending what her daughter had just said. "What?" She shook her head again. "What did you just say?"

"I've decided to stay with Grandma. And I've been looking into attending Interlochen for the summer. It's a great art school, Mom. It's only a few miles away. I can help Grandma. I'll work with her at Dolly's. And she's offered to help with tuition. It will help ease your financial burden, too."

Arden's heart raced. "Is this your grandmother's idea?"

As soon as the words left her mouth, Arden wished they had been attached to a rubber band, and she could just easily retract them, but it was too late.

"No, Mom, this was actually Lexie's idea at first," Lauren said, her eyes wide. "What this has all been about is healing. Grandma's 'influence' has been good for us all. Aren't you happier now than you were a few weeks ago?"

"Yes," Arden said without hesitation.

"So am I. So is Grandma. She needs *me*, Mom. And I think I need her even more."

"What about your internship this summer, Lauren? What about your future?"

"I never applied for one, Mom," Lauren said sheepishly. "I just can't imagine . . ."

Lauren began to cry softly. "I've just been so unhappy, Mom. And I'm happy with Grandma. I'm inspired here. An artist doesn't need an internship. An artist needs inspiration and a safe place to create. I have found that here. My future is here for a little while. Let me find myself this summer. I need you to be okay with that."

Arden looked out over the water, sighed, and then smiled and took her daughter's hand. The two sat in silence and continued to watch the boats pass. As the sun lowered behind the dunes, a chill quickly settled over them.

"Lauren, I admire and love you so much. But do you understand how much care your grandmother will require? Do you understand that her bad days will eventually outweigh her good ones? That is a huge burden on anyone, but especially a young woman whose life is just beginning."

"I know, Mom. I've talked extensively with her doctor about it." Lauren hesitated, but continued. "I've even talked with Jake about it."

"You have?" Arden asked, trying to hide her upset.

"Mom, he echoed the same concerns you did," she said. "But he also said he'd be here to help. I know that eventually Grandma will need more care. And, ultimately, she will likely have to go into a place that can better address her needs. But, right now, what she needs is family. What *I* need is family. What *we all* need is family. I want to be here, Mom. I want to be with her."

"You're a good person, Lauren, but it's such an obligation."

Lauren smiled and looked her mother square on, her blue eyes unflinching. "It's not an obligation to me, Mom. It's a *privilege*. I want her to know— every single day—that it has been my privilege to be her granddaughter."

Arden hugged her daughter. "I can't stay, though. I have to go back to work. Van has been pressing me about coming back."

"We all understand that. It's not about guilt anymore, or running. It's about being a family. Supporting one another. But remember, you need to find yourself, too. You need to write, Mom."

Lauren held her mother by the shoulders. "You need to tell them you're a writer, not an online editor. If they don't let you write, find someplace that will. And you need to finish your book. Even if it's never published, it's important to who you are."

"I have to make a living, honey."

"You're so driven and so talented, Mom. Think of what you could be, not what everyone else wants you to be. Right?"

Over Lauren's shoulder, Arden could see her mother showing Jake how to cup his hand to wave like a princess.

"He's a great guy, Mom. Make the long distance thing work, okay?" Lauren said, giving her mom a gentle shake, before finally noticing her changed appearance. "No glasses? Makeup? Tousled hair? You look amazing, Mom!"

The two hugged again, until Lolly's voice shattered the moment. "Drinks on me! The old crow is taking everyone to the Old Crow!"

Lauren and Arden stood, and the foursome started toward the ancient outdoor bar that overlooked the lake.

"What exactly does royalty drink?" Lauren asked her grandmother, taking her hand in hers, their bracelets tingling.

Lolly smiled. "Anything she darn well wants, my dear, especially," she said, stopping to curtsy and touch her tiara, "when a queen gets to be my age."

epilogue

The Book Charm

To a Story That Will Never End

July 4, 2014—Arden, Lauren, and Lolly

H urry! The show's starting!" my mother yells from the yard.

I peek off the screened porch, and—for a moment—all I can see are fireflies blinking, briefly illuminating the steppingstone path, the dock, and the still waters of Lost Land Lake in the twilight.

But then . . . *BOOM!*

An explosion of colorful fireworks suddenly lights the skies, as if God has plucked out His own crayon box and set to work on coloring the heavens.

I can see my mom standing there just like a kid, slack-jawed, looking up, her hands on her heart. She is barefoot, a jacket wrapped around her waist, her old body perched on a single steppingstone, her red wig mimicking the flaming trail of the fireworks as they fall toward the lake.

This is her night, I say to the old cabin.

Beyond the fireworks, I can see so many changes lingering on the horizon. Come September, the air will turn chilly, and Lauren will be attending art school full time and staying here. Her father has even offered to help us more.

He is happy now, I am happy now, and that has made us kinder, more generous.

We are all happy now. Happiness, I've learned, is not only quite magical, but also contagious.

Yes, my mother requires more help, but she is holding her own right now, and Jake comes every other day. He adores her. He loves *me*.

I have to say it again to myself: He *loves* me.

"Hurry!" I yell into the cabin.

I hear Lauren's charm bracelet first, followed by the squeaks of the wood floor. A large circle of light temporarily blinds me.

"Think we'll need this?" Lauren asks.

My eyes adjust to see she is holding an old flashlight, held together by decades of masking tape. Behind Lauren, I can see her portrait of us hanging on a log wall.

"No," I say, nodding toward the blinking fireflies and fireworks outside. "There's enough light."

"Got it?" Lauren whispers.

"Yep," I say, touching the pocket of my hoodie.

The screen door bangs shut, and Lauren and I join my mother. Slowly, we three make our way to the end of the dock.

There are sounds of summer I now know will stay with me forever, no matter where I live or what I do, sounds that I will hear as I take my last breath. *This* summer orchestra will always remain in my ears: Bullfrogs moaning, cicadas chirping, hummingbirds zipping, fish jumping, dragonflies fluttering like violins, the mournful call of loons, the excited yells of children, and boat engines on the water.

But, mostly, I will forever hear the jangling of my mother's charm bracelet.

It is getting very dark now, and I stumble on the edge of a stepping-stone. I was wrong to have told Lauren to forego the flashlight.

My mother grabs my hand to steady me and our wrists collide, setting our charm bracelets jangling. Lauren giggles, and I can hear her grab her grandmother's other hand.

"You're wearing your bracelet again," my mom says, her voice lifting.

My mother's touch fills me not only with love but also with strength. It centers me. I now know that I have been blessed with the greatest gifts any woman could ever have. It just took a great teacher to show me.

My mother's charms, I now know, aren't just charms. They are pieces of her, hard won through love, loss, and life.

I take my fingers and begin to feel for her charms, trying to guess each one by touch rather than sight, wondering if her lessons have stuck.

"Your sewing machine!" I say.

"To a life bound by family," my mom replies.

"Your kite!" I say.

"To a life filled with high-flying fun!"

"Hmmm," I start, feeling the charm. "Oh! A puzzle piece."

"To a life filled with friends who complete you!"

My fingers continue to move, rifling through her many charms until I no longer simply feel their silhouettes, I can actually feel their power vibrate.

"An ice cream cone, a mustard seed, and a loon!"

"To a life filled with a passion for what you do, to a life filled with faith, and to a life filled with a love that always calls you home!"

My mother slows and sighs. "You came home."

"I never really left," I say.

We take a seat at the end of the dock and dangle our feet in the water, the fireworks lighting up Lost Land Lake.

"Happy birthday, Mom! All those fireworks are for you! The world is celebrating your uniqueness!"

My mother squeezes my hand tightly. She knows that I have remembered her stories.

I pull a little box out of my hoodie pocket and my mother yelps in surprise, reaching out her hands for her present, just like a kid.

"No," Lauren says, laughing. "You have to recite the poem first, Grandma."

"I'm *way* too old for this."

"You will never be too old for this," I say. "Let's do it together!"

This charm
Is to let you know
That every step along the way,
I have loved you so.

So each time you open up,
A little box from me
Remember that it really all
Began with You and Me.

"That's right," I say. "Now, here you go."

My mother tears open the tiny box, and there, sitting atop a little velvet throne, is a silver charm.

"What is it?" my mother asks, squinting in the darkness.

"It's a book," I say.

My mother pulls it from the box and studies it, rubbing her old hands over its delicate outline.

"What's it mean, Arden?"

"It's to a story that will never end," I say.

I smile and lean into my mom. She is warm, safe, and smells of summer, a mixed bag of scents, from perfumed peonies to firewood from making s'mores.

"I put all of our initials on the back of the charm," I say. "We are forever the authors of our very own book."

There is silence as my mom adds the charm to her bracelet. Finally, I say, "And I'm writing again, Mom. Not only at *Paparazzi* but also the story of your charms. The story of us . . . all of us. I finally found my voice again."

I can hear my mother cry softly.

"I'm so happy," she finally says, before adding, very seriously, "Promise me something, girls."

"Anything," we reply in unison.

"Promise me you will always wear your charm bracelets," she says. "That way, we'll never be apart. That way, you'll never forget."

"We'll never forget, Mom," I say.

My mom looks out over the lake as fireworks illuminate the sky once again, and she puts her arms around our shoulders, drawing her girls even closer. As colorful fireworks explode overhead, she kisses our cheeks.

"I will always love you, Arden," she says. "I will always love you, Lauren."

"We love you, too."

A breeze as soft as my mother's kisses rushes across the water and over the lip of the dock to jangle our bracelets.

"You know, some people say they hear the voices of their family in this lake: In the call of the whippoorwill, the cry of the loon, the moan of the bullfrog," my mom whispers. "But I hear my family's voices in the jangling of our charms."

The way she says this makes goose bumps cover my body.

I turn to look at my mom. In the distance, fireworks explode again, a strobe of light illuminating her aging face. I can see her rosy cheeks dotted with summer freckles, even under all that makeup. It is as if a million paparazzi have arrived to capture her image, so I will never forget how she looks at this very moment.

Beautiful. Happy, I think.

I look even closer, and I can still see tears streaming down her face.

"Are you okay, Mom?" I ask.

"Sixty-one years ago today," she whispers over the echoing booms of the fireworks, "was my last birthday with my mom. But you two . . . you two have given me the greatest gift ever. You are my living history. My stories won't die with me."

My heart leaps into my throat, and I can feel myself begin to choke up, too.

I take a deep breath and force my tears to stop their rise.

For I am not sad. I am *blessed.*

I am the keeper of my mother's memories.

And when I am her age, I hope to sit here with my daughter, and my grandchildren, as the fireworks explode.

I will sit patiently and wait for the wind to rattle my charm bracelet— which will be even heavier than my mom's is now—and I will shut my eyes, and I will listen to the voices of my family.

Acknowledgments

I always preach to aspiring writers that they should write what calls to them, no matter what anyone else thinks, because that writing will truly become inspired work and thus inspire others. Moreover, that work will call to you—if not haunt you—until you finish it.

I also tell writers that the end goal of success or money is never the most important thing when you come from this place: Writing *is* the reward. You do it because, well, there is no other choice.

This is so true with *The Charm Bracelet*.

My grandmothers and their charm bracelets were the inspiration for this highly personal novel that honors and pays tribute not only to them (the book bears my grandmother's name as a pseudonym) but also our elders, who we too often take for granted and whose incredible lives we too often overlook.

As I grew older, I—like most of us do—got caught up in things that seemed important but really weren't. In my quietest moments, I could still hear in my mind the jangling of my mother's and grandmothers' bracelets, and that sound reminded me of what was truly important in life, that the smallest things are the greatest gifts.

I spent my summers with my grandparents, usually at an old log cabin in the Ozarks, always without a phone, a TV, a microwave. It was the time before cell phones, wireless, and laptops. We only had inner tubes, books, fishing poles, and one another. But I received the greatest gift of all those summers: I got to know my grandparents as people, beautiful, flawed, wonderful humans whose sacrifices and journeys helped make me who I am.

What I ask of you is this: Take a moment, if you have yet to do so, and ask your elders about their lives. Put down your phones and listen. They will astound you.

I couldn't be prouder of this novel, which took me many years (and tries) to perfect. After writing four memoirs, I learned that writing a novel is—as my esteemed agent, Wendy Sherman, told me—akin to wrestling a bear to the ground. Well, I wrestled the bear to the ground and got pretty torn up along the way. But I learned a lot, too. The journey has been so worth it. An artist, I believe, should always be a bit uncomfortable in their work. It makes you question, worry, wonder, stretch, and ultimately, better.

That's a great transition to Wendy, whom I just can't thank enough . . . not only for being a great agent and friend, of course, but also for being much more than that. See, I didn't think I could do this. And you never stopped believing in me. You guided, you coached, you taught, you listened, you cheered, you worried, but you never dished out false BS. Did you send me packing quite a few times? Yep. But I listened. Over and over. And when I knew you liked it, when I knew you were ready, when I said, "I'm scared," you said, "Let me be your parachute."

To Laurie Chittenden: *Reunited and it feels so gooood* . . . Sorry, but I'm a Peaches & Herb–era guy. Honestly, I couldn't have dreamed of a better fit for this novel, and to be back with you a decade after *America's Boy*—after we have both grown and changed so much—seems as if it has always been part of a bigger plan. Your early enthusiasm for *The Charm Bracelet* (I mean, you have a charm bracelet!) has meant the world. You have also helped make this book infinitely deeper, richer, and more resonant. It's never "work" to work with you.

Speaking of early and ongoing enthusiasm: To the entire team at St. Martin's Press and Thomas Dunne Books—Sally Richardson, Tom Dunne, Pete Wolverton, Jen Enderlin, and Lisa Senz—huge, heartfelt thanks. I have never been met with such a warm embrace, and it means the world.

Thanks also to Melanie Fried (a Michigan girl!) as well as Cameron Mac-Leod Jones, whose charm illustrations were (pardon the pun) absolutely charming and truly captured the beauty and sentimentality of the novel and my family's charms.

To Jenny Meyer: *Gracias! Danke schön! Grazie!* How many ways are there to say thank you? You seem to have found plenty! Truly, an author's dream is to see their work published around the world, and you have made that dream come true. To see offers for *The Charm Bracelet* to be translated into German, Russian, Italian, Polish, Spanish, and on and on has made me cry every time. You are amazing at what you do. And a wonderful person to boot. (Same to you, Shane King!)

Heartfelt thanks to Kim Perel, who offered wonderful early insights and directions for making this book come to life.

Huge hugs to McLean & Eakin Booksellers (Jess, Bess, and Kirstyn . . . and, of course, you, too, Matt!) and Jill Miner and Jody Chwatun at Saturn Booksellers, who were also early readers of the manuscript, and who took time from their insane schedules to offer key, critical feedback that made this book better. I would not be here without you.

Caroline Leavitt: Your talents know no limits. You are not only an amazing writer, you are also a gifted editor. You pushed me, encouraged me, and—more than anything—believed in me when my soul needed a major hug. You also helped me at the drop of a hat more times than I can count with more things than I can count. I am so proud to call you a friend. We are manic, creative, kindred spirits.

Nancy Thayer: I remember how nervous I was reaching out to you. I remember how gracious you were in return. Thank you isn't enough. I adore you.

Debbie Macomber: Reaching out to Debbie for an early blurb was sort of like me saying, "I'm going to fly to the moon." It didn't seem possible. But that's the thing about dreams: They often come true. Thank you, Debbie. Your early support was instrumental in this book's momentum and success. For you to squeeze my book into your insane schedule is beyond humbling. And to Renate Roth: Thanks for helping every step of the way!

Adriana Trigiani: To see a flurry of exclamation points and *x*'s and *o*'s from you and then seeing you would love to blurb my book nearly landed me in the hospital. But being hoarse the next day was so worth it. You are one of my inspirations. Your kindness equals your talent.

To my mutts, Doris and Mabel: You keep me sane. Along with wine, coffee, and lots of running. And wine.

Finally, to Gary: I wouldn't be here—quite literally—without you. I asked you over and over and over if I could write a novel. You never wavered in your support. You never said I was crazy. You never told me to stop. You said, "You can do anything, and you will. Dream big. Write small." You have often joked that you are "my muse." Well, I have news for muse: You are. And you are my heart, soul, spirit, codependent copilot and love of my life. Here's to the next chapter. And the next . . .

As much as *The Charm Bracelet* celebrates my love for my grandmothers, it also celebrates my love for Michigan, its beauty and its people. Michigan isn't just the place where I live. It's also a main character in my writing. It is as real and human and alive and breathing as any of my protagonists. I am my best in Pure Michigan, author, human, husband.

And a final note regarding the poem in *The Charm Bracelet*: Over the years I spent writing this book, many friends sent me photos of their charm bracelets as well as the stories behind their charms to inspire me. Some sent poems that had been given to them by their mothers and grandmothers. Oftentimes, though the poems varied, some of the lines were the same. I pulled some of those beautiful lines together to create the poem, and then, thinking there might be an author behind it since there were so many similarities in what was sent to me, went in search of the poet. But I could never find an attribution. The closest I could come was a link on Yahoo Answers many years ago, in which someone had asked for a poem to go along with a charm bracelet they were giving their stepdaughter. I reached out to the person who had posted that poem, which also contained similar lines, but never received a response. I also posted the poem far and wide, but never found the source.

everything
I ate

(a year in the life of my mouth)

by tucker shaw

CHRONICLE BOOKS
SAN FRANCISCO

Library of Congress Cataloging-in-Publication Data available.
ISBN 0-8118-4772-1
Manufactured in China.

Design by JAY PETER SALVAS
The text of this book was typeset in Gotham 5 3/4/9,
   Berthold Akzidenz Grotesk, and Adobe Caslon

Distributed in Canada by Raincoast Books.
9050 Shaughnessy Street
Vancouver, British Columbia V6P 6E5

10 9 8 7 6 5 4 3 2 1

Chronicle Books L.L.C
85 Second Street
San Francisco, California 94105

www.chroniclebooks.com

Thanks for feedin me.

Dedicated to

all the cooks + kitchens
of New York City.
(You're the real heroes)
Let's eat!

Must write
Thanks to — GRAM who understood.

CHRIS + DOC		· Dan M.
Sam S.		· Mikyla ← hottie
Scott S.	Danny	· Bill L.
Gray C.	Jorge	· Jay Peter !!
Andy	Dad	· Carrie B, Jan H,
Deb	Moms	· Doug O., Beth S,

Alex, Henry, Marc,
Chris, Andrea, Susan,
Tim (A&M), Jay, Steven,
Buzz, everyone @

· Leslie D, Bridget W,
and James.
and Brenda Tucker
Chronicle Rules!!
Gonzo! Yum.

I ♡ my Canon Elph !

In 2004 I took a picture of everything I ate. Everything. Meals, snacks, scraps, appetizers, main courses, desserts, intermezzos, free samples, and amuchies. If I ate it in 2004, I shot it. My camera, my Elph, missed <u>nothing</u>.

And when I was done, I had thousands of pictures of the food I ate. Thousands.

"Are you sure you want us to publish these photos?" asked my editor through my crackly cell phone. "They're pretty personal, you know."

I choked on the egg sandwich I'd just photographed. She's right, I thought. They are pretty personal. I chewed, swallowed, and deliberated. I came to the careful conclusion...

Eh, what the hell?

what the hell? what the hell?

And so what started out as a silly ~~challenge~~ challenge to myself, a simple dare to record every single thing that I ate for a year, had turned into something else: a ridiculously comprehensive, unedited, full-color, skin-on, bone-in chronology of a year in my life.

Sure, it's just a bunch of pictures of food, none of them all that great. But it's the most honest thing I've ever done. There are no secrets in these pictures. Nothing is missing.

There are meals I loved (May 10), meals I hated (July 11), and meals I couldn't afford (December 16). There are months I was too busy and too flush to bother to cook, when I ate out every night. There are the broke months when I made everything myself (and some of it was pretty damn good.)

There's the trout I caught — my first — which I cleaned myself and stuffed with apples, sage, and bacon and cooked over the campfire (July 21). There are steaks (January 10, April 13, May 2), falafels (Sept 10), cookies in Chinatown (March 7, October 6), courtside snacks (April 19, July 29). There are pork shoulders I braised (October 29), zitis I baked (Apr 12) and risottos I mastered (Oct 14).

I celebrated friends' birthdays (Feb 1), career moves (April 1), and holidays (Apr 5, Dec 25). I traveled: to Vegas (April), Italy (May), San Francisco (October). I drove to Montana (July), had oral surgery (May 13), and turned a year older (Dec 5). I had a flicker of romance (April) that burned out too fast. I had Salisbury Steak in the shadow of Mt. Rushmore (July 14) and a hot dog in Central Park

(March 14). I had one last dinner with my grandfather (Sept 3) before attending his funeral. (Oct 2).

There are friends in the pictures. Family. Coworkers, acquaintances, people I barely remember. There's New York City, my best friend ever.

When I look at what I ate, I remember everything. I remember what it tasted like. I remember where I was, who was there, how I felt, whether we laughed. I remember the choices I made and the consequences they brought.

I wanted to remember what I ate in 2004, oatmeal to foie gras. Now maybe I will.

January

January

January

01 2:34 PM **Cold pizza from Two Boots. Sausage and onion.** 02 8:47 PM **Cereal at home.** 03 9:02 PM **Trail mix at home.**

MONTH

JAN

FEB

MAR

APR

MAY

JUN

JUL

AUG

SEP

OCT

NOV

DEC

DATE

01/01

DAY

THU

01 8:28 AM **Oatmeal and OJ at home.** 02 9:40 AM **Brioche and coffee at work.** 03 3:50 PM **Movie snax.**
Calendar Girls **with Jorge.** 04 6:16 PM **Nuts at home.** 05 7:12 PM **Cheese and crackers at Susan and Andrea's.**
06 9:09 PM **Salad, bruschetta, pasta with clams from Tanti Baci.** 07 9:50 PM **Hershey's Hugs at home.**

MONTH

JAN

FEB

MAR

APR

MAY

JUN

JUL

AUG

SEP

OCT

NOV

DEC

DATE

01/02

DAY

FRI

01 10:12 AM "Everything" bagel and coffee from Bagel Buffet. 02 1:00 PM Eggs Nova at Elmo with Alex, Tim, Susan, Andrea, and Henry. 03 3:55 PM Workout Boost shake from Equinox. 04 6:11 PM Peanuts and raisins at home. 05 7:11 PM Spinach at home. 06 8:44 PM Movie snax. *Monster* with Jorge, Wayne, Robert, and Danny. 07 1:00 AM Turkey sandwich at home. 08 1:42 AM Hershey's Kisses at home. 09 2:23 AM Grilled cheese and tomato from Manatus with Danny.

MONTH

JAN
FEB
MAR
APR
MAY
JUN
JUL
AUG
SEP
OCT
NOV
DEC

DATE

01/03

DAY

SAT

01 11:11 AM **Banana and coffee.** 02 1:12 PM **Chips and salsa at Rocking Horse with Alex, Susan, Andrea, and Henry.** 03 1:36 PM **Huevos rancheros at Rocking Horse.** 04 5:14 PM **Odwalla Superfood at home.** 05 5:33 PM **Beef jerky at home.** 06 6:15 PM **Carrot at home.** 07 8:08 PM **Mock cassoulet with spinach at home with Danny, Jorge, and Robert.** 08 9:40 PM **Hot-water gingerbread and ice cream at home.**

MONTH

JAN
FEB
MAR
APR
MAY
JUN
JUL
AUG
SEP
OCT
NOV
DEC

DATE

01/04

DAY

SUN

01 12:16 PM **OJ at home.** 02 12:23 PM **Scrambled eggs at home.** 03 2:37 PM **Wonton soup and mixed vegetables with white rice from Mama Buddha.** 04 8:10 PM **Tekka maki dinner, hijiki on the side, from Monster Sushi.** 05 8:51 PM **Leftover gingerbread at home.** 06 9:59 PM **Entenmann's donut at home with Danny.**

MONTH

JAN
FEB
MAR
APR
MAY
JUN
JUL
AUG
SEP
OCT
NOV
DEC

DATE

01/05

DAY

MON

01 2:15 PM **Pita City falafel on 7th Avenue with Mike and Marc.** 02 8:14 PM **Penne with veal ragout at home.**
03 10:37 PM **Honey Bunches of Oats at home.**

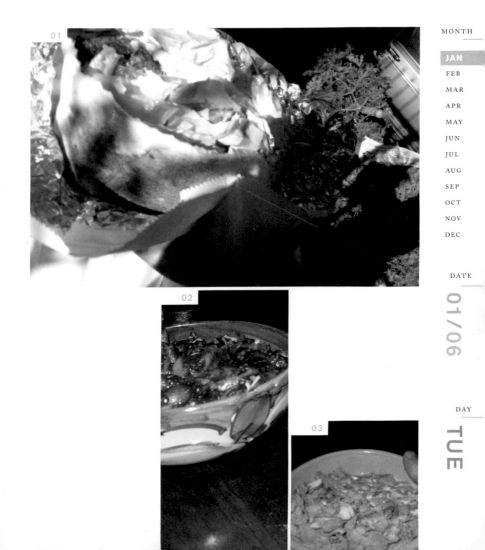

MONTH

JAN
FEB
MAR
APR
MAY
JUN
JUL
AUG
SEP
OCT
NOV
DEC

DATE

01/06

DAY

TUE

01 9:30 AM **Croissant, coffee, Odwalla Wellness at work.** 02 1:03 PM **BLT and Diet Coke at Elmo with Josh.** 03 6:56 PM **Beef jerky at home.** 04 7:24 PM **Popcorn at home.** 05 8:42 PM **Bacon Burger Deluxe from Bus Stop at home.** 06 9:50 PM **Honey Bunches of Oats at home.**

MONTH

JAN

FEB

MAR

APR

MAY

JUN

JUL

AUG

SEP

OCT

NOV

DEC

DATE

01/07

DAY

WED

01 9:34 AM Oatmeal and coffee from Murray's Bagels at work. 02 12:56 PM Lentil soup at Elmo with Andy.
03 1:06 PM Salmon BLT at Elmo. 04 7:53 PM Nuts at home. 05 8:20 PM Bread and olive oil at Gonzo with Chris.
06 8:26 PM Soppressata pizza at Gonzo. 07 8:44 PM Arugula and Parmegiano-Reggiano at Gonzo. 08 8:45 PM
Eggplant caponata; meat plate with speck, bresaola, and boiled ham; crostini at Gonzo. 09 9:18 PM Vanilla
ice cream sandwich with hazelnut meringue at Gonzo. 10 9:39 PM Herbal lozenge on 13th Street. 11 11:39 PM
Hershey's Hugs at home. 12 12:20 AM Honey Bunches of Oats at home.

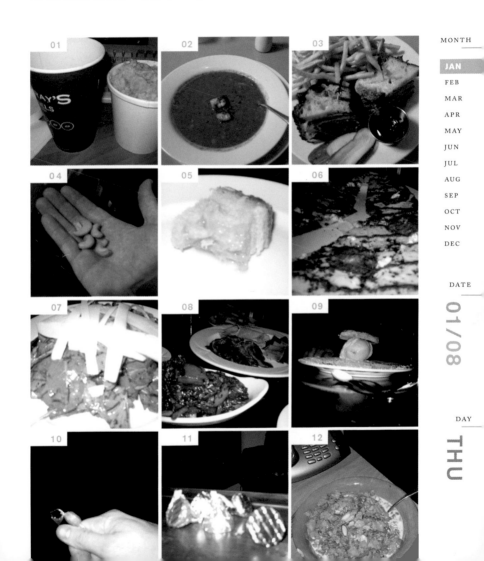

MONTH

JAN
FEB
MAR
APR
MAY
JUN
JUL
AUG
SEP
OCT
NOV
DEC

DATE

01/08

DAY

THU

01 9:39 AM **Brioche and coffee from La Bergamote at work.** 02 10:18 AM **Hungarian bunny cookies from Saryn at work.** 03 1:57 PM **Tomato-eggplant bisque, arugula with lima beans and Brussels sprouts from Whole Foods at work.** 04 2:24 PM **Tibetan tofu wrap from Whole Foods at work.** 05 3:16 PM **Naked Green Machine juice at work.** 06 9:37 PM **Popcorn at home.** 07 10:25 PM **Chicken with carrots, spinach, bacon, roasted potatoes, and turnips at home.** 08 11:20 PM **Cinnamon Life at home.**

MONTH

JAN
FEB
MAR
APR
MAY
JUN
JUL
AUG
SEP
OCT
NOV
DEC

DATE

01/09

DAY

FRI

01 10:11 AM Oatmeal and coffee from Bonsignour at home. 02 1:56 PM Peanut butter protein shake from Equinox. 03 8:12 PM Chopped salad at Ruth's Chris Steakhouse with Tim, Andrea, and Susan. 04 8:31 PM Rib-eye, medium-rare, with sautéed mushrooms and creamed spinach at Ruth's Chris. 05 9:24 PM Caramelized-banana cream pie at Ruth's Chris.

MONTH

JAN
FEB
MAR
APR
MAY
JUN
JUL
AUG
SEP
OCT
NOV
DEC

DATE

01/10

DAY

SAT

01 11:09 AM **Oatmeal at home.** 02 2:48 PM **Nachos at Tamar's.** 03 6:59 PM **Trail mix at home.** 04 9:46 PM **Chips and salsa at Tortilla Flats with Chris.** 05 10:07 PM **Quesadilla 2004 at Tortilla Flats.** 06 10:19 PM **Chicken flautas at Tortilla Flats.**

MONTH

JAN
FEB
MAR
APR
MAY
JUN
JUL
AUG
SEP
OCT
NOV
DEC

DATE

01/11

DAY

SUN

01 12:32 PM **All-Green juice from Elixir.** 02 2:22 PM **Ham and cheese croissant from La Bergamote.** 03 4:10 PM **Trail mix at home.** 04 8:53 PM **Potato-leek soup from Petite Abeille at home with Danny.** 05 9:04 PM **Croque-monsieur and salad with frites from Petite Abeille with Danny.**

MONTH

JAN

FEB

MAR

APR

MAY

JUN

JUL

AUG

SEP

OCT

NOV

DEC

DATE

01/12

DAY

MON

01 9:06 AM **Omega-3 oatmeal from Sacred Chow.** 02 1:14 PM **All-Green juice from Elixir.** 03 2:11 PM **Carrot and ginger soup, wilted greens, scrambled eggs, and bacon at home.** 04 6:18 PM **Orange at home.** 05 7:54 PM **Popcorn at home.** 06 8:46 PM **Pasta carbonara at home.** 07 10:03 PM **Tortuga rum cake at home.**

MONTH

JAN

FEB

MAR

APR

MAY

JUN

JUL

AUG

SEP

OCT

NOV

DEC

DATE

01/13

DAY

TUE

01 1:51 PM **Pumpkin soup and mixed salad from Tossed at work.** 02 8:02 PM **Tuna tartare with chorizo at Alta with Doc and Barry.** 03 8:04 PM **Lamb meatballs at Alta.** 04 8:12 PM **Pork bellies at Alta.** 05 8:21 PM **Caramelized cauliflower at Alta.** 06 8:29PM **Sautéed duck breast at Alta.** 07 9:02 PM **Chiles rellenos and Danish pork ribs at Alta.** 08 9:10 PM **Risotto with shrimp and saffron at Alta.** 09 11:57 PM **Cheerios at home.**

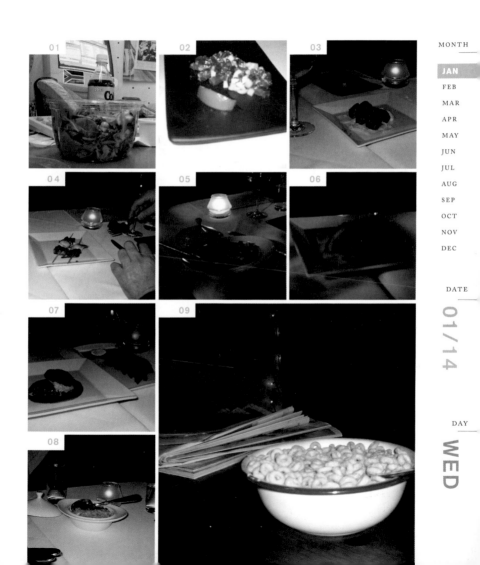

MONTH

JAN
FEB
MAR
APR
MAY
JUN
JUL
AUG
SEP
OCT
NOV
DEC

DATE

01/14

DAY

WED

01 9:19 AM Brioche and coffee from La Bergamote. 02 1:55 PM Salmon, broccoli rabe, roasted cauliflower, and Portuguese muffin with Cheddar cheese from City Bakery. 03 8:19 PM Orange at home. 04 9:19 PM Minestrone soup, burger, and salad from Nadine's. 05 10:22 PM Wheat Chex at home.

MONTH

JAN

FEB

MAR

APR

MAY

JUN

JUL

AUG

SEP

OCT

NOV

DEC

DATE

01/15

DAY

THU

01 9:26 AM **Brioche and coffee from La Bergamote at work.** 02 12:45 PM **Lentil soup at Elmo with Andy.** 03 12:53 PM **BLT at Elmo with Andy.** 04 9:05 PM **Popcorn at home.** 05 10:13 PM **Leftover pasta carbonara doctored up with spinach at home.** 06 12:26 AM **Tortuga rum cake at home.**

MONTH

JAN

FEB

MAR

APR

MAY

JUN

JUL

AUG

SEP

OCT

NOV

DEC

DATE

01/16

DAY

FRI

01 11:17 AM **Eggs over easy, grits, bacon, and biscuits at the Pink Teacup with Chris.** 02 11:46 AM **The rest of Chris's almond brioche from the Sullivan Street Bakery.** 03 3:23 PM **Workout Boost shake from Equinox at home.** 04 6:28 PM **Cheese and crackers at Susan and Andrea's.** 05 8:27 PM **Spaghetti with meatballs and mixed greens at Susan and Andrea's.** 06 9:12 PM **Chocolate chip cookies and frozen yogurt at Susan and Andrea's.** 07 10:56 PM **Popcorn at home.** 08 12:23 AM **Nutter Butters at home.**

MONTH

JAN
FEB
MAR
APR
MAY
JUN
JUL
AUG
SEP
OCT
NOV
DEC

DATE

01/17

DAY

SAT

01 10:02 AM Bacon, egg, and cheese roll and coffee from Spyros Deli at home. 02 12:04 PM Peanut Heaven shake from Equinox at home. 03 3:42 PM Oatmeal with Cheerios mixed in at home. 04 5:27 PM Movie snax. *Triplets of Belleville* with Antonio. 05 7:40 PM Bread and dips at Calcutta with Antonio. 06 7:55 PM Assorted Indian appetizers at Calcutta. 07 8:13 PM Chicken Marsala and vegetarian curry at Calcutta. 08 1:42 AM Popcorn at home.

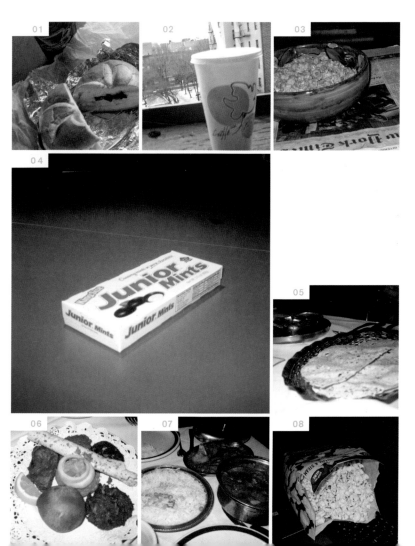

MONTH

JAN

FEB

MAR

APR

MAY

JUN

JUL

AUG

SEP

OCT

NOV

DEC

DATE

01/18

DAY

SUN

01 11:30 AM **Oatmeal at home.** 02 2:27 PM **Bread at I Tre Merli Café with Susan.** 03 2:38 PM **White bean soup at I Tre Merli Café.** 04 2:51 PM **Ham and asparagus panino at I Tre Merli Café.** 05 8:15 PM **Popcorn at home.** 06 9:14 PM **Winter chicken stew at home.** 07 9:24 PM **Spinach at home.** 08 10:44 PM **Wheaties at home.**

MONTH

JAN
FEB
MAR
APR
MAY
JUN
JUL
AUG
SEP
OCT
NOV
DEC

DATE

01/19

DAY

MON

01 9:43 AM Granola bar and apple cider from Whole Foods at work. 02 2:23 PM Tuna roll, salmon roll, arugula with lima beans, goat cheese from Whole Foods at work. 03 3:35 PM Vodka chocolates from Saryn at work. 04 7:58 PM Chips at home. 05 9:24 PM Pizza from Village Pizza at home with Danny. 06 10:08 PM Candy from Puerto Rico at home with Danny. 07 10:47 PM Cheerios at home.

MONTH

JAN
FEB
MAR
APR
MAY
JUN
JUL
AUG
SEP
OCT
NOV
DEC

DATE

01/20

DAY

TUE

01 9:31 AM **Oatmeal and coffee from Murray's at work.** 02 2:15 PM **Salmon, broccoli rabe, pea shoots, roasted carrots, roasted parsnips, and roasted Asian long squash from City Bakery at work.** 03 8:50 PM **Popcorn at home.** 04 9:49 PM **Frittata with bacon and spinach at home.** 05 10:25 PM **Wheaties at home.**

MONTH

JAN

FEB

MAR

APR

MAY

JUN

JUL

AUG

SEP

OCT

NOV

DEC

DATE

01/21

DAY

WED

01 9:14 AM **Brioche from La Bergamote from Ali at work.** 02 2:15 PM **Dan dan noodles and wonton soup from Grand Sichuan at work.** 03 9:09 PM **Crab cakes and chopped salad from Nadine's at home with Danny.** 04 11:18 PM **Häagen Dazs at home with Danny.** 05 11:47 PM **Oatmeal at home.**

01

02

03

04

05

MONTH

JAN
FEB
MAR
APR
MAY
JUN
JUL
AUG
SEP
OCT
NOV
DEC

DATE

01/22

DAY

THU

01 12:28 PM **Chips from Marc at work.** 02 1:16 PM **Spiced grape juice at Union Square Farmers' Market.** 03 1:50 PM **Chicken cutlet with lettuce, tomato, mayo, and mustard and plantain chips from Olympia Deli at work.** 04 6:56 PM **Trail mix at home.** 05 9:34 PM **Ropa vieja, red beans, and tostones from La Nueva Rampa at home.** 06 12:28 AM **Cinnamon Life at home.**

MONTH

JAN

FEB

MAR

APR

MAY

JUN

JUL

AUG

SEP

OCT

NOV

DEC

DATE

01/23

DAY

FRI

01 1:37 PM Bread and butter at Bruxelles with Susan, Andrea, Tim, and Henry. 02 2:04 PM Eggs Benedict, squash, ratatouille, and frites at Bruxelles. 03 6:21 PM Crudités with Annachiara at Susan's. 04 9:41 PM Salad at home. 05 9:49 PM Pasta with bacon, garlic, demi-glace, and greens at home. 06 12:21 AM Caramel candies from Danny at home.

MONTH

JAN

FEB

MAR

APR

MAY

JUN

JUL

AUG

SEP

OCT

NOV

DEC

DATE

01/24

DAY

SAT

01 11:54 AM **Oatmeal at home.** 02 3:09 PM **Egg salad sandwich from Taylor's at home.** 03 7:01 PM **Caramel candies from Danny at home.** 04 10:23 PM **Bacon Cheeseburger Deluxe from Bus Stop with Danny at home.** 05 11:31 PM **Cinnamon Life at home.**

MONTH

JAN
FEB
MAR
APR
MAY
JUN
JUL
AUG
SEP
OCT
NOV
DEC

DATE

01/25

DAY

SUN

01 1:48 PM **Hazelnut-squash soup and mixed-vegetable nori wrap with mixed-nut pâté from Bonobo.**
02 2:20 PM **Ham and Brie sandwich and veggie chips from the conference room.** 03 7:04 PM **Unsalted raisins and peanuts at home.** 04 8:55 PM **Touch of Lime chips at home with Danny.** 05 9:23 PM **Meatloaf, Brussels sprouts, broccoli, and mac and cheese from Mama's at home with Danny.** 06 10:16 PM **Frosted Flakes at home.**

MONTH

JAN

FEB

MAR

APR

MAY

JUN

JUL

AUG

SEP

OCT

NOV

DEC

DATE

01/26

DAY

MON

01 12:39 PM **Dan dan noodles at Grand Sichuan with Andy.** 02 12:54 PM **Wonton soup at Grand Sichuan.**
03 4:27 PM **Goldenberg Peanut Chew from Sara at work.** 04 10:07 PM **Chicken Parmesan over greens at home.**
05 11:05 PM **Caramel at home.** 06 11:39 PM **Cinnamon Life at home.**

MONTH

JAN
FEB
MAR
APR
MAY
JUN
JUL
AUG
SEP
OCT
NOV
DEC

DATE

01/27

DAY

TUE

01 2:33 PM Ham and Cabot Cheddar on brioche, Brussels sprouts, roasted beets, and potato-leek soup from Whole Foods at work. 02 7:23 PM Bread and butter at Gonzo with Deb. 03 7:31 PM White bean spread, Taleggio, Parmesan, and Robiola cheeses at Gonzo. 04 7:34 PM Soppressata, wild mushroom pizza at Gonzo. 05 8:48 PM Chocolate semifreddo at Gonzo.

MONTH

JAN
FEB
MAR
APR
MAY
JUN
JUL
AUG
SEP
OCT
NOV
DEC

DATE

01/28

DAY

WED

01 2:02 PM Salmon sushi, arugula with Brussels sprouts and green beans, and pineapple chunks from Whole Foods at work. 02 3:13 PM Granola bar from Whole Foods at work. 03 9:03 PM Bread and olive oil at Gonzo with Chris and Doc. 04 9:13 PM Half soppressata, half Gorgonzola and potato pizza at Gonzo. 05 9:26 PM Meat plate (speck, bresaola, salami) and grilled onion with Parmesan at Gonzo. 06 9:45 PM Spaghettini with clams at Gonzo. 07 10:15 PM Hazelnut meringue ice cream sandwich at Gonzo. 08 11:49 PM Cinnamon Life at home.

MONTH

JAN
FEB
MAR
APR
MAY
JUN
JUL
AUG
SEP
OCT
NOV
DEC

DATE

01/29

DAY

THU

01 9:56 AM Brioche and coffee from La Bergamote at work. 02 1:29 PM Tossed salad from Guy and Gaillard at work. 03 6:47 PM Balance bar and coffee from the Abingdon Market (née New Opera Deli) on Bleecker and Hudson. 04 6:53 PM Banana at home. 05 9:24 PM Ketchup chips with Danny at home. 06 10:42 PM Chicken curry, calamari, pad Thai, and summer rolls from Spice at home. 07 12:08 AM Frosted Flakes at home.

MONTH

JAN
FEB
MAR
APR
MAY
JUN
JUL
AUG
SEP
OCT
NOV
DEC

DATE

01/30

DAY

FRI

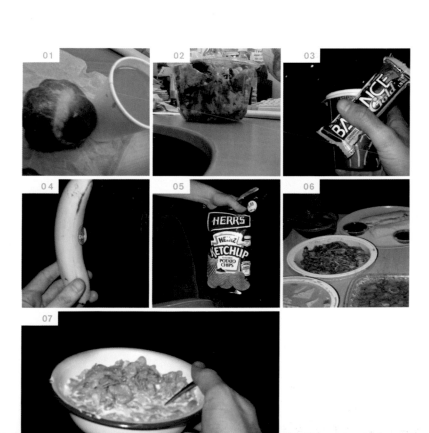

01 1:59 PM **Peanut Heaven shake from Equinox and banana at home.** 02 3:47 PM **Carrots at home.** 03 4:26 PM **Black beans at Havana Chelsea with Chris.** 04 4:35 PM **Cuban sandwich at Havana Chelsea.** 05 5:27 PM **Chocolate cookies and oatmeal-raisin cookie at City Bakery with Chris.** 06 6:13 PM **M&M's on 14th and 6th with Chris.** 07 7:56 PM **Movie snax.** *Latter Days* **with Chris, Jorge, and Wayne.** 08 10:23 PM **Squash soup at Jefferson with Chris, Jorge, Wayne, and Danny.** 09 10:28 PM **Walnut-raisin bread at Jefferson.** 10 10:36 PM **Yellowtail sashimi, tuna tartare, and edamame ravioli at Jefferson.** 11 10:37 PM **Scallops with braised vegetables at Jefferson.** 12 1:14 AM **Grilled cheese with bacon and tomato, fries, and vanilla shake from Manatus with Chris and Danny at home.**

MONTH

JAN
FEB
MAR
APR
MAY
JUN
JUL
AUG
SEP
OCT
NOV
DEC

DATE

01/31

DAY

SAT

Oscars —

Charlize Jubilee
Flan Penn

Crouching Tiger,
Hidden Salmon

Gosford Pork

Mike Pickles
need
more...

february

01 12:23 PM Oatmeal at home. 02 3:46 PM Fuji apple on 22nd Street. 03 6:21 PM Superbowl snax with Danny, Jorge, Wayne, Alex, and Pat at home. 04 6:24 PM Asparagus with wasabi dip, onion dip from Alex at home. 05 8:05 PM Three pizzas—plain, sausage and onion, and pepperoni—at home. 06 8:45 PM Chocolate birthday cake for Jorge from a deli on Christopher Street at home. 07 10:19 PM Godiva chocolates.

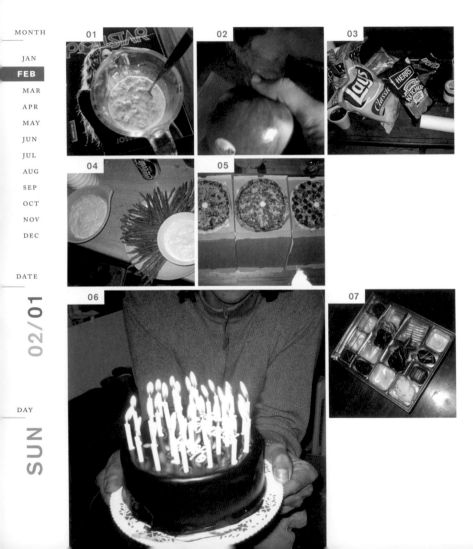

MONTH

JAN
FEB
MAR
APR
MAY
JUN
JUL
AUG
SEP
OCT
NOV
DEC

DATE

02/01

DAY

SUN

01 10:02 AM Brioche and coffee from La Bergamote at work.   02 1:13 PM Salmon BLT with salad at Elmo.
03 6:34 PM Teething biscuit with Henry at Susan and Andrea's.   04 9:24 PM Leftover pizza with Danny at home.
05 11:11 PM Cinnamon Life at home.

MONTH

JAN

FEB

MAR

APR

MAY

JUN

JUL

AUG

SEP

OCT

NOV

DEC

DATE

02/02

DAY

MON

01 9:53 AM Oatmeal and coffee from Murray's Bagels at work. 02 1:32 PM Falafel platter from Pita City at work. 03 8:08 PM Onion rings, small cup of chili at Chat 'N' Chew with Chris and Mom. 04 8:18 PM Bacon cheeseburger deluxe at Chat 'N' Chew. 05 8:48 PM Chocolate cake at Chat 'N' Chew.

MONTH

JAN

FEB

MAR

APR

MAY

JUN

JUL

AUG

SEP

OCT

NOV

DEC

DATE

02/03

DAY

TUE

01

02

03
04

05

01 10:24 AM Yogurt with granola and strawberries from Austin's at work. 02 1:49 PM Black bean soup, ham and Taleggio cheese panino, Mediterranean salad from Whole Foods at work. 03 2:46 PM Granola bar from Whole Foods at work. 04 8:15 PM Bread and olive oil at Gonzo with Andy and Maryam. 05 8:25 PM Mashed potato and Gorgonzola pizza at Gonzo. 06 8:28 PM Eggplant caponata, cannelini beans and smoked tuna, meat plate with speck, bresaola, Robiola cheese, Parmesan, and salami at Gonzo. 07 9:35 PM Hazelnut meringue ice cream sandwich at Gonzo. 08 11:09 PM Hummingbird cake from Magnolia at home with Danny.

MONTH

JAN

FEB

MAR

APR

MAY

JUN

JUL

AUG

SEP

OCT

NOV

DEC

DATE

02/04

DAY

WED

01 1:10 PM Salad with greens, tuna, tomato, and chickpeas at Food on 6th Avenue with Andy. **02** 6:40 PM Banana at home. **03** 8:37 PM Salt-baked potato cake with Fontina core with Scott S. at Alta. **04** 8:42 PM Fried goat cheese and grilled sourdough with serrano ham, Valdeon cheese, and pineapple at Alta. **05** 8:58 PM Tuna tataki at Alta. **06** 9:14 PM Shrimp and tomato risotto at Alta. **07** 9:29 PM Lime-ginger tart at Alta. **08** 11:19 PM Lay's potato chips at home. **09** 11:45 PM Häagen Dazs vanilla at home.

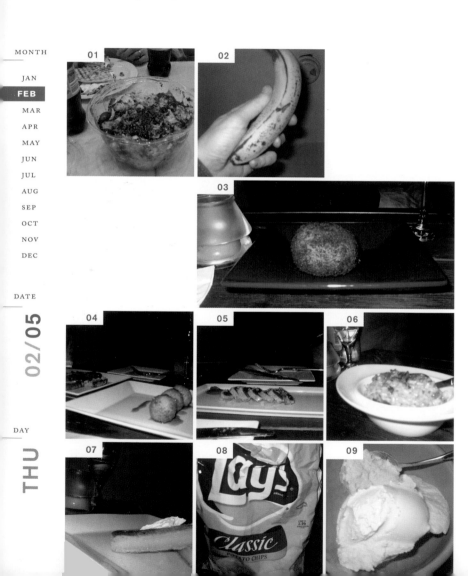

MONTH

JAN

FEB

MAR

APR

MAY

JUN

JUL

AUG

SEP

OCT

NOV

DEC

DATE

02/05

DAY

THU

01 02 03 04 05 06 07 08 09

01 10:29 AM Yogurt with granola and strawberries from Austin's at work. 02 2:04 PM Black bean soup, pepper jack and turkey sandwich from Whole Foods at work. 03 4:18 PM Yellow watermelon from Whole Foods at work. 04 6:32 PM Banana at home. 05 6:35 PM Trail mix at home. 06 8:38 PM Pure protein bar and coffee at home. 07 9:57 PM Ruffles at home. 08 10:15 PM Vegetable pad Thai, spring rolls from Kobma Thai with Danny at home.

MONTH

JAN

FEB

MAR

APR

MAY

JUN

JUL

AUG

SEP

OCT

NOV

DEC

DATE

02/06

DAY

FRI

01 12:21 PM Honey Nut Cheerios at home. 02 2:08 PM Workout Boost shake at home. 03 3:34 PM Classic Dosa from the Hampton Chutney Company with Chris. 04 4:23 PM Almond raisin cake and brownie from Pain Quotidian on Broome Street with Chris. 05 5:08 PM Shawarma and baklava at Mahmouns with Chris. 06 6:42 PM Graham cracker at Susan and Andrea's with Henry. 07 7:25 PM Mandarin orange slices and raspberries at Susan's. 08 9:27 PM Rib-eye with pan sauce, roasted potatoes and endive, wilted greens at home. 09 1:20 AM Raisin Bran at home.

MONTH

JAN

FEB

MAR

APR

MAY

JUN

JUL

AUG

SEP

OCT

NOV

DEC

DATE

02/07

DAY

SAT

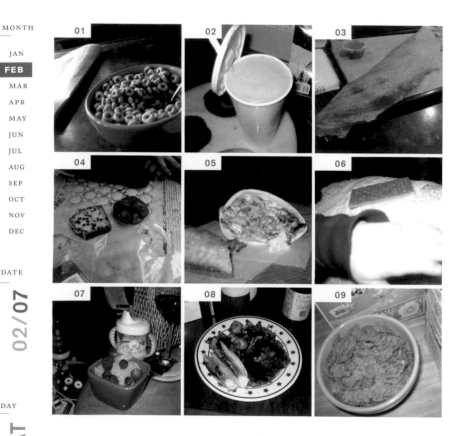

01 11:57 AM Bagel with cream cheese and lox at Susan and Andrea's with Henry. 02 1:28 PM Susan's low-fat cheesecake. 03 4:49 PM Movie snax. *The Dreamers* with Lynn. 04 7:05 PM Frisée salad with calamari at Five Points with Lynn. 05 7:33 PM Duck pâté with cornichons at Five Points. 06 7:47 PM Roasted duck liver at Five Points. 07 8:05 PM Cod bake and potato pizza with truffle oil at Five Points. 08 11:11 PM Raisin Bran at home.

MONTH

JAN

FEB

MAR

APR

MAY

JUN

JUL

AUG

SEP

OCT

NOV

DEC

DATE

02/08

DAY

SUN

01 02 03

04 05 06

07 08

01 1:13 PM Wonton soup with Andy at Green House on 29th Street. 02 1:18 PM Vegetable dumplings at Green House. 03 7:22 PM Peanuts and raisins at home. 04 9:42 PM Ketchup chips at home with Danny. 05 9:46 PM Organic greens at home. 06 10:07 PM Frittata with bacon and potatoes at home. 07 11:29 PM Honey Nut Cheerios at home.

MONTH

JAN

FEB

MAR

APR

MAY

JUN

JUL

AUG

SEP

OCT

NOV

DEC

DATE

02/09

DAY

MON

01 9:44 AM Brioche and coffee from La Bergamote at home. 02 2:11 PM Arugula salad with beans, Southwestern wrap, Fuji apple, black bean soup, and quinoa salad from Whole Foods at work. 03 8:50 PM Chips and tomato salsa with Chris at Mexicana Mama. 04 9:03 PM Pork tacos at Mexicana Mama. 05 10:37 PM Cupcakes from Magnolia with Chris and Danny at home. 06 11:34 PM Raisin Bran at home.

MONTH

JAN
FEB
MAR
APR
MAY
JUN
JUL
AUG
SEP
OCT
NOV
DEC

DATE

02/10

DAY

TUE

01 9:50 AM **Oatmeal at home.** 02 2:27 PM **Smoked turkey with Brie from Champignon at work.** 03 7:03 PM **Raisins and peanuts at home.** 04 9:44 PM **Cheeseburger and salad from Hudson Corner at home.** 05 11:51 PM **Raisin Bran at home.**

MONTH

JAN

FEB

MAR

APR

MAY

JUN

JUL

AUG

SEP

OCT

NOV

DEC

DATE

02/11

DAY

WED

01 2:33 PM Salmon with red peppers, salad, and orange cake from Antique Café at work. 02 6:56 PM Butternut squash soup with Henry at Susan and Andrea's. 03 10:32 PM Pork chop, carrot soup, and calamari from Nadine's with Danny at home. 04 11:31 PM Cinnamon Life at home.

MONTH

JAN

FEB

MAR

APR

MAY

JUN

JUL

AUG

SEP

OCT

NOV

DEC

DATE

02/12

DAY

THU

01 10:04 AM Brioche, chocolate chip cookie, and chocolate-covered marshmallow at work. 02 2:03 PM Grilled chicken sandwich, black bean soup, apple, and granola bar from Whole Foods at work. 03 2:36 PM Chocolate-covered marshmallow at work. 04 8:11 PM Bread and butter with Tim, Susan, and Andrea at Artisanal. 05 8:19 PM Prince Edward Island oysters with Mignonette sauce at Artisanal. 06 8:42 PM Artisanal blend fondue. 07 9:09 PM Gnocchi with salt pork at Artisanal. 08 9:22 PM Sautéed skate on raspberry coulis cauliflower purée at Artisanal. 09 10:29 PM Cheese course (St. Andre, Emmenthaler, and Soumaintran) at Artisanal.

MONTH

JAN

FEB

MAR

APR

MAY

JUN

JUL

AUG

SEP

OCT

NOV

DEC

DATE

02/13

DAY

FRI

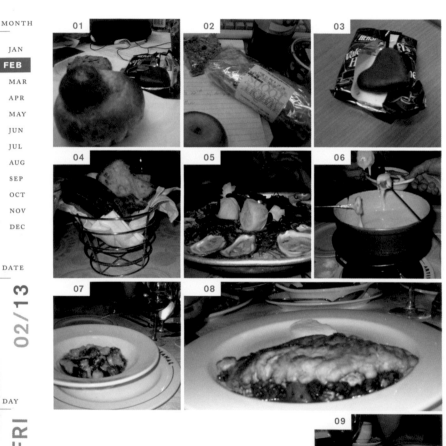

01 9:40 AM Oatmeal at home. 02 12:02 PM Workout Boost shake at home. 03 2:37 PM Leftover pork chop at home. 04 3:36 PM Chocolate-covered cherries (milk and dark), rum roll, and cashew bark from Li-Lac with Chris. 05 4:00 PM Valentine cookies at John Vie. 06 4:25 PM Bouchée and marrons glacé from Maison du Chocolate at Rockefeller Center. 07 4:35 PM Dark chocolate bear from Teuscher. 08 4:42 PM Milk Monju from Minamoto Kitchen. 09 4:43 PM Cherries from Minamoto Kitchen. 10 8:55 PM Jackie's birthday cake at Jorge and Wayne's. 11 12:13 AM Doritos at home. 12 12:32 AM Mozzarella and basil sandwich at home.

MONTH

JAN

FEB

MAR

APR

MAY

JUN

JUL

AUG

SEP

OCT

NOV

DEC

DATE

02/14

DAY

SAT

01 9:56 AM Oatmeal at home. 02 5:48 PM Peanuts and raisins at home. 03 8:28 PM Candy hearts at loft party at the Ukrainian Community Center with Chris, Alex, Rich, and Omar. 04 9:09 PM Pasta with beans, baked beans, tomatoes, and meatballs at the Ukrainian Center. 05 11:05 PM BLT from Bus Stop at home. 06 11:36 PM Cinnamon Life at home.

MONTH

JAN
FEB
MAR
APR
MAY
JUN
JUL
AUG
SEP
OCT
NOV
DEC

DATE

02/15

DAY

SUN

01 10:28 AM Oatmeal at home. 02 11:37 AM Eggs over medium, grits, bacon, biscuits, and pecan pancakes at the Pink Teacup with Chris. 03 8:45 PM Porcini, chestnut, and shrimp soup at Serafina Sandro with Lynn, Tom, Zach, and Micha. 04 9:03 PM Pasta with porcini at Serafina Sandro. 05 9:23 PM Mixed seafood pasta at Serafina Sandro. 06 9:48 PM Grilled artichoke at Serafina Sandro (braised lamb shoulder in background). 07 10:08 PM Roast pork with wilted spinach at Serafina Sandro.

MONTH

JAN

FEB

MAR

APR

MAY

JUN

JUL

AUG

SEP

OCT

NOV

DEC

DATE

02/16

DAY

MON

01 9:24 AM Brioche and coffee from La Bergamote on 20th Street. 02 11:34 AM Banana bread from Sara at work. 03 2:01 PM Roast pork and arugula sandwich with horseradish on five-grain bread and lentil-vegetable soup from Bottino Carry Out at work. 04 8:52 PM Salad at home. 05 9:30 PM Pizza from Domino's with Danny at home. 06 9:57 PM Burger from Manatus with Danny at home.

MONTH

JAN

FEB

MAR

APR

MAY

JUN

JUL

AUG

SEP

OCT

NOV

DEC

DATE

02/17

DAY

TUE

01 10:20 AM Banana at work. 02 1:07 PM BLT and salad at Elmo with Andy. 03 7:23 PM Peanuts and raisins at home. 04 10:05 PM Carrot soup, croque-madame, and salad from La Petite Abeille with Danny at home. 05 11:10 PM Wheaties at home.

MONTH

JAN

FEB

MAR

APR

MAY

JUN

JUL

AUG

SEP

OCT

NOV

DEC

DATE

02/18

DAY

WED

01 1:52 PM No. 6 pork, arugula, and horseradish sandwich on five-grain from Bottino Carry Out at work.
02 8:06 PM Bread and butter at Bivio with Doc. 03 8:26 PM Anchovy toasts with mozzarella cheese at Bivio.
04 8:50 PM Pasta with lobster ragout at Bivio. 05 10:47 PM Wheaties at home.

MONTH

JAN
FEB
MAR
APR
MAY
JUN
JUL
AUG
SEP
OCT
NOV
DEC

DATE

02/19

DAY

THU

01 9:37 AM Breakfast smoothie from the Protein Kitchen at work. 02 2:14 PM Salmon sushi, assorted greens, Bosc pear from Whole Foods at work. 03 8:03 PM Assorted canapés (prosciutto, tapenade) and mixed nuts at Da Silvano Wine Bar with Buzz. 04 9:03 PM Bread, butter, and salt at A.O.C. Bedford with Alex, Buzz, and Patches. 05 9:12 PM Serrano ham with roasted tomatoes and bread at A.O.C. Bedford. 06 9:13 PM Foie gras with herbed oil and roasted pearl onion, salad with anchovy at A.O.C. Bedford. 07 9:44 PM Roasted suckling pig with mashed potatoes and roasted onions at A.O.C. Bedford. 08 9:46 PM Seafood paella at A.O.C. Bedford. 09 10:42 PM Assorted cheeses (two sheep's milk artisanal cheeses, one extra bleu) with bread at A.O.C. Bedford. 10 12:53 AM Wheaties at home.

MONTH

JAN

FEB

MAR

APR

MAY

JUN

JUL

AUG

SEP

OCT

NOV

DEC

DATE

02/20

DAY

FRI

01 9:57 AM Oatmeal at home. 02 12:56 PM Workout Boost shake with Jorge on 12th Street. 03 1:58 PM White bean soup at I Tre Merli on Charles Street with Susan, Andrea, Jorge, and Henry. 04 2:14 PM Prosciutto and Taleggio panino at I Tre Merli. 05 3:08 PM All-Green juice from Elixir. 06 7:41 PM Vodka and caviar party with Alex, Tim, Steven, Jay, Chris, Jeorg, Jorge, Wayne, Danny, Susan, Andrea, John, Buzz, Barry, Patches, Christopher, Marc, and a bunch of other people at Tim M.'s. 07 8:26 PM Mushroom pierogi, beet salad, assorted olives, smoked sable, salami pâté, and black bread at Tim M.'s. *(continued on next page)*

MONTH

JAN

FEB

MAR

APR

MAY

JUN

JUL

AUG

SEP

OCT

NOV

DEC

DATE

02/21

DAY

SAT

08 8:40 PM Osetra caviar, toasts at Tim M.'s. **09** 8:50 PM Potato salad with salmon roe at Tim M.'s. **10** 9:39 PM Assorted cheeses, cucumber and dill salad, olives, pickles at Tim M.'s. **11** 10:28 PM Hazelnut meringues and chocolate biscotti at Tim M.'s. **12** 10:29 PM Vanilla meringues and lace cookies at Tim M.'s. **13** 1:44 AM Grilled cheese at home with Danny.

DATE

02/21

DAY

SAT

01 11:33 AM Egg, cheese, bacon, and tomato on ciabatta from Panino Gusto at home with Danny. 02 8:18 PM Ruffles at home with Danny. 03 9:26 PM Hot dogs and onion rings from PopBurger at home with Danny, Chris, and Jeorg. 04 10:45 PM Chocolate frosting at home.

MONTH

JAN

FEB

MAR

APR

MAY

JUN

JUL

AUG

SEP

OCT

NOV

DEC

DATE

02/22

DAY

SUN

01 10:23 AM Banana and water at work. 02 12:26 PM Raisin scone and pepper butter at Bright Food with Andy. 03 12:41 PM Catfish wrap and black beans. 04 9:35 PM Duck confit salad at Bao 111 with Chris and Jeorg. 05 9:37 PM Seared beef salad at Bao 111. 06 9:52 PM Short ribs on lemongrass skewers at Bao 111. 07 9:54 PM Shrimp-stuffed calamari at Bao 111. *(continued on next page)*

MONTH

JAN

FEB

MAR

APR

MAY

JUN

JUL

AUG

SEP

OCT

NOV

DEC

DATE

02/23

DAY

MON

08 9:57 PM **Spring rolls at Bao 111.** 09 10:08 PM **Whole fish (red snapper) with sweet-and-sour glaze at Bao 111.**
10 10:54 PM **Quail egg with shaved truffle, candied nuts at Jack's Luxury Oyster Bar with Chris and Jeorg.**
11 10:59 PM **Scallops at Jack's.** 12 11:16 PM **Rum-soaked baba with caramel foam and whipped cream at Jack's.**
13 12:14 AM **Honey Bunches of Oats at home.**

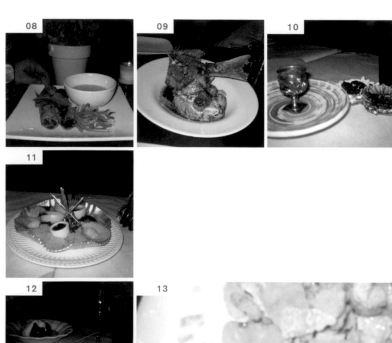

DATE

02/23

DAY

MON

01 9:50 AM Granola bar from Whole Foods at work. 02 2:22 PM Grilled chicken panino from Champignon at work. 03 7:00 PM Ruffles and Rheingold at home. 04 9:11 PM Penne with kitchen-cupboard ragù with Danny at home. 05 10:48 PM Chocolate frosting at home. 06 11:10 PM Berry Burst Cheerios at home.

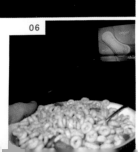

MONTH

JAN

FEB

MAR

APR

MAY

JUN

JUL

AUG

SEP

OCT

NOV

DEC

DATE

02/24

DAY

TUE

01 1:26 PM **Green salad at Patsy's Pizza with Jose.** 02 1:38 PM **Pizza with prosciutto, sausage, and mushrooms at Patsy's.** 03 8:53 PM **Eggplant melanzano salata at Snack Taverna with Jason.** 04 9:10 PM **Lamb's tongue with beans at Snack Taverna.** 05 9:21 PM **Roasted baby pig with vegetables at Snack Taverna.** 06 9:40 PM **Baklava at Snack Taverna.** 07 9:54 PM **Chocolate cake with raspberry sauce at Snack Taverna.**

MONTH

JAN

FEB

MAR

APR

MAY

JUN

JUL

AUG

SEP

OCT

NOV

DEC

DATE

02/25

DAY

WED

01 9:46 AM Brioche and coffee from La Bergamote at work. 02 2:05 PM Turkey club from Guy & Gaillard at work.
03 7:12 PM Peanuts and raisins at home. 04 9:02 PM Odwalla Superfood at home. 05 9:49 PM Omelet with
spinach and bacon at home. 06 11:07 PM Life cereal at home.

01

MONTH

JAN

FEB

MAR

APR

MAY

JUN

JUL

AUG

SEP

OCT

NOV

DEC

02

マッテル?

03

04

DATE

02/26

05

06

DAY

THU

01 1:19 PM Tamale at Salsa y Salsa with Andy. 02 1:37 PM Chicken tacos at Salsa y Salsa. 03 6:56 PM Peanuts and raisins at home. 04 9:44 PM Complimentary salad at Sakura Hana. 05 9:53 PM Two pieces yellowtail, two pieces eel at Sakura Hana with my new *National Geographic*. 06 10:00 PM Kake udon with vegetable tempura at Sakura Hana. 07 1:16 AM Girl Scout cookies.

01 2:39 PM Grilled ham and cheese, fries at Chat 'N' Chew with Susan, Andrea, and Henry. 02 6:33 PM Balance Gold Caramel Nut Blast on Bank Street and Bleecker. 03 6:44 PM Naked Protein Blast on West 10th Street and Greenwich. 04 8:24 PM Trail mix at home. 05 10:38 PM Pork loin and herbed mayonnaise at Scott's birthday party. 06 1:58 AM Eggs and spinach at home. 07 2:16 AM Honey Bunches of Oats at home.

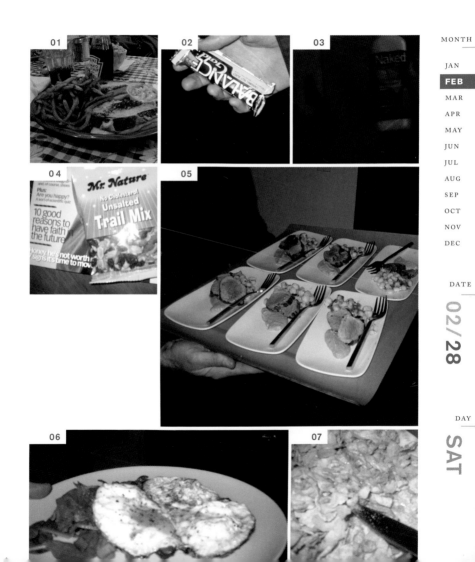

MONTH

JAN

FEB

MAR

APR

MAY

JUN

JUL

AUG

SEP

OCT

NOV

DEC

DATE

02/28

DAY

SAT

01 11:12 AM **Peach smoothie from Amy's. 02** 1:18 PM **Toasted poppy-seed bagel from Brew Bar at home. 03** 3:19 PM **Movie snax.** *The Passion of the Christ* **with Jason. 04** 6:53 PM **Oscar snax (sea salt and vinegar chips) at home with Danny and Chris. 05** 8:41 PM **Burgers from Nadine's at home with Danny and Chris. 06** 10:18 PM **Entenmann's cookies at home. 07** 10:49 PM **Girl Scout Cookies at home.**

MONTH

JAN

FEB

MAR

APR

MAY

JUN

JUL

AUG

SEP

OCT

NOV

DEC

DATE

02/29

DAY

SUN

01 2:01 PM **Turkey club with avocado, broccoli rabe, and spinach from Deli Marche at work.** 02 7:09 PM **Trail mix at home.** 03 9:20 PM **Ketchup chips at home with Danny.** 04 10:39 PM **Sesame chicken and wonton soup from Mama Buddha at home with Danny.** 05 11:21 PM **Life cereal at home.**

MONTH

JAN
FEB
MAR
APR
MAY
JUN
JUL
AUG
SEP
OCT
NOV
DEC

DATE

03/01

DAY

MON

01

02

03

04

05

01 10:18 AM Oatmeal from Murray's at work. 02 1:41 PM Tuna salad on whole-grain from Guy & Gaillard at work. 03 8:39 PM Marinated peppers and sautéed mushrooms at Gonzo with Roger. 04 8:55 PM Spaghettini with clams at Gonzo. 05 10:48 PM French toast from Manatus at home with Danny. 06 11:48 PM Granola at home.

MONTH

JAN

FEB

MAR

APR

MAY

JUN

JUL

AUG

SEP

OCT

NOV

DEC

DATE

03/02

DAY

TUE

01 9:50 AM Brioche and coffee from La Bergamote at work. 02 1:55 PM Tuna roll, seaweed salad, and tofu garden salad from Whole Foods at work. 03 5:03 PM Naked Pomegranate-Blueberry juice at work. 04 6:41 PM Cheese and crackers, squash, corn, bananas, and apples with Henry at Susan and Andrea's. 05 8:50 PM Susan's "pot roast pasta" and salad. 06 11:14 PM Granola at home.

MONTH

JAN

FEB

MAR

APR

MAY

JUN

JUL

AUG

SEP

OCT

NOV

DEC

DATE

03/03

DAY

WED

01 1:44 PM Carrot-squash soup, no. 6 pork sandwich with arugula and horseradish on five-grain from Bottino Carry Out at work. 02 1:47 PM Curried tofu rice wrap from Marci at work. 03 9:06 PM Duck spring rolls at Chow Bar with Jason. 04 9:08 PM Seaweed salad at Chow Bar. 05 9:09 PM Barbecued ribs at Chow Bar. 06 9:32 PM Prawns with crispy spinach at Chow Bar. 07 10:04 PM Cherry Blow Pop on West 4th Street with Jason. 08 11:08 PM Granola at home.

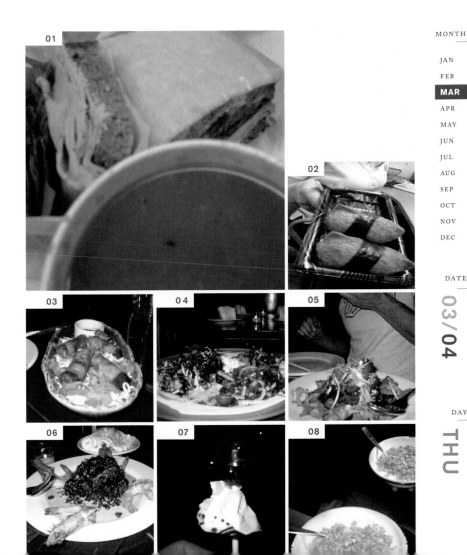

MONTH

JAN
FEB
MAR
APR
MAY
JUN
JUL
AUG
SEP
OCT
NOV
DEC

DATE

03/04

DAY

THU

01 10:23 AM Croissant and coffee from Champignon at work. 02 12:52 PM Bread and garlic oil at Le Zie with Gladys and Joe F. 03 1:15 PM Tricolore salad with bacon and feta cheese at Le Zie. 04 1:29 PM Pasta with sausage and fennel at Le Zie. 05 7:00 PM Beef jerky at home. 06 8:52 PM Olives and almonds at Barbuto with Chris. 07 9:01 PM Polenta with sautéed mushrooms and mascarpone at Barbuto (sardines and escarole in background). 08 9:15 PM Burrata from Apulia over dandelion leaves at Barbuto. 09 9:37 PM Slow-cooked pork ribs over fennel, broccoli rabe at Barbuto (wood-grilled rib-eye in background). 10 10:03 PM Chocolate pot de crème and lemon cake with whipped cream at Barbuto. 11 12:34 PM Maple & Brown Sugar Frosted Mini-Wheats at home.

MONTH

JAN

FEB

MAR

APR

MAY

JUN

JUL

AUG

SEP

OCT

NOV

DEC

DATE

03/05

DAY

FRI

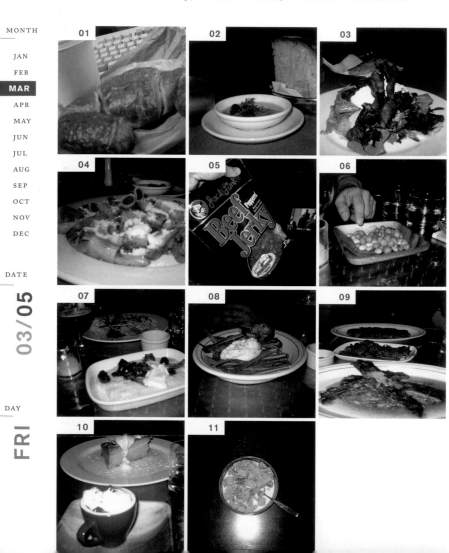

01 9:16 AM Oatmeal at home. **02** 1:29 PM Two eggs over medium, bacon, potatoes, toasted English muffin, and mixed greens at the Village Den with Susan, Andrea, and Henry. **03** 5:26 PM Peach Dream smoothie from Elixir, green-tea energy bar from Sacred Chow by the river. **04** 8:20 PM Beef jerky at home. **05** 9:39 PM Hamentaschen at home. **06** 11:45 PM Maple & Brown Sugar Frosted Mini-Wheats at home. **07** 12:21 AM Popcorn at home.

MONTH

JAN
FEB
MAR
APR
MAY
JUN
JUL
AUG
SEP
OCT
NOV
DEC

DATE

03/06

DAY

SAT

01 2:45 PM Almond cookie and lemon cookie at Rocco's with Chris. 02 3:24 PM Dried fruit samples (plum, mango, mandarin peel) at Munchie Paradise on Mott Street. 03 3:49 PM Fried spring rolls at Dim Sum Go Go with Chris. 04 3:57 PM Pork buns and pork-rib chunks with black beans at Dim Sum Go Go. 05 4:35 PM Pork and crab juicy buns at Joe's Shanghai. 06 4:52 PM Sesame cookie from May May Bakery on Pell St. 07 4:54 PM Walnut cookie from May May. 08 8:32 PM Chips, salsa, salsa fresca, and guacamole at El Sombrero with Alex and Tim. 09 8:48 PM Carnitas, rice and beans at El Sombrero. 10 11:07 PM Granola at home.

MONTH

JAN

FEB

MAR

APR

MAY

JUN

JUL

AUG

SEP

OCT

NOV

DEC

DATE

03/07

DAY

SUN

01 1:37 PM Chicken cutlet on roll with lettuce, tomato, mayo, and mustard at work. 02 3:35 PM Pistachios at work.
03 8:01 PM Popcorn at home. 04 9:13 PM White Rose mac and cheese at home. 05 10:43 PM Wheaties at home.

MONTH

JAN

FEB

MAR

APR

MAY

JUN

JUL

AUG

SEP

OCT

NOV

DEC

DATE

03/08

DAY

MON

01 2:12 PM Chicken club and Mediterranean tofu salad with feta cheese from Whole Foods at work.
02 2:59 PM Naked Green Machine at work. 03 4:23 PM Granola bar from Whole Foods at work. 04 10:20 PM
Croque-monsieur and frites from La Petite Abeille with Danny at home. 05 10:48 PM Wheaties at home.

MONTH

JAN

FEB

MAR

APR

MAY

JUN

JUL

AUG

SEP

OCT

NOV

DEC

DATE

03/09

DAY

TUE

01 9:48 AM Brioche from La Bergamote and coffee at work. 02 1:03 PM Apple cider from the farmers' market in Union Square. 03 1:53 PM Roasted fennel, roasted radicchio, sautéed long beans, and breaded catfish from City Bakery at work. 04 3:34 PM Chocolate chip cookie from City Bakery at work. 05 6:34 PM Tuna tataki salad at Nobu Next Door with Susan K. 06 6:47 PM Yellowtail sashimi with jalapeño. 07 6:52 PM Rock shrimp tempura. 08 7:09 PM Black cod with miso sauce. 09 7:35 PM Banana sesame harumaki with milk chocolate and honey. 10 9:23 PM Bread, oil, and vinegar at Pepe Verde with Jason. 11 9:27 PM Air-dried beef, arugula, and feta cheese; Caesar salad. 12 11:27 PM Wheaties at home.

MONTH

JAN

FEB

MAR

APR

MAY

JUN

JUL

AUG

SEP

OCT

NOV

DEC

DATE

03/10

DAY

WED

01 9:37 AM Croissant from La Bergamote on 21st Street. 02 2:22 PM Falafel sandwich with hummus from Pita City at work. 03 7:08 PM Blueberry cheesecake Pure Protein bar on the way home. 04 9:38 PM Jason's leftover pasta with meat sauce from Pepe Verde at home. 05 11:19 PM Entenmann's Popems with Danny at home.

MONTH

JAN

FEB

MAR

APR

MAY

JUN

JUL

AUG

SEP

OCT

NOV

DEC

DATE

03/11

DAY

THU

01 2:13 PM Southwestern wrap with pepper jack and Mediterranean salad with extra arugula and extra feta cheese from Whole Foods at work. 02 4:25 PM Last-day cupcake from Magnolia with Saryn, Marci, Sara, and Marc at work. 03 10:25 PM Hot dogs, French fries, and chocolate shake from PopBurger with Danny at home. 04 10:49 PM Twin burgers from PopBurger.

01

02

03

04

MONTH

JAN

FEB

MAR

APR

MAY

JUN

JUL

AUG

SEP

OCT

NOV

DEC

DATE

03/12

DAY

FRI

01 11:02 AM Oatmeal at home. 02 3:19 PM Plain bagel with scallion cream cheese and lox from Bagels & More at home. 03 8:52 PM Cocktail nuts at Campbell's Apartment at Grand Central with Chris and Doc. 04 10:18 PM Bread and yellow bell pepper soup at Hearth with Chris and Doc. 05 10:34 PM Ribollita with black cabbage and white beans, foie gras with citrus mustard, and red wine–braised octopus at Hearth. 06 10:58 PM Roasted cod with bacalau and salsa verde at Hearth. 07 11:18 PM Duck leg confit with roasted veggies at Hearth. 08 11:50 PM Pear and huckleberry crisp with vanilla ice cream at Hearth. 09 12:00 AM Cordial cookies at Hearth.

MONTH

JAN

FEB

MAR

APR

MAY

JUN

JUL

AUG

SEP

OCT

NOV

DEC

DATE

03/13

DAY

SAT

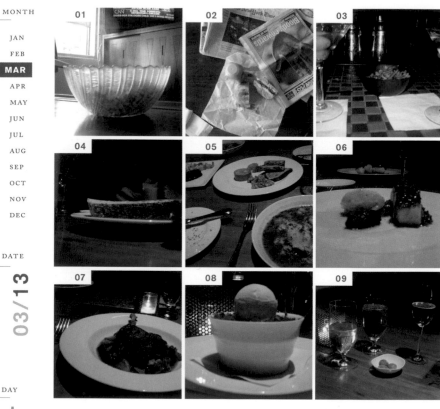

01 3:00 PM Hot dog in Central Park with Mom, Eric, Connie, Lewis, and Ruby. 02 3:23 PM Pretzel on Columbus Circle. 03 3:42 PM Roasted nuts on 7th Ave and 41st Street. 04 4:42 PM Egg salad and reduced-fat chips from Abingdon Market (formerly New Opera Deli) at home. 05 10:35 PM Pork mushu and egg roll from Mama Buddha with Danny at home. 06 11:45 PM Muesli at home.

MONTH

JAN

FEB

MAR

APR

MAY

JUN

JUL

AUG

SEP

OCT

NOV

DEC

DATE

03/14

DAY

SUN

01 10:33 AM Oatmeal at home. 02 1:21 PM Baked sardines with celery oil, peekytoe crab on cumin crisps, and beet-greens ravioli at Jo Jo with Lynn. 03 1:39 PM Lobster in carrot-citrus broth, black bass with carrots. 04 2:04 PM Warm chocolate cake with vanilla ice cream, passion-fruit Pavlova. 05 5:17 PM Sunflower seeds by the river. 06 9:38 PM Popcorn at home with Danny. 07 9:55 PM Pad Thai with shrimp and spring rolls from Kobma Thai at home with Danny. 08 10:55 PM Entenmann's carb-counting chocolate chip cookie.

MONTH

JAN

FEB

MAR

APR

MAY

JUN

JUL

AUG

SEP

OCT

NOV

DEC

DATE

03/15

DAY

MON

01 9:49 AM Oatmeal at home. 02 1:39 PM Bread basket with Brett at Pastis. 03 1:43 PM Frisée salad with lardons and soft-boiled egg, side of sautéed spinach. 04 5:18 PM Purefruits from Taylor's at home. 05 9:27 PM Kitchen-cupboard linguini with spinach and spicy sausages with Danny at home. 06 10:56 PM Wheaties at home.

01

02

03

04

05

06

MONTH

JAN

FEB

MAR

APR

MAY

JUN

JUL

AUG

SEP

OCT

NOV

DEC

DATE

03/16

DAY

TUE

01 9:41 AM Muesli at home. **02** 1:30 PM Peppermill turkey with roasted red peppers on whole-grain, microwaved spinach with sea salt at home. **03** 4:12 PM Roasted peanuts and almonds from the stand at 14th Street and 5th Avenue. **04** 4:58 PM Apple on West 11th Street. **05** 6:09 PM Teething biscuit with Henry at Susan and Andrea's. **06** 7:27 PM Strawberry C-Monster at home. **07** 9:30 PM Miso soup at East with Karl. **08** 9:36 PM Chuka seaweed salad and edamame at East. **09** 9:42 PM Sushi and sashimi combo platter at East. **10** 9:51 PM Eel and avocado roll at East. **11** 12:16 AM Popcorn at home. **12** 12:45 AM Wheaties at home.

MONTH

JAN

FEB

MAR

APR

MAY

JUN

JUL

AUG

SEP

OCT

NOV

DEC

DATE

03/17

DAY

WED

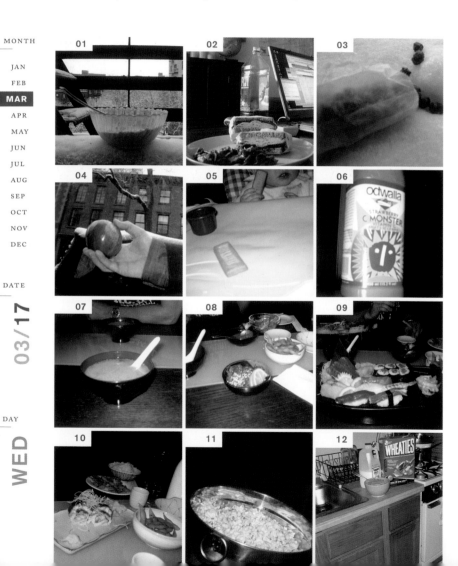

01 10:47 AM **Banana** at home. 02 12:05 PM **Oatmeal** at home. 03 2:19 PM **Pastrami with mustard, plantain chips, Diet Vanilla Coke** at home. 04 4:20 PM **Apple** at home. 05 5:08 PM **Dried orange peel from Munchies Paradise on Mott Street.** 06 5:45 PM **Individual quiche from Patisserie Claude in Sheridan Square.** 07 6:37 PM **Pistachios** at home. *(continued on next page)*

MONTH

JAN
FEB
MAR
APR
MAY
JUN
JUL
AUG
SEP
OCT
NOV
DEC

DATE

03/18

DAY

THU

08 9:40 PM Yellowtail sashimi with jalapeño at Nobu with Jason. 09 9:52 PM Rock shrimp tempura with ponzu at Nobu. 10 10:04 PM Black cod with miso sauce at Nobu. 11 10:18 PM Red snapper, yellowtail, and fresh-water eel at Nobu. 12 10:41 PM Yellowtail and king salmon at Nobu. 13 10:57 PM Banana and sesame harumaki with milk chocolate and honey at Nobu. 14 11:58 PM Wheaties at home.

DATE

03/18

DAY

THU

01 9:31 AM **Banana at home.** 02 10:58 AM **Oatmeal at home.** 03 1:26 PM **Egg salad and potato chips from Abingdon Market at home.** 04 5:33 PM **Biscotti at Susan and Andrea's.** 05 5:58 PM **Doritos and sour cream and onion Ruffles with Alex on the West Side Highway.** 06 8:20 PM **Martini and selection of cheeses with Buzz, Alex, Barry, Susan, Andrea, and Henry at Buzz and Barry's house in Sullivan County.** 07 10:10 PM **Pasta, salad, and roasted asparagus.** 08 11:13 PM **Ice cream and chocolate chip cookie.** 09 11:48 PM **More cookies.**

MONTH

JAN

FEB

MAR

APR

MAY

JUN

JUL

AUG

SEP

OCT

NOV

DEC

DATE

03/19

DAY

FRI

01 10:45 AM Bacon, eggs, and Alex's cheese biscuits at Buzz's. **02** 2:19 PM Sausage pizza from Napoli. **03** 4:25 PM Rum-and-Coke pound cake at Buzz and Barry's. **04** 6:19 PM Cheeses at Buzz and Barry's. **05** 9:50 PM Braised short ribs, mashed potatoes, and broiled Brussels sprouts at Buzz and Barry's. **06** 10:33 PM Andrea's sticky toffee pudding at Buzz and Barry's.

MONTH

JAN

FEB

MAR

APR

MAY

JUN

JUL

AUG

SEP

OCT

NOV

DEC

DATE

03/20

DAY

SAT

01 10:15 AM **French toast and strawberries at Buzz's.** 02 3:02 PM **Balance bar outside Susan and Andrea's on 6th Avenue.** 03 4:02 PM **Egg salad, chips, and Superfood from Abingdon Market at home.** 04 10:25 PM **Pizza from Village Pizza at home with Danny.** 05 10:56 PM **Cookies at home with Danny.**

MONTH

JAN

FEB

MAR

APR

MAY

JUN

JUL

AUG

SEP

OCT

NOV

DEC

DATE

03/21

DAY

SUN

01 8:50 AM **Banana and Superfood at home.** 02 1:26 PM **Ham and cheese crêpe from the stand outside the New York Public Library on 49th Street.** 03 4:10 PM **Baby arugula at home.** 04 4:51 PM **Teriyaki beef jerky at home.** 05 10:38 PM **Pork dumplings, fried rice, and wonton soup from Mama Buddha with Danny at home.**

MONTH

JAN

FEB

MAR

APR

MAY

JUN

JUL

AUG

SEP

OCT

NOV

DEC

DATE

03/22

DAY

MON

01 8:48 AM Oatmeal at home. 02 10:43 AM Workout Boost shake from Equinox at home. 03 12:47 PM Tomato bisque at Florent with Andy. 04 12:57 PM Bacon and Swiss omelet, string beans, five-grain toast. 05 4:37 PM Purefruits from Taylor's at construction site on 11th and Greenwich Streets. 06 8:18 PM Bread and herbed spread at Chubo with Doc and Sam. 07 8:28 PM Seared shrimp with crisp noodle pancake and bok choy at Chubo; warm frisée salad with grapefruit and bacon in background. *(continued on next page)*

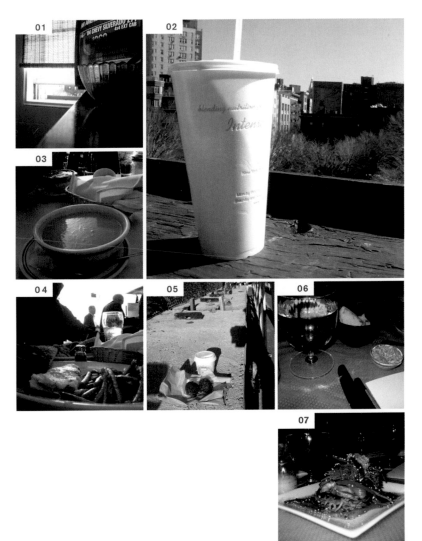

MONTH

JAN

FEB

MAR

APR

MAY

JUN

JUL

AUG

SEP

OCT

NOV

DEC

DATE

03/23

DAY

TUE

08 8:34 PM Broth with soba and beef-barley dumpling at Chubo. **09** 8:46 PM Roast pork at Chubo. **10** 8:47 PM Short ribs with kimchi orzo at Chubo. **11** 8:48 PM Grilled Cornish game hen alla Diavola at Chubo. **12** 9:14 PM Twin German mango pancakes at Chubo. **13** 10:00 PM Sesame and ginger chews at Chubo. **14** 12:22 AM Entenmann's donuts with Danny at home.

DATE

03/23

DAY

TUE

01 10:29 AM Oatmeal at home. 02 3:43 PM Smoky Joe sandwich (smoked turkey and smoked Gouda cheese) from Abingdon Market, apple at home. 03 9:51 PM Chicken fajita burrito from Burritoville at home with Danny. 04 10:12 PM Shredded Wheat at home.

MONTH

JAN

FEB

MAR

APR

MAY

JUN

JUL

AUG

SEP

OCT

NOV

DEC

DATE

03/24

DAY

WED

01 9:34 AM Oatmeal at home. 02 11:35 AM Corn flakes at the *New York Times* photo studio. 03 2:40 PM BLT and greens at Westville with Antonio. 04 2:59 PM Homemade sandwich cookie at Westville. 05 7:50 PM Spring rolls at Hue with Michael. 06 8:00 PM Seared beef salad (bon luc loc) at Hue. 07 8:12 PM Curried shrimp with pineapple and coconut sticky rice at Hue. 08 8:25 PM Duck two ways (grilled and confit) at Hue. 09 9:18 PM Fried coconut ice cream at Hue.

MONTH

JAN
FEB
MAR
APR
MAY
JUN
JUL
AUG
SEP
OCT
NOV
DEC

DATE

03/25

DAY

THU

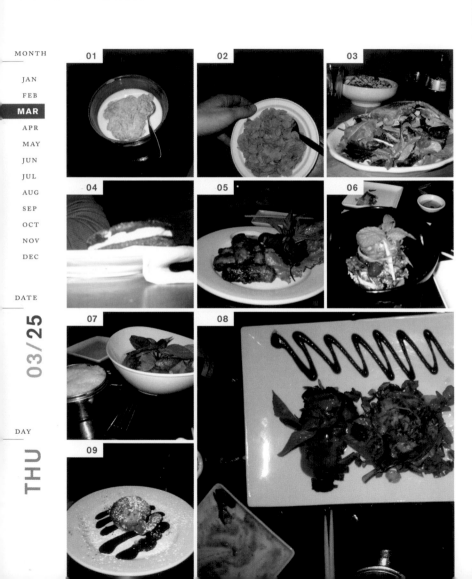

01 9:14 AM **Oatmeal at home.** 02 11:23 AM **Odwalla B-Monster on 12th Street.** 03 1:45 PM **Chicken and avocado sandwich from Pinnacle Deli with Jim at the 120th Street hard courts.** 04 6:24 PM **Cold sesame noodles from Mama Buddha at the park outside home, Hudson and Bank Streets.** 05 9:07 PM **Movie snax.** *Dawn of the Dead* with Jorge. 06 1:43 AM **Grilled cheese with bacon and tomato from Manatus with Danny at home.** 07 2:04 AM **Life cereal at home.**

MONTH

JAN

FEB

MAR

APR

MAY

JUN

JUL

AUG

SEP

OCT

NOV

DEC

DATE

03/26

DAY

FRI

01 11:21 AM **Grilled bagel with butter from Brew Bar.** 02 2:32 PM **Soppressata, mozzarella, and pesto on Italian bread from Barocco Hots at Bleecker Street Playground with Susan, Alex, Paul, and Henry.** 03 2:46 PM **Beet salad and chocolate chip cookie at Bleecker Street Playground.** 04 8:48 PM **Lay's Thick Cut Sea Salted chips at home.** 05 10:21 PM **Linguine carbonara with spinach at home.**

MONTH

JAN

FEB

MAR

APR

MAY

JUN

JUL

AUG

SEP

OCT

NOV

DEC

DATE

03/27

DAY

SAT

01

02

03

04

05

01 11:22 AM Plain bagel with cream cheese and Nova lox from Murray's at home. 02 5:16 PM Ham and cheese croissant from La Bergamote on 21st Street. 03 6:05 PM Lay's Thick Cut Sea Salted chips at home. 04 6:49 PM Cape Cod reduced-fat potato chips with Danny at home. 05 7:32 PM Baby carrots with Danny at home. 06 8:05 PM Onion soup with poached egg and Gruyère cheese at home. 07 9:29 PM Pepperidge Farm Brussels cookies at home. 08 9:40 PM Honey Nut Shredded Wheat at home.

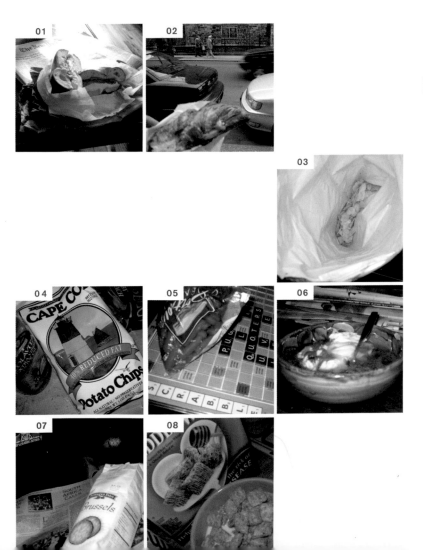

MONTH

JAN
FEB
MAR
APR
MAY
JUN
JUL
AUG
SEP
OCT
NOV
DEC

DATE

03/28

DAY

SUN

01 10:00 AM Oatmeal with sautéed bananas with Andy at Pastis. 02 3:01 PM Hot soppressata sandwich with mozzarella, red onion, and pesto at Barocco Hots. 03 6:04 PM Girl Scout Thin Mints from Jason at home. 04 9:07 PM Steak frites at Le Singe Vert with Karl. 05 10:33 PM Thin Mints with Danny at home. 06 11:05 PM Life cereal at home.

MONTH

JAN

FEB

MAR

APR

MAY

JUN

JUL

AUG

SEP

OCT

NOV

DEC

DATE

03/29

DAY

MON

01

02

03

04

05

06

01 11:30 AM Greek yogurt with berries and honey from Karen's on Astor Place. 02 2:37 PM BLT at Westville with Susan and Henry. 03 3:01 PM Homemade Little Debbie at Westville. 04 8:38 PM Risotto with bacon, spinach, and shrimp at home with Danny. 05 9:48 PM Honey Nut Shredded Wheat at home.

01

02

03

04

05

MONTH

JAN

FEB

MAR

APR

MAY

JUN

JUL

AUG

SEP

OCT

NOV

DEC

DATE

03/30

DAY

TUE

01 8:48 AM **Banana at home.** 02 12:52 PM **Beef consommé at Remi with Steven.** 03 1:04 PM **Roasted grouper at Remi.** 04 1:29 PM **Berry tiramisu at Remi.** 05 8:23 PM **Toro sashimi tartare at Megu with Chris.** 06 8:45 PM **Chef's selection of sushi at Megu.** 07 8:54 PM **Squid skewers and chef's grill at Megu.** 08 8:57 PM **Breaded pork at Megu.** *(continued on next page)*

MONTH

JAN
FEB
MAR
APR
MAY
JUN
JUL
AUG
SEP
OCT
NOV
DEC

DATE

03/31

DAY

WED

09 9:14 PM Sea urchin sashimi at Megu. 10 9:33 PM Seared toro skewer at Megu. 11 10:10 PM Quail egg at Jack's with Chris. 12 10:13 PM Bay scallops on the half-shell at Jack's. 13 10:21 PM Iced tea sorbet at Jack's. 14 10:46 PM Baba au rhum at Jack's (taken with no flash after great big scary maitre d' told me to quit taking pictures). 15 12:22 AM Pepperidge Farm Chocolate Chunk cookies at home with Danny.

01 1:22 PM **Purée of cauliflower soup with mushroom garni at Gotham with Dan.** 02 1:47 PM **Roasted sea bass with whipped potatoes and vegetables at Gotham with Dan.** 03 2:12 PM **Assorted sorbets at Gotham with Dan (chocolate cake in background).** 04 9:24 PM **Jorge's mixed greens at home with Danny and Jorge.** 05 9:39 PM **Spaghetti with pancetta and peperoncini at home.** 06 10:15 PM **Entenmann's chocolate chip cookies at home.**

MONTH

JAN

FEB

MAR

APR

MAY

JUN

JUL

AUG

SEP

OCT

NOV

DEC

DATE

04/01

DAY

THU

01 9:17 AM **Oatmeal at French Roast with Andy.** 02 2:27 PM **Peanut Heaven shake at Equinox.** 03 4:36 PM **Smoky Joe sandwich (smoked turkey, smoked Gouda cheese, sun-dried tomatoes, and arugula on wheat) from Abingdon Market at home.** 04 7:51 PM **Mixed salted nuts at home.** 05 9:22 PM **Carrot and squash soup at Antonio's.** 06 9:51 PM **Bacalau à Bráz and mixed greens at Antonio's.** 07 10:29 PM **Strawberries and low-carb ice cream at Antonio's.** 08 12:52 AM **Honey Nut Shredded Wheat at home.**

MONTH

JAN

FEB

MAR

APR

MAY

JUN

JUL

AUG

SEP

OCT

NOV

DEC

DATE

04/02

DAY

FRI

01 10:51 AM **Grilled bagel from Brew Bar at home.** 02 2:35 PM **Banana bread and hot-spiced grape juice at the farmers' market in Union Square with Chris.** 03 4:47 PM **Oatmeal at home.** 04 9:40 PM **Chips at home with Danny.** 05 9:42 PM **Buffalo jerky at home with Danny.** 06 10:33 PM **Cod, chips, and onion rings from A Salt and Battery at home with Danny.** 07 11:19 PM **Deep-fried Mars bar from A Salt and Battery.**

MONTH

JAN

FEB

MAR

APR

MAY

JUN

JUL

AUG

SEP

OCT

NOV

DEC

DATE

04/03

DAY

SAT

01 11:01 AM Bacon, egg, and cheese on a roll from Spyros at home. 02 1:31 PM Movie snax at 34th Street with Jason. *Hellboy.* 03 5:41 PM Potato chips at home with Danny. 04 7:31 PM Bacon Cheeseburger Deluxe from Manatus at home with Danny. 05 10:58 PM Rice Krispies at home with Moses.

MONTH

JAN
FEB
MAR
APR
MAY
JUN
JUL
AUG
SEP
OCT
NOV
DEC

DATE

04/04

DAY

SUN

01 9:03 AM Muesli with fresh fruit and café au lait at Le Gamin with Andy. 02 11:13 AM Quiche at Patisserie Claude with Tina. 03 4:13 PM Turkey and Havarti wrap from D'Agostino's at home. 04 7:35 PM Seder plate (horseradish, parsley, chicken bone, charoset, and egg) at Jeffrey's seder, with a whole bunch of people. 05 8:23 PM Matzo, horseradish and charoset, and egg. 06 8:30 PM Gefilte fish with horseradish. 07 9:09 PM Matzo ball soup. 08 9:34 PM Beef brisket, potatoes, carrots and raisins, and asparagus. 09 10:11 PM Macaroons and almond cookies. 10 10:15 PM Jelly candy. 11 11:55 PM Rice Krispies at home.

MONTH

JAN

FEB

MAR

APR

MAY

JUN

JUL

AUG

SEP

OCT

NOV

DEC

DATE

04/05

DAY

MON

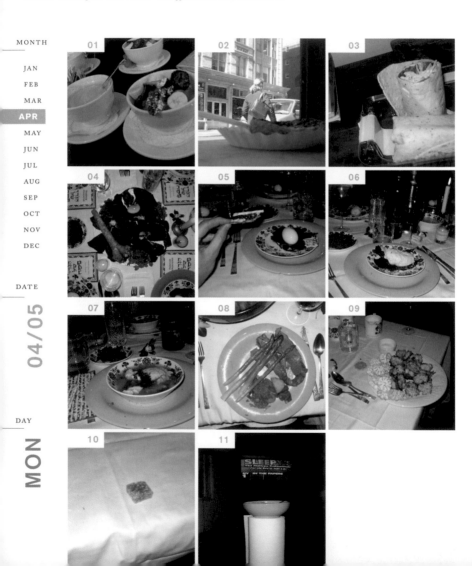

01 9:36 AM **Fried eggs at home.** 02 10:16 AM **Banana at home.** 03 10:23 AM **Macaroons at home.** 04 1:28 PM **BLT with mixed greens at Elmo with Andy.** 05 9:40 PM **Risotto with shrimp and sausage and poached egg at home with Jorge and Danny.** 06 9:56 PM **Macaroons at home.** 07 11:13 PM **Rice Krispies at home.**

MONTH

JAN
FEB
MAR
APR
MAY
JUN
JUL
AUG
SEP
OCT
NOV
DEC

DATE

04/06

DAY

TUE

01 9:07 AM **Croissant at Joe.** 02 12:32 PM **Peach smoothie with creatine from Equinox.** 03 2:42 PM **Ham, asparagus, and Taleggio panino at I Tre Merli Café with Susan, Tim, and Henry.** 04 8:38 PM **Popcorn at home with Danny.** 05 9:29 PM **Leftover risotto croquettes with fried eggs and spinach at home with Danny.** 06 12:08 AM **Cracklin' Oat Bran at home.**

MONTH

JAN

FEB

MAR

APR

MAY

JUN

JUL

AUG

SEP

OCT

NOV

DEC

DATE

04/07

DAY

WED

01 10:18 AM Oatmeal at home. 02 3:05 PM Dan dan noodles and pork soup dumplings from Grand Sichuan at Andy's office apartment. 03 5:16 PM Peach Dream smoothie from Elixir on Hudson Street. 04 9:15 PM Ketchup chips at home. 05 9:42 PM Chicken fajita burrito with extra guacamole and salsa fresca from Benny's Burritos at home with Danny. 06 10:18 PM Honey Nut Shredded Wheat at home.

MONTH

JAN
FEB
MAR
APR
MAY
JUN
JUL
AUG
SEP
OCT
NOV
DEC

DATE

04/08

DAY

THU

01 10:18 AM **Banana and OJ at home.** 02 3:12 PM **Smoky Joe sandwich from Abingdon Market.** 03 3:45 PM **Salted roasted almonds at home.** 04 7:28 PM **Movie snax.** *Eternal Sunshine of the Spotless Mind* with Antonio. 05 7:35 PM **Starburst assorted fruit flavors.** 06 10:10 PM **Assorted dips and bread at Calcutta with Antonio.** 07 10:19 PM **Keema nan and mincemeat samosas at Calcutta.** 08 10:39 PM **Chicken tikka makhnl, chicken kurma, black beans, nan at Calcutta.** 09 1:49 AM **Salted roasted almonds at home with Danny and Mark.**

MONTH

JAN
FEB
MAR
APR
MAY
JUN
JUL
AUG
SEP
OCT
NOV
DEC

DATE

04/09

DAY

FRI

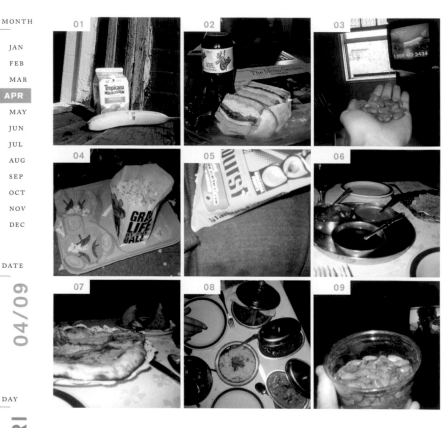

01 10:19 AM Banana and OJ at home. 02 3:09 PM Hot soppressata sandwich from Barocco Hots at home. 03 4:11 PM Doritos along the Hudson River with Jason. 04 5:29 PM Hot dog with Jason. 05 10:03 PM Antipasto plate at John's with Gray and John. 06 10:04 PM Bruschetta with goat cheese at John's. 07 10:29 PM Pappardelle with Tuscan meat sauce at John's.

MONTH

JAN
FEB
MAR
APR
MAY
JUN
JUL
AUG
SEP
OCT
NOV
DEC

DATE

04/10

DAY

SAT

01 11:31 AM **Grilled plain bagel with butter from Brew Bar at home.** 02 2:44 PM **Easter eggs at home with Danny, Jorge, Wayne, and Chris.** 03 5:01 PM **Chorizo at Rich's with Mac, Carlos, Steve, Rich K., Rich, Chris, Omar, Jorge, Wayne, Danny, and a bunch of other people.** 04 5:48 PM **Ham, turkey, asparagus, beet, cucumber, potatoes au gratin, and ambrosia at Rich's.** 05 6:02 PM **Chocolate eggs.** 06 6:33 PM **Mac's three-layer lemon, pistachio, and white chocolate Lady Baltimore cake.** 07 7:21 PM **Easter cupcakes for the road.** 08 8:37 PM **Entenmann's cheese-filled crumb cake at home with Danny.**

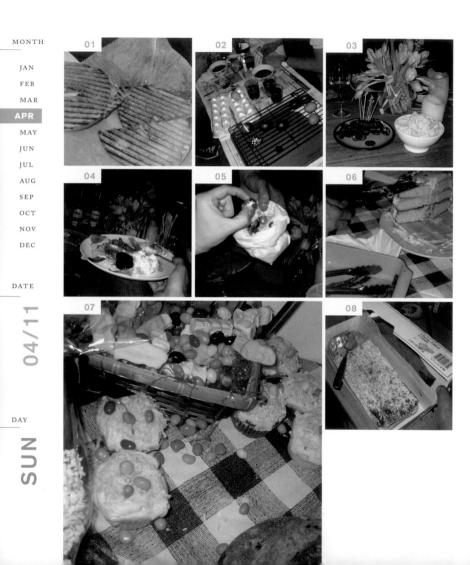

MONTH

JAN

FEB

MAR

APR

MAY

JUN

JUL

AUG

SEP

OCT

NOV

DEC

DATE

04/11

DAY

SUN

01 10:53 AM **Sugar toast with Dan at Panya.** 02 1:07 PM **Wheatgrass shot at Elixir.** 03 1:15 PM **Egg salad sandwich at home.** 04 4:09 PM **Purefruits from Taylor's at home.** 05 7:14 PM **Cape Cod reduced-fat chips at home.** 06 8:04 PM **Easter egg at home.** 07 8:57 PM **Baked ziti at home with Danny.** 08 10:19 PM **Leftover coffee cake at home with Danny.** 09 10:31 PM **Peeps at home with Danny.** 10 11:41 PM **Cracklin' Oat Bran at home.**

MONTH

JAN
FEB
MAR
APR
MAY
JUN
JUL
AUG
SEP
OCT
NOV
DEC

DATE

04/12

DAY

MON

01 7:43 AM Banana at home. 02 10:17 AM Oatmeal at home. 03 1:28 PM Leftover ziti at home. 04 6:57 PM Duck-liver pâté with Port jelly at BLT Steakhouse with Deb. 05 7:31 PM Gruyère popovers at BLT Steakhouse. 06 7:49 PM Assorted oysters at BLT Steakhouse. 07 8:04 PM Rib-eye for two (medium-rare) with roasted garlic and marrow, onion rings at BLT Steakhouse. 08 8:52 PM Steamed banana pudding, rum-raisin ice cream, chocolate cookies at BLT Steakhouse. 09 11:21 PM Cheerios at home.

MONTH

JAN

FEB

MAR

APR

MAY

JUN

JUL

AUG

SEP

OCT

NOV

DEC

DATE

04/13

DAY

TUE

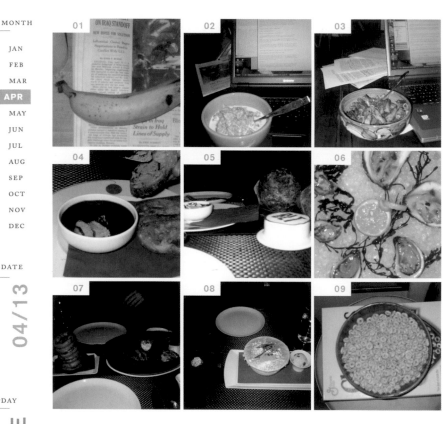

01 8:35 AM **Poppy-seed Danish from Lafayette Bakery on Greenwich Avenue.** 02 12:46 PM **Roast pork and broccoli rabe panino from Buon Italia in Chelsea Market.** 03 2:57 PM **Banana by the mailbox at home.** 04 7:29 PM **Japanese snapper sushi at Taka with J.J.** 05 7:31 PM **Fried squid at Taka.** 06 7:34 PM **Shrimp shumai at Taka.** 07 7:41 PM **Udon with tempura and egg at Taka.** 08 11:04 PM **Vanilla Almond Special K at home.**

MONTH

JAN
FEB
MAR
APR
MAY
JUN
JUL
AUG
SEP
OCT
NOV
DEC

DATE

04/14

DAY

WED

01 8:15 AM **Nutrigrain blueberry at St. Vincent's E.R. with Danny.** 02 10:48 AM **Nutrisnack apricot-oat bar at St. Vincent's.** 03 2:16 PM **Club sandwich from Blimpie's outside St. Vincent's.** 04 3:59 PM **Shot of wheatgrass and small All-Green at Elixir with Jorge.** 05 4:41 PM **Potato knish from the 2nd Avenue Deli at home.** 06 8:44 PM **Eggplant caponata, chicken liver pâté, white bean spread, and fava beans with walnuts at Gonzo with Tim, Alex, Susan, Andrea, and Tim A.** 07 8:45 PM **Soppressata pizza and artichoke pizza at Gonzo.** 08 8:53 PM **Roasted clams with garlic toast at Gonzo.** 09 9:18 PM **Pizza rustica with baked egg at Gonzo.** 10 9:22 PM **Braised escarole at Gonzo.** 11 9:58 PM **Hazelnut meringue–ice cream birthday sandwich at gonzo.** 12 11:31 PM **Cinnamon Life cereal at home.**

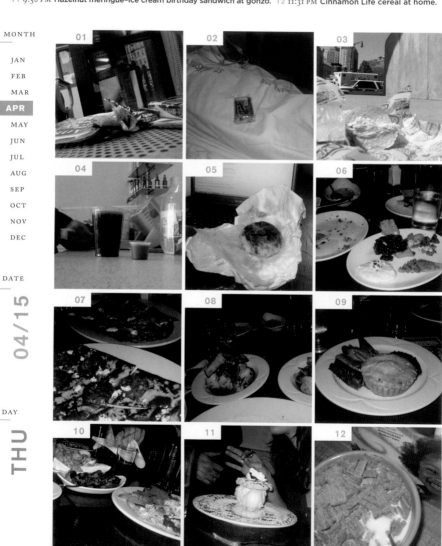

MONTH

JAN
FEB
MAR
APR
MAY
JUN
JUL
AUG
SEP
OCT
NOV
DEC

DATE

04/15

DAY

THU

01 8:57 AM **Banana at home.** 02 9:33 AM **Granola with fresh fruit at Pastis with Andy.** 03 1:47 PM **Soppressata and provolone from Barocco at home.** 04 2:27 PM **Hershey's caramel kisses at home.** 05 3:27 PM **Cheerios in Abingdon Square with Henry.** 06 5:32 PM **Pisatchios at home.** 07 8:31 PM **Tzatziki, spanakopita, eggplant at Opa! Souvlaki in Queens with John.** 08 8:37 PM **Saganaki at Opa! Souvlaki.** 09 8:38 PM **Broiled octopus at Opa!** 10 9:30 PM **Baklava and galaktobouriko at Opa!**

MONTH

JAN
FEB
MAR
APR
MAY
JUN
JUL
AUG
SEP
OCT
NOV
DEC

DATE

04/16

DAY

FRI

01 9:36 AM Toasted bagel from Bagels and More at home. 02 2:13 PM Gyro platter from Hudson Falafel.
03 2:55 PM Coconut "Cupcake for Kerry" at Democratic bake sale on Bleecker Street with Alex, Chris, and Susan.
04 5:00 PM Yogurt-covered pretzels. 05 7:45 PM Mixed nuts at the Mandarin Oriental with Marc, Chris, Tim A.,
Paul, Alex, Susan, Andrea, and Janice. 06 10:46 PM Cheeseburger Deluxe from Bus Stop at home. 07 11:51 PM
Cinnamon Life at home.

MONTH

JAN

FEB

MAR

APR

MAY

JUN

JUL

AUG

SEP

OCT

NOV

DEC

DATE

04/17

DAY

SAT

01 3:17 PM **Asparagus and chips at Susan and Andrea's with Tim A., Christopher, Marc, Tim M., Paul, Alex, John, Wes, and Henry (not pictured: deviled egg).** 02 3:30 PM **Cheeseburgers and hot dogs at Susan and Andrea's.** 03 3:32 PM **Potato salad, green salad, and coleslaw at Susan and Andrea's.** 04 6:41 PM **Mixed greens at home.** 05 9:42 PM **Low-carb chocolates at Karl's.** 06 9:44 PM **Low-carb cheesecake at Karl's.** 07 12:14 AM **Vanilla Almond Special K at home.**

01 10:20 AM **Banana on the 1 train.** 02 10:51 AM **Corn muffin from the coffee stand on 116th and Broadway at the 120th Street courts.** 03 2:59 PM **Smoky Joe sandwich from Abingdon Market at home.** 04 7:47 PM **Beef jerky at home.** 05 8:39 PM **Popcorn at home.** 06 9:56 PM **Eggs with spinach, salsa, and tortillas at home.** 07 11:35 PM **Vanilla Almond Special K at home.** 08 1:53 AM **Vanilla wafer cookies at home.**

MONTH

JAN
FEB
MAR
APR
MAY
JUN
JUL
AUG
SEP
OCT
NOV
DEC

DATE

04/19

DAY

MON

01 9:35 AM Granola with fruit at French Roast with Andy. 02 3:49 PM Cobb salad from Chop't along the Hudson with Henry. 03 7:45 PM Spicy tuna and Asian pear at Matsuri with Doc and Chris. 04 7:47 PM Oysters with crushed yuzu ice at Matsuri. 05 7:59 PM Lotus root with sesame and chiles at Matsuri. 06 8:12 PM Selection of sashimi—toro, sweet shrimp, urchin, eel-avocado roll, dried squash roll—at Matsuri. 07 8:31 PM Sliced Kobe beef with mustard sauce at Matsuri. 08 8:36 PM Skewered chicken with chiles at Matsuri. 09 8:39 PM Eel tempura with green-tea salt at Matsuri. 10 8:45 PM Miso-glazed black cod at Matsuri. 11 8:51 PM Salmon collar with shiso and broccoli rabe at Matsuri. 12 9:15 PM Roasted pineapple, beignets, and citrus sauce at Matsuri (ginger crème brûlée, Valrhona chocolate tart in background).

MONTH

JAN
FEB
MAR
APR
MAY
JUN
JUL
AUG
SEP
OCT
NOV
DEC

DATE

04/20

DAY

TUE

01 10:26 AM **Oatmeal at home.** 02 2:26 PM **Smoked salmon on pumpernickel on Crosby Street from Dean & DeLuca.** 03 3:15 PM **Peach Dream smoothie from Elixir on Hudson Street.** 04 5:04 PM **Pistachios at home.** 05 8:47 PM **Fried pork dumplings, steamed vegetable dumplings, mushu pork and mushu chicken (extra plum sauce) from Mama Buddha at home with Danny.** 06 10:10 PM **Cheerios at home.**

MONTH

JAN

FEB

MAR

APR

MAY

JUN

JUL

AUG

SEP

OCT

NOV

DEC

DATE

04/21

DAY

WED

01 11:51 AM **Popeye Eggs at Sarabeth's with Mom.** 02 2:48 PM **Immune Booster smoothie from Elixir on Hudson Street.** 03 6:29 PM **Microwave popcorn at home.** 04 7:43 PM **Green salad, bruschetta, spaghetti with pesto from Tanti Baci at home.** 05 9:04 PM **Cheerios at home.**

MONTH

JAN
FEB
MAR
APR
MAY
JUN
JUL
AUG
SEP
OCT
NOV
DEC

DATE

04/22

DAY

THU

01 9:39 AM **Oatmeal at home.** 02 2:27 PM **Smoked salmon sandwich from Taylor's at home.** 03 7:55 PM **Mixed nuts with Jorge at home.** 04 8:45 PM **Movie snax (popcorn, Reese's Pieces, Sour Patch Kids).** *Kill Bill Part 2* at 19th and Broadway with Jorge and Wayne. 05 12:33 AM **Beef jerky at home with Danny.** 06 1:18 AM **Grilled cheese, bacon, tomato from Manatus at home with Danny.**

MONTH

JAN
FEB
MAR
APR
MAY
JUN
JUL
AUG
SEP
OCT
NOV
DEC

DATE

04/23

DAY

FRI

01 9:40 AM **Fuji apple cider at the Abingdon Farmers' Market.** 02 12:03 PM **Eggs and tortillas at home.** 03 3:24 PM **Lime Frozfruit and Strawberry Frozfruit on Washington Street with Jason.** 04 3:48 PM **Cherry Frozfruit on Spring Street with Jason.** 05 6:24 PM **Maple-cured turkey and Swiss from Abingdon Market at home.** 06 10:23 PM **Mongolian beef from Spice at home with Danny.**

MONTH

JAN
FEB
MAR
APR
MAY
JUN
JUL
AUG
SEP
OCT
NOV
DEC

DATE

04/24

DAY

SAT

01 9:24 AM Croissant at Panino Gusto on Hudson Street. 02 2:09 PM Chips and cheese dip at Rocking Horse with Susan, Andrea, and Henry. 03 2:19 PM Carnitas with guacamole and red onion at Rocking Horse. 04 4:54 PM Mixed nuts at home with Jorge. 05 6:25 PM Hard licorice stick at Chelsea Market with Jorge. 06 7:10 PM Brazilian chocolate-banana candy from Paul at home. 07 8:03 PM Quick quesadilla with D'Agostino's Mexican Blend shredded cheese with Jason and the Queen Mary 2. 08 8:52 PM Pepperoni, onion, and tomato pizza at home with Danny. 09 9:41 PM Entenmann's lemon crunch cake at home with Danny.

MONTH

JAN
FEB
MAR
APR
MAY
JUN
JUL
AUG
SEP
OCT
NOV
DEC

DATE

04/25

DAY

SUN

01 7:28 AM **Oatmeal at home.** 02 11:40 AM **Hamburger and honey sandwich, broccoli, green beans, and bug juice with Ms. Zimmermann's first-grade class at Allen-Stevenson.** 03 11:49 AM **Popsicle at Allen-Stevenson.** 04 7:36 PM **Low-fat chips at home.** 05 8:02 PM **Quick quesadilla with smoked Gouda at home.** 06 9:04 PM **Fusilli with ham, smoked Gouda, diced tomatoes, and broccoli rabe with Danny at home.** 07 10:05 PM **Stella D'oro swiss fudge cookies with Danny at home.** 08 10:11 PM **Leftover lemon crunch cake at home.** 09 11:02 PM **Life cereal at home.**

MONTH

JAN

FEB

MAR

APR

MAY

JUN

JUL

AUG

SEP

OCT

NOV

DEC

DATE

04/26

DAY

MON

01 8:16 AM **Oatmeal at home.** 02 1:09 PM **Berry Lean shake with extra vitamin C from Elixir on Hudson Street.** 03 3:04 PM **Ham and cheese on tortilla, spinach with arugula, and carrots at home.** 04 7:39 PM **Apple at home.** 05 7:49 PM **Dried salted peas at home.** 06 8:09 PM **Ketchup chips at home with Danny.** 07 8:48 PM **White Rose pasta dinner doctored up with ham and smoked Gouda.** 08 10:19 PM **Life cereal at home.**

MONTH

JAN
FEB
MAR
APR
MAY
JUN
JUL
AUG
SEP
OCT
NOV
DEC

DATE

04/27

DAY

TUE

01 8:44 AM **Brioche and coffee at La Bergamote.** 02 10:50 AM **Strawberries at home.** 03 1:20 PM **Orange at home.** 04 1:49 PM **Snickers on Jane Street.** 05 2:47 PM **Peanut Heaven smoothie from Equinox on Bank Street.** 06 7:09 PM **Apple at home.** 07 9:00 PM **Peasant bread at Il Buco with Barry, Alex, Lalita, Paul, Liz, Steven, Patches, Wesley, Andrea, and birthday-boy Buzz.** *(continued on next page)*

MONTH

JAN

FEB

MAR

APR

MAY

JUN

JUL

AUG

SEP

OCT

NOV

DEC

DATE

04/28

DAY

WED

08 9:10 PM Grilled octopus salad with asparagus at Il Buco. **09** 9:12 PM Pizzetta with sprouts and red bell peppers, fried oysters and lemon slices at Il Buco. **10** 9:39 PM Artichoke-heart salad at Il Buco. **11** 9:48 PM Country sausages with peas and onions at Il Buco. **12** 10:29 PM Grilled rib-eye with dandelion leaves and roasted garlic at Il Buco. **13** 11:18 PM Chocolate birthday cake, lemon tart, rhubarb tart at Il Buco. **14** 12:24 AM Life cereal at home.

DATE

04/28

DAY

WED

01 9:43 AM **Oatmeal with fried bananas at Pastis.** 02 11:54 AM **Balance Gold on the 7th Avenue subway.**
03 3:40 PM **Soppressata with tomatoes, arugula, and mustard from Barocco Hots.** 04 8:09 PM **Fried calamari at Meet with Jason.** 05 8:30 PM **Gnocchi with crispy pancetta, fries, and mussels with tomato at Meet.**
06 11:13 PM **Cheerios at home.**

MONTH

JAN

FEB

MAR

APR

MAY

JUN

JUL

AUG

SEP

OCT

NOV

DEC

DATE

04/29

DAY

THU

New York to Las Vegas **01** 8:12 AM **Egg McMuffin at JFK with Andrea, Susan, and Alex. 02** 10:14 AM **Peanuts and coffee over Ohio with Andrea, Susan, and Alex. 03** 1:48 PM **Nachos at Kahunaville at Treasure Island with Tim, Alex, Susan, and Andrea. 04** 2:08 PM **Crunchy chicken, bacon, and pecan salad with creamy bacon dressing at Kahunaville. 05** 7:48 PM **Cornbread muffins and rolls at Emeril's at MGM Grand with Tim, Alex, Susan, and Andrea. 06** 7:58 PM **Oysters at Emeril's MGM. 07** 8:08 PM **Gazpacho with lobster and greens at Emeril's MGM. 08** 8:21 PM **Soft-shell crab with succotash and cocktail sauce at Emeril's MGM. 09** 8:39 PM **Creole-spiced salmon over potatoes** *(continued on next page)*

MONTH

JAN

FEB

MAR

APR

MAY

JUN

JUL

AUG

SEP

OCT

NOV

DEC

DATE

04/30

DAY

FRI

at Emeril's MGM. 10 9:01 PM Seared ahi tuna with white beans at Emeril's MGM. 11 9:21 PM Beef tenderloin with roasted garlic and wine-reduction sauce at Emeril's MGM. 12 9:58 PM Rustic blueberry tart, citrus puff pastry, and banana cream pie at Emeril's MGM.

MAY

- call Susan
- raincoat
- sweater
- need blazer
- get heel repaired on boots
- Mother's day

- extraction
- braces 5/25

- deadline 5/
- Vegas # - r
- Passport
- Milano, Torino, Bologna, Florence -
- car to Kennedy (Newark?)
- Old Homestead

call Bumps, Ed. Cool

Las Vegas **01** 11:45 AM Granola and banana at Kahunaville Cabana at Treasure Island with Susan, Andrea, and Alex. **02** 3:06 PM Nachos and two salsas at El Sombrero with Susan, Andrea, and Alex. **03** 3:30 PM Burrito with pork verde and red sauce at El Sombrero. **04** 3:44 PM Vanilla pudding with raisins and rum at El Sombrero. **05** 10:03 PM Roasted peanuts at the Peppermill Lounge with Susan. **06** 10:29 PM Shrimp cocktail at the Peppermill Lounge. **07** 11:06 PM Patty melt at the Peppermill Lounge with Susan, Andrea, Alex, and Tim. (Tim's Cobb salad in background.) **08** 1:44 AM Snax at Treasure Island.

MONTH

JAN

FEB

MAR

APR

MAY

JUN

JUL

AUG

SEP

OCT

NOV

DEC

DATE

05/01

DAY

SAT

Las Vegas **01** 12:50 PM **Fruit plate at Kahunaville with Susan, Andrea, Tim, and Alex. 02** 2:00 PM **Monterey chicken wrap at Kahunaville. 03** 5:41 PM **Cappuccino at Zefferino at the Venetian with Susan. 04** 7:02 PM **Champagne snax with Andrea, Susan, Tim, and Alex at Treasure Island. 05** 8:44 PM **Avocado and onion salad; oysters; roasted red peppers; Caesar salad; fava beans with Parmesan, prosciutto, and bread at Craft Steak at the MGM with Susan, Andrea, Tim, and Alex.** *(continued on next page)*

01

02

03

04

05

MONTH

JAN
FEB
MAR
APR
MAY
JUN
JUL
AUG
SEP
OCT
NOV
DEC

DATE

05/02

DAY

SUN

06 9:09 PM Porterhouse with marrow, New York strip, rib-eye, braised short ribs, sautéed morels, grilled asparagus, steamed peas, Yukon gold potato purée, frites, and potatoes au gratin at Craft Steak. **07** 10:07 PM Angel food birthday cake at Craft Steak. **08** 10:08 PM Chocolate cake with vanilla sauce, mixed berry crumble, monkey bread with caramel sauce, assorted ice creams at Craft Steak. **09** 10:09 PM Mixed berries at Craft Steak. **10** 10:10 PM Brioche bread pudding at Craft Steak.

DATE

05/02

DAY

SUN

Las Vegas to New York City **01** 9:26 AM **Orange juice at Treasure Island. 02** 3:30 PM **Peanuts and apple juice over Nebraska. 03** 4:23 PM **Turkey sandwich with roasted red peppers, potato chips, and lemon cookie over Chicago. 04** 11:02 PM **Fried eggs at home. 05** 11:53 PM **Honey Nut Cheerios at home.**

MONTH

JAN
FEB
MAR
APR
MAY
JUN
JUL
AUG
SEP
OCT
NOV
DEC

DATE

05/03

DAY

MON

New York City to Milano 01 8:45 AM Grilled bagel with butter from Brew Bar at home. 02 12:59 PM Smoky Joe sandwich from Abingdon Market, Workout Boost shake from Elixir at home. 03 4:46 PM Strawberries from Panini Express at JFK. 04 6:58 PM Europe Central Time, Alitalia flight 605 to Milan. Steamed sea bass, spinach, bow-tie pasta in red sauce, poached chicken with carrots, Babybel cheese, roll, crackers, mixed fruit.

MONTH

JAN
FEB
MAR
APR
MAY
JUN
JUL
AUG
SEP
OCT
NOV
DEC

DATE

05/04

DAY

TUE

Milano to Torino **01** 6:14 AM Focaccia with ham, cinnamon roll on flight 605. **02** 1:12 PM Swordfish carpaccio, salad, and grape tomatoes with Francesco at Chiara and Francesco's apartment. **03** 2:06 PM Mascerated fruit and olives with Francesco. **04** 8:35 PM Cheese sticks and puffed rice at Locanda Mongreno restaurant with Chiara, Francesco, and John. **05** 8:51 PM Smoked duck with citrus and ginger at Locanda Mongreno. *(continued on next page)*

01 02 03

04 05

MONTH

JAN
FEB
MAR
APR
MAY
JUN
JUL
AUG
SEP
OCT
NOV
DEC

DATE

05/05

DAY

WED

06 9:07 PM Octopus ravioli with sun-dried tomatoes and consommé at Locanda Mongreno. **07** 9:31 PM Linguine with asparagus and nutmeg at Locanda Mongreno. **08** 9:56 PM Local trout with apples and tea at Locanda Mongreno. **09** 10:17 PM Assorted bonbons (ginger, almond, lavender, cardamom, preserved orange slices) at Locanda Mongreno. **10** 10:31 PM Bitter-chocolate tart with unsweetened whipped cream, berries, and cocoa powder at Locanda Mongreno.

Torino to Bologna 01 9:47 AM Baked apple and croissant at Victoria Hotel, Torino, with Francesco and Chiara. 02 12:54 PM Macaroons, a gift from visiting students at the 2004 Torino Book Fair (Fiera Internazionale del Libro). 03 1:19 PM Pastry from visiting students at the 2004 Torino Book Fair. 04 1:39 PM Lasagne Bolognese, sautéed zucchini, and roasted potatoes at Ciao! with Lisa, Gianluca, Alessandro, and Francesca. 05 9:41 PM Antipasto (chick peas, white beans, tomatoes, green beans, and polenta) at Questo & Quello, Bologna, with Lisa and John. 06 9:50 PM Broccoli soufflés with sautéed fennel at Questo & Quello. 07 10:06 PM Veal carpaccio with warm tomato relish at Questo & Quello. 08 10:16 PM Ravioli with asparagus and artichoke at Questo & Quello. 09 10:42 PM Rabbit braised with olives and leeks at Questo & Quello. 10 11:30 PM Chocolate torte with citrus marmalade at Questo & Quello.

MONTH

JAN
FEB
MAR
APR
MAY
JUN
JUL
AUG
SEP
OCT
NOV
DEC

DATE

05/06

DAY

THU

Bologna to Firenze 01 8:13 AM Croissant and yogurt at Hotel Excelsior, Bologna. 02 11:01 AM Pressed roasted vegetable sandwich at Libreria Veronese, Bologna, with a bunch of schoolchildren. 03 1:25 PM Salad of cracked wheat, ricotta, and vegetables at Divinis, Bologna, with Lisa and John. 04 1:47 PM Mixed salami at Divinis. 05 8:49 PM Assorted bruschetta at Enzo e Piero, Firenze, with Alessandro, Francesca, and John. 06 9:09 PM Ribollita at Enzo e Piero. 07 9:39 PM Bistecca alla Fiorentina at Enzo e Piero. 08 10:21 PM Panna cotta with strawberries at Enzo e Piero.

MONTH

JAN
FEB
MAR
APR
MAY
JUN
JUL
AUG
SEP
OCT
NOV
DEC

DATE

05/07

DAY

FRI

Firenze 01 9:18 AM Cake, biscuits, and coffee at Hotel Locanda degli Artisti. 02 11:18 AM Pressed roasted vegetable sandwich with assembled Florentine students at Biblioteca Isolotto. 03 1:33 PM Scallopini of pork and mixed salad at Enzo e Piero with Francesco, Chiara, and John. 04 8:35 PM Pappa di pomodoro at unnamed restaurant in Firenze with Alessandro and Francesca. 05 9:07 PM Bistecca alla fiorentina.

MONTH

JAN

FEB

MAR

APR

MAY

JUN

JUL

AUG

SEP

OCT

NOV

DEC

DATE

05/08

DAY

SAT

Firenze to Milano 01 9:37 AM Croissant and yogurt at Hotel Locanda degli Artisti with Alessandro and Francesca. 02 1:36 PM Salami, artichoke, and toasted bread at Trattoria Pallotino, Firenze, with Alessandro and Francesca. 03 1:49 PM Rigatoni alla Pallotino with tomato, pancetta, and basil at Trattoria Pallotino. 04 2:05 PM Tomatoes and eggs at Trattoria Pallotino. 05 7:30 PM Panino with salami from panini stand in Firenze. 06 12:00 AM Kit Kat at Hotel Cavour, Milano.

MONTH

JAN

FEB

MAR

APR

MAY

JUN

JUL

AUG

SEP

OCT

NOV

DEC

DATE

05/09

DAY

SUN

Milano 01 10:01 AM Croissant, breads, and muesli at Hotel Cavour, Milano. 02 12:39 PM Crackers with Lisa at the Disney Worldwide office. 03 1:13 PM Marinated sardines with Lisa, Alessandro, Laura, and other members of the Disney publishing team, at Mediateca restaurant in Milano. 04 1:39 PM Arugula with ricotta and speck at Mediateca. 05 1:57 PM Chocolate torte at Mediateca. 06 7:46 PM Francesco's marinated anchovies, olive bread, home-dried tomatoes, and olives at Chiara and Francesco's with Francesco, Chiara, John, and Alessandro. 07 8:09 PM Francesco's pasta alla frutti di mare. *(continued on next page)*

MONTH

JAN
FEB
MAR
APR
MAY
JUN
JUL
AUG
SEP
OCT
NOV
DEC

DATE

05/10

DAY

MON

08 8:33 PM **Arugula and grape tomatoes.** 09 8:45 PM **Francesco's grilled branzino.** 10 9:10 PM **Francesco's grilled calamari.** 11 9:30 PM **Sardinian pecorino secco cheese with bitter honey and bread.** 12 9:53 PM **Mascerated fruit.** 13 10:05 PM **Assorted chocolates.**

Milano to New York City **01** 7:01 AM Croissant and breads at Hotel Cavour, Milano. **02** 11:48 AM EUROPE CENTRAL TIME. Whitefish with zucchini, pasta with red sauce, smoked salmon, cheese, crackers, roll, and mixed fruit on Alitalia flight 604. **03** 11:19 AM EASTERN DAYLIGHT TIME. Pastry with red sauce, almond cake on flight 604. **04** 7:04 PM Reduced-fat potato chips at home. **05** 9:26 PM Pad Thai with shrimp, spring rolls at home with Danny. **06** 10:08 PM Wheaties at home.

MONTH

JAN

FEB

MAR

APR

MAY

JUN

JUL

AUG

SEP

OCT

NOV

DEC

DATE

05/11

DAY

TUE

01 9:42 AM **Oatmeal at home.** 02 2:25 PM **Bread at I Tre Merli with Susan, Henry, and Tim.** 03 2:55 PM **Milano panino with Taleggio and salami at I Tre Merli.** 04 8:24 PM **Sardinian pecorino secco at home.** 05 9:06 PM **Garlic bread at Old Homestead with Chris.** 06 9:17 PM **Chopped salad at Old Homestead.** 07 9:56 PM **Porterhouse for two, sautéed mushrooms, baked potato at Old Homestead.** 08 10:24 PM **Cheesecake with blueberries at Old Homestead.**

MONTH

JAN
FEB
MAR
APR
MAY
JUN
JUL
AUG
SEP
OCT
NOV
DEC

DATE

05/12

DAY

WED

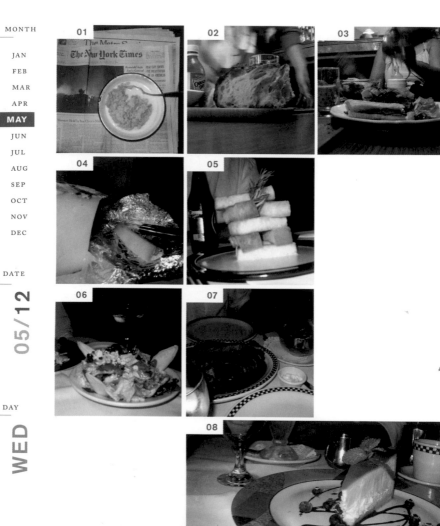

01 2:09 PM **Yogurt and Odwalla Superfood at home.** 02 2:44 PM **Tomato soup at home.** 03 6:43 PM **Yoplait vanilla custard style at home.** 04 8:49 PM **Scrambled eggs, spinach, and chicken stock at home.** 05 10:39 PM **Häagen Dazs tres leches ice cream at home.**

01

02

03

04
05

MONTH

JAN

FEB

MAR

APR

MAY

JUN

JUL

AUG

SEP

OCT

NOV

DEC

DATE

05/13

DAY

THU

01 10:11 AM **Oatmeal and coffee at home.** 02 12:50 PM **Odwalla Protein 2004, vanilla yogurt at deli on 23rd Street with Andy.** 03 4:56 PM **Mozzarella and tomato salad from Taylor's, Power Apple smoothie from Elixir at home.** 04 7:11 PM **Lemon yogurt at home.** 05 8:25 PM **Tomato soup with poached egg at home.** 06 10:20 PM **Movie snax at Kips Bay theater.** *Troy* **with Jorge.** 07 2:24 AM **Häagen Dazs tres leches ice cream at home.**

MONTH

JAN

FEB

MAR

APR

MAY

JUN

JUL

AUG

SEP

OCT

NOV

DEC

DATE

05/14

DAY

FRI

01 10:12 AM Odwalla Superfood, lemon yogurt at home. 02 1:22 PM Onion consommé with Parmesan crisp at Eleven Madison with Heather and Johanne. 03 1:38 PM One-side-seared tuna tartare at Eleven Madison. 04 8:10 PM Gumbo at Bayou with Heather, Sally, Mary Kay, and Johanne. 05 8:29 PM Fried catfish, hush puppies, and fries at Bayou. 06 9:20 PM Lemon icebox cake, pecan pie, and bread pudding with whiskey sauce at Bayou. 07 12:42 AM Häagen Dazs tres leches ice cream at home.

MONTH

JAN
FEB
MAR
APR
MAY
JUN
JUL
AUG
SEP
OCT
NOV
DEC

DATE

05/15

DAY

SAT

01 1:27 PM **Belated Mother's Day raspberry-and-coconut shake at Norma's with Mom.** **02** 1:55 PM **Four-cheese omelet at Norma's.** **03** 10:40 PM Pasta with olive oil and salt at home.

MONTH

JAN
FEB
MAR
APR
MAY
JUN
JUL
AUG
SEP
OCT
NOV
DEC

DATE

05/16

DAY

SUN

01 9:37 AM La Yogurt Sabor Latino and orange juice on the library steps, 5th Avenue. 02 4:13 PM Odwalla Superfood, yogurt, and banana in Abingdon Square. 03 9:18 PM Bruschetta from Tanti Baci at home. 04 9:58 PM Spaghetti Bolognese from Tanti Baci at home.

MONTH

JAN

FEB

MAR

APR

MAY

JUN

JUL

AUG

SEP

OCT

NOV

DEC

DATE

05/17

DAY

MON

01

02

03

04

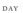

01 9:39 AM Omega-3 oatmeal from Sacred Chow at Bleecker Street playground. **02** 2:10 PM Soppressata sandwich with mozzarella, arugula, and red onion marmalade from Barocco Hots at home. **03** 4:13 PM Cherry yogurt at home. **04** 8:34 PM Crab cakes at Florent with Jason. **05** 8:45 PM Vegetarian chili at Florent. **06** 11:09 PM Häagen Dazs tres leches ice cream at home.

MONTH

JAN
FEB
MAR
APR
MAY
JUN
JUL
AUG
SEP
OCT
NOV
DEC

DATE

05/18

DAY

TUE

01 10:25 AM **Oatmeal** at home. 02 1:14 PM **Soppressata** at home. 03 2:34 PM **Cherry-vanilla yogurt** at home.
04 3:57 PM **Carrot-ginger soup** at home. 05 7:11 PM **Banana** at home. 06 9:11 PM **Pecorino secco** at home.
07 10:02 PM **Azteca combo (green taco, chile relleno, beans and rice)** from Mary Ann's at home with Danny.
08 10:44 PM **Soggy Wheaties** at home.

MONTH

JAN

FEB

MAR

APR

MAY

JUN

JUL

AUG

SEP

OCT

NOV

DEC

DATE

05/19

DAY

WED

01 8:45 AM Vanilla yogurt at home. 02 12:33 PM Breaded chicken on Italian bread with herbed mayonnaise and onions at Sandwiches with Andy. 03 2:13 PM Cheerios by the river with Henry. 04 8:07 PM Bread at Arezzo with Chris. 05 8:15 PM Fried calamari and zucchini at Arezzo. 06 8:16 PM Wood oven-toasted focaccia with Robiola cheese, spinach, and truffle oil at Arezzo. 07 8:28 PM Fresh pea cavatelli with tomatoes, sausages, and Parmesan at Arezzo. 08 8:49 PM Wood oven-roasted striped bass, braised escarole, and potatoes at Arezzo. 09 10:31 PM Wheaties at home.

MONTH

JAN

FEB

MAR

APR

MAY

JUN

JUL

AUG

SEP

OCT

NOV

DEC

DATE

05/20

DAY

THU

01 8:44 AM Oatmeal at home. 02 12:58 PM Cobb salad at Moonstruck Diner on 9th Ave with Betsy and Andy.
03 6:50 PM Banana at home. 04 7:55 PM Potato chips at home. 05 9:46 PM Spaghetti with spinach, pancetta,
and three cheeses (grano, Parmesan, ricotta) at home. 06 11:11 PM Entenmann's cheese-filled crumb cake
at home.

MONTH

JAN

FEB

MAR

APR

MAY

JUN

JUL

AUG

SEP

OCT

NOV

DEC

DATE

05/21

DAY

FRI

01

02

03

04

05

06

01 11:42 AM Greek yogurt and honey at home. 02 3:16 PM Leftover pasta, refried, at home. 03 9:28 PM Assorted oysters at Strip House with Susan, Andrea, and Tim. 04 9:57 PM Assorted breads at Strip House. 05 10:20 PM Watermelon ice at Strip House. 06 10:28 PM Sautéed langostinos at Strip House. 07 10:44 PM Tomato, onion, and cucumber salad at Strip House. 08 11:01 PM Rib chop, creamed spinach, and goose-fat potatoes at Strip House. 09 11:37 PM Cheesecake at Strip House. 10 11:58 PM Assorted chocolates at Strip House.

MONTH

JAN
FEB
MAR
APR
MAY
JUN
JUL
AUG
SEP
OCT
NOV
DEC

DATE

05/22

DAY

SAT

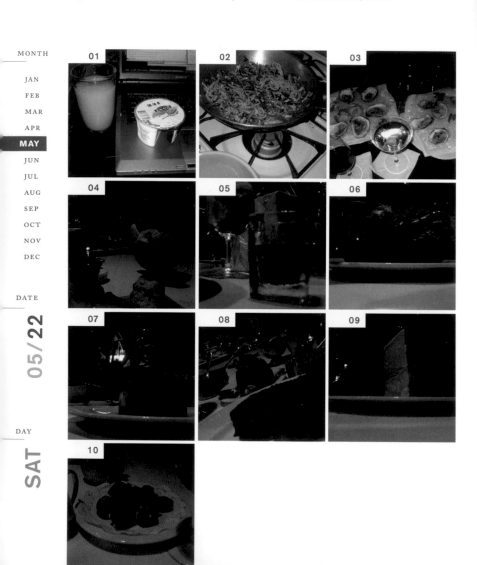

01 2:04 PM Oatmeal at home. 02 3:54 PM Vanilla yogurt at home. 03 7:34 PM Potato chips at home. 04 8:29 PM Mixed salad with grape tomatoes at home. 05 10:25 PM Denver omelet at home. 06 11:15 PM Wheaties at home. 07 11:38 PM Häagen Dazs coffee ice cream at home.

MONTH

JAN

FEB

MAR

APR

MAY

JUN

JUL

AUG

SEP

OCT

NOV

DEC

DATE

05/23

DAY

SUN

01 10:22 AM Oatmeal at home. 02 1:08 PM Nutrament on Bank Street. 03 6:03 PM Greek yogurt and honey at home. 04 6:50 PM Banana at home. 05 7:27 PM Avocado at home. 06 7:46 PM D'Agostino's white bean soup at home. 07 8:35 PM Soppressata at home. 08 9:08 PM Omelet with three cheeses, tomatoes, and sautéed onions at home. 09 10:36 PM Häagen Dazs vanilla fudge ice cream at home.

MONTH

JAN
FEB
MAR
APR
MAY
JUN
JUL
AUG
SEP
OCT
NOV
DEC

DATE

05/24

DAY

MON

01 11:18 AM **Banana** at home. 02 12:27 PM **Workout Boost shake** from Equinox at home. 03 1:53 PM **Tomato soup with poached egg** at home. 04 6:28 PM **Monterey jack cheese** at home. 05 9:00 PM **Catfish and scallion** at 5 Ninth with Doc. 06 9:10 PM **Peas with bacon and fava beans, pork belly with scallion and jellyfish** at 5 Ninth (roasted oysters in background). 07 9:40 PM **Braised lamb shoulder with cavatelli** at 5 Ninth (Squab Two Ways in background). 08 10:34 PM **Strawberry shortcake with shaved coconut** at 5 Ninth (fried calamari in background). 09 11:41 PM **Häagen Dazs dulce de leche ice cream** at home.

MONTH

JAN
FEB
MAR
APR
MAY
JUN
JUL
AUG
SEP
OCT
NOV
DEC

DATE

05/25

DAY

TUE

01 11:34 AM **Oatmeal at home.** 02 3:38 PM **Dark-meat turkey on sourdough with herbed mayo, lettuce, and tomato and side of gazpacho and chips from Sandwiches on Greenwich Ave. at home.** 03 9:44 PM **Grilled cheese and tomato, fries from Bus Stop at home.** 04 11:01 PM **Häagen Dazs chocolate peanut butter ice cream at home.**

MONTH

JAN
FEB
MAR
APR
MAY
JUN
JUL
AUG
SEP
OCT
NOV
DEC

DATE

05/26

DAY

WED

01

02

03

04

01 10:20 AM Oatmeal at home. 02 1:40 PM Turkey on wheat with herbed mayo, lettuce, red onion, tomato, and hot sauce from Sandwiches at home. 03 6:30 PM Greek yogurt and honey at home. 04 8:56 PM Sautéed eggplant with mozzarella at Grano Trattoria with Jason (sautéed artichoke with pancetta and Parmesan in background). 05 9:14 PM Pappardelle with lamb ragout at Grano Trattoria (four-cheese ravioli in background). 06 9:47 PM Biscotti and espresso at Grano Trattoria. 07 11:28 PM Häagen Dazs cherry vanilla at home.

MONTH

JAN
FEB
MAR
APR
MAY
JUN
JUL
AUG
SEP
OCT
NOV
DEC

DATE

05/27

DAY

THU

01 1:35 PM **Lentil soup at Moustache with Chris.** 02 1:40 PM **Babaganoush and hummus at Moustache.** 03 2:05 PM **Buttercreams from Li-Lac with Chris.** 04 5:47 PM **White bean soup with egg at home.** 05 9:03 PM **Sour cream and onion chips at home.** 06 9:53 PM **Chicken-and-sausage stew at home.** 07 11:17 PM **Life cereal at home.**

MONTH

JAN
FEB
MAR
APR
MAY
JUN
JUL
AUG
SEP
OCT
NOV
DEC

DATE

05/28

DAY

FRI

01 8:48 AM **Croissant and coffee from Brew Bar at home.** 02 1:05 PM **Yogurt at home.** 03 2:35 PM **Falafel platter at Hudson Falafel with Jorge.** 04 4:48 PM **Yogurt with honey at home.** 05 8:03 PM **Leftover stew at home.** 06 9:42 PM **Pernil, yellow rice, red beans, and sweet plantains from La Nueva Rampa at home.** 07 11:29 PM **Life cereal at home.**

MONTH

JAN
FEB
MAR
APR
MAY
JUN
JUL
AUG
SEP
OCT
NOV
DEC

DATE

05/29

DAY

SAT

01 11:14 AM Oatmeal at home. 02 1:52 PM Omelet with arugula and D'Agostino's Mexican cheeses blend.
03 5:16 PM Tomato soup with spinach, day-old bread, and Parmesan rind at home. 04 9:32 PM Sausage,
sautéed mushrooms, and potato salad at loft party at the Ukrainian Community Center on 2nd Avenue.
05 11:29 PM Life cereal at home. 06 11:48 PM Häagen Dazs dulce de leche ice cream at home.

MONTH

JAN
FEB
MAR
APR
MAY
JUN
JUL
AUG
SEP
OCT
NOV
DEC

DATE

05/30

DAY

SUN

01 10:32 AM Banana at home. 02 12:45 PM Greek yogurt at home. 03 2:31 PM Oatmeal at home. 04 6:09 PM Candy from Amsterdam at home with Danny. 05 8:16 PM Plain pizza from Village Pizza at home with Danny. 06 10:00 PM Häagen Dazs chocolate peanut butter ice cream at home.

MONTH

JAN
FEB
MAR
APR
MAY
JUN
JUL
AUG
SEP
OCT
NOV
DEC

DATE

05/31

DAY

MON

JUNE

01 10:00 AM **Banana at home.** 02 1:35 PM **Tomato-vegetable soup, catfish and salmon with roasted carrots at City Bakery with Dan.** 03 3:35 PM **Peach Dream smoothie from Elixir.** 04 5:41 PM **Peanut Heaven smoothie from Equinox at home.** 05 9:43 PM **Pâté Choux Swan from Payard at performance of Cooking for Kings at 59E59 with Chris and Doc.** 06 10:22 PM **Lobster gnocchi at Da Silvano with Chris and Doc.** 07 10:32 PM **Octopus stew at Da Silvano.** 08 10:40 PM **Braised rabbit with polenta at Da Silvano.** 09 11:05 PM **Panna cotta with chocolate drizzle at Da Silvano.**

MONTH

JAN
FEB
MAR
APR
MAY
JUN
JUL
AUG
SEP
OCT
NOV
DEC

DATE

06/01

DAY

TUE

01 9:19 AM **Banana at home.** 02 1:11 PM **Cherry ice from hielo man on Houston and the East River with JJ.** 03 2:02 PM **Super Soy Berry shake from Amy's on Astor Place.** 04 3:52 PM **Greek yogurt at home.** 05 7:12 PM **Bacalau crostini with arugula at Barbuto with Deb (olives and almonds in the background).** 06 7:28 PM **White asparagus with prosciutto and parsley at Barbuto.** 07 8:02 PM **Florida shrimp with fiddlehead ferns and lemon at Barbuto.** 08 8:29 PM **Spaghetti with walnuts and arugula at Barbuto.** 09 8:51 PM **Scallops with fava beans at Barbuto.** 10 9:21 PM **Quail with peas and red peppers at Barbuto.** 11 9:41 PM **Assorted sorbets at Barbuto.**

MONTH

JAN
FEB
MAR
APR
MAY
JUN
JUL
AUG
SEP
OCT
NOV
DEC

DATE

06/02

DAY

WED

01 9:41 AM Oatmeal at home. 02 1:06 PM Smoked salmon sandwich from Taylor's at home. 03 4:19 PM **Soy Berry Smoothie from Elixir at home.** 04 9:08 PM Chips, salsas, and guacamole at Palapa wih Jason. 05 9:43 PM **Black bean and chicken quesadilla at Palapa.** 06 9:47 PM Fish tacos at Palapa (taquitos in the background). 07 11:49 PM Kinder Bueno at home with Danny.

MONTH

JAN

FEB

MAR

APR

MAY

JUN

JUL

AUG

SEP

OCT

NOV

DEC

DATE

06/03

DAY

THU

01 9:25 AM Oatmeal at home. 02 12:41 PM METR-x shake from GNC Smoothie Bar on 7th Avenue. 03 4:02 PM Caramel Nut Blast Balance bar at Central Park courts with JJ. 04 8:43 PM Fried calamari and tuna rolls at Elmo with Tim, Alex, Paul, and Balazs. 05 8:44 PM Mac and cheese at Elmo. 06 8:45 PM Shrimp cocktail at Elmo. 07 9:28 PM Meatloaf with mashed potatoes, spinach, carrots, and mushroom gravy at Elmo. 08 12:28 AM Ring Dings at home with Danny. 09 12:36 AM Häagen Dazs dulce de leche ice cream at home.

MONTH

JAN

FEB

MAR

APR

MAY

JUN

JUL

AUG

SEP

OCT

NOV

DEC

DATE

06/04

DAY

FRI

01 10:06 AM **Croissant at home.** 02 1:42 PM **Yogurt at home.** 03 3:55 PM Barocco Hots no. 6 (soppressata with red onion relish and basil–cum–panzanella) at home. 04 9:33 PM **Pasta with sausages, spinach, and Parmesan at home with Danny.** 05 10:19 PM Early-summer crumble (blueberries and peaches) at home.

MONTH

JAN
FEB
MAR
APR
MAY
JUN
JUL
AUG
SEP
OCT
NOV
DEC

DATE

06/05

DAY

SAT

01 9:25 AM **Croissant at home with Danny.** 02 12:39 PM **Yogurt at home with Danny.** 03 3:09 PM **Mozzarepa on 72nd Street, Queens, with Alex.** 04 3:19 PM **Collards, plantains, yams, and macaroni and cheese on 74th Street, Queens, with Alex.** 05 5:23 PM **Oatmeal on the Go at home with Danny.** 06 8:13 PM **Frittata at home with Danny.** 07 9:13 PM **Stroopwafel at home with Danny.** 08 9:26 PM **Corn flakes at home.**

MONTH

JAN
FEB
MAR
APR
MAY
JUN
JUL
AUG
SEP
OCT
NOV
DEC

DATE

90/90

DAY

SUN

01 9:59 AM **Oatmeal at home.** 02 12:55 PM **BLT and salad at Westville with Andy.** 03 1:22 PM **Homemade sandwich cookie at Westville.** 04 4:07 PM **Leftover pasta with sausages at home.** 05 9:19 PM **More leftover pasta at home.** 06 9:57 PM **Wheaties at home.**

MONTH

JAN
FEB
MAR
APR
MAY
JUN
JUL
AUG
SEP
OCT
NOV
DEC

DATE

06/07

DAY

MON

01 8:27 AM Oatmeal at home. 02 2:00 PM Breaded chicken, lettuce, tomato, red onion, and herb mayo on sourdough from Sandwiches at home. 03 10:00 PM Kraft mac and cheese at home. 04 10:24 PM Corn flakes at home.

MONTH

JAN

FEB

MAR

APR

MAY

JUN

JUL

AUG

SEP

OCT

NOV

DEC

DATE

06/08

DAY

TUE

01 9:27 AM **Mango-fig muffin from Bonsignour at home.** 02 12:09 PM **Odwalla C Monster at Riverside Park with Jim.** 03 1:54 PM **Egg salad on whole-wheat from Taylor's at home.** 04 5:49 PM **La Yogurt at home.** 05 7:51 PM **Crostini at Novita with Roger and David.** 06 8:28 PM **Asparagus soup at Novita.** 07 8:51 PM **Roasted branzino with vegetables and thyme at Novita.** 08 9:23 PM **Chocolate tart with pistachio sauce and vanilla ice cream at Novita.** 09 10:59 PM **Wheaties at home.**

MONTH

JAN
FEB
MAR
APR
MAY
JUN
JUL
AUG
SEP
OCT
NOV
DEC

DATE

06/09

DAY

WED

01 12:06 PM **Mango at home.** 02 2:47 PM **Nutty Healthy Shake from 3rd Avenue Natural with Henry.** 03 3:51 PM **Chocolate chip cookie from City Bakery at Susan and Andrea's with Henry.** 04 6:14 PM **Leftover Kraft Dinner at home.** 05 9:37 PM **Movie snax.** *Baadasss* **at Union Square with Jason.** 06 11:04 PM **General Tso's chicken, white rice from Mama Buddha with Danny at home.**

01
02
03

04
05
06

MONTH

JAN
FEB
MAR
APR
MAY
JUN
JUL
AUG
SEP
OCT
NOV
DEC

DATE

06/10

DAY

THU

01 8:42 AM Oatmeal-blueberry scone at home. 02 1:51 PM Smoked turkey with Brie and mustard from Abingdon Market at home. 03 8:49 PM Reduced-fat potato chips at home with Danny. 04 10:45 PM Pad see ell with chicken and pad Thai with shrimp at home with Danny. 05 11:37 PM Corn flakes at home.

MONTH

JAN

FEB

MAR

APR

MAY

JUN

JUL

AUG

SEP

OCT

NOV

DEC

DATE

06/11

DAY

FRI

01 10:58 AM **Yogurt at home.** 02 12:17 PM **Peruvian produce at Susan and Andrea's with Erlinda and Henry.** 03 1:32 PM **Dark-meat turkey with lettuce and red onion on seven-grain from Sandwiches at Hudson River Park with Alex, Tim, Susan, Andrea, and Henry.** 04 4:40 PM **Peanut butter, honey, and Wheaties sandwich at home.** 05 6:51 PM **Workout Boost shake from Equinox at home.** 06 9:47 PM **Eggs, fries, and beans at home.** 07 11:24 PM **Wheaties at home.**

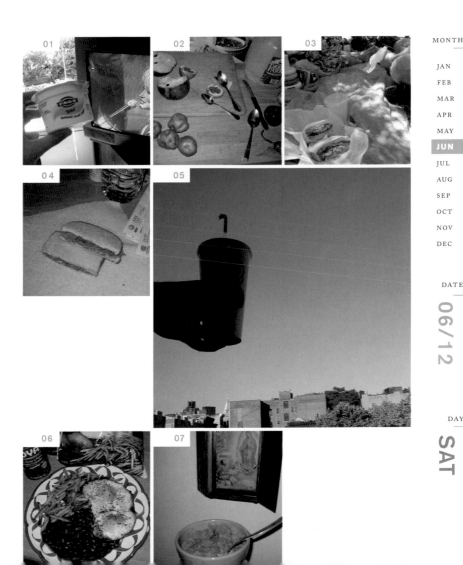

MONTH

JAN
FEB
MAR
APR
MAY
JUN
JUL
AUG
SEP
OCT
NOV
DEC

DATE

06/12

DAY

SAT

01 10:24 AM **Croissant and coffee from Lafayette Bakery on Greenwich Avenue.** 02 12:37 PM **Ham-and-cheese croissant from La Bergamote with Chris at home.** 03 1:50 PM **Hot dogs with ketchup and onions from Crif Dogs on St. Mark's Place with Chris.** 04 2:58 PM **Two scoops: Coconut-almond and mint chocolate chip from Mary's Dairy on W. Fourth with Chris.** 05 6:57 PM **Movie snax.** *Saved* **at Union Square with Jorge, Danny, Wayne, and Robert.** 06 10:02 PM **Cheeseburger Deluxe from Bus Stop at home.** 07 10:37 PM **Cheerios at home.**

MONTH

JAN

FEB

MAR

APR

MAY

JUN

JUL

AUG

SEP

OCT

NOV

DEC

DATE

06/13

DAY

SUN

01 9:17 AM **Oatmeal at home.** 02 1:34 PM **Peach Dream smoothie from Elixir on Hudson Street.** 03 3:12 PM **Cold sesame noodles from Mama Buddha on Hudson Street.** 04 8:27 PM **Panzanella, grilled green onions at August with Susan and Buzz.** 05 8:28 PM **Grilled octopus with lemon and chickpeas, mixed salami plate at August.** 06 8:31 PM **Blue Point oysters at August.** 07 9:04 PM **Roasted squab with almonds, steak with watercress and radish at August.** 08 9:41 PM **Assorted cheeses, strawberries with mascarpone and balsamic vinegar, rhubarb panzanella at August.** 09 12:01 AM **Cheerios at home.**

MONTH

JAN
FEB
MAR
APR
MAY
JUN
JUL
AUG
SEP
OCT
NOV
DEC

DATE

06/14

DAY

MON

01 9:18 AM **Oatmeal at home.** 02 1:01 PM **Grilled shrimp with watercress, corn, green beans, and jicama at Sarabeth's with Brett.** 03 5:23 PM **Peanut butter and honey sandwich at home.** 04 10:25 PM **Kitchen-cupboard panzanella at home.** 05 10:56 PM **Cheerios at home.**

MONTH

JAN

FEB

MAR

APR

MAY

JUN

JUL

AUG

SEP

OCT

NOV

DEC

DATE

06/15

DAY

TUE

01 9:21 AM **Oatmeal at home.** 02 1:41 PM **Tuna fish sandwiches at home.** 03 6:30 PM **White peach at home.**
04 11:35 PM **Sesame chicken at home with Danny.**

01

02

03

04

MONTH

JAN

FEB

MAR

APR

MAY

JUN

JUL

AUG

SEP

OCT

NOV

DEC

DATE

06/16

DAY

WED

01 9:43 AM **Oatmeal at home.** 02 2:31 PM **Fried-egg sandwich at home.** 03 7:44 PM **Salt-and-vinegar potato chips at home.** 04 9:52 PM **Kitchen-cabinet risotto with shrimp at home with Danny.** 05 10:32 PM **Blueberry-and-peach cobbler at home with Danny.**

MONTH

JAN

FEB

MAR

APR

MAY

JUN

JUL

AUG

SEP

OCT

NOV

DEC

DATE

06/17

DAY

THU

01 1:48 PM **Lemon Frozfruit on 10th Street.** 02 2:19 PM **Falafel sandwich, spinach pie from Mahmoun's in Union Square.** 03 6:37 PM **Quiche from Patisserie Claude at home.** 04 9:13 PM **Caviar flight at 5757 with Susan, Tim, Eva, Alex, and Bobby.** 05 11:32 PM **Leftover risotto at home.** 06 11:45 PM **Potato chips at home.** 07 12:09 AM **Cinnamon Toast Crunch at home.**

MONTH

JAN
FEB
MAR
APR
MAY
JUN
JUL
AUG
SEP
OCT
NOV
DEC

DATE

06/18

DAY

FRI

01 11:02 AM Scone and coconut cookie from Thé Adore with Chris. 02 11:18 AM Cherries in the Union Square Farmers' Market with Chris. 03 11:42 AM Egg salad with bacon at Eisenberg's. 04 5:02 PM Yogurt with blueberries and honey at home. 05 8:43 PM Pickled quail egg at Jack's Luxury Oyster Bar with Susan. (Note: All pictures from this meal are fuzzy because the maitre d' asked me not to take pictures, so I had to sneak them. It was the second time I'd been busted at Jack's.) 06 8:46 PM Pimiento cheese with black bread at Jack's. 07 8:48 PM Oysters Rockefeller presented on a spoon at Jack's. *(continued on next page)*

MONTH

JAN
FEB
MAR
APR
MAY
JUN
JUL
AUG
SEP
OCT
NOV
DEC

DATE

06/19

DAY

SAT

08 8:57 PM **Blue Point oysters, Kumamoto oysters, and shrimp with toast and caviar at Jack's.** 09 9:07 PM **Crayfish soup velouté at Jack's.** 10 9:28 PM **Lobster tail on toast at Jack's.** 11 9:45 PM **Halibut with pink peppercorns at Jack's.** 12 10:20 PM **Iced-tea sorbet at Jack's.** 13 10:36 PM **Baba au rhum with whipped cream at Jack's.** 14 12:25 AM **Cinnamon Toast Crunch at home.**

01 11:13 AM **Oatmeal at home.** 02 1:31 PM **Strawberry Frozfruit in Hudson River Park with Danny.** 03 3:00 PM **Cherries at home.** 04 5:01 PM **Tuna fish sandwich at home.** 05 7:17 PM **Banana at home.** 06 11:24 PM **Smoked turkey wrap, sour cream and onion potato chips at home with Danny.** 07 11:50 PM **Bran flakes at home.**

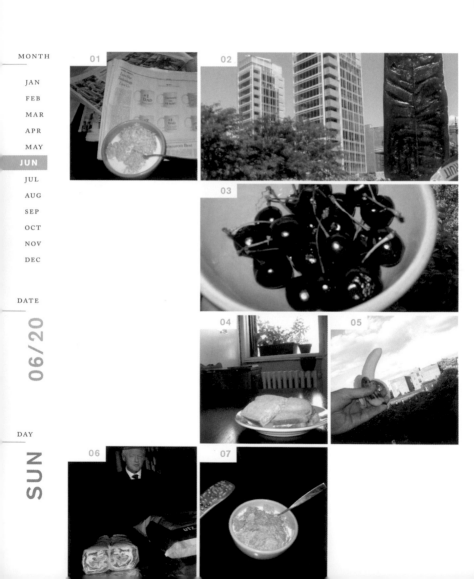

MONTH

JAN
FEB
MAR
APR
MAY
JUN
JUL
AUG
SEP
OCT
NOV
DEC

DATE

06/20

DAY

SUN

01 9:58 AM Oatmeal at home. 02 5:16 PM Tuna fish sandwiches at home. 03 8:58 PM Olives at Barbuto with Chris, Doc, and Jeorg. 04 9:03 PM Prosciutto and figs at Barbuto. 05 9:44 PM Florida shrimp with chile oil and avocado at Barbuto. 06 10:04 PM Wood oven–roasted black sea bass with grilled lemon at Barbuto. 07 10:43 PM Chocolate pudding at Barbuto. 08 11:47 PM Donuts at home with Danny.

MONTH

JAN
FEB
MAR
APR
MAY
JUN
JUL
AUG
SEP
OCT
NOV
DEC

DATE

06/21

DAY

MON

01 9:32 AM **Oatmeal at home.** 02 1:38 PM **Slice from Joe's Pizza on Bleecker Street.** 03 4:38 PM **Peanut butter and jelly at home.** 04 6:33 PM **Sour cream and onion chips at home.** 05 9:12 PM **Franks and beans at home with Danny.** 06 10:01 PM **Donuts at home with Danny.** 07 10:10 PM **Wheaties at home.**

MONTH

JAN
FEB
MAR
APR
MAY
JUN
JUL
AUG
SEP
OCT
NOV
DEC

DATE

06/22

DAY

TUE

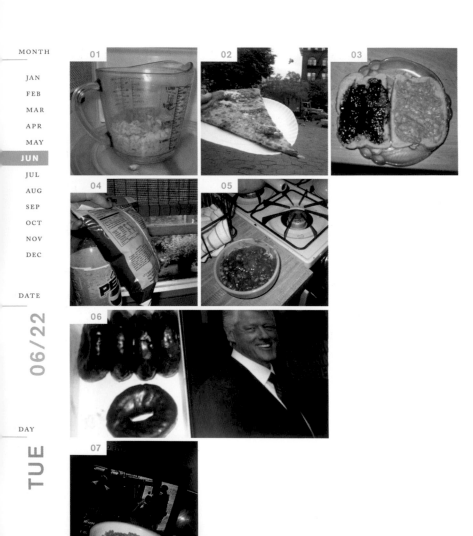

01 9:03 AM Oatmeal at home. 02 1:09 PM Fried-egg sandwiches with spinach at home. 03 5:27 PM Peanut butter and jelly on hot-dog bun at home. 04 7:55 PM Grape leaves, falafels, lamb canapés, vegetable canapés, and baklava at Andy and Maryam's with a hundred of their friends. 05 8:27 PM Chocolate cookies at Andy and Maryam's. 06 9:06 PM Spring rolls and shrimp ravioli with chile sauce at O Mai with Brett and Jake. 07 9:18 PM Spicy beef, shrimp with pork ribs at O Mai. 08 11:02 PM Vanilla Almond Special K at home.

MONTH

JAN
FEB
MAR
APR
MAY
JUN
JUL
AUG
SEP
OCT
NOV
DEC

DATE

06/23

DAY

WED

01 8:47 AM Oatmeal at home. 02 10:10 AM Mixed-fruit juice, blueberry muffin at Sarabeth's with Mom. 03 2:19 PM Chocolate pound cake sample at Central Park Tennis Center with JJ. 04 5:11 PM Tuna fish salad on hot-dog rolls at home. 05 9:07 PM Hot dog at home with Danny. 06 9:37 PM Soup with ramen, spinach, spring onion, and egg at home with Danny. 07 10:31 PM Vanilla Almond Special K at home.

MONTH

JAN
FEB
MAR
APR
MAY
JUN
JUL
AUG
SEP
OCT
NOV
DEC

DATE

06/24

DAY

THU

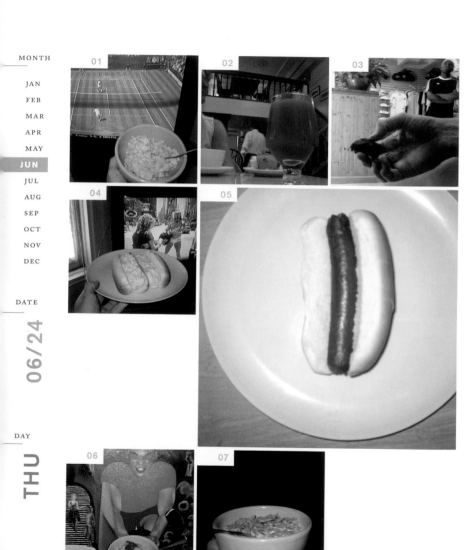

01 10:24 AM Oatmeal at home. 02 12:26 PM Leftover tuna salad at home. 03 12:47 PM Peanut butter and jelly on hot-dog bun at home. 04 2:45 PM Leftover baklava at Andy's. 05 7:49 PM Salt-and-vinegar potato chips at home. 06 9:58 PM Movie snax. *The Notebook* at Chelsea Cinemas with Danny. 07 1:05 AM Scrambled eggs, fries, and sliced tomatoes at home with Danny.

MONTH

JAN
FEB
MAR
APR
MAY
JUN
JUL
AUG
SEP
OCT
NOV
DEC

DATE

06/25

DAY

FRI

01 10:13 AM New Jersey peach at home. 02 11:57 AM Oatmeal at home. 03 2:43 PM Meatloaf on seven-grain from Sandwiches at Hudson River Park with Susan, Andrea, Henry, Tim, Alex, Paul, and Balazs. 04 3:58 PM Brownie and bread pudding. 05 6:47 PM Yogurt with honey at home. 06 8:45 PM Cold sesame noodles from Mama Buddha at home with Danny. 07 2:18 AM Bran flakes at home.

MONTH

JAN
FEB
MAR
APR
MAY
JUN
JUL
AUG
SEP
OCT
NOV
DEC

DATE

06/26

DAY

SAT

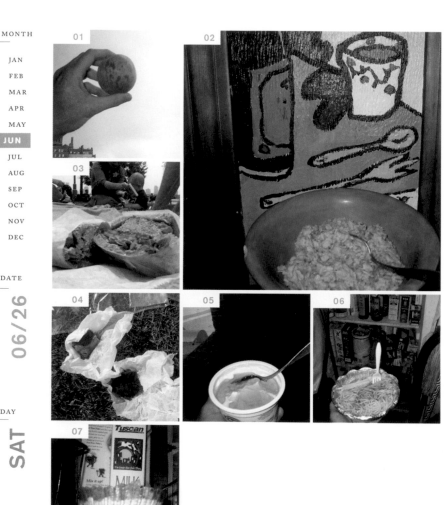

01 11:27 AM **Oatmeal at home.** 02 5:47 PM **Ketchup chips at home.** 03 6:04 PM **Yogurt at home.** 04 11:58 PM **Fried eggs on toast at home.** 05 12:12 AM **Bran flakes at home.**

MONTH

JAN

FEB

MAR

APR

MAY

JUN

JUL

AUG

SEP

OCT

NOV

DEC

DATE

06/27

DAY

SUN

01

02

03

04

05

01 1:17 PM Cherries from the farmers' market in Union Square. 02 1:55 PM Grilled chicken on whole-wheat at Sandwiches on Greenwich Avenue. 03 4:44 PM Strawberry Frozfruit on W. 10th St. 04 5:52 PM Peanut butter and jelly at home. 05 11:35 PM Olives at Casa Mono with Lynn. 06 11:39 PM Fried bacalau with lemon aioli at Casa Mono. 07 12:03 AM Lamb with fava beans, grilled green onions with chiles, sweetbreads with chickpeas at Casa Mono. 08 12:04 AM Roasted red peppers at Casa Mono.

MONTH

JAN
FEB
MAR
APR
MAY
JUN
JUL
AUG
SEP
OCT
NOV
DEC

DATE

06/28

DAY

MON

01 10:30 AM Banana at home. 02 3:02 PM Tuna, white beans, tomatoes, and Parmesan wedges at home. 03 6:22 PM Potato chips at home with Danny. 04 7:41 PM Favas and edamame at Matsuri with Scott. 05 7:56 PM Kobe beef with wasabi, scallop sashimi at Matsuri. 06 8:00 PM Sautéed oshitashi (pickled spinach), okra with bonito flakes at Matsuri. 07 8:10 PM Chicken skewers at Matsuri. 08 8:29 PM Tuna and toro sashimi with shrimp sushi at Matsuri. 09 8:59 PM Miso-glazed black cod at Matsuri. 10 11:02 PM Bran flakes at home.

MONTH

JAN
FEB
MAR
APR
MAY
JUN
JUL
AUG
SEP
OCT
NOV
DEC

DATE

06/29

DAY

TUE

01 10:10 AM **Applesauce at home.** 02 2:30 PM **Strawberry Frozfruit on 7th Ave and 18th Street.** 03 3:39 PM **Tuna and white beans at home.** 04 9:07 PM **Salt-and-vinegar potato chips at home with Danny.** 05 9:51 PM **Shrimp-and-spinach risotto at home with Danny.** 06 10:32 PM **Banana Nut Crunch at home.** 07 10:48 PM **Nestlé chocolate morsels at home.**

MONTH

JAN
FEB
MAR
APR
MAY
JUN
JUL
AUG
SEP
OCT
NOV
DEC

DATE

06/30

DAY

WED

01 9:10 AM Oatmeal at home. 02 12:49 PM BLT with salad at Westville with Michael. 03 2:59 PM Plum at home. 04 5:36 PM Lemon Frozfruit on W. 10th Street. 05 9:19 PM Bread at La Petite Abeille with Alex. 06 9:30 PM Frisée salad with bacon and poached egg at Petite Abeille. 07 9:47 PM Mussels with celery, fennel, and lemon, frites at Petite Abeille.

MONTH

JAN
FEB
MAR
APR
MAY
JUN
JUL
AUG
SEP
OCT
NOV
DEC

DATE

07/01

DAY

THU

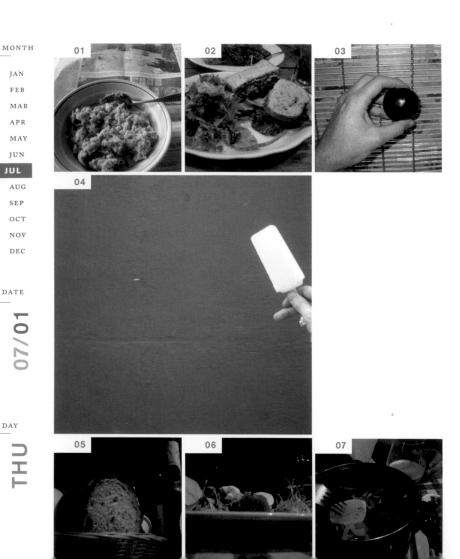

New York City to Tinkwig, Pennsylvania **01** 9:11 AM Oatmeal at home. **02** 3:43 PM Blueberries along Route 590, PA, with Tim, Marc, and Chris. **03** 5:59 PM Peanuts at Jay and Steven's with Tim, Marc, Chris, Jay, and Steven. **04** 7:26 PM Cool Ranch Doritos at I.G.A. with Jay and Marc. **05** 7:50 PM Provolone at Jay and Steven's with Tim. **06** 8:10 PM Hummus, pita, artichoke hearts, roasted peppers, sliced onions, and tomatoes at Jay and Steven's. **07** 10:45 PM Grilled shrimp with chiles, grilled pork with garlic and sage at Jay and Steven's. **08** 10:51 PM Grilled vegetables at Jay and Steven's. **09** 10:52 PM Grilled pork, tomato and jalapeño raita, cucumber and cilantro raita, couscous at Jay and Steven's. **10** 11:56 PM Nilla wafers with Tim. **11** 12:06 AM Bananas and cherries Foster with banana ice cream and cherry ice cream.

MONTH

JAN
FEB
MAR
APR
MAY
JUN
JUL
AUG
SEP
OCT
NOV
DEC

DATE

07/02

DAY

FRI

Tinkwig, Pennsylvania 01 11:09 AM **Plain yogurt at Jay and Steven's.** 02 2:27 PM **Italian hoagie from Hoagie Hut at Jay and Steven's.** 03 2:33 PM **Salt-and-vinegar potato chips at with Jay and Tim.** 04 4:34 PM **American cheese at I.G.O. with Susan.** 05 5:26 PM **Vanilla and chocolate twist at Dairy Twist with Susan and Marc.** 06 8:06 PM **Brie, smoked Gouda, crackers, hummus, radishes, butter, and salt at Jay and Steven's with Jay, Steven, Tim, Marc, Christopher, Susan, Andrea, and Henry.** 07 8:18 PM **Edamame at Jay and Steven's.** 08 10:12 PM **Grilled pork tenderloin with peaches and peppers at Jay and Steven's.** 09 10:13 PM **Watermelon and arugula salad with feta at Jay and Steven's.** 10 10:14 PM **Lentils with red onions and red peppers at Jay and Steven's.** 11 11:51 PM **Glazed plums at Jay and Steven's.**

MONTH

JAN
FEB
MAR
APR
MAY
JUN
JUL
AUG
SEP
OCT
NOV
DEC

DATE

07/03

DAY

SAT

Tinkwig, Pennsylvania 01 9:47 AM Pecan ring at Jay and Steven's. 02 10:16 AM Nectarine at Jay and Steven's. 03 3:13 PM Chocolate and vanilla twist with chocolate sprinkles at Dairy Twist with Christopher and Marc. 04 4:23 PM Pretzels, Ruffles, leftover raitas, and nuts at Jay and Steven's. 05 5:23 PM Assorted cheeses at Jay and Steven's. 06 8:17 PM Chilled cucumber-and-dill soup at Jay and Steven's with Jay, Steven, Tim, Marc, Christopher, Susan, Andrea, Regina, and Jonny. 07 9:13 PM Barbecued chicken at Jay and Steven's. 08 9:14 PM Potato salad, coleslaw, and baked beans at Jay and Steven's. 09 9:15 PM Hamburgers and hot dogs at Jay and Steven's. 10 10:09 PM Honeydew and lemon verbena popsicle. 11 10:34 PM Red, white, and blue shortcake (with strawberries, blueberries, and white peaches) at Jay and Steven's.

MONTH

JAN
FEB
MAR
APR
MAY
JUN
JUL
AUG
SEP
OCT
NOV
DEC

DATE

07/04

DAY

SUN

Tinkwig, Pennsylvania, to New York City 01 1:09 PM **Applesauce at home.** 02 1:54 PM **Peach Dream smoothie from Elixir on Hudson Street.** 03 2:32 PM **Meatloaf on seven-grain at Sandwiches on Greenwich.** 04 8:59 PM **Potato chips at home.** 05 9:55 PM **Spinach and Cheddar omelet with salsa at home.** 06 10:54 PM **Banana Nut Crunch at home.**

MONTH

JAN
FEB
MAR
APR
MAY
JUN
JUL
AUG
SEP
OCT
NOV
DEC

DATE

07/05

DAY

MON

01
02
03
04
05
06

01 9:43 AM Brioche from Lafayette Patisserie on Greenwich Street. 02 1:46 PM Slice from Joe's Pizza on Carmine Street. 03 3:50 PM Peanut butter and jelly on whole-wheat, peach at home. 04 10:09 PM Kitchen-cupboard pasta at home. 05 12:01 AM Shredded Wheat at home.

MONTH

JAN
FEB
MAR
APR
MAY
JUN
JUL
AUG
SEP
OCT
NOV
DEC

DATE

07/06

DAY

TUE

01 8:46 AM **Peach at home.**   02 12:33 PM **Yogurt at home.**   03 6:38 PM **Peanut butter and jelly sandwich at home.**
04 11:00 PM **Cheese omelet at home.**

MONTH

JAN

FEB

MAR

APR

MAY

JUN

JUL

AUG

SEP

OCT

NOV

DEC

DATE

07/07

DAY

WED

01

02

03

04

01 8:41 AM Oatmeal at home. 02 12:34 PM Tuna fish sandwich at home. 03 1:38 PM Vegetable dumplings from 6th Avenue deli at Susan and Andrea's. 04 4:26 PM Meatball with Susan at Susan and Andrea's. 05 8:45 PM Potato chips at home. 06 10:12 PM Frites from La Petite Abeille with Danny at home. 07 10:28 PM Croque-monsieur and salad from La Petite Abeille at home.

MONTH

JAN
FEB
MAR
APR
MAY
JUN
JUL
AUG
SEP
OCT
NOV
DEC

DATE

07/08

DAY

THU

01 9:43 AM Oatmeal at home. 02 11:49 AM Yogurt at home. 03 4:55 PM Chicken cutlet on roll with mustard, mayo, lettuce, and tomato from Village Deli at home. 04 8:58 PM Crudités at Pure Food & Wine with Doc and Chris. 05 9:18 PM Tomato tartare and avocado rolls at Pure Food. 06 9:19 PM Collard-wrapped summer rolls with tamarind sauce, seaweed salad with sour cherries at Pure Food. 07 9:20 PM Spring rolls with carrot puree at Pure Food. *(continued on next page)*

MONTH

JAN
FEB
MAR
APR
MAY
JUN
JUL
AUG
SEP
OCT
NOV
DEC

DATE

07/09

DAY

FRI

08 9:48 PM Zucchini and tomato "lasagna," summer squash pasta with truffles at Pure Food. 09 9:49 PM Chanterelle "ravioli" at Pure Food. 10 9:50 PM Avocado and pepper "tacos" at Pure Food. 11 10:27 PM Chocolate cookie with chocolate and pistachio "ice cream," lemon ice, and ginger-walnut sundae at Pure Food. 12 10:29 PM Marinated cherries at Pure Food. 13 12:24 AM Banana Nut Crunch at home.

New York to Tinkwig, Pennsylvania 01 9:48 AM **Oatmeal at home.** 02 2:26 PM **Ramen noodles with egg drop at home.** 03 6:26 PM **Pringles on Route 6 with Alex and Boris.** 04 8:49 PM **Orzo salad at Jay and Steven's with Jay, Steven, Chris, and Marc.** 05 9:31 PM **Skirt steak with pesto, grilled scallops, New Jersey corn at Jay and Steven's.** 06 11:24 PM **Chocolate chip cookies at Jay and Steven's.**

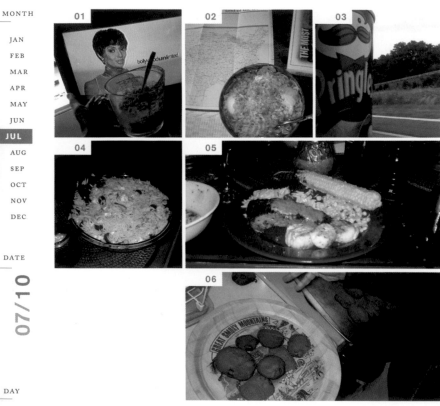

MONTH

JAN
FEB
MAR
APR
MAY
JUN
JUL
AUG
SEP
OCT
NOV
DEC

DATE

07/10

DAY

SAT

Tinkwig, Pennsylvania, to La Porte, Indiana 01 10:15 AM Egg McMuffin, hash browns, OJ at McDonald's in Almedia, PA. 02 12:36 PM Birthday Cake ice cream at Snappy's in Clearfield, PA. 03 3:28 PM Turkey club, chocolate chip cookie from Au Bon Pain in Youngstown, OH. 04 8:17 PM Garden salad with blue cheese dressing at Roskowe's in La Porte with Alex. 05 8:32 PM Fried perch, roasted new potatoes, and broccoli at Roskowe's. 06 8:59 PM Cherry pie at Roskowe's.

MONTH

JAN
FEB
MAR
APR
MAY
JUN
JUL
AUG
SEP
OCT
NOV
DEC

DATE

07/11

DAY

SUN

La Porte, Indiana, to Albert Lea, Minnesota 01 8:08 AM **Cheerios and sausages at Blue Heron Inn, La Porte.** 02 12:29 PM **Potato chips on I-90 near Beloit, WI.** 03 1:48 PM **Crispy fried cookie from fruit stand near Spring Green, WI.** 04 2:10 PM **More cookies, Taliesin, WI.** 05 4:27 PM **Rumble Burger with root beer from Rumbleseats drive-in, Gotham, WI.** 06 6:56 PM **Another crispy cookie on the Mississippi at La Crosse, WI.** 07 9:41 PM **Chips and salsa at Mexico Lindo in Albert Lea with Alex.** 08 10:04 PM **Chopped beef, refried beans, rice, and complimentary tostada at Mexico Lindo.** 09 10:40 PM **The rest of the cookies.** 10 10:55 PM **Complimentary Days Inn cookie.**

MONTH

JAN

FEB

MAR

APR

MAY

JUN

JUL

AUG

SEP

OCT

NOV

DEC

DATE

07/12

DAY

MON

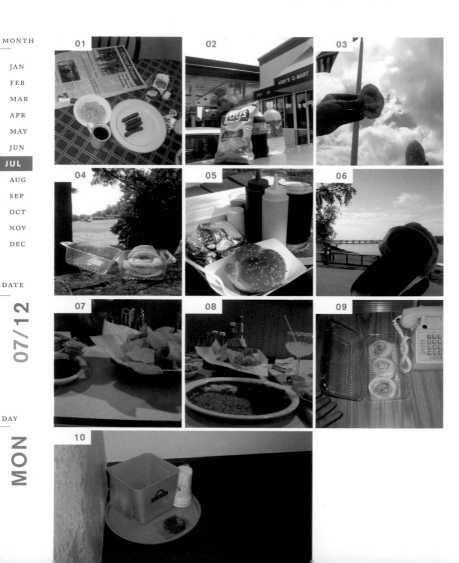

Albert Lea, Minnesota, to Interior, South Dakota 01 8:42 AM Donut and coffee at Donut Hut in Albert Lea with Alex. 02 11:44 AM Dill pickle chips on I-80 with Alex. 03 12:49 PM Corn lollipop at Corn Palace in Mitchell, SD. 04 2:03 PM Deep-fried cheese "curds" at Culver's in Mitchell with Alex. 05 2:08 PM Double Butterburger, crinkle-cut fries at Culver's. 06 4:38 PM Chocolate soft-serve at Badlands Trading Post in Cactus Flats, SD. 07 8:11 PM Fritos in the Badlands with Alex. 08 9:19 PM Sautéed rib-eye and frozen green beans at Interior Campground, Badlands, with Alex. 09 10:09 PM Chocolate chip ice cream with Hershey's chocolate sauce at Interior Campground.

MONTH

JAN

FEB

MAR

APR

MAY

JUN

JUL

AUG

SEP

OCT

NOV

DEC

DATE

07/13

DAY

TUE

The Badlands to the Black Hills 01 8:23 AM Bisquick biscuits at Interior Campground with Alex. 02 4:04 PM Salisbury steak, corn, and mixed vegetables at Mount Rushmore. 03 5:19 PM Fritos at Crazy Horse Memorial, SD. 04 7:48 PM Linguine with meat sauce, boiled snap peas, mixed greens, cottage cheese, pears, potato salad, and buttered bread at Camp Michael in Nemo, SD with Alex, Michael, and Michael.

MONTH

JAN

FEB

MAR

APR

MAY

JUN

JUL

AUG

SEP

OCT

NOV

DEC

DATE

07/14

DAY

WED

01

02

03

04

The Black Hills to Three Forks, Montana 01 8:23 AM Eggs with cheese and tomato, bacon, herbed potatoes, and pancakes at Camp Michael with Alex, Michael, and other guests. 02 1:57 PM Potato soup at Cashway Café in Broadus, MT, with Alex. 03 2:07 PM Daily-special soft taco with beef-chili filling at Cashway Café. 04 2:22 PM Bread pudding at Cashway Café. 05 4:48 PM Ice cream sandwich at Little Big Horn, MT. 06 8:35 PM Chex Mix outside Bozeman, MT. 07 9:00 PM Quarter Pounder with Cheese meal at McDonald's in Belgrade, MT, with Alex.

MONTH

JAN
FEB
MAR
APR
MAY
JUN
JUL
AUG
SEP
OCT
NOV
DEC

DATE

07/15

DAY

THU

Three Forks to Bigfork, Montana **01** 8:35 AM Donut and coffee at Sacajawea Hotel in Three Forks, MT. **02** 12:56 PM Granola bar outside Norris Hot Springs, MT. **03** 1:43 PM Two beef-and-bean burritos, Salsa Verde Doritos, and Hostess cherry pie at Smokey's Tobacco Exchange, Boulder, MT. **04** 3:08 PM Peach pie at Avon Café in Avon, MT. **05** 8:12 PM Bread and butter at Showthyme in Bigfork, MT, with Alex. **06** 8:32 PM Arugula salad with house-smoked duck breast and Parmesan crisp at Showthyme. **07** 8:53 PM Rack of lamb roasted with cherries, mashed potatoes, and asparagus at Showthyme (venison medallions with polenta cakes in background). **08** 9:27 PM Sticky toffee pudding with ginger ice cream at Showthyme.

MONTH

JAN
FEB
MAR
APR
MAY
JUN
JUL
AUG
SEP
OCT
NOV
DEC

DATE

07/16

DAY

FRI

Bigfork to the Yaak Valley, Montana 01 8:35 AM Cinnamon roll and coffee at Brookie's Cookies in Bigfork, MT. 02 2:13 PM Potato pancakes at Libby Diner in Libby, MT, with Alex. 03 6:04 PM Apricot at the Yaak Wilderness Ranch. 04 9:00 PM Cherries at the Yaak. 05 9:36 PM Rib-eye, grilled zucchini, grilled onions, and baked potatoes at the Yaak with Alex. 06 11:16 PM Cherry Bisquick Surprise at the Yaak with Alex.

MONTH

JAN

FEB

MAR

APR

MAY

JUN

JUL

AUG

SEP

OCT

NOV

DEC

DATE

07/17

DAY

SAT

The Yaak Wilderness Ranch 01 11:03 AM **Oatmeal with huckleberry syrup with Alex at the Yaak.** 02 2:41 PM **Potatoes and fried eggs at the Yaak.** 03 7:13 PM **Chips and guacamole at the Yaak.** 04 9:01 PM **Burritos and blue cheese salad at the Yaak.** 05 10:08 PM **Cherry Bisquick Surprise Part 2 at the Yaak.**

MONTH

JAN

FEB

MAR

APR

MAY

JUN

JUL

AUG

SEP

OCT

NOV

DEC

DATE

07/18

DAY

SUN

The Yaak Wilderness Ranch 01 10:34 AM Fried eggs, bacon, and biscuits at the Yaak. 02 1:36 PM Ketchup chips at the Yaak. 03 2:14 PM Banana at the Yaak. 04 3:40 PM Peanut butter and jelly sandwich at the Yaak. 05 4:19 PM Peach at the Yaak. 06 7:28 PM Grilled corn and black bean salsa with chips at the Yaak. 07 10:02 PM Hamburgers, grilled zucchini, and grilled onions at the Yaak. 08 11:11 PM Freeze-dried ice cream at the Yaak.

MONTH

JAN

FEB

MAR

APR

MAY

JUN

JUL

AUG

SEP

OCT

NOV

DEC

DATE

07/19

DAY

MON

The Yaak Wilderness Ranch 01 9:23 AM **Oatmeal with huckleberry syrup at the Yaak.** 02 2:19 PM **Omelet with grilled corn salsa at the Yaak.** 03 7:55 PM **Corn chips at the Yaak with Alex.** 04 9:55 PM **Wood-grilled rib-eyes, potato and onion hobo packs at the Yaak.** 05 10:11 PM **Alex's coleslaw at the Yaak.** 06 10:53 PM **Candy bars at the Yaak.**

MONTH

JAN
FEB
MAR
APR
MAY
JUN
JUL
AUG
SEP
OCT
NOV
DEC

DATE

07/20

DAY

TUE

The Yaak Wilderness Ranch 01 10:09 AM Fried eggs, corn bread, and cantaloupe at the Yaak with Alex. 02 1:07 PM Banana at the Yaak. 03 2:42 PM Tuna fish sandwich at the Yaak with Alex. 04 7:23 PM Brown trout at the Yaak. 05 9:40 PM Brown trout stuffed with sage, apples, and bacon, grilled leeks, toasted corn bread, and leftover coleslaw at the Yaak with Alex. 06 11:35 PM Life cereal at the Yaak.

MONTH

JAN

FEB

MAR

APR

MAY

JUN

JUL

AUG

SEP

OCT

NOV

DEC

DATE

07/21

DAY

WED

The Yaak Wilderness Ranch 01 9:49 AM Scrambled eggs and salsa with Alex at the Yaak. 02 2:07 PM Steak sandwich and cucumbers with Alex at the Yaak. 03 7:56 PM Jalapeño chips and corn chips with leftover grilled corn salsa with Alex at the Yaak. 04 9:48 PM Frittata, sautéed cauliflower, and mixed green salad with Alex at the Yaak. 05 10:44 PM Kit Kat at the Yaak. 06 10:56 PM Hershey's bar with Alex at the Yaak. 07 11:09 PM Life cereal at the Yaak.

MONTH

JAN
FEB
MAR
APR
MAY
JUN
JUL
AUG
SEP
OCT
NOV
DEC

DATE

07/22

DAY

THU

The Yaak Wilderness Ranch 01 9:27 AM Oatmeal with Alex at the Yaak. 02 2:28 PM Triple-decker PBJ at the Yaak. 03 6:18 PM Banana at the Yaak. 04 6:58 PM Ketchup chips at the Yaak. 05 8:27 PM Cheese and crackers, sliced cucumbers with Alex at the Yaak. 06 8:54 PM Kitchen-sink chili, roasted potatoes, sautéed broccoli with Alex at the Yaak. 07 10:04 PM Apple crisp at the Yaak.

MONTH

JAN

FEB

MAR

APR

MAY

JUN

JUL

AUG

SEP

OCT

NOV

DEC

DATE

07/23

DAY

FRI

The Yaak Valley to Glacier National Park, Montana 01 9:49 AM **Fried eggs, bacon, and fried green tomatoes with Alex at the Yaak.** 02 1:16 PM **Local cherries in Whitefish, MT.** 03 3:01 PM **Peanut butter and jelly with Alex in Glacier Nat'l Park.** 04 5:19 PM **Trail mix in Glacier Nat'l Park.** 05 7:17 PM **Cracked peppercorn potato chips in Glacier Nat'l Park.** 06 9:18 PM **Rib-eyes, grilled onions and zucchini, potato hobo packs with Alex in Glacier Nat'l Park.** 07 10:20 PM **S'mores in Glacier Nat'l Park.**

MONTH

JAN
FEB
MAR
APR
MAY
JUN
JUL
AUG
SEP
OCT
NOV
DEC

DATE

07/24

DAY

SAT

Glacier National Park to Williston, North Dakota 01 7:02 AM Maple and brown sugar oatmeal with Alex in Glacier Nat'l Park. 02 2:03 PM Cheeseburger, fries, fry bread from 4-H booth with Alex at Marias County Fair and Rodeo in Shelby, MT. 03 2:31 PM Fry bread at Marias County Fair and Rodeo in Shelby, MT. 04 9:12 PM Fried onions with spicy horseradish sauce with Alex at Applebee's in Williston, ND. 05 9:23 PM Bacon Cheeseburger Deluxe at Applebee's in Williston. 06 9:50 PM Hershey's bar in Williston.

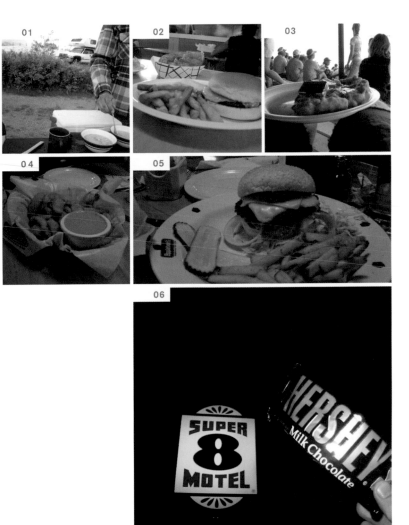

MONTH

JAN
FEB
MAR
APR
MAY
JUN
JUL
AUG
SEP
OCT
NOV
DEC

DATE

07/25

DAY

SUN

Williston, North Dakota, to Duluth, Minnesota 01 8:47 AM Fried eggs, hash browns, bacon, and white toast at Gramma Sharon's in Williston, ND. 02 2:55 PM Fried Canadian walleye sandwich, fries, wild rice at Whitey's in Grand Forks, MN. 03 5:57 PM Fresh smoked whitefish at Ball Drop Lake, MN. 04 9:34 PM Bread and olive oil at Bellisio's in Duluth. 05 9:56 PM Roasted pork chops, potatoes, mixed vegetables at Bellisio's in Duluth.

MONTH

JAN
FEB
MAR
APR
MAY
JUN
JUL
AUG
SEP
OCT
NOV
DEC

DATE

07/26

DAY

MON

Duluth, Minnesota, to Whitmore Lake, Michigan 01 8:53 AM **Egg McMuffin in Superior, WI.** 02 3:34 PM **Chicago-style hot dog at Chicago-Style Hot Dog and Gyro with Alex in Escanaba, MI.** 03 5:48 PM **Moosetracks ice cream at Mildwood Pasties in Epoufette, MI.** 04 8:45 PM **Tabasco cheese popcorn on Route 23 near Saginaw, MI.** 05 10:53 PM **Pizza with pepperoni, onions, and peppers from Marco's with Alex in Whitmore Lake.**

MONTH

JAN

FEB

MAR

APR

MAY

JUN

JUL

AUG

SEP

OCT

NOV

DEC

DATE

07/27

DAY

TUE

Whitmore Lake, Michigan, to New York City **01** 9:48 AM **Egg McMuffin in Whitmore Lake.** **02** 2:23 PM **Ham and bean soup with Alex at Dutch Pantry in DuBois, PA.** **03** 2:31 PM **Pantry Cordon Bleu, mashed potatoes with gravy, corn, and roll at Dutch Pantry.** **04** 2:52 PM **Apple fritters at Dutch Pantry.** **05** 9:40 PM **Sesame chicken, mixed greens from Mama Buddha at home.**

MONTH

JAN

FEB

MAR

APR

MAY

JUN

JUL

AUG

SEP

OCT

NOV

DEC

DATE

07/28

DAY

WED

01 9:13 AM **Oatmeal at home.** 02 1:26 PM **Zone Perfect (peanut butter chocolate) at Central Park Tennis Center.** 03 5:26 PM **Leftover Chinese greens at home.** 04 8:31 PM **Smoked whitefish with Chris at home.** 05 8:48 PM **Fancy chocolates with Chris at home.** 06 9:14 PM **Leftover Chinese fry-up at home.**

MONTH

JAN
FEB
MAR
APR
MAY
JUN
JUL
AUG
SEP
OCT
NOV
DEC

DATE

07/29

DAY

THU

01 8:46 AM **Oatmeal at home.** 02 2:40 PM **Meatloaf sandwich and lemonade from Sandwiches at home.**
03 7:54 PM **Pasta with quick tomato sauce at home.**

MONTH

JAN

FEB

MAR

APR

MAY

JUN

JUL

AUG

SEP

OCT

NOV

DEC

DATE

07/30

DAY

FRI

01 9:47 AM Egg and cheese on roll from Spyros at home. 02 1:43 PM Toasted challah, heirloom tomato, and tuna fish at home. 03 8:53 PM Guacamole and chips at Susan and Andrea's with Susan, Andrea, and Alex. 04 9:30 PM Tomato, mozzarella, and basil salad at Susan and Andrea's. 05 10:36 PM Skirt steak with cilantro, roasted peppers, and toasted tortillas at Susan and Andrea's. 06 11:16 PM Tres leches panna cotta with strawberries at Susan and Andrea's. 07 2:16 AM Häagen Dazs tres leches ice cream at home.

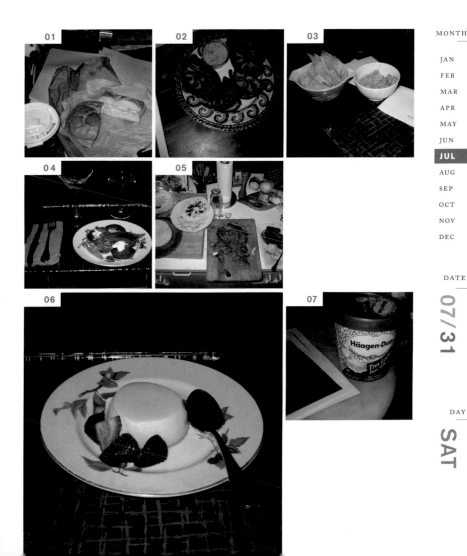

MONTH

JAN
FEB
MAR
APR
MAY
JUN
JUL
AUG
SEP
OCT
NOV
DEC

DATE

07/31

DAY

SAT

august

01 11:53 AM Bacon, egg, and cheese on a roll, fried potatoes from Manatus at home. 02 4:29 PM Tuna fish sandwiches at home. 03 5:53 PM Greek yogurt and white Jersey nectarine at home. 04 6:52 PM Tostitos at home. 05 9:06 PM Ramen noodles with spinach at home. 06 10:10 PM Entenmann's cheese bun at home. 07 11:23 PM Bite-size Frosted Mini-Wheats at home.

MONTH

JAN

FEB

MAR

APR

MAY

JUN

JUL

AUG

SEP

OCT

NOV

DEC

DATE

08/01

DAY

SUN

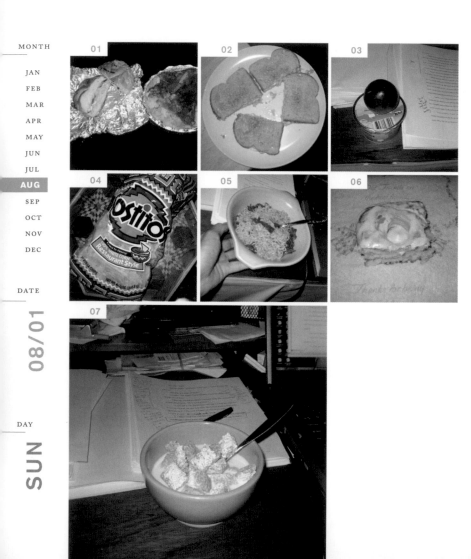

01 11:11 AM **Banana** at home. 02 2:00 PM **Flaked tuna on toast with tomato and mayo** at home. 03 9:05 PM **Sun Chips** at home with Danny. 04 9:52 PM **Meatloaf and mashed potatoes** at home with Danny. 05 10:38 PM **Peach crumble** at home with Danny.

MONTH

JAN
FEB
MAR
APR
MAY
JUN
JUL
AUG
SEP
OCT
NOV
DEC

DATE

08/02

DAY

MON

01 9:44 AM **Oatmeal at home.** 02 12:47 PM **Fried egg sandwiches at home.** 03 2:16 PM **Leftover peach crumble at home.** 04 5:46 PM **Greek yogurt at home.** 05 8:15 PM **Leftover meatloaf at home.** 06 12:38 AM **Fudge swirl soy "ice cream" with Marc and Danny at home.** 07 1:12 AM **Frosted Mini-Wheats at home.**

MONTH

JAN

FEB

MAR

APR

MAY

JUN

JUL

AUG

SEP

OCT

NOV

DEC

DATE

08/03

DAY

TUE

01 9:46 AM Oatmeal at home. 02 2:09 PM Meatloaf sandwiches with Sun Chips at home. 03 4:29 PM Greek yogurt with honey at home. 04 8:58 PM Guacamole with chips, goat cheese empanadas with chile sauce at Suenos with Scott. 05 9:40 PM Pan-roasted pork with fried onions and chile sauce at Suenos. 06 10:03 PM Banana and chocolate empanada with whipped cream at Suenos. 07 1:25 AM Frosted Mini-Wheats at home.

MONTH

JAN

FEB

MAR

APR

MAY

JUN

JUL

AUG

SEP

OCT

NOV

DEC

DATE

08/04

DAY

WED

01 10:20 AM **Free-sample Krispy Kreme donut on Worth Street.** 02 2:13 PM **Mixed greens with croutons, onions, avocado, carrots, and house vinaigrette at Hale & Hearty Soups, Chelsea Market.** 03 5:07 PM **Sour cream–and-onion potato chips at home.** 04 9:32 PM **Heirloom tomato salad with basil at Yard with Joe.** 05 9:51 PM **Grilled shrimp, mixed greens, and coleslaw at Yard.** 06 12:08 AM **Honey Nut Cheerios at home.**

MONTH

JAN

FEB

MAR

APR

MAY

JUN

JUL

AUG

SEP

OCT

NOV

DEC

DATE

08/05

DAY

THU

01 8:45 AM Oatmeal at home. 02 1:53 PM PBJ at home. 03 4:56 PM Sour cream–and–onion potato chips at home. 04 7:31 PM Kettle Chips at Hudson River Park with Chris. 05 10:13 PM Frittata with onions, red potatoes, and tomatoes with Danny at home. 06 12:52 AM Honey Nut Cheerios at home.

01 10:00 AM Oatmeal at home. **02** 1:15 PM Guacamole and chips, cherries at house party with Henry, Susan, Andrea, Tim M., Tim A., Alex, Christopher, Marc, David, John, Ted, and other guests. **03** 1:49 PM Fried chicken, coleslaw, and macaroni and cheese from Mama's; Cowboy beans, macaroni salad, deviled eggs, and tossed salad at Tim's. **04** 2:20 PM Cherry popsicle at Tim's. **05** 2:29 PM Ice-cream cake from Emack & Bolio's at Tim's. **06** 8:17 PM Potato chips at home. **07** 9:01 PM Spaghetti with grape tomatoes, peppers, and goat cheese with Danny at home. **08** 12:43 AM Honey Nut Cheerios at home.

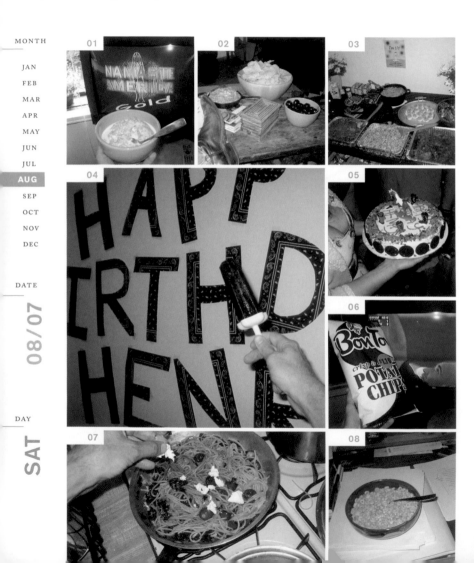

MONTH

JAN
FEB
MAR
APR
MAY
JUN
JUL
AUG
SEP
OCT
NOV
DEC

DATE

08/07

DAY

SAT

01 11:12 AM **Oatmeal at home.** 02 3:55 PM **Mozzarepa on Christopher Street.** 03 5:19 PM **Strawberry Frozade, Lemon Frozade in Hudson River Park with Jason.** 04 8:53 PM **Pizza rolls with Danny at home.** 05 9:21 PM **Croque-monsieur, tomato soup, mixed greens, and fries from La Petite Abeille with Danny at home.** 06 10:05 PM **Entenmann's dulce de leche cake with Danny at home.** 07 10:38 PM **Honey Nut Cheerios at home.**

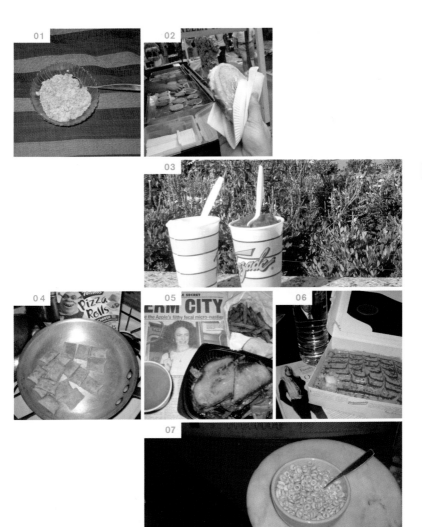

MONTH

JAN

FEB

MAR

APR

MAY

JUN

JUL

AUG

SEP

OCT

NOV

DEC

DATE

80/80

DAY

SUN

01 1:21 PM **Black bean soup at Bar 6 with Daniel.** 02 1:32 PM **Grilled chicken sandwich with arugula and tomato at Bar 6.** 03 5:25 PM **Greek yogurt with honey at home.** 04 9:06 PM **Pasta with spinach, bacon, and Parmigiano cheese at home.** 05 11:07 PM **Honey Bunches of Oats at home.**

MONTH

JAN
FEB
MAR
APR
MAY
JUN
JUL
AUG
SEP
OCT
NOV
DEC

DATE

08/09

DAY

MON

01 9:32 AM **Oatmeal at home.** 02 3:10 PM **Leftover pasta with spinach, bacon, and Parmigiano at home.** 03 5:03 PM **Strawberry popsicle at home.** 04 7:00 PM **Leftover goat cheese at home.** 05 8:47 PM **Salt-and-vinegar potato chips at home.** 06 9:54 PM **Bacon Cheeseburger Deluxe from Hudson Corner at home with Danny.** 07 11:04 PM **Honey Bunches of Oats at home.**

MONTH

JAN
FEB
MAR
APR
MAY
JUN
JUL
AUG
SEP
OCT
NOV
DEC

DATE

08/10

DAY

TUE

01 11:02 AM **Oatmeal at home.** 02 2:24 PM **Tuna fish sandwich on toasted potato bread at home.** 03 4:58 PM **Greek yogurt at home.** 04 9:19 PM **Scrambled eggs, tomatoes, and toast at home.** 05 11:01 PM **Cheerios at home.**

MONTH

JAN

FEB

MAR

APR

MAY

JUN

JUL

AUG

SEP

OCT

NOV

DEC

DATE

08/11

DAY

WED

01

02

03

04

05

New York City to Nantucket 01 8:21 AM Oatmeal at home. 02 3:17 PM Swordfish sandwich with Dad in Nantucket.
03 4:05 PM Grapes with Dad in Nantucket. 04 5:41 PM Crackers and cheese with Eric and Ruby at Eric and
Connie's. 05 7:10 PM Crackers and cheese with Gram and Geoff in Nantucket. 06 7:46 PM Lamb chops, pasta
with olive oil, cucumbers and tomatoes with Dad, Heather, Gram, and Geoff in Nantucket. 07 8:52 PM Butter
crunch ice cream in Nantucket.

MONTH

JAN

FEB

MAR

APR

MAY

JUN

JUL

AUG

SEP

OCT

NOV

DEC

DATE

08/12

DAY

THU

Nantucket 01 10:28 AM **Grapes in Nantucket.** 02 2:19 PM **Cheeseburger and fries with Dad, Heather, and Geoff at the West End, Nantucket.** 03 6:16 PM **Salmon dip and bluefish dip with Eric, Connie, Lewis, Ruby, Dad, Heather, Gram, and Geoff at Eric and Connie's house.** 04 8:16 PM **Lobster and corn at Eric and Connie's.** 05 9:21 PM **Mixed-fruit tart with whipped cream at Eric and Connie's.**

MONTH

JAN

FEB

MAR

APR

MAY

JUN

JUL

AUG

SEP

OCT

NOV

DEC

DATE

08/13

DAY

FRI

Nantucket to New York City 01 8:03 AM **Blueberries in Nantucket.** 02 9:35 AM **Toast with jelly in Nantucket.**
03 4:44 PM **Peanut butter and jelly at home.** 04 8:49 PM **Black beans with poached eggs, French fries at home.**
05 10:24 PM **Refried noodles with minced onions at home.** 06 11:05 PM **Cheerios at home.**

MONTH

JAN

FEB

MAR

APR

MAY

JUN

JUL

AUG

SEP

OCT

NOV

DEC

DATE

08/14

DAY

SAT

01 12:21 PM **Oatmeal at home.** 02 3:35 PM **Peanut butter and jelly at home.** 03 3:45 PM **Yogurt at home.**
04 7:27 PM **Two Boots pizza with andouille sausage, tomato, spinach, onion, and garlic at home.**
05 9:11 PM **Peach upside-down cake at home.**

MONTH

JAN
FEB
MAR
APR
MAY
JUN
JUL
AUG
SEP
OCT
NOV
DEC

DATE

08/15

DAY

SUN

01 1:59 PM Leftover pizza at home. 02 8:37 PM Tuna tartare with truffle oil at the Mermaid Inn with Doc and Chris. 03 8:49 PM Fried oysters with coleslaw, seared sardines with tomatoes, oysters, and crab salad with tartar sauce and cocktail sauce at the Mermaid Inn. 04 9:06 PM Chilled pea soup with lobster at the Mermaid Inn. 05 9:22 PM Bacon-crusted halibut with mashed potatoes and onion broth at the Mermaid Inn. 06 9:47 PM Chocolate pudding at the Mermaid Inn. 07 11:35 PM Cheerios at home. 08 11:46 PM Leftover peach upside-down cake at home.

MONTH

JAN
FEB
MAR
APR
MAY
JUN
JUL
AUG
SEP
OCT
NOV
DEC

DATE

08/16

DAY

MON

01 10:42 AM **Oatmeal at home.** 02 2:49 PM **Tuna-tomato panzanella made with leftover pizza crust.** 03 8:21 PM **Chips and salsa with Danny at home.** 04 9:01 PM **Roasted pork with black beans and yellow rice with Danny at home.** 05 10:08 PM **Moon pie from Westville at home with Danny.** 06 10:32 PM **Cheerios at home.**

MONTH

JAN

FEB

MAR

APR

MAY

JUN

JUL

AUG

SEP

OCT

NOV

DEC

DATE

08/17

DAY

TUE

01 10:20 AM Oatmeal at home. 02 1:37 PM Shakeburger and fries at Shake Shack with Chris. 03 6:59 PM Tostitos with Jorge at home. 04 9:00 PM Tekka maki dinner with miso soup, oshitashi (pickled spinach), and shumai (crab dumplings) with Jorge at home. 05 10:30 PM Fried parsnips from Ready to Eat with Danny and Jorge at home. 06 10:49 PM Cheerios at home.

MONTH

JAN

FEB

MAR

APR

MAY

JUN

JUL

AUG

SEP

OCT

NOV

DEC

DATE

08/18

DAY

WED

01 8:38 AM **Oatmeal at home.** 02 2:09 PM **Polenta with peas and corn, panino with soppressata and tapenade, tramezzini with tomato and pancetta at 'inoteca with Deb.** 03 2:38 PM **Cheeses at 'inoteca.** 04 3:15 PM **Chocolate pudding with whipped cream and figs at 'inoteca.** 05 9:48 PM **Hot dogs and fries with Danny at home.** 06 10:48 PM **Strawberry popsicle at home.**

MONTH

JAN

FEB

MAR

APR

MAY

JUN

JUL

AUG

SEP

OCT

NOV

DEC

DATE

08/19

DAY

THU

New York to Fire Island 01 8:49 AM Oatmeal at home. 02 12:21 PM Peanut butter and jelly at home. 03 3:54 PM Cote d'Or chocolate with Chris on the LIRR to Sayville. 04 5:01 PM Tortilla chips with Chris at Garth's house. 05 7:45 PM Goat cheese and crackers with Chris at Garth's. 06 9:39 PM Pasta with pancetta and eggs with Chris at Garth's. 07 12:21 AM Lemon cake with Chris at Garth's.

MONTH

JAN

FEB

MAR

APR

MAY

JUN

JUL

AUG

SEP

OCT

NOV

DEC

DATE

08/20

DAY

FRI

Fire Island 01 10:51 AM **Toast with butter with Chris at Garth's.** 02 3:16 PM **Goat cheese, avocado, and tomato sandwich and tortilla chips with Chris at Garth's house.** 03 3:57 PM **Chips and salsa with Garth at Garth's house.** 04 6:15 PM **Cote d'Or chocolate with Chris at Garth's house.** 05 9:29 PM **Chicken with ginger, garlic, saffron, and cilantro with Chris, Garth, and Phil at Garth's house.** 06 9:40 PM **Couscous at Garth's.** 07 9:41 PM **Cucumber and golden raisin raita at Garth's.** 08 12:26 AM **Spice cake at Garth's.**

MONTH

JAN
FEB
MAR
APR
MAY
JUN
JUL
AUG
SEP
OCT
NOV
DEC

DATE

08/21

DAY

SAT

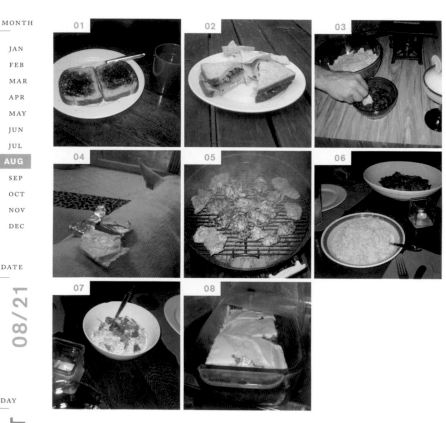

Fire Island to New York City 01 10:53 AM Scrambled eggs with zucchini, onions, and mixed herbs, bacon, and English muffin with Chris, Tony, Joe, and Garth at Garth's house. 02 1:33 PM Cherry Frozfruit with Chris at Sayville station. 03 5:23 PM Banana at home. 04 5:28 PM Panzanella with tuna and tomatoes at home. 05 9:08 PM Kitchen-cupboard pasta with shaved Parmigiano at home. 06 10:36 PM Lemon cake at home.

MONTH

JAN

FEB

MAR

APR

MAY

JUN

JUL

AUG

SEP

OCT

NOV

DEC

DATE

08/22

DAY

SUN

01 10:31 AM **Oatmeal at home.** 02 2:07 PM **Egg salad at home.** 03 8:39 PM **Chicken soup at home.**
04 9:08 PM **Chips, salsa, and guacamole from Benny's Burritos with Danny and Jorge at home.**

MONTH

JAN

FEB

MAR

APR

MAY

JUN

JUL

AUG

SEP

OCT

NOV

DEC

DATE

08/23

DAY

MON

01

02

03

04

01 1:35 PM Goat cheese, bacon, tomato, and avocado sandwiches, radishes and green beans in Central Park with Mom. 02 1:59 PM Peaches and birthday cookies (chocolate chip) with Mom. 03 8:13 PM Potato chips with Danny at home. 04 9:42 PM Catfish po'boy with salad and fries from Westville with Danny at home. 05 10:11 PM Chocolate chip cookies with Danny at home.

01
02
03

MONTH

JAN
FEB
MAR
APR
MAY
JUN
JUL
AUG
SEP
OCT
NOV
DEC

04

DATE

08/24

05

DAY

TUE

01 6:45 AM **Oatmeal at home.** 02 12:17 PM **Chicken salad sandwich from Taylor's with Buzz at Abingdon Square Park.** 03 8:51 PM **Ritz Chips with Danny at home.** 04 9:07 PM **Open-faced bacon, egg, tomato, and avocado sandwich with warm potato salad with Danny at home.** 05 10:14 PM **Entenmann's Star Puffs with Danny at home.** 06 10:58 PM **Kix at home.**

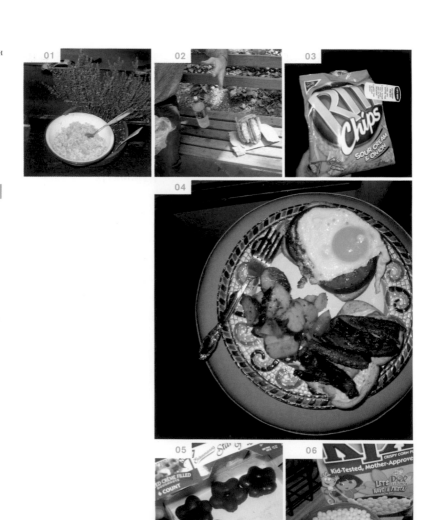

MONTH

JAN
FEB
MAR
APR
MAY
JUN
JUL
AUG
SEP
OCT
NOV
DEC

DATE

08/25

DAY

WED

01 9:57 AM **Oatmeal at home.** 02 3:00 PM **Shrimp with leeks at home.** 03 4:06 PM **Ramen noodles with chicken broth at home.** 04 9:22 PM **Arugula and red endive salad with avocado with Jorge and Julian at Jorge's.** 05 9:44 PM **Catfish with olives, tomatoes, lemons, and Kashi pilaf at Jorge's.** 06 10:26 PM **Pound cake with ice cream and jam at Jorge's.** 07 11:53 PM **Kix at home.**

MONTH

JAN
FEB
MAR
APR
MAY
JUN
JUL
AUG
SEP
OCT
NOV
DEC

DATE

08/26

DAY

THU

01 10:58 AM Oatmeal at home. 02 1:49 PM Peanut butter and jelly sandwiches at home. 03 4:57 PM Green beans at home. 04 5:42 PM Baked Lay's with Jorge at home. 05 6:55 PM Movie snax. *Open Water* at Chelsea Cinema with Jorge. 06 10:22 PM Egg, potato, and onion fry-up at home. 07 11:02 PM Chocolate chip cookies at home.

MONTH

JAN
FEB
MAR
APR
MAY
JUN
JUL
AUG
SEP
OCT
NOV
DEC

DATE

08/27

DAY

FRI

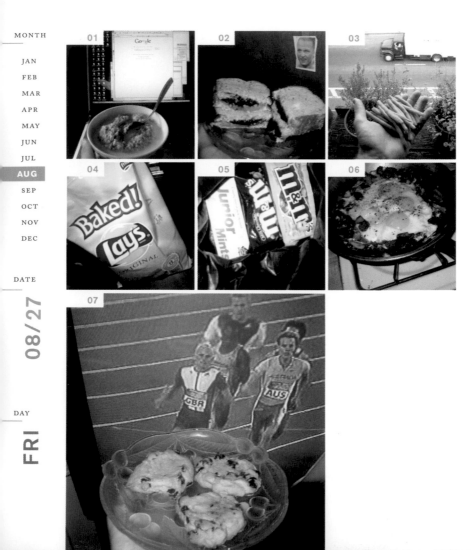

01 9:39 AM **Brioche from La Bergamote with Danny and Chris on Hudson Street.** 02 9:54 AM **Cinnamon old-fashioned from Donut Hut at 7th Avenue and 14th Street with Chris.** 03 10:21 AM **Peach at Union Square Farmers' Market with Chris.** 04 2:06 PM **Chocolate chip cookie at home.** 05 3:27 PM **Chilaquiles with Janice, Andrea, Susan, Tim, and Henry at La Palapa.** 06 9:31 PM **Fried calamari, chips with guacamole at Elmo with Tim and Alex.** 07 10:09 PM **Macaroni and cheese, iceberg lettuce salad with blue cheese dressing at Elmo.** 08 10:19 PM **Shrimp cocktail at Elmo.** 09 10:30 PM **Fried chicken with spinach, mashed potatoes, and carrots, onion rings at Elmo.** 10 11:09 PM **Pecan brownie with pecan ice cream, Key lime pie at Elmo.**

MONTH

JAN
FEB
MAR
APR
MAY
JUN
JUL
AUG
SEP
OCT
NOV
DEC

DATE

08/28

DAY

SAT

01 10:25 AM **Oatmeal at home.** 02 11:12 AM **Strawberry popsicle on Bleecker Street.** 03 11:52 AM **Lime Frozfruit with Chris and Alex on 7th Avenue.** 04 1:56 PM **Fruit salad with Chris, Alex, Rich, Mac, and Omar on 7th Avenue.** 05 5:20 PM **Ham and cheese with Russian dressing in Hudson River Park.** 06 9:03 PM **Domino's pepperoni pizza with Danny at home.** 07 9:43 PM **Kix at home.**

MONTH

JAN
FEB
MAR
APR
MAY
JUN
JUL
AUG
SEP
OCT
NOV
DEC

DATE

08/29

DAY

SUN

01 10:07 AM **Oatmeal at home.** 02 2:51 PM **Meatloaf sandwiches at home.** 03 8:34 PM **Potato chips at home.**
04 9:12 PM **Carrot-ginger soup from Pastis with Danny at home.** 05 9:21 PM **Burger with cheddar cheese, tomato, onion, and lettuce; fries; and fried calamari from Pastis at home.** 06 10:48 PM **Kix at home.**

MONTH

JAN
FEB
MAR
APR
MAY
JUN
JUL
AUG
SEP
OCT
NOV
DEC

DATE

08/30

DAY

MON

01 9:17 AM **Oatmeal at home.** 02 1:44 PM **Joe's Pizza on Bleecker Street.** 03 2:23 PM **Tuna fish sandwiches with sliced cucumber at home.** 04 6:40 PM **Banana in Union Square.** 05 8:08 PM **Potato chips with Danny at home.** 06 8:59 PM **Pasta with tomatoes, spinach, and garlic with Danny at home.** 07 9:57 PM **Frosted Mini-Wheats at home.**

MONTH

JAN
FEB
MAR
APR
MAY
JUN
JUL
AUG
SEP
OCT
NOV
DEC

DATE

08/31

DAY

TUE

01 9:22 AM Oatmeal at home. **02** 1:51 PM Peanut butter and jelly sandwiches at home. **03** 2:53 PM Reese's on E. 13th Street. **04** 3:22 PM Cherry Frozfruit at Madison Square Park. **05** 5:29 PM Yogurt at home. **06** 7:37 PM Salt and vinegar chips at home. **07** 7:56 PM Spicy tomato soup at home. **08** 8:57 PM Short ribs with Kennebec potatoes and onions at home. **09** 10:05 PM Frosted Mini-Wheats at home.

MONTH

JAN
FEB
MAR
APR
MAY
JUN
JUL
AUG
SEP
OCT
NOV
DEC

DATE

09/01

DAY

WED

New York City to Bonita Springs, Florida 01 8:43 AM Bran muffin at LaGuardia Airport with Mom. 02 9:35 AM Blueberry Nutri-Grain at LaGuardia. 03 11:25 AM Orange juice and pretzels on US Airways flight 269 with Mom. 04 3:35 PM Grilled chicken sandwich with cheese and bacon, grilled vegetables at Bob Jones Restaurant with Mom. 05 8:21 PM Chips and salsa at Iguana Mia with Mom. 06 8:36 PM Guacamole at Iguana Mia. 07 8:45 PM Pork tacos with rice and beans at Iguana Mia.

MONTH

JAN
FEB
MAR
APR
MAY
JUN
JUL
AUG
SEP
OCT
NOV
DEC

DATE

09/02

DAY

THU

Bonita Springs, Florida 01 8:26 AM Bran cereal with raisins, strawberry yogurt at Holiday Inn Express with Mom.
02 12:53 PM Chef's club sandwich with coleslaw at Worthington Grille Room with Edwina and Mom. 03 1:14 PM
Chocolate chip cookie at Worthington Grille Room. 04 3:18 PM Apple-cinnamon Nutri-Grain bar at Holiday Inn
Express. 05 6:49 PM Rotisserie chicken, roasted potatoes, frozen green beans, dinner rolls, and salad at Bumpa
and Edwina's condo with Bumpa, Edwina, Clint, and Mom. 06 7:50 PM Chocolate cream pie with Cool Whip at
Bumpa and Edwina's condo with Bumpa, Edwina, Clint, Mom, Georgeann, and Ron.

MONTH

JAN

FEB

MAR

APR

MAY

JUN

JUL

AUG

SEP

OCT

NOV

DEC

DATE

09/03

DAY

FRI

Bonita Springs, Florida, to New York City 01 8:01 AM Bran cereal with raisins, blueberry yogurt at Holiday Inn Express with Mom. 02 11:42 AM Strawberry Nutri-Grain at Southwest Florida International Airport. 03 1:34 PM Pretzels on US Airways flight 1058. 04 7:56 PM Tortilla chips with Danny at home. 05 8:10 PM Peanut butter and honey tortilla with Danny at home. 06 8:22 PM Apple butter tortilla with Danny at home. 07 10:34 PM Grilled cheese with tomato and bacon from Manatus with Danny at home. 08 10:43 PM Belgian waffle from Manatus at home.

MONTH

JAN
FEB
MAR
APR
MAY
JUN
JUL
AUG
SEP
OCT
NOV
DEC

DATE

09/04

DAY

SAT

01 10:50 AM Oatmeal at home. 02 2:52 PM Salt and vinegar potato chips at home with Danny. 03 4:14 PM Blueberry Nutri-Grain at home. 04 4:53 PM Slice at Joe's Pizza. 05 8:15 PM Spicy tomato soup at home. 06 9:21 PM Meatloaf with zucchini, carrots, and peekaboo weenies at home with Danny. 07 10:03 PM Tres leches cake at home. 08 10:54 PM More tres leches cake at home.

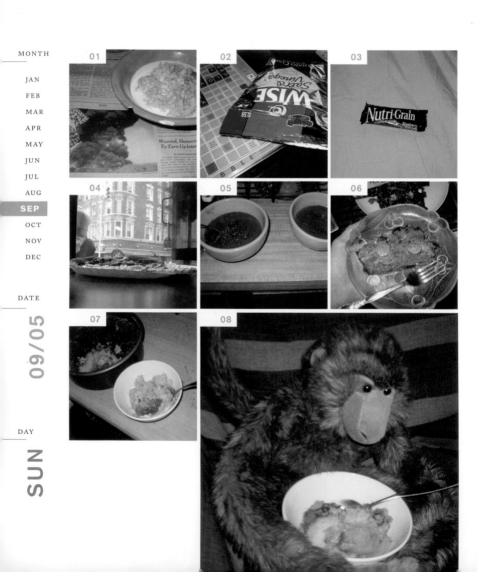

MONTH

JAN
FEB
MAR
APR
MAY
JUN
JUL
AUG
SEP
OCT
NOV
DEC

DATE

09/05

DAY

SUN

01 12:16 PM Scrambled eggs with salsa and tortillas at home. 02 2:47 PM Meatloaf sandwiches at home.
03 5:55 PM Nuts with Danny at the US Open Tennis Center in Queens. 04 7:43 PM Hot dog at the US Open.
05 8:32 PM Potato chips at the US Open. 06 10:25 PM Pork mu shu from Mama Buddha at home with Danny.
07 11:03 PM Tres leches cake at home.

MONTH

JAN
FEB
MAR
APR
MAY
JUN
JUL
AUG
SEP
OCT
NOV
DEC

DATE

09/06

DAY

MON

01 12:54 PM Tuna fish sandwiches at home. 02 4:36 PM Popsicle on Central Park West with JJ. 03 7:49 PM Salt and vinegar potato chips at home. 04 9:18 PM Potato, broccoli, and red onion frittata at home. 05 10:29 PM Tres leches cake at home with Danny.

MONTH

JAN
FEB
MAR
APR
MAY
JUN
JUL
AUG
SEP
OCT
NOV
DEC

DATE

09/07

DAY

TUE

01 9:19 AM Scrambled eggs, bacon, home fries, and toasted English muffin with John at Bonbonniere. 02 12:01 PM Movie snax. *Hero.* Union Square Theater. 03 3:15 PM Meatloaf sandwiches at home. 04 8:54 PM Pasta with pancetta, pepperoncini, and arugula at home with Danny. 05 9:42 PM Israeli chocolate bar at home with Danny. 06 9:54 PM Plum cake at home.

MONTH

JAN

FEB

MAR

APR

MAY

JUN

JUL

AUG

SEP

OCT

NOV

DEC

DATE

09/08

DAY

WED

01 9:43 AM **Oatmeal at home.** 02 12:23 PM **Dark-meat turkey on wheat bread at Sandwiches with Andy.**
03 5:41 PM **Leftover spaghetti at home.** 04 9:49 PM **Sour cream and onion potato chips at home.** 05 9:58 PM
Leftover spaghetti at home. 06 10:18 PM **Hot dogs at home with Danny.** 07 10:54 PM **Plum cake at home.**

MONTH

JAN

FEB

MAR

APR

MAY

JUN

JUL

AUG

SEP

OCT

NOV

DEC

DATE

09/09

DAY

THU

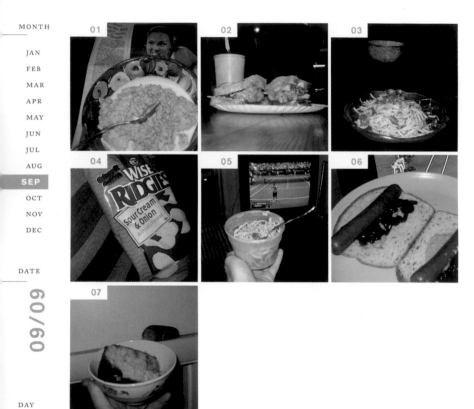

01 9:19 AM Oatmeal at home. 02 1:48 PM Falafel and hummus sandwich, almond-honey cake from Rainbow Falafel in Union Square with Paul. 03 8:52 PM Antipasti platter (onions agrodolce, braised fennel with bread crumbs, roasted peppers with pickled anchovies) at Pace with Chris and Doc. 04 9:05 PM Blue Point oysters at Pace. 05 9:26 PM Risotto with veal cheeks and marrow, agnolotti with pork at Pace. 06 9:58 PM Red mullet with tomatoes in "crazy water" at Pace. 07 9:59 PM Roasted boar with mashed potatoes and mixed vegetables at Pace. 08 10:00 PM Sweetbreads with prosciutto and sage with Marsala sauce at Pace. 09 10:10 PM Broad beans with spinach at Pace. 10 10:48 PM Zeppole with two chocolate sauces, chocolate torte with vanilla ice cream, and assorted cookies at Pace. 11 12:02 AM Plum cake at home.

MONTH

JAN
FEB
MAR
APR
MAY
JUN
JUL
AUG
SEP
OCT
NOV
DEC

DATE

09/10

DAY

FRI

01 11:10 AM Eggs over easy, bacon, home fries, salad, and toasted English muffin with Chris at Village Den. 02 2:09 PM Edy's strawberry popsicle at home. 03 3:08 PM Apple sample at Union Square Farmers' Market with Chris. 04 3:29 PM Grilled Swiss with bacon at Eisenberg's with Chris. 05 9:06 PM Bruschetta from Tanti Baci at home with Danny. 06 9:16 PM Linguine with clam sauce from Tanti Baci at home with Danny. 07 12:02 AM Entenmann's fudge cookies at home.

MONTH

JAN
FEB
MAR
APR
MAY
JUN
JUL
AUG
SEP
OCT
NOV
DEC

DATE

09/11

DAY

SAT

01 10:27 AM **Oatmeal at home.** 02 1:11 PM **Cherry Blow Pop in Hudson River Park with Jason.** 03 3:16 PM **Spring rolls, spring salad, and Thai wide noodles with chicken from Kelly and Ping with Jason in Washington Square Park.** 04 7:45 PM **Potato chips at home.** 05 9:27 PM **Omelet with broccoli and tomatoes at home.** 06 11:19 PM **Grape-Nuts Flakes at home.**

MONTH

JAN
FEB
MAR
APR
MAY
JUN
JUL
AUG
SEP
OCT
NOV
DEC

DATE

09/12

DAY

SUN

01 8:26 AM Oatmeal at home.　02 3:37 PM Tuna fish sandwiches at home.　03 9:34 PM Bacon, tomato, avocado, and egg sandwich, sautéed broccoli with zucchini, home fries at home with Danny.　04 10:26 PM Entenmann's chocolate chip cookies at home.

MONTH

JAN

FEB

MAR

APR

MAY

JUN

JUL

AUG

SEP

OCT

NOV

DEC

DATE

09/13

DAY

MON

01 1:21 PM **Egg salad sandwich at home.** 02 8:23 PM **Tostitos at home with Danny.** 03 10:19 PM **"Danny's spaghetti" with garlic, onions, tomatoes, and spinach at home with Danny and Jorge.** 04 11:47 PM **Grape-Nuts Flakes at home.**

MONTH

JAN

FEB

MAR

APR

MAY

JUN

JUL

AUG

SEP

OCT

NOV

DEC

DATE

09/14

DAY

TUE

01 12:40 PM **Chorizo and goat cheese sandwich at French Roast with Susan.** 02 3:04 PM **Broken Nilla wafers at Susan and Andrea's with Susan.** 03 8:49 PM **Cucumber with Lawry's at home.** 04 9:39 PM **Leftover "Danny's pasta" at home.** 05 10:10 PM **Vanilla wafers at home with Danny.** 06 10:58 PM **Rosh Hashanah apples and honey at home with Danny.** 07 11:16 PM **Grape-Nuts Flakes at home.**

MONTH

JAN

FEB

MAR

APR

MAY

JUN

JUL

AUG

SEP

OCT

NOV

DEC

DATE

09/15

DAY

WED

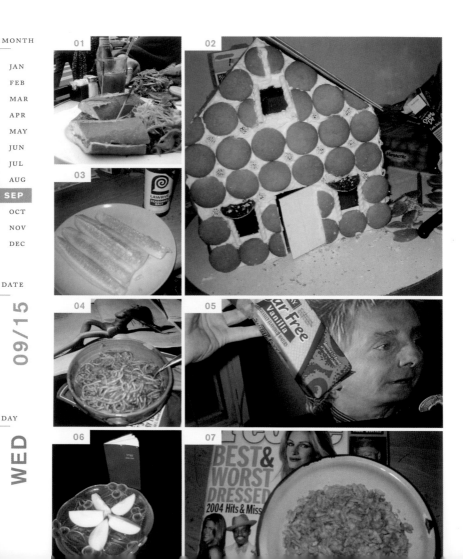

01 9:35 AM Oatmeal at home. 02 1:22 PM Double Shack Burger at Shake Shack with Chris. 03 4:31 PM Peanut butter and banana sandwich at home. 04 9:28 PM Artichoke dip with bread and devils on horseback at Freeman's with Christopher and Marc. 05 9:55 PM Roasted pork with baked apples, raisins, and spinach, heirloom tomatoes, fresh corn and basil salad at Freeman's (roasted trout in background). 06 9:56 PM Codfish shepherd's pie, sautéed zucchini at Freeman's. 07 11:36 PM Salt and vinegar potato chips at home. 08 11:50 PM Grape-Nuts Flakes at home.

MONTH

JAN

FEB

MAR

APR

MAY

JUN

JUL

AUG

SEP

OCT

NOV

DEC

DATE

09/16

DAY

THU

01 10:07 AM **Oatmeal at home.** 02 2:19 PM **Falafel sandwich with hummus from Rainbow in Union Square Park with Jason R.** 03 3:04 PM **Raspberries with Jason R. at Union Square Farmers' Market.** 04 8:48 PM **Potato chips at home.** 05 10:16 PM **Chicken and white bean stew at home.** 06 11:27 PM **Cornflakes at home.**

MONTH

JAN
FEB
MAR
APR
MAY
JUN
JUL
AUG
SEP
OCT
NOV
DEC

DATE

09/17

DAY

FRI

01 8:42 AM **Oatmeal at home.** 02 1:28 PM **Quiche from Pâtisserie Claude in Sheridan Square with Chris.** 03 1:50 PM **Cream puff at Beard Papa with Chris.** 04 2:07 PM **Two pork, two chicken dumplings at Dumpling Man with Chris.** 05 2:14 PM **House hummus at Hummus Place with Chris.** 06 2:40 PM **Deconstructed ramen soup with pork at Mamafoku.** 07 3:32 PM **Vietnamese Special sandwich at Nicky's Vietnamese Sandwiches.** 08 10:17 PM **Chopped salad at Ruth's Chris Steak House with Susan, Andrea, Tim, Patches, Alex, and Eva.** 09 10:37 PM **Rib-eye at Ruth's Chris.**

MONTH

JAN
FEB
MAR
APR
MAY
JUN
JUL
AUG
SEP
OCT
NOV
DEC

DATE

09/18

DAY

SAT

01 12:09 PM **Omelet with mixed cheeses and spinach, dry toast at home.** 02 3:33 PM **Raspberries at home.**
03 3:40 PM **Peanut butter and jelly sandwich at home.** 04 9:52 PM **Leftover chicken stew with egg over easy at home.** 05 10:56 PM **Cornflakes at home.**

MONTH

JAN
FEB
MAR
APR
MAY
JUN
JUL
AUG
SEP
OCT
NOV
DEC

DATE

09/19

DAY

SUN

01 9:14 AM Oatmeal at home. 02 10:30 AM Banana on 14th Street. 03 2:35 PM Tuna fish sandwiches and potato chips at home. 04 9:59 PM Macaroni and cheese with chorizo and peas at home. 05 11:02 PM Reese's Pieces at home.

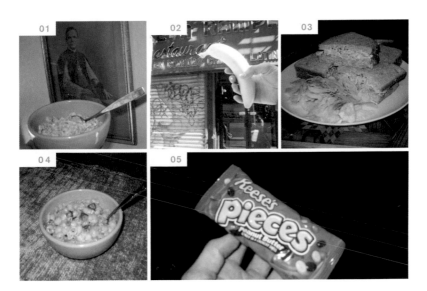

MONTH

JAN
FEB
MAR
APR
MAY
JUN
JUL
AUG
SEP
OCT
NOV
DEC

DATE

09/20

DAY

MON

01 9:41 AM **Oatmeal at home.** 02 2:00 PM **Tropicana strawberry smoothie on Delancey Street with JJ.** 03 2:24 PM **Pure Protein bar at East River Park with JJ.** 04 4:05 PM **Cherry helado on Houston Street with JJ.** 05 8:47 PM **Chips and guacamole, shrimp cocktail with avocado, and macaroni and cheese at Elmo with Buzz and Tim.** 06 9:08 PM **Cheeseburger with Cheddar, bacon, avocado, lettuce, tomato, onion, and French fries at Elmo.**

MONTH

JAN
FEB
MAR
APR
MAY
JUN
JUL
AUG
SEP
OCT
NOV
DEC

DATE

09/21

DAY

TUE

01 10:03 AM Zucchini muffin from Yura in Central Park with Mom. 02 1:10 PM Egg salad on toast with lettuce and tomato, pickle from Eisenberg's in Madison Square Park with Chris. 03 2:02 PM Edy's cherry popsicle at home. 04 9:54 PM Ziti with sauce of chopped take-out fried chicken from Elmo, carrots, spinach, bacon, and Parmesan at home with Danny. 05 10:39 PM Snickers Fun Size at home with Danny. 06 10:57 PM Entenmann's lemon crunch cake at home with Danny.

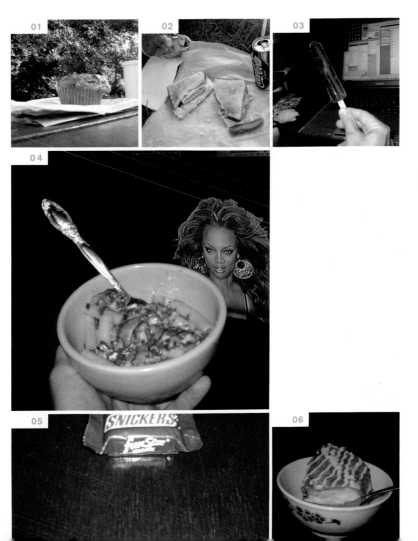

MONTH

JAN

FEB

MAR

APR

MAY

JUN

JUL

AUG

SEP

OCT

NOV

DEC

DATE

09/22

DAY

WED

01 9:05 AM Oatmeal at home. 02 2:23 PM Meatloaf sandwich at home. 03 7:01 PM Strawberry popsicle at home. 04 8:37 PM Potato chips at home. 05 10:09 PM Braised pork ribs with carrots and celery, mac and cheese, broccoli rabe at home. 06 11:13 PM Cheerios at home.

MONTH

JAN
FEB
MAR
APR
MAY
JUN
JUL
AUG
SEP
OCT
NOV
DEC

DATE

09/23

DAY

THU

01 8:26 AM Oatmeal at home. 02 10:14 AM Pumpkin pudding at food shoot with Susan, Laura, and Jeff.
03 12:56 PM Two spicy tuna rolls, yellowtail roll with scallion, green salad with carrot dressing from Monster
Sushi at food shoot with Susan, Laura, and Jeff. 04 4:19 PM Peach yogurt at food shoot. 05 5:54 PM Strawberries
at home. 06 10:26 PM Potato chips at home with Danny. 07 11:04 PM Linguine carbonara with spinach, spicy
German mustard, and Parmesan wedge at home with Danny. 08 11:59 PM Cornflakes with brown sugar at home.

MONTH

JAN
FEB
MAR
APR
MAY
JUN
JUL
AUG
SEP
OCT
NOV
DEC

DATE

09/24

DAY

FRI

01 12:33 PM **Oatmeal with raspberries at home.** 02 3:27 PM **Leftover linguine carbonara at home.** 03 3:51 PM **Orange popsicle at home.** 04 5:19 PM **Yogurt at home.** 05 9:52 PM **Braised chicken thighs with spicy German mustard and carrots, roasted potatoes, and spinach at home with Danny.** 06 10:46 PM **Peach bread pudding at home.**

MONTH

JAN
FEB
MAR
APR
MAY
JUN
JUL
AUG
SEP
OCT
NOV
DEC

DATE

09/25

DAY

SAT

01 12:09 PM Bread basket with assorted jams and butter at Olives with Scott S. 02 12:28 PM Scrambled eggs, bacon, rosemary potato hash, and white toast at Olives. 03 4:29 PM Cherry popsicle at home. 04 9:34 PM Potato chips at home with Danny. 05 10:34 PM Sausage, broccoli rabe, and bread-crumb bake at home with Danny. 06 11:08 PM Leftover peach bread pudding at home.

01
02
03
04
05
06

MONTH

JAN
FEB
MAR
APR
MAY
JUN
JUL
AUG
SEP
OCT
NOV
DEC

DATE

09/26

DAY

SUN

01 9:37 AM Oatmeal with raspberries at home. 02 1:57 PM Turkey, Swiss cheese, and lettuce sandwich with Susan and Henry at Susan and Andrea's. 03 4:05 PM Babybel cheese at Susan and Andrea's. 04 4:41 PM Rice, chicken, applesauce, and cheese with Henry at Susan and Andrea's. 05 9:58 PM Pizza with pepperoni and onions from Village Pizza at home with Danny. 06 10:45 PM Stella D'oro Swiss Fudge cookies with peanut butter at home.

MONTH

JAN
FEB
MAR
APR
MAY
JUN
JUL
AUG
SEP
OCT
NOV
DEC

DATE

09/27

DAY

MON

01

02

03

04

05

06

01 9:38 AM Pretzel croissant at City Bakery with Danielle. 02 12:50 PM Cobb salad at Elmo with Tamar. 03 8:17 PM Bread, butter, peppers, and blue cheese at Frank's Steak House with Alex and Tim. 04 8:53 PM Shrimp cocktail and escargots at Frank's. 05 9:14 PM T-Bone for two at Frank's. 06 9:15 PM Potatoes baked with Parmesan cheese and goose fat, sautéed mushrooms, and creamed spinach at Frank's. 07 11:09 PM Cornflakes at home.

MONTH

JAN

FEB

MAR

APR

MAY

JUN

JUL

AUG

SEP

OCT

NOV

DEC

DATE

09/28

DAY

TUE

01 9:48 AM **Oatmeal with raisins at Florent with Andy.** 02 3:06 PM **Steak sandwich at home.** 03 7:18 PM **Yogurt at home.** 04 10:49 PM **Omelet with sausage and cheese, toasted tortillas at home.** 05 11:29 PM **Entenmann's chocolate chip cookies at home with Danny.** 06 11:38 PM **Cornflakes at home.**

MONTH

JAN
FEB
MAR
APR
MAY
JUN
JUL
AUG
SEP
OCT
NOV
DEC

DATE

09/29

DAY

WED

01 9:45 AM **Oatmeal at home.** 02 2:09 PM **Shrimp, pineapple, water chestnuts, bok choy, and black bean sauce with brown rice from Asian Station in the Time-Life Building cafeteria with Jorge.** 03 7:17 PM **Potato chips at home.** 04 9:35 PM **Tim's leftover filet mignon, creamed spinach, and goose-fat potatoes from Frank's at home.**

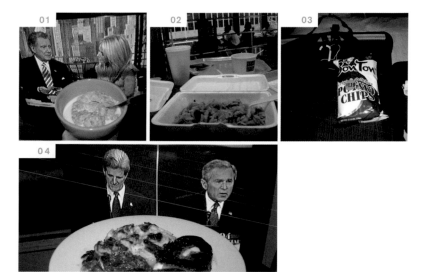

MONTH

JAN
FEB
MAR
APR
MAY
JUN
JUL
AUG
SEP
OCT
NOV
DEC

DATE

09/30

DAY

THU

New York City to Kearsarge, New Hampshire 01 9:27 AM Banana bread from Starbucks in town car with Mom. 02 1:37 PM Split pea soup at Horsefeathers in North Conway, NH, with Mom and Eric. 03 1:49 PM Fried crab and Havarti on white with French fries and pickle at Horsefeathers. 04 3:35 PM White chocolate/mint "bark" sample at the Rocky Mountain Chocolate Factory in North Conway, NH. 05 6:22 PM Dinner rolls at The Lobster Trap in Kearsarge, NH, with Mom, Eric, Dan, Nancy, Ron, Georgeann, Edwina, Donald, and Susan. *(continued on next page)*

MONTH

JAN
FEB
MAR
APR
MAY
JUN
JUL
AUG
SEP
OCT
NOV
DEC

DATE

10/01

DAY

FRI

06 6:52 PM Clam chowder at The Lobster Trap. 07 7:05 PM Fried scallops with tartar sauce and coleslaw at The Lobster Trap. 08 8:12 PM Mint chocolate chip ice cream in waffle cone at the Rocky Mountain Chocolate Factory. 09 8:27 PM "Penuche" fudge with mixed nuts from the Rocky Mountain Chocolate Factory at the Red Jacket Inn in Kearsarge, NH.

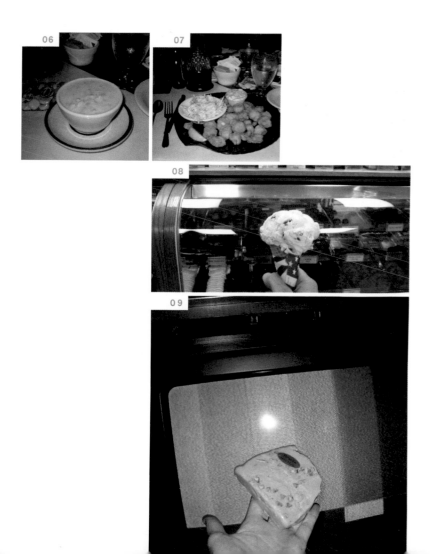

01 8:23 AM **Eggs Benedict, home fries, and bacon at the Red Jacket Inn with Eric.**
02 12:53 PM **Funeral Buffet I, prepared by the Sweenys (chocolate mint bars, chocolate cookies, tuna wraps, chocolate chip cookies, ginger cookies, potato chips, selection of cheeses and fruits) with Edwina, Georgeann, Clint, Dan, Eric, Mom, Tim, Wendy, Chad, Aiden, and 100 guests at Bumpa's house in Kearsarge, NH.** 03 12:54 PM **Funeral Buffet II (ham sandwiches, potato salad, lemon squares, and crackers) at Bumpa's house in Kearsarge, NH.** 04 6:43 PM **Leftover buffet items (ham sandwich, cheese cubes, and potato salad) at Bumpa's with Edwina, Georgeann, Ron, Nancy, Dan, Eric, and Mom.** 05 9:27 PM **Old-fashioned chocolate fudge from the Rocky Mountain Chocolate Factory at the Red Jacket Inn with Eric and Mom.**

MONTH

JAN

FEB

MAR

APR

MAY

JUN

JUL

AUG

SEP

OCT

NOV

DEC

DATE

10/02

DAY

SAT

Kearsarge, New Hampshire, to New York City 01 7:27 AM Glazed donut from Dunkin' Donuts at the Eastern Slopes Regional Airport in Frieburg, ME, with Mom and Eric. 02 8:04 AM Another donut above Lake Sebago, ME, with Eric. 03 10:27 AM Ginger cookie from Bumpa's funeral at the White Plains train station. 04 1:27 PM Panzanella made from leftover funeral buffet sandwiches at home with Bumpa's obituary. 05 6:35 PM Salt and vinegar potato chips at home with Jorge. 06 9:24 PM Garlic bread at home with Jorge, Wayne, and Danny. 07 9:28 PM Spaghetti with sausage and tomato sauce, Parmigiano cheese at home with Jorge, Wayne, and Danny. 08 10:06 PM Lemon-orange cake at home with Jorge, Wayne, and Danny.

MONTH

JAN
FEB
MAR
APR
MAY
JUN
JUL
AUG
SEP
OCT
NOV
DEC

DATE

10/03

DAY

SUN

01 12:47 PM Roasted corn and eggplant soup at Bright Food Shop with Susan. 02 1:00 PM Catfish wrap with watercress and black beans at Bright. 03 7:32 PM Panzanella made from leftover funeral buffet sandwiches at home. 04 8:29 PM Leftover spaghetti-and-garlic-bread sandwich at home. 05 9:10 PM Chocolate cookie from Bumpa's funeral at home. 06 9:22 PM Lemon-orange cake at home.

MONTH

JAN
FEB
MAR
APR
MAY
JUN
JUL
AUG
SEP
OCT
NOV
DEC

DATE

10/04

DAY

MON

01 9:02 AM Oatmeal at home. 02 2:14 PM Vegetable dumplings with green onions at Republic with Buzz. 03 2:21 PM Duck soup with Chinese greens and ginger at Republic. 04 9:40 PM Risotto with sausage, roasted broccoli, and poached egg at home with Danny. 05 10:17 PM Cornflakes at home. 06 10:31 PM Entenmann's dulce de leche cake at home.

MONTH

JAN

FEB

MAR

APR

MAY

JUN

JUL

AUG

SEP

OCT

NOV

DEC

DATE

10/05

DAY

TUE

01 9:55 AM Brioche from La Bergamote at home. 02 1:39 PM Dim sum (crab dumplings, vegetable dumplings, pork dumplings) at Triple-Eight with Andy. 03 1:52 PM Dim sum (shrimp dumplings, glazed eggplant) at Triple-Eight with Andy. 04 2:33 PM Walnut cookie from a Chinese bakery on Pell Street. 05 5:53 PM Yogurt at home. 06 8:28 PM Potato chips at home. 07 9:34 PM Spicy tomato soup at home. 08 10:32 PM Apple crisp at home.

MONTH

JAN
FEB
MAR
APR
MAY
JUN
JUL
AUG
SEP
OCT
NOV
DEC

DATE

10/06

DAY

WED

01 8:56 AM **Oatmeal at home.** 02 12:14 PM **California avocado sandwich, rosemary chips from Pret a Manger in Bryant Park with Marc.** 03 4:29 PM **Leftover apple crisp at home.** 04 9:37 PM **Refried risotto at home.** 05 11:04 PM **Entenmann's dulce de leche cake at home.**

MONTH

JAN

FEB

MAR

APR

MAY

JUN

JUL

AUG

SEP

OCT

NOV

DEC

DATE

10/07

DAY

THU

01 8:44 AM Oatmeal at home. 02 1:19 PM Bread at La Bonne Soupe with Patches. 03 1:20 PM Saffron and mussel soup at La Bonne Soupe. 04 1:33 PM Salade Niçoise at La Bonne Soupe. 05 6:01 PM Potato chips at home. 06 8:04 PM Scallops with microgreens and ginger sauce at Gotham with Buzz. 07 8:29 PM Miso-glazed cod with sprouts, spinach, sticky rice, and tomato broth at Gotham. 08 9:00 PM Toasted brioche with ice cream and almond cookie, cordial cookies at Gotham. 09 11:51 PM Cornflakes at home.

MONTH

JAN
FEB
MAR
APR
MAY
JUN
JUL
AUG
SEP
OCT
NOV
DEC

DATE

10/08

DAY

FRI

New York City to Liberty, New York 01 1:24 PM **Cashews on Palisades Parkway with Buzz.** 02 2:18 PM **Bread and olive oil at Cosimo's in Middletown, NY, with Buzz.** 03 2:25 PM **Mixed sausage pizza, fresh mozzarella and pancetta pizza at Cosimo's.** 04 8:30 PM **White bean and sausage soup at Buzz's house with Buzz.** 05 9:03 PM **Braised pork loin with smoked chile reduction at Buzz's.** 06 11:01 PM **Mildred Pierce pear pie at Buzz's.**

MONTH

JAN
FEB
MAR
APR
MAY
JUN
JUL
AUG
SEP
OCT
NOV
DEC

DATE

10/09

DAY

SAT

Liberty, New York, to New York City 01 11:35 AM **Leftover pie at Buzz's.** 02 1:07 PM **Leftover soup and leftover pizza at Buzz's.** 03 2:00 PM **More pie.** 04 8:25 PM **Ruffles at home with Danny.** 05 9:05 PM **Cheeseburger Deluxe and French fries from Manatus, leftover tomato soup at home with Danny.** 06 9:48 PM **Chocolate donut at home with Danny.**

MONTH

JAN
FEB
MAR
APR
MAY
JUN
JUL
AUG
SEP
OCT
NOV
DEC

DATE

10/10

DAY

SUN

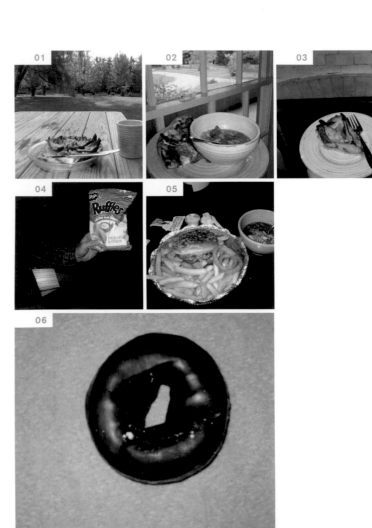

01 9:44 AM **Scrambled eggs, bacon, potatoes, and English muffin at Bonbonniere with John.** 02 12:29 PM **New England clam chowder at The Oyster Bar with Dan and Mikyla.** 03 12:41 PM **Clams casino at The Oyster Bar.** 04 4:39 PM **Strawberry popsicle at home.** 05 7:49 PM **Papaya salad with chiles and basil, seared beef salad with watercress and tomato at O Mai with Chris.** 06 7:55 PM **Vegetable dumpling soup, grilled eggplant, and seared shrimp with pork ribs at O Mai.** 07 9:18 PM **Grilled cheese at home.** 08 11:01 PM **Cornflakes at home.**

MONTH

JAN
FEB
MAR
APR
MAY
JUN
JUL
AUG
SEP
OCT
NOV
DEC

DATE

10/11

DAY

MON

01 10:00 AM **Oatmeal at home.** 02 2:55 PM **Tuna melt at home.** 03 8:31 PM **Potato chips at home.** 04 9:43 PM
Frittata with chorizo, spinach, and leftover cheese from Bumpa's funeral at home.

MONTH

JAN

FEB

MAR

APR

MAY

JUN

JUL

AUG

SEP

OCT

NOV

DEC

DATE

10/12

DAY

TUE

New York City to San Francisco 01 7:45 AM Mixed fruit at JFK Terminal 7. 02 9:51 AM Apple pancakes, sausage, apple danish, mixed fruit on United Airlines flight 27. 03 1:03 PM Ruffles, turkey sandwich on UA flight 27. 04 2:24 PM Huevos Montana with refried beans and avocado at Anchorage Café, Sausalito, CA, with Dad. 05 3:09 PM Coffee ice cream at Dave's Ice Cream in Sausalito with Dad. 06 5:59 PM Bread at Absinthe with Heather, Geoff, and Dad. 07 6:14 PM Cabbage soup at Absinthe. 08 6:55 PM Blanquette de veau with mixed vegetables and quinoa at Absinthe. 09 11:14 PM Cookies & cream ice cream at Dad's.

MONTH

JAN
FEB
MAR
APR
MAY
JUN
JUL
AUG
SEP
OCT
NOV
DEC

DATE

10/13

DAY

WED

Tiburon 01 8:21 AM **Corn muffin at Dad's.** 02 8:45 AM **Oatmeal with butter at Dad's.** 03 12:28 PM **Bread at Zuni Café with Heather and Dad.** 04 12:47 PM **Anchovies with Parmesan cheese, celery, and olives at Zuni Café.** 05 12:53 PM **Wood-oven pizza with cheese and tomatoes at Zuni Café.** 06 1:32 PM **Espresso granita at Zuni Café.** 07 7:15 PM **Lamb chops, risotto with mixed vegetables at Dad's with Heather, Geoff, and Dad.** 08 8:06 PM **Tarte Tatin at Dad's.**

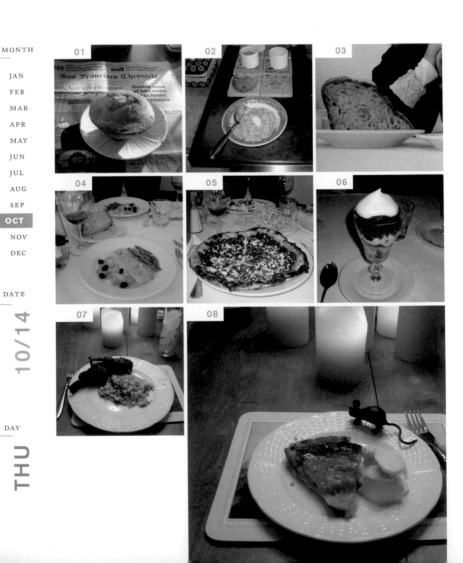

MONTH

JAN

FEB

MAR

APR

MAY

JUN

JUL

AUG

SEP

OCT

NOV

DEC

DATE

10/14

DAY

THU

Tiburon 01 7:54 AM Shredded wheat at Dad's. 02 12:17 PM Porchetta sandwich with mixed greens from Mondo Caffe in Chronicle Books' big conference room with Brenda and Jane. 03 4:01 PM Olive oil sample from McEvoy's at the San Francisco Ferry Building with Heather. 04 7:28 PM Braised pork with roasted potatoes and rainbow chard at Dad's with Heather, Geoff, and Dad. 05 8:21 PM Bread and figs at Dad's. 06 8:26 PM Vanilla ice cream at Dad's.

MONTH

JAN

FEB

MAR

APR

MAY

JUN

JUL

AUG

SEP

OCT

NOV

DEC

DATE

10/15

DAY

FRI

Tiburon 01 8:11 AM Shredded wheat at Dad's. 02 2:02 PM Club sandwich at the San Francisco Yacht Club with Heather and Dad. 03 7:38 PM Sliced steak and Gruyère potatoes at Dad's with Heather, Geoff, and Dad. 04 8:27 PM Chocolate cake at Dad's.

MONTH

JAN
FEB
MAR
APR
MAY
JUN
JUL
AUG
SEP
OCT
NOV
DEC

DATE

10/16

DAY

SAT

San Francisco to New York City 01 8:57 AM Apple pancakes, sausage, mixed fruit, and coffee cake on United Airlines flight 16. 02 2:12 PM Wheat Thins, Oreos, raisins, Milky Way, cheese spread, and bread sticks on UA flight 16. 03 7:00 PM Potato chips at home with Danny, Jorge, and Robert. 04 8:36 PM Spaghetti with sausage and red sauce at home with Danny. 05 9:21 PM Cornflakes at home. 06 9:36 PM Entenmann's chocolate chip cookies at home with Danny.

MONTH

JAN
FEB
MAR
APR
MAY
JUN
JUL
AUG
SEP
OCT
NOV
DEC

DATE

10/17

DAY

SUN

01 7:49 AM Oatmeal at home. 02 2:31 PM Spaghetti with sausage and red sauce at home. 03 8:30 PM Potato chips at home with Danny. 04 9:08 PM Rainy-night stew with chicken thighs, chorizo, white beans, and mixed vegetables at home. 05 10:07 PM Cornflakes at home.

MONTH

JAN
FEB
MAR
APR
MAY
JUN
JUL
AUG
SEP
OCT
NOV
DEC

DATE

10/18

DAY

MON

01 10:01 AM **Oatmeal at home.** 02 1:47 PM **Chicken soup with rice, grilled cheese with bacon and tomato at Village Den with Andy.** 03 7:02 PM **Tadik and salad at Andy's house with Danny, Andy, Natasha, and Nicky.** 04 7:06 PM **Zareshk at Andy's.** 05 10:09 PM **Entenmann's Halloween cake at home with Danny.**

MONTH

JAN
FEB
MAR
APR
MAY
JUN
JUL
AUG
SEP
OCT
NOV
DEC

DATE

10/19

DAY

TUE

01 9:26 AM Oatmeal with fried eggs at home. 02 2:36 PM Leftover chicken, chorizo, and white bean stew at home.
03 7:03 PM Appetizer meatballs from Balducci's at Jorge and Wayne's for Ken and Brad's going-away party.
04 8:51 PM Amuse-bouche samosa at Cafe Gray with Chris and Doc. 05 8:57 PM. Scallop and oyster appetizer,
flaxseed bread at Cafe Gray. 06 9:27 PM Sea trout with chervil sauce at Cafe Gray (fluke with puffed-rice crust
in background). *(continued on next page)*

MONTH

JAN

FEB

MAR

APR

MAY

JUN

JUL

AUG

SEP

OCT

NOV

DEC

DATE

10/20

DAY

WED

07 9:49 PM **Lamb chop on eggplant pedestal with carrot emulsion at Cafe Gray.** 08 10:05 PM **Raspberry financier with Gruyère cream and cold raspberry soup at Cafe Gray.** 09 10:24 PM **Hazelnut soufflé with oranges and ice cream at Cafe Gray.** 10 10:32 PM **Cordial cookies at Cafe Gray.** 11 11:26 PM **Potato chips at home.** 12 11:48 PM **Life cereal at home.**

DATE

10/20

DAY

WED

01 10:54 AM **Two eggs, bacon, and cheese on a roll from Spyros at home.** 02 12:40 PM **Steamed Thai dumplings at Pam Real Thai Food with Chris.** 03 12:46 PM **Spicy papaya salad at Pam Real Thai.** 04 12:48 PM **Oxtail soup at Pam Real Thai.** 05 9:24 PM **Potato chips at home.** 06 10:06 PM **Burger with Cheddar cheese, bacon, and guacamole from Cowgirl Hall of Fame at home with Danny.** 07 10:44 PM **Kit Kat at home.** 08 10:56 PM **Life cereal at home.**

MONTH

JAN
FEB
MAR
APR
MAY
JUN
JUL
AUG
SEP
OCT
NOV
DEC

DATE

10/21

DAY

THU

New York City to Tinkwig, Pennsylvania 01 8:17 AM **Croissant in Abingdon Square Park.** 02 10:01 AM **Oatmeal at home.** 03 12:22 PM **Prosciutto and smoked turkey sandwich, potato chips, cherry yogurt from Abingdon Market at home.** 04 8:52 PM **Pepperoni pizza from Bruno's Pizza at Chris and Marc's with Chris and Marc.** 05 8:53 PM **Everything pizza from Bruno's Pizza at Chris and Marc's.** 06 12:25 AM **Krispy Kreme Mini Crullers at Chris and Marc's.**

MONTH

JAN

FEB

MAR

APR

MAY

JUN

JUL

AUG

SEP

OCT

NOV

DEC

DATE

10/22

DAY

FRI

Tinkwig, Pennsylvania 01 11:46 AM **Onion bagel with butter at Chris and Marc's.** 02 1:29 PM **Extra-chocolate cake with leftover apple butter cream with Marc at Chris and Marc's.** 03 2:02 PM **Apple at Chris and Marc's.** 04 2:25 PM **Corn bread and bacon at Chris and Marc's with Marc.** 05 6:58 PM **Mushroom tart and Stilton tart with cranberry chutney at Chris and Marc's with Chris, Marc, Patches, Balazs, Tim, Regina, Johnny, Karen, Susan, Andrea, Henry, Jay, Stephen, Alex, and some other people.** *(continued on next page)*

MONTH

JAN

FEB

MAR

APR

MAY

JUN

JUL

AUG

SEP

OCT

NOV

DEC

DATE

10/23

DAY

SAT

06 7:55 PM **Cheeses at Chris and Marc's.** 07 9:36 PM **Pork roast stuffed with corn bread, apples, and bacon at Chris and Marc's.** 08 9:37 PM **Potato gratin and French lentils at Chris and Marc's.** 09 10:00 PM **Beef tenderloin with red wine sauce at Chris and Marc's.** 10 12:13 AM **German chocolate birthday cake, apple cider cake at Chris and Marc's.**

Tinkwig, Pennsylvania, to New York City 01 11:38 AM **Orange at Chris and Marc's.** 02 12:37 PM **Bagel with cream cheese at Tim's in Blooming Grove, PA.** 03 12:39 PM **Coffee cake at Tim's.** 04 5:34 PM **Potato chips at home.** 05 8:19 PM **Lamb and white bean stew with sage and turnips at home.** 06 9:14 PM **Apple cake at home.**

MONTH

JAN
FEB
MAR
APR
MAY
JUN
JUL
AUG
SEP
OCT
NOV
DEC

DATE

10/24

DAY

SUN

01 3:14 PM **Fried egg omelet with spinach and jack cheese at home.** 02 8:21 PM **Jack cheese at home.**
03 8:42 PM **Tortilla chips, guacamole, and chile con carne burrito at home.** 04 9:59 PM **Apple cake at home.**

MONTH

JAN

FEB

MAR

APR

MAY

JUN

JUL

AUG

SEP

OCT

NOV

DEC

DATE

10/25

DAY

MON

01 8:57 AM Brioche from Lafayette Pâtisserie in Abingdon Square Park. 02 3:41 PM Dark-meat turkey with herbed mayonnaise, roasted peppers, lettuce, and tomato on sourdough with chips from The Original Sandwich Shoppe (formerly Sandwiches) at home. 03 6:31 PM Potato chips at home. 04 9:25 PM Chicken leg with mustard and turnips, corn bread muffin at home. 05 10:46 PM Apple cake at home.

MONTH

JAN

FEB

MAR

APR

MAY

JUN

JUL

AUG

SEP

OCT

NOV

DEC

DATE

10/26

DAY

TUE

01 10:34 AM **Oatmeal at home.** 02 2:40 PM **Soppressata with pesto on white bread, mixed greens at Barocco Hots with Christopher.** 03 7:43 PM **Yogurt at home.** 04 9:53 PM **Sesame chicken, steamed vegetable dumplings from Mama Buddha at home.** 05 10:45 PM **Apple cake at home.** 06 10:51 PM **Wheaties at home.**

MONTH

JAN

FEB

MAR

APR

MAY

JUN

JUL

AUG

SEP

OCT

NOV

DEC

DATE

10/27

DAY

WED

01 1:38 PM **Tuscan roast beef sandwich from Pax Deli in Madison Square Park.** 02 5:01 PM **Lavender candies from Madrid at Dan's office with Dan.** 03 7:35 PM **Potato chips at home.** 04 10:28 PM **Grilled cheese with bacon and tomato, French fries at home.** 05 12:07 AM **Wheaties at home.**

MONTH

JAN
FEB
MAR
APR
MAY
JUN
JUL
AUG
SEP
OCT
NOV
DEC

DATE

10/28

DAY

THU

01 2:50 PM Chicken cutlet with mustard and mayonnaise on roll from Spyros Deli at home. 02 5:24 PM Prosciutto, speck, and cheeses with Chris and Doc at home. 03 9:02 PM Braised pork shoulder with white beans and sage, corn bread, fingerling potatoes at home with Chris and Doc. 04 10:12 PM Apple cake "French toast" with pumpkin ice cream and maple caramel with Chris and Doc at home.

MONTH

JAN

FEB

MAR

APR

MAY

JUN

JUL

AUG

SEP

OCT

NOV

DEC

DATE

10/29

DAY

FRI

01 12:03 PM Apple cake "sandwich" with grapefruit conserve at home. 02 2:29 PM Quiche at Pâtisserie Claude with Chris. 03 2:48 PM Snail pastry at Sullivan Street Bakery with Chris. 04 3:28 PM Coconut gelato from Laboratorio del Gelato on Ludlow Street with Chris. 05 4:00 PM Vietnamese sandwich from Little Nicky's with Chris. 06 6:15 PM Leftover speck and cheese at home. 07 7:59 PM Potato chips at home. 08 8:37 PM Frittata with chorizo, spinach, and cheese at home. 09 11:20 PM Chocolate chip cookies at home. 10 11:36 PM Corn Chex at home.

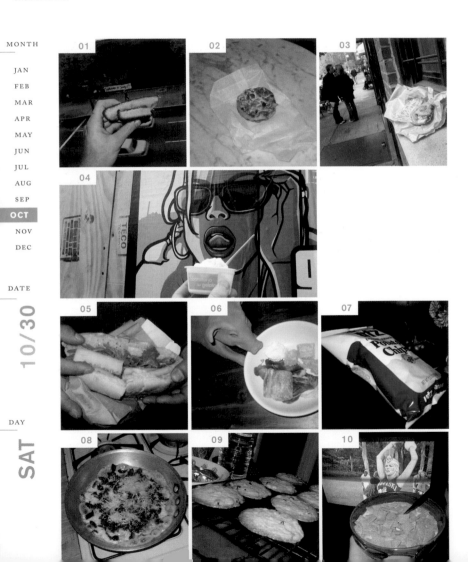

MONTH

JAN
FEB
MAR
APR
MAY
JUN
JUL
AUG
SEP
OCT
NOV
DEC

DATE

10/30

DAY

SAT

01 10:25 AM Bacon, egg, and cheese on a roll from Spyros outside Bleecker Street Playground. 02 1:40 PM Banana with Henry. 03 2:00 PM Babybel Cheese with Henry. 04 4:22 PM Chocolate chip cookie at home. 05 5:15 PM Potato chips at home. 06 8:23 PM Leftover speck at home. 07 9:21 PM Leftover pork roast and potatoes with fried egg at home. 08 9:58 PM Coconut cookies at home.

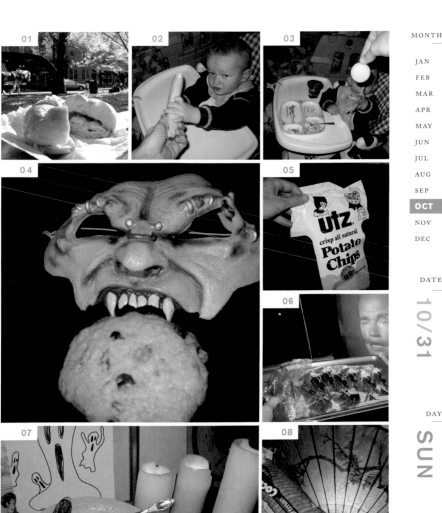

MONTH

JAN
FEB
MAR
APR
MAY
JUN
JUL
AUG
SEP
OCT
NOV
DEC

DATE

10/31

DAY

SUN

reheat soup
remove pork, put potatoes in

serve soup
serve pork + potatoes
(don't forget
cornbread)
warm up cake
warm syrup

Nov.

01 2:08 PM **Southwestern chicken soup from Dean & DeLuca at Rockefeller Center.** 02 6:45 PM **Potato chips at home.** 03 9:03 PM **Vegetable pad Thai, spring rolls from Kobma Thai at home.** 04 10:41 PM **Corn Chex at home.**

MONTH

JAN

FEB

MAR

APR

MAY

JUN

JUL

AUG

SEP

OCT

NOV

DEC

DATE

11/01

DAY

MON

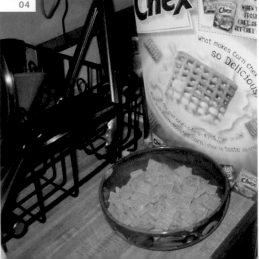

01 9:43 AM Croissant from 49th Street coffee cart at work. 02 1:02 PM Grilled chicken salad with chickpeas, spinach, and orange at work. 03 7:33 PM Potato chips at home. 04 8:10 PM Crab chips at home with Danny. 05 9:21 PM Tortilla chips and guacamole from Cowgirl Hall of Fame at home with Danny. 06 9:32 PM Chicken quesadilla from Cowgirl at home with Danny. 07 10:11 PM Cannoli from Danny's office at home with Danny. 08 10:21 PM Chocolate chip cookies at home with Danny.

MONTH

JAN

FEB

MAR

APR

MAY

JUN

JUL

AUG

SEP

OCT

NOV

DEC

DATE

11/02

DAY

TUE

01 9:45 AM Corn muffin from 51st Street coffee cart at work. 02 2:31 PM Pulled pork, corn pudding, broccoli, and lentil salad from Time Inc. Cafeteria at work. 03 8:38 PM Tortilla chips at home. 04 10:31 PM Pasta with red sauce and pancetta at home with Danny. 05 11:06 PM Louisiana crunch cake at home with Danny. 06 11:31 PM Chocolate truffle and chocolate éclair from Danny's office at home. 07 11:37 PM Corn Chex at home.

MONTH

JAN

FEB

MAR

APR

MAY

JUN

JUL

AUG

SEP

OCT

NOV

DEC

DATE

11/03

DAY

WED

01 10:09 AM **Cinnamon-raisin oatmeal from Time Inc. Cafeteria at work.** 02 2:35 PM **Tabbouleh, grilled chicken salad, roasted eggplant, and fruit salad from Time Inc. Cafeteria at work.** 03 7:15 PM **Potato chips at home.** 04 9:37 PM **Leftover pasta at home.** 05 10:27 PM **Corn Chex at home.**

MONTH

JAN

FEB

MAR

APR

MAY

JUN

JUL

AUG

SEP

OCT

NOV

DEC

DATE

11/04

DAY

THU

01 9:57 AM Yogurt with granola and fruit from Pax deli at work. 02 1:19 PM Panino with prosciutto and Taleggio cheese, potato chips, and blueberry yogurt from Bocco at work. 03 8:06 PM Potato chips at home. 04 10:02 PM Scrambled eggs at home. 05 10:27 PM Leftover pad Thai from Kobma Thai at home. 06 11:07 PM Coconut cookies and vanilla ice cream at home.

MONTH

JAN

FEB

MAR

APR

MAY

JUN

JUL

AUG

SEP

OCT

NOV

DEC

DATE

11/05

DAY

FRI

01 11:12 AM Two eggs fried over easy, potatoes, bacon, toasted English muffin, and mixed greens at the Village Den with Andrea, Susan, and Henry. 02 3:07 PM Carrot cookie at Union Square Farmers' Market with Jorge. 03 3:17 PM Tomatillo at Union Square Farmers' Market. 04 5:20 PM Potato chips at home with Jorge. 05 6:08 PM Pâté and crackers at Jorge and Wayne's with Jorge and Wayne. 06 7:32 PM Movie snax. *Alfie* with Jorge, Danny, Wayne, and Robert. 07 11:09 PM Two hotdogs with onions, twin burgers, and fries from PopBurger at home with Danny. 08 12:01 AM Vanilla cupcake from PopBurger at home.

MONTH

JAN
FEB
MAR
APR
MAY
JUN
JUL
AUG
SEP
OCT
NOV
DEC

DATE

11/06

DAY

SAT

01 1:42 PM Quiche from Pâtisserie Claude on W. 4th Street with Danny. 02 4:33 PM Bite of John's pistachio cupcake from Sugar Sweet Sunshine on Rivington with Jason and John. 03 7:49 PM Onion and garlic potato chips at home. 04 8:31 PM Chicken legs with artichoke hearts, mustard powder, and potatoes at home with Danny. 05 9:16 PM Fried pound cake with pumpkin ice cream at home with Danny.

MONTH

JAN
FEB
MAR
APR
MAY
JUN
JUL
AUG
SEP
OCT
NOV
DEC

DATE

11/07

DAY

SUN

01 9:52 AM **Croissant at work.** 02 1:51 PM **Chicken sandwich with Russian dressing on rye from Pret a Manger on 6th Avenue.** 03 7:37 PM **Onion and garlic chips at home.** 04 8:37 PM **Smoked turkey, prosciutto, and jack cheese on whole wheat from Abingdon Market at home.** 05 12:57 AM **Tres leches ice cream at home.**

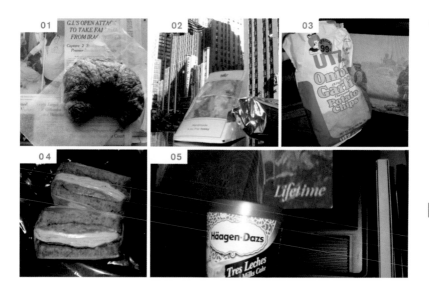

MONTH

JAN

FEB

MAR

APR

MAY

JUN

JUL

AUG

SEP

OCT

NOV

DEC

DATE

11/08

DAY

MON

01 1:14 PM **Turkey chili, roasted Brussels sprouts, and yogurt from Citarella at work.** 02 7:27 PM **Potato chips at home.** 03 9:47 PM **Tortilla chips, salsa, and guacamole from Burritoville at home with Danny and Jorge.** 04 9:55 PM **Grilled chicken burrito with red beans and spinach from Burritoville.** 05 11:02 PM **Puffed wheat at home.**

MONTH

JAN
FEB
MAR
APR
MAY
JUN
JUL
AUG
SEP
OCT
NOV
DEC

DATE

11/09

DAY

TUE

01 2:06 PM Turkey chili and sourdough roll from Citarella at work. 02 4:30 PM Chocolate ice cream cake from Carvel at work with Heather, Regan, Lisa, Liza, Emily, and about twenty-five other people. 03 4:31 PM Assorted candies at work. 04 5:38 PM Red-and-white Hershey's Kiss at work. 05 7:36 PM Tortilla chips at home. 06 9:00 PM Bread and olive oil at Gonzo with Susan and Andrea. 07 9:06 PM Robiola cheese, Parmigiano-Reggiano, and prosciutto with toasts at Gonzo. 08 9:21 PM Half mashed potato/half soppressata pizza, eggplant caponata at Gonzo. 09 9:39 PM Spaghetti with manila clams, glazed short ribs at Gonzo. 10 10:59 PM Grape-Nuts Flakes at home.

MONTH

JAN
FEB
MAR
APR
MAY
JUN
JUL
AUG
SEP
OCT
NOV
DEC

DATE

11/10

DAY

WED

01 10:16 AM Oatmeal from Time Inc. Cafeteria at work. 02 2:19 PM Pulled pork, coleslaw, and roll from Daisy May's BBQ at work. 03 8:41 PM Fried artichokes, pizza with prosciutto and arugula at Giorgione with Chris. 04 9:00 PM Veal and raisin meatballs, Romaine salad with Parmesan cheese at Giorgione. 05 9:41 PM Caramel-chocolate bar from Taylor's on Hudson Street with Chris. 06 10:56 PM Grape-Nuts Flakes at home.

MONTH

JAN

FEB

MAR

APR

MAY

JUN

JUL

AUG

SEP

OCT

NOV

DEC

DATE

11/11

DAY

THU

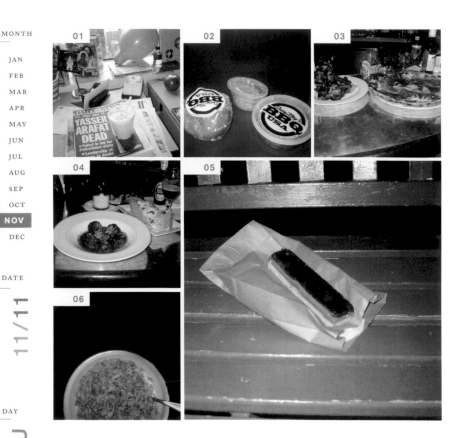

01 9:52 AM Cinnamon-raisin oatmeal from Time Inc. Cafeteria at work. 02 2:32 PM Tofu summer rolls and beef summer rolls from Little Saigon with Liza at work. 03 10:19 PM Vegetable soup, bread from Pastis at home with Danny. 04 10:33 PM Cheeseburger and fries from Pastis at home with Danny. 05 11:16 PM Grape-Nuts Flakes at home.

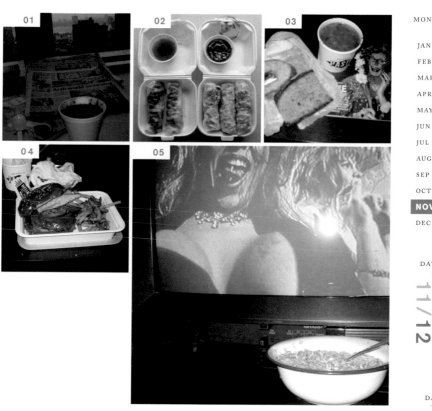

MONTH

JAN

FEB

MAR

APR

MAY

JUN

JUL

AUG

SEP

OCT

NOV

DEC

DATE

11/12

DAY

FRI

01 11:15 AM French toast with bananas, strawberries, and apples at Paris Commune with Wayne, Jorge, Danny, and Carol. 02 5:37 PM Oatmeal cookie on 7th Avenue with Jorge. 03 5:51 PM Tortilla chips and salsa at home with Jorge. 04 8:24 PM Potato chips at home. 05 10:24 PM Whole-wheat pasta carbonara at home with Danny. 06 11:12 PM Banana crunch cake at home.

MONTH

JAN

FEB

MAR

APR

MAY

JUN

JUL

AUG

SEP

OCT

NOV

DEC

DATE

11/13

DAY

SAT

01 10:45 AM Greek yogurt with honey at home. 02 12:03 PM Bacon, egg, and cheese on a roll from Spyros at home. 03 3:21 PM Movie snax. *Saw* with Jorge. 04 7:32 PM Tostitos Hint of Lime at home with Jorge, Wayne, Danny, and Bill. 05 8:25 PM French onion soup with Gruyère crouton at home with Jorge, Wayne, Danny, and Bill. 06 8:40 PM Veal meatballs with tomato sauce and sautéed broccoli rabe at home with Jorge, Wayne, Danny, and Bill. 07 9:08 PM Warm chocolate babka with whipped cream at home with Jorge, Wayne, Danny, and Bill. 08 9:52 PM Banana crunch cake at home.

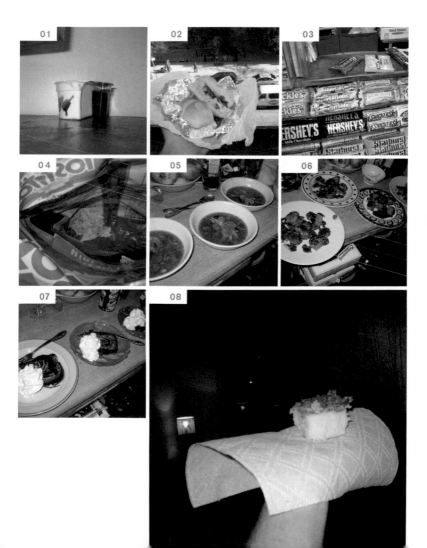

MONTH

JAN
FEB
MAR
APR
MAY
JUN
JUL
AUG
SEP
OCT
NOV
DEC

DATE

11/14

DAY

SUN

01 9:59 AM **Fruit salad and mixed berry yogurt from Time Inc. Cafeteria at work.** 02 1:44 PM **Seafood tomato bisque from Hale & Hearty Soups at work.** 03 7:50 PM **Honey BBQ chips at home.** 04 9:03 PM **Leftover onion soup with poached egg at home.** 05 10:01 PM **Honey Bunches of Oats at home.**

MONTH

JAN
FEB
MAR
APR
MAY
JUN
JUL
AUG
SEP
OCT
NOV
DEC

DATE

11/15

DAY

MON

01 10:27 AM Corn muffin from coffee cart on 51st Street at work. 02 1:12 PM New England clam chowder with oyster crackers from Hale & Hearty Soups. 03 8:16 PM Goat cheese, salami, grapes, and crackers at Susan and Andrea's with Susan, Andrea, Tim A., Mark, Alex, and Patches. 04 9:25 PM Pepperoni and onion pizza from Two Boots at Susan and Andrea's.

MONTH

JAN
FEB
MAR
APR
MAY
JUN
JUL
AUG
SEP
OCT
NOV
DEC

DATE

11/16

DAY

TUE

01 10:05 AM Cinnamon-raisin oatmeal from Time Inc. Cafeteria at work. **02** 3:11 PM Couscous with grilled chicken, roasted eggplant, red onion, and tomato; cherry yogurt from Time Inc. Cafeteria at work. **03** 8:40 PM Potato chips at home. **04** 9:28 PM Fried cod and chips from A Salt & Battery at home with Danny. **05** 10:00 PM Deep-fried Mars bar from A Salt & Battery at home. **06** 10:10 PM Wheat Chex at home.

MONTH

JAN
FEB
MAR
APR
MAY
JUN
JUL
AUG
SEP
OCT
NOV
DEC

DATE

11/17

DAY

WED

01 9:52 AM Corn muffin from coffee cart on 50th Street. 02 12:46 PM California BLT from Pret a Manger in Rockefeller Center with Chris. 03 1:06 PM Hakuunnohotori (bean cake with milk) from Minamoto Kitchen on 48th Street with Chris. 04 8:36 PM Kalamata olives at home. 05 9:57 PM Spaghetti with bacon, eggplant, mushrooms, tomato, mustard greens, olives, and smoked fresh mozzarella at home. 06 10:34 PM Corn Chex at home.

MONTH

JAN
FEB
MAR
APR
MAY
JUN
JUL
AUG
SEP
OCT
NOV
DEC

DATE

11/18

DAY

THU

01 9:15 AM Corn muffin from coffee cart on 47th Street at work. 02 2:20 PM Greek salad with chicken, red onion, and feta; broccoli from Time Inc. Cafeteria at work. 03 8:53 PM Taro chips at Kalustyan's Café with Chris and Doc. 04 8:55 PM Minced chicken puffs with cilantro yogurt at Kalustyan's Café. 05 8:58 PM Pineapple soup with fish dumplings and green onions at Kalustyan's Café. 06 9:13 PM Duck breast with barley and grapes, baby Brussels sprouts with mushrooms at Kalustyan's Café. 07 9:27 PM Grilled shrimp with shaved cucumber in Indian spices at Kalustyan's Café. 08 9:44 PM Veal vindaloo with rice cakes, cod steamed with green tomatoes and green beans at Kalustyan's Café. 09 10:13 PM Caramel Khafi with stewed raisins at Kalustyan's Café. 10 11:59 PM Honey Bunches of Oats at home.

MONTH

JAN
FEB
MAR
APR
MAY
JUN
JUL
AUG
SEP
OCT
NOV
DEC

DATE

11/19

DAY

FRI

01 12:02 PM Maple candies at Union Square Farmers' Market with Chris. 02 12:31 PM Egg salad with bacon, lettuce, and tomato on white toast at Eisenberg's with Chris. 03 12:58 PM Peanut butter cookie, chocolate cookie, and vanilla cookie from City Bakery on 18th Street with Chris. 04 4:05 PM Potato chips at home. 05 8:20 PM Leftover spaghetti at home. 06 11:41 PM Wheat Chex at home. 07 11:47 PM French fries and Chicken McNuggets from McDonald's at home with Danny. 08 12:33 AM Entenmann's chocolate chip cookies at home with Danny.

MONTH

JAN
FEB
MAR
APR
MAY
JUN
JUL
AUG
SEP
OCT
NOV
DEC

DATE

11/20

DAY

SAT

01 1:03 PM Oatmeal at home. **02** 4:36 PM Leftover spaghetti at home. **03** 5:01 PM Potato chips at home. **04** 10:32 PM Grilled cheese with bacon and tomato, fries from Manatus at home with Danny. **05** 11:02 PM Wheat Chex at home.

MONTH

JAN
FEB
MAR
APR
MAY
JUN
JUL
AUG
SEP
OCT
NOV
DEC

DATE

11/21

DAY

SUN

01 10:00 AM Corn muffin from coffee cart on 50th Street at work. 02 1:55 PM Mixed greens with chickpeas, avocado, bacon, and tomatoes from Tossed at work. 03 4:36 PM Hakuunnohotori (bean cake with milk) from Minamoto Kitchen at work. 04 7:18 PM Potato chips at home with Jorge. 05 10:25 PM Burger with cheddar and bacon, fries from Hudson Corner at home with Jorge and Danny. 06 11:26 PM Corn Chex at home.

01

02

03

04

05

06

MONTH

JAN

FEB

MAR

APR

MAY

JUN

JUL

AUG

SEP

OCT

NOV

DEC

DATE

11/22

DAY

MON

01 8:38 AM Brioche at La Bergamote. 02 1:00 PM Meatloaf sandwich with Russian dressing and coleslaw with Andy at Carve. 03 7:12 PM Shaved Brussels sprouts with red cabbage and hazelnuts at Barbuto with Mom. 04 7:22 PM Duck sausage with polenta and cabbage at Barbuto. 05 7:40 PM Braised beef cheeks and carrots at Barbuto. 06 8:09 PM Pear galette with coffee ice cream at Barbuto. 07 10:04 PM Corn Chex at home.

MONTH

JAN
FEB
MAR
APR
MAY
JUN
JUL
AUG
SEP
OCT
NOV
DEC

DATE

11/23

DAY

TUE

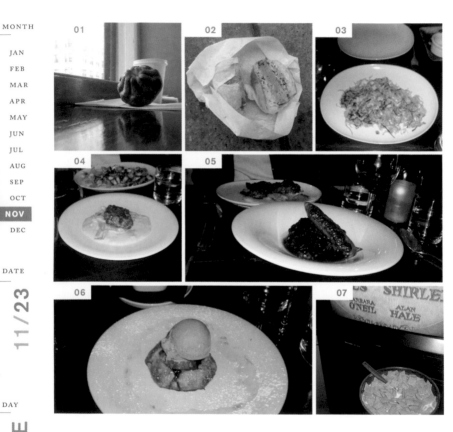

01 9:16 AM Brioche from La Bergamote on 20th Street. 02 10:15 AM Thanksgiving turkey cookie from Regan's boyfriend's mother at work. 03 2:40 PM Breaded chicken sandwich with lettuce, tomato, and sautéed onions on seven grain from the Original Sandwich Shoppe at home. 04 6:18 PM Potato chips at home. 05 8:22 PM Miso soup from Monster Sushi at home with Danny. 06 8:36 PM Two tuna rolls from Monster Sushi at home with Danny. 07 11:14 PM Amaretti cookies at home.

MONTH

JAN

FEB

MAR

APR

MAY

JUN

JUL

AUG

SEP

OCT

NOV

DEC

DATE

11/24

DAY

WED

New York City to Tinkwig, Pennsylvania **01** 12:18 PM Smoked salmon on poppy seed bagel at Chris and Marc's with Chris, Marc, Susan, Andrea, and Henry. **02** 12:27 PM Smoked tuna at Chris and Marc's. **03** 1:44 PM Sesame cracker with Marc. **04** 2:25 PM Pâté sucre with Marc. **05** 4:06 PM Crudités with artichoke dip and tomato dip, spiced nuts medley at Chris and Marc's with Alex, Patches, Chris, Marc, Susan, Andrea, Henry, Jay, Steven, and Tim A. **06** 4:07 PM Asparagus with wasabi dip at Chris and Marc's. **07** 5:43 PM Fennel tart at Chris and Marc's. **08** 6:48 PM Celery root soup with sautéed mushrooms at Chris and Marc's. **09** 7:19 PM Turkey with cornbread stuffing at Chris and Marc's. **10** 8:03 PM Three stuffings (cornbread, oyster, and vegan), mashed potatoes at Chris and Marc's. *(continued on next page)*

MONTH

JAN

FEB

MAR

APR

MAY

JUN

JUL

AUG

SEP

OCT

NOV

DEC

DATE

11/25

DAY

THU

11 8:18 PM Creamed onions with bread crumbs, lima bean casserole, braised baby Brussels sprouts with root vegetables, and mashed potatoes at Chris and Marc's. 12 8:19 PM Two chutneys (golden raisin and nectarine-currant) at Chris and Marc's. 13 8:20 PM Green bean casserole at Chris and Marc's. 14 8:21 PM Mashed butternut squash at Chris and Marc's. 15 8:29 PM Thanksgiving as plated (clockwise from top): Oyster stuffing, turkey, butternut squash, green bean casserole, Brussels sprouts with baby carrots and baby turnips, creamed onions, beet salad, mashed potatoes, and gravy at Chris and Marc's. 16 8:45 PM Vegetarian lasagna at Chris and Marc's. 17 10:03 PM Pumpkin pie with plums, maple butter cake, shaved apple tart, pumpkin trifle, and crème anglaise at Chris and Marc's.

Tinkwig 01 11:18 AM **Maple cake at Chris and Marc's.** 02 11:59 AM **Shaved apple tart at Chris and Marc's.** 03 1:36 PM **Leftover turkey at Chris and Marc's.** 04 4:27 PM **Cheese ball at Chris and Marc's with Chris and Marc.** 05 6:04 PM **Mixed nuts medley at Chris and Marc's with Alex, Tim A., Jay, Steven, Chris, and Marc.** 06 6:43 PM **Glazed ham with maple at Chris and Marc's with Alex, Patches, Jay, Steven, Chris, Marc, Tim A., Buzz, Barry, and Dolores.** 07 6:56 PM **Raclette fixins: Potatoes, pineapple, cornichons, sliced ham, and Brussels sprouts at Chris and Marc's.** 08 6:57 PM **Raclette and Gruyère cheeses at Chris and Marc's.** 09 8:03 PM **Pumpkin pie with plums at Chris and Marc's.** 10 8:15 PM **Pumpkin trifle at Chris and Marc's.**

MONTH

JAN
FEB
MAR
APR
MAY
JUN
JUL
AUG
SEP
OCT
NOV
DEC

DATE

11/26

DAY

FRI

Tinkwig, Pennsylvania, to New York City 01 10:46 AM Plain bagel with vegetable cream cheese at Jay and Steven's with Jay, Steven, Tim A., Alex, Patches, Chris, and Marc. 02 1:14 PM Hot pretzel at Stroudsburg Flea Market with Patches. 03 1:32 PM Zesty tortilla soup sample at Stroudsburg Flea Market with Patches. 04 2:07 PM Apple fritter at Stroudsburg Flea Market with Patches, Jay, Steven, Alex, Tim A., Chris, and Marc. 05 6:27 PM Scrambled eggs with butter at home with Danny. 06 11:25 PM Grilled cheese with bacon and fries from Manatus at home with Danny. 07 11:50 PM M&M's at home with Danny.

MONTH

JAN
FEB
MAR
APR
MAY
JUN
JUL
AUG
SEP
OCT
NOV
DEC

DATE

11/27

DAY

SAT

01 1:07 PM **Two eggs and tomato on toasted onion bagel from Bagel Buffet at home with Danny.** 02 8:03 PM **Tamari roasted almonds at home.** 03 8:13 PM **Chicken stew with tomato sauce and spinach at home with Danny.** 04 9:15 PM **Tres leches cake at home with Danny.**

MONTH

JAN
FEB
MAR
APR
MAY
JUN
JUL
AUG
SEP
OCT
NOV
DEC

DATE

11/28

DAY

SUN

01 2:06 PM **Chicken broth at home.** 02 4:17 PM **Chicken broth at home.** 03 5:42 PM **Chicken broth at home.**
04 9:03 PM **Pasta with olive oil and mozzarella cheese at home.**

MONTH

JAN

FEB

MAR

APR

MAY

JUN

JUL

AUG

SEP

OCT

NOV

DEC

DATE

11/29

DAY

MON

01 9:03 AM Brioche at La Bergamote. **02** 2:45 PM Chicken gyro from cart on 50th Street at work. **03** 3:06 PM Fruit salad from Time Inc. Cafeteria at work. **04** 4:07 PM Japanese chestnut sweet from Minamoto Kitchen at work. **05** 9:56 PM Chocolate truffle at Glo with Danny and Jorge. **06** 11:02 PM Tortilla chips and salsa from Burritoville at home with Danny. **07** 11:05 PM Mystical chicken burrito from Burritoville at home with Danny. **08** 11:39 PM Tres leches cake at home. **09** 11:48 PM Puffed wheat at home.

MONTH

JAN
FEB
MAR
APR
MAY
JUN
JUL
AUG
SEP
OCT
NOV
DEC

DATE

11/30

DAY

TUE

december

01 10:04 AM Oatmeal and granola from Time Inc. Cafeteria at work. 02 2:31 PM Lamb gyro from cart on 50th Street at work. 03 4:10 PM Cherry yogurt at work. 04 8:37 PM Potato chips at home. 05 9:26 PM Large pie (half pepperoni, spinach, and onion, half plain) from Village Pizza at home with Danny. 06 10:17 PM Entenmann's chocolate chip cookies at home with Danny.

MONTH

JAN

FEB

MAR

APR

MAY

JUN

JUL

AUG

SEP

OCT

NOV

DEC

DATE

12/01

DAY

WED

01 10:13 AM Croissant from Citarella at work. 02 12:38 PM Broccoli, beef empanada, roasted eggplant, chickpea salad, and Brazilian chicken salad at Dishes on 45th Street with Chris. 03 12:57 PM Peanut butter cookie from Dishes. 04 8:56 PM Potato chips at home. 05 9:52 PM Bo luc loc from Café Asean at home with Jorge. 06 10:28 PM Entenmann's chocolate chip cookies at home. 07 11:16 PM Puffed wheat at home.

MONTH

JAN

FEB

MAR

APR

MAY

JUN

JUL

AUG

SEP

OCT

NOV

DATE

12/02

DAY

THU

01 8:58 AM Brioche from La Bergamote on 20th Street. **02** 2:06 PM Spanish lentils with sausage from Hale & Hearty Soups at work. **03** 8:03 PM Leftover pizza at home. **04** 9:14 PM Movie snax. *Hero* at Chelsea Cinemas with Jorge. **05** 12:35 AM Red-potato hash, fried eggs at home. **06** 12:43 AM Puffed wheat at home.

MONTH

JAN

FEB

MAR

APR

MAY

JUN

JUL

AUG

SEP

OCT

NOV

DEC

DATE

12/03

DAY

FRI

01 2:08 PM Oatmeal at home. 02 5:49 PM Fig bars on Spring Street with Jorge. 03 6:21 PM Bread and olive oil at Provence with Julian and Jorge. 04 6:40 PM Baked salt cod with potatoes and toast at Provence. 05 7:07 PM Cassoulet at Provence. 06 7:47 PM Ile flotante (meringue with caramel floating in crème anglaise) at Provence. 07 7:50 PM Assorted cheeses with grapes and toasts at Provence. 08 9:17 PM Pound cake with nuts at Julian's with Jorge and Julian.

MONTH

JAN
FEB
MAR
APR
MAY
JUN
JUL
AUG
SEP
OCT
NOV
DEC

DATE

12/04

DAY

SAT

01 10:24 AM Pain au chocolate from Sullivan Street Bakery. **02** 12:00 PM Two eggs, bacon, and cheese on a roll from Spyros at home. **03** 2:44 PM White chocolate and peppermint bark from Williams-Sonoma on 7th Avenue with Jorge. **04** 3:17 PM Avocado roll from Chelsea Market with Jorge. **05** 5:45 PM Potato chips in taxi with Jorge on 14th Street. **06** 7:04 PM Lobster chunk at Jorge and Wayne's. **07** 7:29 PM Parmesan cheese chunk at Jorge and Wayne's. *(continued on next page)*

MONTH

JAN
FEB
MAR
APR
MAY
JUN
JUL
AUG
SEP
OCT
NOV
DEC

DATE

12/05

DAY

SUN

08 7:49 PM Taste of chocolate-cherry gooey cake at Jorge and Wayne's. **09** 7:58 PM Mixed greens, tomato, and Parmesan cheese at Jorge and Wayne's. **10** 8:42 PM Lobster, champagne, and saffron risotto at Jorge and Wayne's with Jorge and Danny. **11** 9:25 PM Chocolate-cherry birthday gooey cake at Jorge and Wayne's. **12** 9:30 PM Chocolate Bar chocolates from Danny at Jorge and Wayne's. **13** 9:42 PM More gooey at Jorge and Wayne's.

01 1:03 PM Siciliano panino, broccoli, and broccoli rabe from Bocca at work. **02** 8:32 PM Peanuts at home. **03** 9:47 PM Bacon Cheeseburger Deluxe and fries from the Village Den at home. **04** 10:53 PM Wheaties and amaretti cookies at home.

MONTH

JAN

FEB

MAR

APR

MAY

JUN

JUL

AUG

SEP

OCT

NOV

DEC

DATE

12/06

DAY

MON

01 10:28 AM Mixed fruit salad, cherry yogurt from Time Inc. Cafeteria at work. 02 1:32 PM Chicken and barley soup from Hale & Hearty Soups at work. 03 6:44 PM Bread and butter at the Grand Central Oyster Bar with Mom. 04 6:48 PM Manhattan clam chowder at the Oyster Bar. 05 7:03 PM Grilled halibut and mixed vegetables at the Oyster Bar. 06 7:25 PM Chocolate animal cookies from Mom. 07 11:03 PM Wheaties at home.

MONTH

JAN

FEB

MAR

APR

MAY

JUN

JUL

AUG

SEP

OCT

NOV

DEC

DATE

12/07

DAY

TUE

01 10:23 AM Oatmeal at work. 02 2:23 PM Tortilla chicken soup, vegetable soup, turkey sandwich from Dean & DeLuca in Rockefeller Center with Jorge. 03 2:43 PM Hakuunnohotori (bean cake with condensed milk) and chestnut sweet from Minamoto on 48th Street with Jorge. 04 8:19 PM Potato chips at home with Danny. 05 10:24 PM Tortilla chips and guacamole from Mary Ann's at home with Danny. 06 10:30 PM Cheesy burrito, refried beans, and rice from Mary Ann's at home with Danny. 07 11:30 PM Wheaties at home.

MONTH

JAN
FEB
MAR
APR
MAY
JUN
JUL
AUG
SEP
OCT
NOV
DEC

DATE

12/08

DAY

WED

01

02

03

04

05

06

07

01 10:15 AM **Corn muffin at work.** 02 1:09 PM **Flat bread and olives at Stella Osteria with Laura.** 03 1:32 PM **Lamb and pignoli tortelli at Stella.** 04 8:34 PM **Potato chips at home with Danny and Robert.** 05 9:01 PM **Caramel bar at home.** 06 9:11 PM **Twin burgers and fries from PopBurger at home with Danny and Robert.** 07 11:12 PM **Life cereal at home.**

MONTH

JAN
FEB
MAR
APR
MAY
JUN
JUL
AUG
SEP
OCT
NOV
DEC

DATE

12/09

DAY

THU

01 10:23 AM Cherry yogurt and granola at work. 02 2:23 PM Chicken salad sandwich with bacon, sea-salt chips from Pret a Manger at work. 03 7:51 PM Olives, feta with red peppers and herbs, and bread at Snack Taverna with Susan, Andrea, Alex, and Flat Stanley. 04 7:54 PM Grilled sardines with herbs and olive oil, saganaki (fried cheese) with lemon and tomato, tzatziki, and olives at Snack Taverna. 05 8:16 PM Potatoes with red onions and parsley, pig cheeks with olive tapenade at Snack. 06 8:17 PM Greek sausage with fennel, moussaka at Snack. 07 8:19 PM Braised lamb with green and white onions at Snack. 08 8:48 PM Baklava with raspberry sauce, wine-poached figs with pistachios and sheep's milk cheese at Snack. 09 10:24 PM Pear and almond torte at Bruxelles with Eric and Connie. 10 10:33 PM Mussels with garlic, frites at Bruxelles with Eric and Connie.

MONTH

JAN
FEB
MAR
APR
MAY
JUN
JUL
AUG
SEP
OCT
NOV
DEC

DATE

12/10

DAY

FRI

01 9:28 AM Orange cake trimmings at home. **02** 3:05 PM Pistachio pinwheel at home. **03** 4:02 PM Maple caramel bar, lemon star, and sparkle cookie at home. **04** 4:04 PM Figgy thumbprint with pine nuts and lavender at home. **05** 7:11 PM Sesame chicken and rice from Mama Buddha at home with Danny. **06** 12:17 AM Frittata with chorizo and spinach at home. **07** 12:41 AM Life cereal at home.

MONTH

JAN
FEB
MAR
APR
MAY
JUN
JUL
AUG
SEP
OCT
NOV
DEC

DATE

12/11

DAY

SAT

01 11:04 AM Oatmeal with cherries at home. **02** 12:55 PM Chocolate-cherry knob at home. **03** 1:42 PM Crispy brittle cookie at home. **04** 1:57 PM Pistachio pinwheel at home. **05** 3:01 PM Toppled chocolate-orange tipsy cake at home. **06** 5:39 PM Chocolate chip cookies, chocolate-cherry knobs at home with Danny, Chris, Ellie, Douglas, and 40-plus cookie-party guests. **07** 5:39 PM Holiday almond M&M's, mixed nuts at the cookie party. **08** 5:39 PM Caramel maple bars at the cookie party. **09** 5:39 PM Peanut brittle at the cookie party. **10** 5:39 PM Lemon stars, coconut pop-ems at the cookie party. *(continued on next page)*

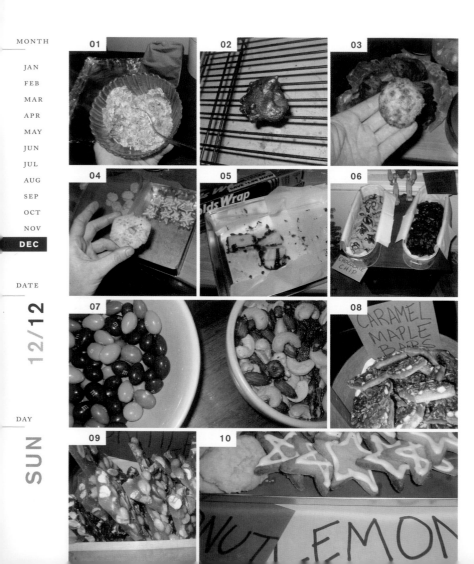

MONTH

JAN

FEB

MAR

APR

MAY

JUN

JUL

AUG

SEP

OCT

NOV

DEC

DATE

12/12

DAY

SUN

11 5:39 PM Hoot's hot-water gingerbread squares at the cookie party. **12** 5:40 PM Figgy thumbprints with pine nuts and lavender, pistachio pinwheels at the cookie party. **13** 5:40 PM Sparkling butter cookies, crispy brittle cookies at the cookie party. **14** 5:40 PM Green diamonds at the cookie party. **15** 5:40 PM Chocolate-orange tipsy cakes at the cookie party. **16** 6:57 PM Hanukkah wafers, red cross cookies at the cookie party. **17** 8:20 PM Chocolate-peppermint rounds from Sam at the cookie party with Sam. **18** 10:56 PM Pizza (half plain, half pepperoni) from Domino's at home with Danny. **19** 11:13 PM Hoot's hot-water gingerbread squares at home.

01 10:13 AM Corn muffin from cart on 51st Street at work. **02** 2:13 PM California BLT from Pret a Manger at work. **03** 8:45 PM Potato chips at home. **04** 9:45 PM Chicken Parmesan sandwich from Village Pizza at home with Danny. **05** 10:51 PM Chocolate-cherry knob at home.

MONTH

JAN
FEB
MAR
APR
MAY
JUN
JUL
AUG
SEP
OCT
NOV
DEC

DATE

12/13

DAY

MON

01 10:10 AM Brioche from Payard on Lexington Avenue. 02 1:42 PM Spinach and leek soup with sourdough bread from Hale & Hearty Soups at work. 03 8:33 PM Brie cheese and crackers at home. 04 9:43 PM Pasta with tomato and ground chicken sauce at home with Danny and Jorge. 05 10:13 PM Chocolate-cherry knob at home. 06 10:37 PM Chocolate chip cookies at home. 07 11:10 PM Life cereal at home.

MONTH

JAN
FEB
MAR
APR
MAY
JUN
JUL
AUG
SEP
OCT
NOV

DATE

12/14

DAY

TUE

01 9:58 AM Muesli from Time Inc. Cafeteria at work. **02** 2:10 PM Pita with zaatar from Bread & Olives at work. **03** 2:43 PM Yogurt at work. **04** 3:53 PM Hakuunnohotori (bean cake with condensed milk) from Minamoto on 48th Street. **05** 5:47 PM Sally's great-aunt's Mystery Thumbprints from Sally at home. **06** 6:37 PM Clementine at home. **07** 8:34 PM St. Andre cheese with crackers at home. **08** 9:16 PM Leftover ground chicken pasta doctored up with chorizo chunks at home. **09** 10:31 PM Holiday almond M&M's at home. **10** 10:36 PM Chocolate chip cookie at home. **11** 10:43 PM Life cereal at home.

MONTH

JAN
FEB
MAR
APR
MAY
JUN
JUL
AUG
SEP
OCT
NOV
DEC

DATE

12/15

DAY

WED

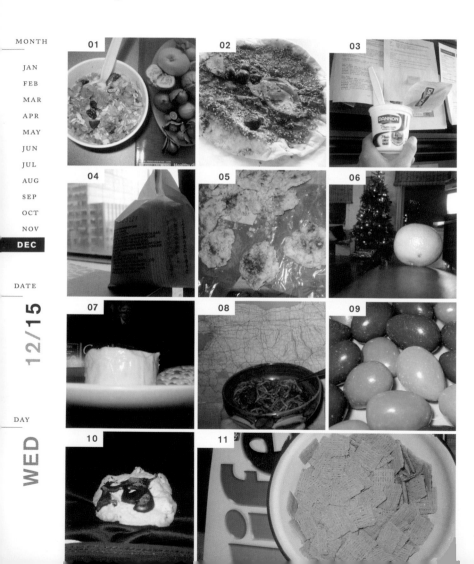

01 10:03 AM Cherry yogurt and fruit salad at work. 02 1:14 PM Smoked salmon spread and toasts at Le Bernardin with Chris and Doc. 03 1:25 PM Oysters with cocktail and mignonette sauces at Le Bernardin. 04 1:40 PM Scallops marinated in lemon juice and olive oil, seaweed Caesar at Le Bernardin. 05 1:40 PM Fluke four ways at Le Bernardin. 06 1:40 PM Layers of crab, avocado, and potato with yellow pepper sauce at Le Bernardin. 07 2:02 PM Pan-roasted codfish with artichoke, garlic, sage, and pistachios at Le Bernardin. 08 2:02 PM Wild striped bass with okra in pineapple nage at Le Bernardin. 09 2:02 PM Black bass in duck bouillon with maitake and enoki mushrooms at Le Bernardin. *(continued on next page)*

MONTH

JAN
FEB
MAR
APR
MAY
JUN
JUL
AUG
SEP
OCT
NOV
DEC

DATE

12/16

DAY

THU

10 2:47 PM Chocolate and praline with sherry-soaked prunes at Le Bernardin. **11** 2:47 PM Madeleines and cookies at Le Bernardin. **12** 2:47 PM Banana crème brûlée with beurre noisette ice cream and caramel. **13** 9:59 PM Kielbasa with mustard-mayonnaise sauce, roasted potatoes at home. **14** 11:05 PM Life cereal at home.

01 1:35 PM Parmesan chicken potpie at Heartland Brewery with Zena. 02 7:14 PM Clementine at home. 03 10:10 PM Pretzels from Eric and Connie at home with Danny. 04 10:19 PM Croque monsieur, frites, green salad, and spinach-leek soup from Petite Abeille at home with Danny. 05 10:58 PM Almond macaroons from Eric and Connie at home with Danny.

MONTH

JAN
FEB
MAR
APR
MAY
JUN
JUL
AUG
SEP
OCT
NOV
DEC

DATE

12/17

DAY

FRI

01 11:19 AM Croissant from Sullivan Street Bakery at home. 02 3:20 PM Egg salad sandwich with bacon, lettuce, and tomato at Eisenberg's with Jorge and Julian. 03 3:23 PM Pickles at Eisenberg's. 04 5:31 PM Clementines at home. 05 7:30 PM Olive assortment at 5757 for Night of 1,000 Bars with Susan, Andrea, Alex, Patches, and Belazs. 06 8:59 PM Mixed nuts at the Peninsula Hotel. 07 10:56 PM Mixed nuts at Campbell's apartment in Grand Central. 08 12:17 AM Scrambled eggs at home.

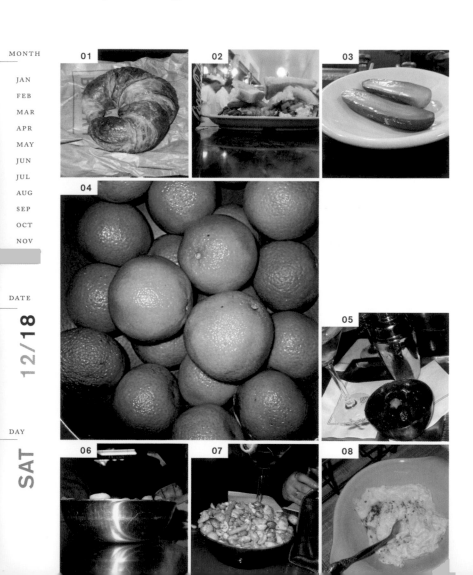

01 9:51 AM Brioche from Lafayette Bakery in Sheridan Square. 02 12:01 PM Bacon, egg, and cheese on a roll from Spyros. 03 6:22 PM Potato chips at home. 04 8:12 PM Braised short ribs with white beans and spinach at home with Danny. 05 9:21 PM Vanilla chocolate chunk cookies at home with Danny.

MONTH

JAN

FEB

MAR

APR

MAY

JUN

JUL

AUG

SEP

OCT

NOV

DEC

DATE

12/19

DAY

SUN

01 10:03 AM Muesli from Time Inc. Cafeteria at work. 02 2:14 PM Chicken, bacon, and avocado sandwich from Pret a Manger at work. 03 3:42 PM Gingerbread family from Regan's boyfriend's mother at work. 04 4:16 PM Make-your-own sundae at work with Liza, Regan, and Emily. 05 8:35 PM Tortilla chips and hummus at Mom's with Mom and Buffy and Sophie. 06 8:49 PM Vegetarian manicotti, meat lasagna, green beans with garlic, and Caesar salad from the Vinegar Factory at Mom's. 07 9:10 PM Dipped Oreo at Mom's. 08 11:07 PM Pretzels dipped in chocolate at home with Danny.

MONTH

JAN
FEB
MAR
APR
MAY
JUN
JUL
AUG
SEP
OCT
NOV
DEC

DATE

12/20

DAY

MON

01

02

03

04

05

06

07

08

01 10:08 AM Croissant from Citarella at work. 02 1:10 PM Pork soup buns at Joe's Shanghai with Patches. 03 1:26 PM Pork, mushroom, and noodle soup at Joe's Shanghai. 04 7:39 PM Mixed nuts at home. 05 8:07 PM Pickles at 2nd Avenue Deli with Danny and Chris. 06 8:08 PM Coleslaw at 2nd Avenue Deli. 07 8:18 PM Chicken liver pâté at 2nd Avenue Deli. 08 8:30 PM Matzo ball soup at 2nd Avenue Deli. 09 8:31 PM Potato soup with dill at 2nd Avenue Deli. *(continued on next page)*

MONTH

JAN
FEB
MAR
APR
MAY
JUN
JUL
AUG
SEP
OCT
NOV
DEC

DATE

12/21

DAY

TUE

10 8:46 PM Pastrami and corned beef half-sandwiches at 2nd Avenue Deli. **11** 8:51 PM Kreplach with fried onions at 2nd Avenue Deli. **12** 8:55 PM Kasha varnishkas at 2nd Avenue Deli. **13** 9:28 PM Raisin-nut rugelach at 2nd Avenue Deli. **14** 9:29 PM Chocolate babka at 2nd Avenue Deli.

DATE

12/21

DAY

TUE

01 10:00 AM Granola from Time Inc. Cafeteria at work. 02 1:05 PM Chocolate from Maison du Chocolate with Amy in Amy's office. 03 5:10 PM Hakuunnohotori (bean cake with condensed milk) from Minamoto on 48th Street. 04 6:25 PM Potato chips at home. 05 9:02 PM Bread at John's Restaurant with Buzz, Barry, Alex, and Patches. 06 9:03 PM Caprese salad at John's. 07 9:08 PM Garlic bread at John's. 08 9:11 PM Colossal shrimp cocktail at John's. 09 9:31 PM Pappardelle with Tuscan meat sauce at John's. 10 9:32 PM Osso bucco at John's. 11 9:35 PM Tomato and goat cheese ravioli at John's. 12 1:08 AM Wheaties at home.

MONTH

JAN
FEB
MAR
APR
MAY
JUN
JUL
AUG
SEP
OCT
NOV

DATE

12/22

DAY

WED

01 10:47 AM Oatmeal from Sacred Chow at home. **02** 2:41 PM Bread at Noho Star with Danny. **03** 2:42 PM Triple celery soup at Noho Star. **04** 3:00 PM Tomato-mozzarella panino and olives at Noho Star. **05** 8:27 PM Italian honey pastries at Jorge and Wayne's with Jorge, Wayne, Danny, Ken, and David B. **06** 9:03 PM Chocolate-covered cherries at Jorge and Wayne's. **07** 9:42 PM Spaghetti with tomato sauce, chicken paillard with white wine and capers at Jorge and Wayne's. **08** 10:11 PM Sugar cookie at Jorge and Wayne's. **09** 10:13 PM Sugar cookie at Jorge and Wayne's. **10** 12:03 AM Assorted Belgian chocolates at Jorge and Wayne's. **11** 12:57 AM Wheaties at home.

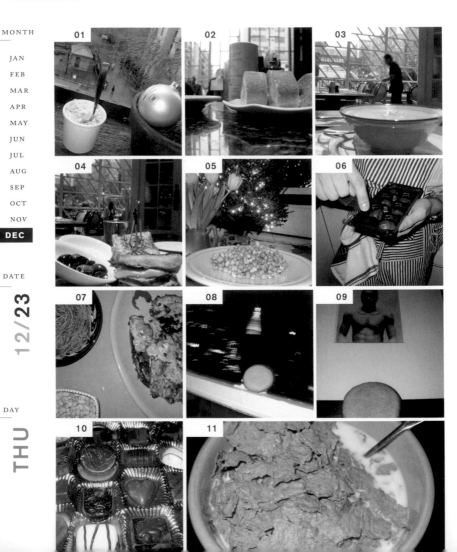

MONTH

JAN
FEB
MAR
APR
MAY
JUN
JUL
AUG
SEP
OCT
NOV
DEC

DATE

12/23

DAY

THU

New York City to San Francisco 01 9:05 AM Bacon, egg, and cheese on a roll from Spyros at home. 02 2:53 PM Gourmet Party Mix on United Airlines flight 9 from JFK to SFO. 03 4:23 PM Pasta with red sauce, boiled shrimp salad with tomato and celery, mixed greens, chocolate brownie, dinner roll on flight 9. 04 5:58 PM French fries at Firewood Grill at SFO with Geoff and Dad. 05 8:57 PM Split pea soup at Dad's with Dad, Heather, Geoff, and Gram. 06 8:59 PM Smoked salmon, toasts, and crème fraîche at Dad's. 07 9:30 PM Chocolate bouche de Noël from Sweden House at Dad's.

MONTH

JAN

FEB

MAR

APR

MAY

JUN

JUL

AUG

SEP

OCT

NOV

DEC

DATE

12/24

DAY

FRI

Tiburon 01 8:55 AM Grapefruit at Dad's with Dad, Heather, Geoff, and Gram. 02 8:57 AM Two poached eggs, bacon at Dad's. 03 9:01 AM Croissants from Sweden House, preserved persimmon from Minamoto Kitchen at Dad's. 04 2:39 PM Red and green grapes at Dad's with Heather. 05 3:10 PM Leftover smoked salmon, toasts, and crème fraîche at Dad's with Heather. 06 3:21 PM Heather's fruitcake at Dad's with Geoff and Heather. 07 6:45 PM Gram's Waldorf salad at Dad's with Dad, Heather, Geoff, and Gram. 08 7:15 PM Spit-roasted standing rib roast, Yorkshire pudding, roasted root vegetables, and peas at Dad's. 09 8:09 PM Christmas trifle with raspberries and toasted almonds at Dad's. 10 8:20 PM White chocolate bunny at Dad's.

MONTH

JAN
FEB
MAR
APR
MAY
JUN
JUL
AUG
SEP
OCT
NOV
DEC

DATE

12/25

DAY

SAT

San Francisco to New York City 01 10:13 AM Omelet with tomato and green onion, two sausages, hush puppies, melon, and cherry Danish on United Airlines flight 956. 02 3:55 PM Wheat Thins, Oreos, Milky Way, cheese, and bread sticks on UA flight 956 (not eaten: raisins). 03 7:53 PM Potato chips at home. 04 8:32 PM Burrata cheese at home. 05 8:58 PM Pasta with pancetta, Swiss chard, eggs, and Parmigiano-Reggiano cheese at home. 06 9:17 PM Assorted butter cookies from Bruno's Bakery at home. 07 9:33 PM Total at home.

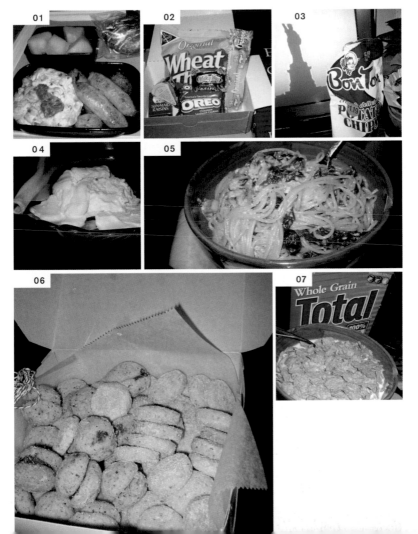

MONTH

JAN
FEB
MAR
APR
MAY
JUN
JUL
AUG
SEP
OCT
NOV
DEC

DATE

12/26

DAY

SUN

01 9:36 AM **Brioche from Le Bergamote on 20th Street.** 02 10:35 AM **Cream of Wheat from Time Inc. Cafeteria at work.** 03 1:05 PM **Crispy duck with pineapple, red onion, and green onions at Pam's Real Thai with Chris.** 04 1:08 PM **Oxtail soup at Pam's.** 05 1:57 PM **Waffle cookie from Minamoto Kitchen in Rockefeller Center.** 06 5:41 PM **Leftover pasta at home.** 07 7:16 PM **Green salad with Parmigiano-Reggiano at Jorge and Wayne's with Jorge, Wayne, and Danny.** 08 7:31 PM **Lamb potpie at Jorge and Wayne's.** 09 8:03 PM **Assorted chocolates at Jorge and Wayne's.** 10 11:25 PM **More cookies from Bruno's at home with Danny.**

MONTH

JAN

FEB

MAR

APR

MAY

JUN

JUL

AUG

SEP

OCT

NOV

DATE

12/27

DAY

MON

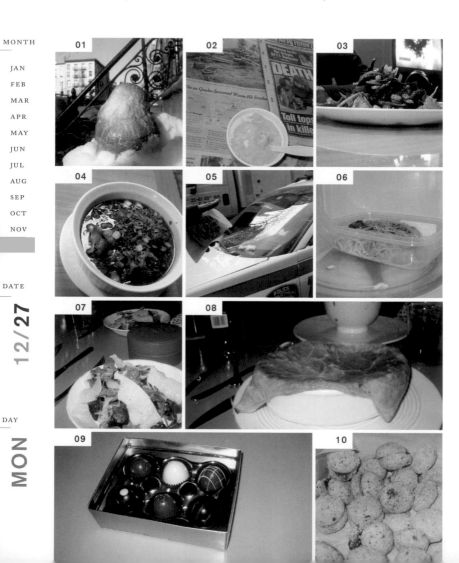

01 10:11 AM Blueberry muffin from coffee cart on 50th Street at work. **02** 2:00 PM Miso soup, spicy tuna roll, and salmon roll from Yummy Sushi at work. **03** 6:49 PM Sea salt and vinegar potato chips at home. **04** 8:55 PM Bacon Cheeseburger Deluxe and fries from the Village Den at home. **05** 10:54 PM Total cereal at home.

MONTH

JAN

FEB

MAR

APR

MAY

JUN

JUL

AUG

SEP

OCT

NOV

DEC

DATE

12/28

DAY

TUE

01 10:22 AM Strawberry smoothie from Maui Wow at work. **02** 2:08 PM Jambalaya at Hale & Hearty Soups.
03 4:50 PM Reese's peanut butter cups at work. **04** 7:58 PM Goat cheese and pesto crackers at home.
05 9:28 PM Chicken stew with white beans, mustard, and spinach at home. **06** 9:52 PM Assorted rugelach
from Lisa with Danny at home. **07** 10:39 PM Life cereal at home.

MONTH

JAN

FEB

MAR

APR

MAY

JUN

JUL

AUG

SEP

OCT

NOV

DEC

DATE

12/29

DAY

WED

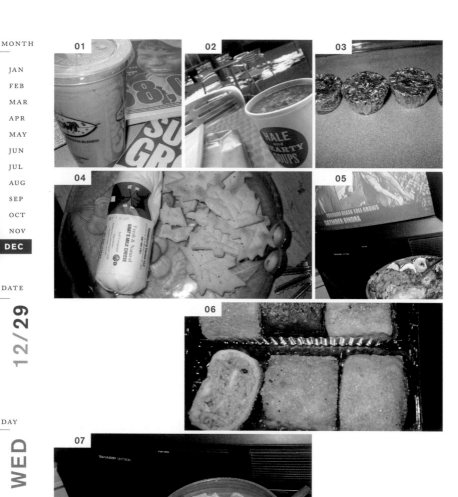

01 11:54 AM Chocolate chip cookies at Jorge and Wayne's. 02 1:53 PM Vegetarian chili and corn bread at Cucina & Co. in Macy's Cellar with Jorge. 03 6:02 PM Heather's fruitcake at home. 04 8:15 PM Macaroni and cheese from Westville at Susan and Andrea's with Henry. 05 8:31 PM Breaded chicken with mixed greens, roasted tomato, and mayonnaise from Westville at Susan and Andrea's. 06 9:10 PM Homemade Oreo cookie from Westville at Susan and Andrea's. 07 12:22 AM Rugelach from Lisa at home. 08 12:43 AM Life cereal at home.

MONTH

JAN

FEB

MAR

APR

MAY

JUN

JUL

AUG

SEP

OCT

NOV

DATE

12/30

DAY

THU

01 9:50 AM Brioche from Lafayette Pâtisserie on Greenwich Avenue. **02** 1:42 PM Mushroom quiche from Pâtisserie Claude on W. 4th Street. **03** 3:58 PM Sticky rice with pork wrapped in bamboo leaf at Sammy's Noodle Shop with Jorge. **04** 4:09 PM Pork noodle soup at Sammy's. **05** 4:11 PM Little juicy pork buns at Sammy's. **06** 6:58 PM Caviar with crème fraîche at home with Danny. **07** 7:57 PM Wild mushroom soup with shaved truffle dumpling at Kittichai with Jorge, Wayne, and Danny. **08** 8:13 PM Cod with red pepper–coconut sauce and Thai greens at Kittichai. **09** 8:39 PM Steak with red wine vinegar sauce, turnips, carrots, beets, and pan squash at Kittichai. **10** 9:29 PM White chocolate and clementine soufflé with Thaiparinha ice cream at Kittichai. **11** 2:36 AM Life cereal at home.

MONTH

JAN
FEB
MAR
APR
MAY
JUN
JUL
AUG
SEP
OCT
NOV
DEC

DATE

12/31

DAY

FRI

01

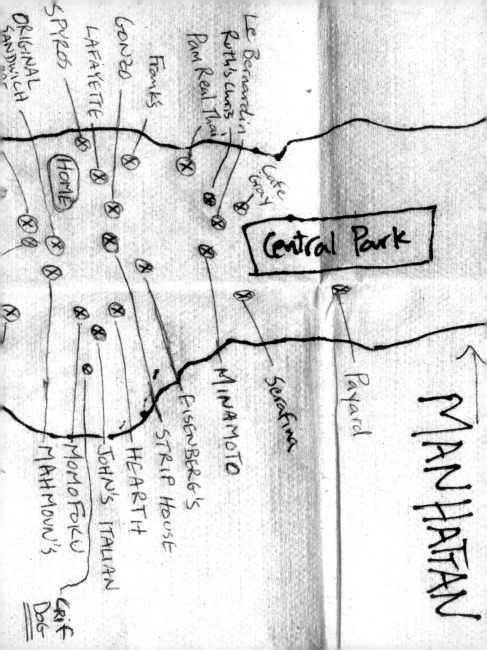

I LOVE STEAK *

STEAK IS GREAT

★ Steaks of the year, 2004
in no particular order ★

- Porterhouse at Craft Steak   w/ Alex Andrea
        VEGA$ (MAY 2)   Susan + Tim

- Ribeye @ Ruth's Chris (January 10)
      w/ Tim, Andrea, Susan.

(JULY 13) — RIBEYE — BADLANDS
                    INTERIOR, S.D.

(JULY 24) — STEAK RIBEYE
w/Alex   AT GLACIER NAT'L PARK

        And finally: T-Bone

on (Sept 28) at
Frank's on
10th Ave
with Alex +
Tim M.

check the pix

FOOD IS MY SHEP-HERD (I shall not want)

2day 4 lunch grilled Swiss + bacon at Eisenberg's

Dos Leches cake

(skip the whole milk, just use condensed + evaporated)

+ nutmeg

Danny's pasta: simple tomato sauce + Pepperoncini + 1 Tbs molasses.

yum

MAY 10 →

Francesco ← best cook in Italy sez:

boil pasta in rabbit stock for maximum frutti di mare ness.

Hi Patches!

Pork shoulder w/beans

butter
diced onion
diced carrot
  " celery
  " garlic
chopped leek
spinach
chicken stock

chorizo
~~diced~~ chop
white wine
red pepper ~~flakes~~
can
white beans
& pork shoulder

- brown pork
- sautee veg (xcept spinach)
  w/ chorizo & pepper flakes
  ~~deglaze~~
- deglaze w/ wine & then chix stock
- return pork, cover,

- cook @ 300 for 2/3 hrs
- stir in beans
- cook 1 hr more
- stir in spinach, serve
  over potatoes
-

follow with cake (fried)

yum Hakuunnohotori @ Minamoto

- RUM SOAKED BABA with
  EXTRA whipped cream at
  JACK's   YUM | Feb 23 | Nov 18

- (Nov 7) ⇒ FRIED POUND CAKE AT Home

- BRIOCHE from Patisserie
  yum | Dec 31 | ⟵ Lafayette

- BRIOCHE @ Payard Dec 14

- OXTAIL SOUP @ Pam Real Thai
  mmm   w/ chris | Oct 21 |

  QUICHE from Patisserie Claude
  (Mar 18) yum yum

01

1070746738